The BLOOD THIEF

THE FITHEACH TRILOGY
BOOK TWO

LUANNE BENNETT

The Word Lounge
Atlanta, Georgia

First Printing, May 2016

ISBN 978-0-692-71373-0

Printed in the United States of America

You are their blood;
Through the veins,
Through the past,
Through the bonds of power.

The BLOOD THIEF

ONE

There was nothing remarkable looking about it, really. There were no red flags or warning signs of the consequences of stepping in its path, nothing that screamed *stay back*. But I swear the damn thing moved every time I came near it.

"Just pick it up," I instructed my trembling hand.

I groaned and flopped back down on the bed. You'd think by now I'd get it through my thick head that I was its master. I called the shots, not that piece of metal shining back at me from the morning light hitting it through the window.

The last month had been a blur. Between finding out who killed my mother and discovering that I was some kind of homicidal assassin on the inside, I'd become a bit of a recluse. I'd resorted to consuming way too much popcorn and red wine while binge watching half a dozen shows on my laptop, all this self-destruction carefully planned around my schedule at Shakespeare's Library.

Greer had been uncharacteristically patient with my self-imposed therapy, and everyone else in my life tiptoed around me like I was some fragile china doll an inch away from shattering. An intervention was imminent if I didn't snap out of it.

My cell phone notification went off, reminding me that if I didn't get off the bed and out the door, Katie was going to throttle me.

"All right." I snatched the amulet off the dresser and put it around my neck. We'd had it back for weeks, but I couldn't bring myself to wear it until now. It would probably still be in Greer's vault if I hadn't threatened to leave if he didn't hand it over. *It'll get you killed*, he'd argued. But he was dead wrong. It was my birthright, and no one would ever take it from me again—not even him.

I was the Oracle, and I intended to start acting like it.

The smell traveling up from the first floor was an effective distraction from the anxiety, and I was out the bedroom door before it could grip me again. I took the stairs two at a time and headed for the kitchen.

"Good morning, Sophia." My eyes automatically went to the source of the smell. French toast was my weakness, and Sophia's was unsurpassed.

"You hungry, Miss Alex?"

After months of raised eyebrows and contemptuous stares, Greer's Italian housekeeper and cook extraordinaire had finally lowered her guard and welcomed me in. We still had our occasional ups and downs, and with her you never knew if your grace points reset back to zero every day, having to be re-earned. But I'd finally reached that coveted point where she trusted me and knew I wasn't there to bilk her employer like some groupie from Crusades, Greer's club playground and legitimizer for all his wealth. I admit, it was nice living in the big house with all the beautiful things, and having my meals prepared by a world-class cook like Sophia. But I really didn't care about the money. A one-bedroom apartment would have suited me just fine. She also knew Greer and I weren't sleeping in the same bed—a cardinal sin in her Catholic book of morals.

"Starving." I grabbed a piece of French toast off the plate

and headed back out of the kitchen. "I'm late. I'll be home around five."

After passing my unofficial probationary period at Shakespeare's Library and declaring my intent to stay, I'd earned the responsibility of opening the shop on the days when I had the morning shift. Katie usually got there early, but I had the key so arriving late wasn't an option.

"Sit down. I bring you coffee and a plate," Sophia said in the thick Italian accent she would take to her grave. I liked the way she spoke, her no-nonsense approach to making statements instead of questions.

Her hand extended as I whizzed past her, grabbing my arm in that way a mother confiscates a ricocheting child.

"Can't. I'm late."

She released my arm. "Always in a rush. Your food will not stick."

"You're right. But go I must."

She gave me a pointed look as I downed the breakfast in my hand and headed for the door.

My boldness wavered as I stepped outside and felt the separation from the sanctity of Greer's fortress. Even with my new skill set, I thought it wise to exercise a little extra caution. I tucked the amulet under my shirt and took the steps leading to the sidewalk with a little less bounce than usual, knowing that there were hunters out there waiting for me to come outside and play.

Greer had warned me about the risks, but I'd proven I could handle myself, and his bad habit of trying to control me had pretty much been nipped in the bud. From now on, I made my own decisions: where, when, and with whom. I mean, it wasn't like I was leaping off of buildings or looking for a fight. I was just a girl working in a used bookstore who happened to have the weight of the world resting on her shoulders.

I hit the sidewalk and headed toward Columbus Avenue. It was a perfect spring morning, and I managed to smile at every fellow New Yorker I passed. Some ignored me, but just as many smiled back.

Despite my rocky reintroduction to my birthplace, I loved this city. It had everything you could possibly need—food, shopping, culture—and there was no other place I wanted to be. Except for maybe a cottage at the seaside. I'd get there someday, but right now I had bigger fish to fry. I had a vessel to find and a prophecy to secure.

A bird kept flying over my head. That wasn't so unusual, but given my history with them and the fact that it was aiming dangerously low, I thought it best to stay alert and get ready to duck if it tried to take a clump out of my scalp.

I shook off the paranoia and focused on the beautiful weather. The trees were just starting to show signs of life: green tips protruding from the lifeless limbs jutting from the trunks, bark no longer as ashen and gray as it looked over the winter. I supposed the bark never did look that dead, but winter has a way of tricking the eye. What a surprise when it all comes bouncing back to life.

About twenty feet ahead, I spotted something on the sidewalk. It was a pigeon, still and dead-looking.

"Oh no," I whispered, half out of concern for it, and half from the uncomfortable reality that I had no idea what I'd do with it if it was just injured. The cowardly part of me hoped it was dead.

I never understood how people could drive right past injured animals, like they were nothing, just trash on the side of the road. Growing up in Indiana farm country, I saw a lot of cruelty, a lot of cast-offs dumped to fend for themselves, to live off of garbage or rodents. I guess people just assumed the farms would take them in.

I reached the mound of feathers and took a breath before bending down to examine it. A woman approached and smiled sympathetically as I crouched next to the still bird. She said nothing as she continued past me, probably relieved that it was someone else's problem. I gave her a weak smile back and considered doing the same, but it was wrong for so many reasons to just leave it on the sidewalk. But what's a girl to do in the middle of Manhattan without a shovel or a patch of dirt? It's not like there are drop-off locations for dead or injured pigeons.

Some Oracle I was. I couldn't even deal with a harmless bird.

As my fingers grazed its side, a wing fanned out and flapped wildly against my skin. It made the most unsettling sound as its beak opened and its flat little eyes turned to look at me.

"Thank God," I muttered as it jumped up and flew a few feet away. "I guess you're not terminal, after all."

A shadow blew past my face, and the sound of air fluttering above my head made me stumble back. I looked up and all I could see was a kaleidoscope of gray and white, fanning together in a riot of feathers, then receding to allow the morning sky to peek back through. The birds were colliding and bouncing off of each other as if their flight navigation had gone all haywire.

I wanted to think it was all about them, but I knew that whenever the odd and strange occurred in my presence, it was usually somehow connected to me.

"Not today," I groaned, wishing for just one normal day.

The bird on the sidewalk seemed to take its cue and lifted into the air. It circled me and then shit, the marbled excrement hitting the cement a few inches from my shoe. The commotion grew as the cauldron of pigeons came together in the sky, circling in neat formation just below the building line. I decided to get out of target range and ran toward the flow of pedestrians at the far end of the block where it intersected with Columbus Avenue.

I heard a dull thump, and one of the birds landed on the sidewalk a few yards in front of me, barely giving me time to stop before I trampled it. With its still body and oddly cocked neck, I was pretty sure this one was dead.

My brain was telling me not to bother and keep moving, but my curiosity compelled me to look back into the sky. Right about the time my eyes lifted, another one came crashing down, smashing against something hard before bouncing to the sidewalk just like the other one.

I winced as the sound of beating hail filled my ears. My eyes flew wide when I looked up and saw blood smeared around the sky. It was literally smeared in the air above me. I reached toward the red stains and gasped as more birds hit the sky and bounced off of it, blocking my view with a slurry of blood and feathers. My index finger ran clean across the smooth surface. The blood was on the outside. Like a mime, I felt along the invisible wall curving around me like a giant bubble.

"Well, what do you know," I whispered in disbelieve.

When extraordinary things happened, I was usually on the undesirable end. It was nice to be on the beneficial side for a change.

The pounding started up again, and so did the hail of pigeons. The damn birds were gunning for me. For *me*.

For a moment I was paralyzed, unable to take a simple step for fear that I'd smash into the invisible wall. But then my instincts kicked in, and I ran toward the crowd at the end of the block. Thankfully, the bubble moved with me instead of trapping me in place under the hailstorm of kamikaze pigeons.

The sound of the birds was replaced by the steady hum of shoes and traffic as I turned into the sea of people at the intersection. I glanced up, and the blood and feathers were gone. So were the dead birds that should have been littering the street behind me. Not a single feather remained. The entire avian slaughter had just vanished, and I questioned whether it really happened or if someone was feeding me hallucinations as a distraction. Either way, it was effective.

"Clever," I said aloud. A man looked at me as I stood in the middle of the crowd talking to myself. I just smiled as he passed and continued with my statement. "They really are clever little bastards."

My hunters *were* getting cleverer, finding new ways to come at me in broad daylight.

"Damn it." I had to look twice at my phone. I wasn't just late; I was *late* late.

I picked up the paced toward the shop. A block away I could see Katie standing by the front door, sans any irate customers, but less than pleased with my tardiness.

"You're late," she grumbled as I walked up.

"I know, I know. I'm sorry, but there was this dead pigeon, and—"

Her eyes rolled and landed back on mine. "Just open the door."

Katie had become a good friend. We'd known each other less than two months, but she's the reason I knew what I was. She's the one who found my birthmark, never asking for an explanation of why I had a strange mark on the back of my head, buried like a concealed tattoo under my thick hair. How good a friend is that?

Regardless of her respect for my secrets, I knew it was only a matter of time before I had to bring her into my world or cut her off completely. There would be no halfway with Katie Bishop. She wasn't the kind of girl who followed blind faith, and eventually there would be a reckoning of all the strange things she'd see if she hung around me long enough.

There were dozens of books scattered on the floor, so I got busy sorting them into orderly stacks on the library table in the center of the room.

Apollo had closed the night before, and he was notorious for leaving the previous night's mess for the day shift. He was the shop manager, which meant he usually played catch-up on business after the doors closed, sometimes not getting out of there until close to midnight. His bad housekeeping wasn't from laziness or lack of consideration for his co-workers. He just had a selective priority for simple tasks, meaning he was brilliant at things like finance and linear algebra, but God help him if he ever had to balance his checkbook or compose a grocery list.

We spent the next half hour drinking bad coffee from the deli across the street while I recounted my quasi-tale about a dead pigeon. I came close to telling her the entire ludicrous story, but I liked having a good friend, and today wasn't the right day for testing that bond.

I was spared from making that stupid mistake by the sound of the front door chimes. A man came in with a young girl and asked if we had any books from *The Boxcar Children* series.

"I think we do," Katie said. They followed her to the children's book section at the back of the store.

With everything in order and no other customers in the shop, I grabbed the paper off the counter and scanned the front page. The headline was too strange to ignore: RATS ATTACK HOMELESS MAN IN CENTRAL PARK.

I snorted. "I got that one beat."

The chimes on the door sounded again. "Can I help—" I looked up from the paper, but whoever it was had already disappeared into the stacks. "Guess not," I muttered, getting back to the article.

Katie and her customers came back to the front desk. "This was one of my favorite books when I was your age," she said to the girl. "You're going to love it."

She handed the man his bag and waved to the girl as they turned to leave.

"She was cute," I said as she smiled back at us and followed her father out of the shop. "Almost makes me want one."

"Yep, she was a charmer," Katie agreed.

We watched the girl through the window as she walked

down the sidewalk holding her father's hand. They stopped at the intersection, and the girl reached for the bag. When her father refused to hand it over, her face twisted into a furious knot. She managed to grab the bag out of his hand and threw it on the curb before marching into the street.

"Yeah . . ." Katie tightened her lips and shook her head. "I don't think so."

She motioned toward the aisle on the other side of the shop, the one that housed the section on magic and metaphysics. "What's she looking for?"

I glanced in the same direction. "I don't know."

"Wiccan," Katie observed.

"Wick what?"

"A witch. Definitely a witch." Katie stretched her neck, but the woman was too deep down the aisle for her to see.

"How can you tell?"

"My friends?" she snickered. "Please. Half of them are witches, or Druids, or some kind of hoodoo doctors."

"Your friends are into voodoo?"

"*Hoo*doo. Folk magic. They're the ones always sprinkling red brick dust on their window sills."

Maybe my secrets wouldn't be such a stretch after all, only I think the witches she was familiar with were a little different than mine.

I got up and walked down the aisle on the other side of where the woman was browsing. She'd walked in and disappeared into the stacks before I got a look at her, and I was curious to see what kind of witch she was. Most of them made a beeline straight for me, but not this one. I'd say this one was avoiding me.

My fingers walked along the book spines until I found a fat one. I quietly pulled it from the shelf to get a window to the other side. All I could see was the top of her head, so I put my ear to the shelf to listen. She was quietly humming.

A minute went by as I listened, trying to recall the tune I was sure I'd heard before, like a familiar scent I couldn't quite place. And then it all came back. My mother used to hum that same song.

What is this?

Her head lifted slightly, and I saw the bright green band wrapped around her hair.

"I know who you are." I hadn't planned to just blurt it out, but my emotions and the impulse got the best of me before I could devise a more strategic way to confront her.

The humming stopped, and I could feel her standing behind the shelf with a smug grin on her face and her brown eyes fixed on me through the wall of books. She was here for me, but there was no fun in just walking into the shop and introducing herself, seeing how she never bothered to tell me her name when we first met. It was really more of an encounter. I ran into her at the hotel I was staying at the first week I arrived in New York. She gave me the creeps, with her morbid eyes and penetrating stare. If it wasn't for Greer, I still wouldn't know who she was.

She pulled another book from her side of the shelf, and then another until her face was completely visible. Her head cocked as she looked back at me through the empty space, never blinking her large brown eyes.

"You don't look so well, Alex."

She put the books back in place. The sound of her shoes disappeared down the aisle just before she came around to my side.

Lumen was a small woman, but I knew better than to discount her based on her size. She looked younger than me. But when Greer showed me a picture of her standing next to my mother thirty years ago, looking exactly like she did today, I knew she was anything but the innocuous girl she purported to be.

"What do you want, Lumen?"

"That's not a very nice way to greet family, is it?" She stayed at the other end of the aisle, leaving a good ten feet between us like I was contagious.

Greer said she was a member of my mother's coven, but he never said anything about family.

"As far as I'm concerned, I don't have any family," I responded with contempt. "If I did, I wouldn't have spent all those years living in other people's houses. If I had a family, they would have looked for me, protected me. Would you like me to continue?"

She said nothing. Instead, she looked me up and down and jammed those creepy little fingers in my brain like she did the first time we met. "Got a lot of ginger in there, don't you? A lot of Maeve Kelley, too." She continued feeling her way around my head, siphoning my thoughts like a thief. "You got something else in there, too. Something not so pretty. But I guess that's to be expected."

"Get out of my head," I whispered.

She was right. She knew exactly who I was, and I hated that she could see me so clearly without earning that privilege.

"They're coming for you. I wouldn't burn too many bridges, if I were you," she warned.

"Who is it now?" I asked. "More dogs? Because I already took care of the first pair that tried that. I don't think they're coming back."

A look of genuine surprise spread over her face, and I knew that didn't happen very often. "You don't even know, do you?"

"Know what?"

She hesitated before continuing, elevating the anticipation as I waited to find out who was next in line to come for me. I thought I'd seen it all, at least the worst of it. But the look she gave me told me I was in for something very different. Maybe I was overreacting—I hoped so.

"The dark ones." Her chilly grin flattened. "And they won't

stop, Alex. They'll put every one of their warriors on the line until they have you. They'll sacrifice every . . . last . . . one."

Her warning left me with a dull ache in the center of my forehead. I'd already had a really bad day and it wasn't even noon. I just wanted her to leave.

"You're going to need your family, Alex. And when you do—"

"And we're related how?" I interrupted. "I don't think you ever clarified that."

Her pupils dilated wildly as her chest expanded from a massive intake of air. "By blood!" she spat, stomping down the aisle toward me.

"Everything all right over here?" Katie appeared where Lumen had just been standing, the baseball paperweight from the front desk in her right hand. She tossed it up in the air and caught it on its way back down, a warning to the petite tyrant stalking toward her friend.

"We're good, Katie. She was just leaving."

Lumen smiled at me with about as much family affection as a rodent consuming her own young. "When the shit hits the fan," she sneered, leaning closer, "I'll be waiting."

TWO

I'd like to say I was fine, but the conversation with Lumen stuck in my head as disturbingly as those pigeons. Even with my new skills, I was no match for an army she referred to as warriors. I'd spent the next few hours ambling around the shop in a funk, returning books to the wrong sections and jumping every time the front door sounded. Katie knew I was shaken by the encounter, and probably got tired of following behind me to make sure I didn't rearrange the entire shop. With the caveat that I had to tell her everything the next day, she'd pushed me toward the door and told me to go home.

I headed over to Crusades instead to find Greer and get some clarification on what these *dark ones* were. When I walked through the door, Thomas was at the bar lining up rows of clean glasses and checking the booze stock for the night. He put his clipboard down and waved me over.

"Thomas," I said as I planted myself on one of the barstools, "would you think less of me if I asked you for a shot of Lagavulin in the middle of the afternoon?"

"Not if I can join you." He poured two shots of the single malt and handed one to me. I downed it and asked for another.

"Slow down, sugar. I assume you're here to see Greer?"

"I am."

He glanced at the bottle. "Then you might want to go easy on that stuff."

Thomas was well acquainted with my temper, and he knew how volatile Greer and I could be when we butted heads. A powwow with the boss was best had with full control of my faculties, and a belly full of scotch would do nothing but leave me with the disadvantage.

"Boss." Thomas nodded as Greer came down the stairs.

Greer looked at the bottle on the bar and then turned his attention to me. Seeing me in the middle of the day meant there was a problem. He knew it. Thomas knew it. The walls knew it.

"Something happened this morning." I did my best to sound casual, but Greer had this annoying talent for cutting through bullshit and sniffing out the truth. He was a living lie detector.

He read my face and then turned to go back up the stairs. I followed him to the mezzanine. He preferred the open space of the VIP room so he could pace the expansive floor while being given undesirable news. I preferred it too, because it put more space between us when I was the one giving it.

He pulled his seat up to mine and sat facing me, silently waiting for me to lead the discussion. No third degree or inquisition, just an open invitation to speak freely.

I decided to get the easy stuff out of the way first. "I was attacked on my way to the shop."

He looked me up and down. "You look fine to me."

"By pigeons. They just came out of nowhere and tried to scalp me." His expression remained flat and I could just smell his agitation. "Okay, they didn't actually touch me because this invisible barrier was wrapped around me. They just kept bouncing off of it, breaking their little necks. It was really sad, Greer."

He stared at me silently while I described the barrier in detail and how the birds kept crashing into it. As I spoke, his eyes wandered around the space above my head as if he could see it.

"A shield," he finally explained. "A spontaneous shield. They're extremely rare. But then, so are you. Were you able to control it, throw it up at will?"

"Uh . . . no. I didn't even know I had one until it was there. It just . . . sprang up out of the blue."

"That's usually how they work. Triggered by a spike of fear." He looked at me suspiciously. "And you said pigeons attacked you?"

"Have you ever had a bunch of pigeons dive-bomb your head, Greer? It's pretty damn traumatic. I've seen *The Birds*. With Tippi Hedren?"

"Well, you may never see another one of those shields again. But if you do, I need to know about it. It may come in handy."

"You mean I might be able to control it?"

"It's not unheard of," he said with a shrug. "It's just difficult for *people* to control them."

"You'll be the first to know," I said, preparing for the good part. "Are you ready for the rest?"

His eyes shut as he rubbed his forehead, "There's more?"

"Lumen paid me a visit this morning."

I expected him to explode, but he remained curiously quiet. Strange, considering her reputation for being a special envoy to my people. At least that's the impression I got from him the last time she showed up.

"What the hell is a *dark one*?"

He froze and looked at me like I'd just crossed some forbidden line. It wasn't easy to surprise Greer Sinclair, but the mention of those two words seemed to do the trick. "Where did you hear that?" he asked a little too softly for my comfort.

"She came to the bookstore. She just waltzed in and told me they were coming for me. And by the way, were you planning to tell me she's part of my family? Is it true?"

As if on cue, he got up and started wearing out the floor. "Word for word, Alex. I need to know exactly what she said."

I told him everything, down to the last detail of Katie coming to my rescue. That part got a laugh.

"I like your friend Katie."

He walked to the enormous window that stretched from one end of the club to the other, his hands in the pockets of his pants, and I could see his jaw working in conjunction with the thoughts running through his mind. The last few months had been stressful for everyone, and lines were beginning to form on his handsome face, though they would eventually smooth out and recede. Greer would look the same a hundred years from now. When my body was old and crumbling, his would look the same.

He looked back at me from over his shoulder, and I got up and stood next to him at the window. "I need to know what I'm dealing with, Greer."

He sighed heavily. "Do you remember our conversation the night you moved into the house?"

I remembered it well, only I'd hardly say I moved in. Greer made that decision for me and pretty much transferred me like a prisoner from Crusades to his brownstone on the Upper West Side. That was the night I found out Ava was still alive, and I'd been lied to for years by the one person I trusted the most. Greer and I spent that evening dancing around my questions, and to this day I have no idea what he is. But I know what he isn't, and for now that's good enough.

"I remember you avoiding most of my questions," I said.

"Do you remember what I told you about the Rogues? The attack in the park?" His jaw tightened as his eyes focused on something across the club.

Thomas was behind the bar, wiping the inside of a glass while his eyes stared back at Greer's. I could feel a storm coming. Greer and Thomas were like two parallel charged wires working together to kept the hurricane turning.

"And?" I persisted. The small, innocuous word must have pushed his red button.

"Fuck!" he roared.

Thomas' thoughts must have synced with Greer's, because he sent the glass in his hand sailing against the far wall of the club.

Greer stormed out of the room and took the stairs three at a time to the main level. I looked back through the window as he reached the bar and barked an order at Thomas. I couldn't hear what he said, but Thomas nodded once and took off through the back door.

Greer's fist came down on the bar, sending a small quake through the building as he looked up at me through the glass. He was about to come back for me, and there was something in his eyes that told me I needed to get out of that room before he did.

I headed for the room on the third floor, the one where I'd slept before moving into the big house. I slammed the door and engaged the flimsy lock. A sheet of wood with hinges wouldn't stop him, but it bought me a few minutes to think and try to figure out what was happening. To my knowledge, I hadn't done anything wrong, but I knew that look—the one that said *you are so fucked.*

His shoes pounded the floor as he came down the hall, making me eye the window with a stupid thought.

"Don't make me break the door, Alex."

"You're scaring me, Greer!"

"Five seconds," he warned, and as a man of his word, the door blew through the useless lock and swung open with a loud crack.

*   *   *

We drove in silence. Something very bad was happening, and I knew there'd be plenty of discussion once we got to the house.

Sophia looked at me strangely as we walked through the door, a question mark suspended behind her expression. I was relieved to see Rhom sitting on the sofa and then Leda coming out of the kitchen with a drink in her hand.

"It's for you, dear. You're going to need it." She handed me the glass.

"For the love of God, will someone please tell me what's going on?"

"Rogues. The dark ones are Rogues," Greer announced matter-of-factly. "You're officially on lockdown."

Ah, I thought. *Now I see what all the fuss is about.* The night he moved me into his house, he told me about them. The man who'd tried to rape me in Central Park was a Rogue, and now they were coming for me. I guess they were after the amulet, too. Why not? Everyone else was. But so far, I'd managed to hold my own with all of them. It was still around my neck, wasn't it?

"No one's locking me anywhere. And why does everyone keep handing me alcohol every time I get bad news?" I handed the drink back to Leda. "If I want a drink, I'll ask for one."

"Don't be temperamental, Alex. We're just trying to make this easier for you." Leda was just being herself—pragmatic to the core.

"You know I love you, Leda, but stop talking to me like I haven't earned my stripes. I think I've demonstrated what I'm capable of when someone pisses me off." I looked at Greer. "Haven't I?"

"A wolf is nothing compared to a Rogue," Rhom said.

"He's right, Alex." Leda looked at me sympathetically. "Think *Greer* with a mean streak."

I snorted.

"Well, maybe that's a bad example," she countered. "Think *Rhom* with an evil side."

Rhom had never been anything but kind to me, but I imagined him capable of some pretty bad things. The thought of him lacking a moral compass was downright frightening.

"I have a job, Greer. I can't just disappear."

"Not anymore," he declared as if I had no say in it.

"Oh yeah? Watch me walk out that door."

"Go. Everyone out." No one questioned the command. He looked at me as I fell into line to leave with everyone else. "Not you."

When the room cleared, he took my hand and led me to the sofa. "Sit down, Alex."

I sank into the cushion and stared at the painting on the opposite wall. I was tired of defending my right to be set free from the glass dome he was always trying to keep me under. My powers were getting stronger, but even that wasn't enough to convince him that I was capable of taking care of myself. True, my power had a mind of its own and only manifested out of fear, but that's when it mattered—right?

"If it's a fight you're looking for, Alex, forget it. I won't debate my decision to do whatever it takes to keep you safe." He took my chin and turned my face up to his. "I won't."

"Then teach me. Teach me how to control it. We can take as much time as we need, but you've got to let me live my life, Greer."

We were deadlocked. Either we compromised, or I had to leave. He knew I'd do it. One morning I'd just be gone.

"If we do this," he looked at me pointedly, "we do it my way."

"Deal. One thing, though." I cut him off before he could open his mouth to argue. "I'm not quitting my job."

I'd convinced Greer to give me one more day to try to salvage my job before he cut me off from the world. Shakespeare's

Library was my refuge, and it was the only job I'd ever actually liked.

"Can you give me an hour?" I asked Rhom.

"You take as much time as you need, Alex. I'll be waiting right here."

I reached for the door and gave him a weak smile. "You always know exactly what I need."

"Alex," he called out before I disappeared into the shop. "I'd do the same thing if I were in Greer's shoes."

I nodded and walked inside, swallowing the bitter pill of acquiescence.

"Morning, sunshine," Katie greeted while eyeing the Starbucks cups I was holding. "Is this your way of distracting me from the elephant in the kitchen?" We usually went for the cheap stuff across the street, but today seemed like a good day to splurge.

"I think it got a little cold." I handed her one of the cups.

"You ready to tell me what's going on?" she asked, taking it.

The shop was empty, so it was as good a time as any to see if Katie Bishop would still be my friend after I told her the truth. I grabbed an extra stool and sat with her behind the counter.

"You know that guy I live with? Well, he's not just some guy."

"They never are," she muttered around a sip of lukewarm coffee.

I decided to approach the conversation from a different angle. "You were right about the woman who came in here yesterday. She's a witch."

She grinned. "I knew there was a reason I like you so much. You've got that . . . vibe."

"I have a vibe?"

"Yeah. I was just thinking the other day: Alex is in the

broom closet. Let me guess." She tapped her finger against her chin. "Gardnerian?"

"I don't think you understand, Katie."

"Not Dianic." Her face twisted like she'd eaten something bitter. "Please don't tell me you're Dianic."

"I don't know what any of those things are," I said, "but I am a witch. I'm just not the kind you think I am."

She lifted off the stool and headed for the stack of books on the library table. "Alex, come on. Either tell me or don't, but cut the bullshit. God, I hate being placated."

"I can kill things with my eyes," I blurted out. "Well, that's how it starts. This blue light shoots out of my eyes."

Katie looked up from the books she was stacking and waited for my next preposterous comment.

"My mother was murdered here—twenty-one years ago. That's why I came back. That's how I met Greer." I'd mentioned him a few times but gave few details on our living arrangements. I described him like you would a roommate, and left it at that.

Katie walked back to the counter, giving me a sympathetic smile as she cupped the curve of my forearm. "And the birthmark?" She was the one who found it buried under my hair. But a girl can only take so much, and even though she never asked questions because she was smart enough to know that I wasn't ready to answer them yet, it was only a matter of time before she did.

"It's the sign of the Oracle." There, I said it. "We all thought my mother was the Oracle, but it's me." I reached inside of my shirt and pulled out the amulet. "This is what everyone wants. It's the key."

"Key to what?"

My shoulders sagged at the thought of it. "To everything."

I dumped it all on the table: my disappearance after my mother's murder, the attack in Central Park, the prophecy. I even told her about Arthur Richmond, leaving out the part about how I killed him, because I thought it might be a little too much, too soon.

Katie reached for the amulet.

I jerked back involuntarily. "No!"

"I just wanted to look at it, Alex. Jeez."

"If you touch it, you're a target," I warned. "Believe me, Katie. You don't want that."

"No hands," she said with her palms in the air. "Looks pretty plain for something like that."

"I know," I agreed. "Believe me, no one was more shocked than I was to find out what it was."

She pointed to the thin line running down the center. "What does that line mean?"

"See, that's the problem. No one knows. I guess we'll figure it out when we find the vessel."

Katie shuddered and walked back to the library table. "This is all very 007-meets-Harry-Potter, Alex. I'll let you know tomorrow if I believe any of it." She continued sorting through the books left over from the night before. "God, I hope you're not crazy, Alex. I have enough crazy friends."

Tomorrow was a delicate subject. I'd come to the shop to explain Lumen, among other things, but the real reason was to see about getting some time off. Apollo was the store manager, but I wanted to run it by Katie first to see if she had any advice on how to approach him. It wasn't like I was some highly prized professional going on hiatus. I was a clerk in a used bookstore, and my job could be filled by the next warm body that walked through the door. I figured I'd be out for a couple of weeks at the most, but the shop couldn't operate with only two people for that long.

"Yeah, about tomorrow." I let out a deep sigh. "I love working here, but—"

"Really?" she said. "Love is a strong word for a used bookstore gig. Think big, Alex."

"I need some time off." I gauged her reaction before continuing. "There are these guys after me, and I kind of need to do something about it. A couple of weeks, tops."

"God, Alex. No!" She dropped a pile of books back on the table. "You're the only one who stuck. Do you know how hard it is to get someone in here who we actually like?"

"Yeah . . . well . . . these guys—"

"Apollo is going to shit!"

"What am I going to shit about?" Apollo walked through the front door and dropped his backpack on the counter. A mass of brown curls hit his forehead as he turned around, making him look more like a high school boy than a man with a master's degree. "Problem, ladies?"

Katie motioned for me to spill the good news, and I explained that I needed to take a couple of weeks off for health reasons. It wasn't exactly a lie.

Apollo reacted about the same as Katie had, only he managed to do it silently with a look that showed how disappointed he was with me. He was the manager, and I knew it was hard for him to tell me that he had no choice but to find a replacement.

"I hate this, Alex, but I don't own the place."

"What about a temp?" Katie suggested.

"We can't afford a temp." With their agency fees on top of the hourly wage, temps were expensive. A small mom-and-pop like Shakespeare's Library just didn't have the budget for one.

"Then I guess this is it." I felt sick from the realization that my job at the shop was over.

"You're leaving today?" Katie asked.

I'd let them down, burdened everyone with double shifts because Greer wouldn't budge on starting my training that afternoon. *Every minute we wait, you're a walking target.* I knew he was right.

I left the shop and met Rhom outside. He wrapped his arm around my shoulders as I cried, politely allowing me the luxury of grief.

THREE

I opened my eyes to pitch black. Not a single thing stood out from the darkness. I felt weightless because without any reference points, my body had nothing to anchor to.

The air was cool and smelled like fresh paint and rubber. I tried to move my arms but they were stuck, tied behind the chair I was sitting in.

"Greer?" There was no answer, but I already knew I was alone. I would have smelled him if he was in the room.

Rhom and I left Shakespeare's Library that morning with the intention of going straight back to the house. We stopped at the corner market to pick up some magazines to get me through the isolation period I was about to endure. The last thing I remembered before waking up in the chair was walking out of the market and looking for Rhom.

"Okay, Greer. That's enough!"

I wasn't too concerned. I knew who'd tied me up. At least I thought I did. But my ease was disintegrating as more time ticked by, and the dead silence of the room started to do a number on my head.

My heart raced as my eyes worked to adjust to the darkness.

But without even the tiniest hint of light in the room, there was nothing to adjust to.

I heard a faint sound, and a thin sliver of light appeared in the center of the room, illuminating a haze of translucent, floating dust. By the time I followed the light to its source, the door had shut. Either someone just entered the room, or someone just left.

"I know you're in here. I can hear you." I couldn't hear anything, but I thought I'd give the bluff a shot.

A footstep on the other side of the room confirmed that I wasn't alone. Another one hit the floor, and then another, each one subtly moving across the length of the room. It must have been a large space, because the footsteps went on forever, getting quieter as they moved away and louder as they came back.

As my nerves kicked in, I started counting the steps. Seventeen in each direction, each one evenly spaced and timed for perfect rhythm.

My breath caught as I heard the footsteps moving toward me again. I could hear them right next to me, pausing for a moment before continuing. When they stopped directly behind me, I thought I'd be sick.

"Say something. Please," I pleaded, trying not to sound too desperate. "Just say something."

A pair of hands cupped my shoulders and slowly moved up to where my clavicle bone curved toward my neck. Thumbs sank into the muscles of my back, while fingers wrapped over the top of my shoulders and gripped my skin.

I sniffed the air, but it wasn't Greer I smelled.

"Shhhh." A breath warmed my ear as a scarf fell over my eyes.

Why use a blindfold in a pitch-black room? Maybe I was being moved somewhere else.

He was walking again. I could hear him behind me, moving farther away toward the back of the room. A cold chill ran through my body as I recognized the sound of steel brushing against steel. I could almost hear the blade moving through the air as he picked it up and started walking toward me again. I tried to say something profound that might trigger any humanity or mercy in him before I felt the edge of that knife against my skin, but my vocal cords froze. I didn't think that could actually happen. How could you just lose your ability to speak?

He stopped behind me, and I felt the tip of the steel press against my bare shoulder. The blade dragged down my biceps and across my restrained forearm, pushing with just enough pressure to keep it from penetrating the surface of my skin. It moved past my wrist, and the tip of the blade settled in the center of my hand. I screamed as the steel punctured the thick flesh of my palm with a steady cut that continued upward until it reached the scarf wrapped around my wrists. With a swift flick, the tie was severed and my hands were free.

Something burned inside of me, but it wasn't coming from my hand. I stood up, still blindfolded, and walked straight ahead. I stopped and reached for the wall a foot away, my eyes burning like lit lanterns. My lids remained shut as I removed the scarf. When the burning finally stopped, I opened them.

I turned my hand to look at the cut, and a bright glow illuminated the blood as it ran down my fingers like black oil tinged with purple and blue. The entire room was lit up by the sapphire disco balls in my eyes, allowing me a good look at my captor.

The man on the other side of the room crooked his finger at me. "Come and get me, little girl," he taunted.

Little girl? Game on.

I ran straight at him because his throat was still intact. But before I could reach for his jugular, I felt the blow of an invisible wall slam against my face, sending me to the floor.

He bent down and hovered over me as the pain did its job. "You're not the only one with a shield," he said.

He straightened back up and extended his hand. I took it

and then grabbed the knife in his other hand. A short laugh burst from his throat as he looked at his empty hand and then at the knife in mine, grinning as he processed his careless faux pas. "Touché," he complimented with a strange sense of pride. "You're better than I thought."

"You're fucking right I am."

He pulled me to my feet and stepped back. I took a deep breath and anticipated my next move. It would be my last for the evening—his, too. The knife lifted over my head. I considered gutting him with an upward jab, but an overhead was a sure thing. My arm stopped as I brought it back down. The tension around my wrist increased as another guy standing behind me confiscated the stolen knife.

"Fuck." I looked back and forth between the two of them. Without a weapon I was dead. The door to my right was a long shot, but I took my chances and ran for it. I reached it first and ran through it, straight outside into the night air. I was thankful for that because stairs or an elevator might have gotten me killed.

They were right behind me, closing the distance between us as I looked around to get my bearings. If we were in Manhattan, I should have run straight into a building or a street, anything but the black void directly in front of me. There was a short wall directly in my path, maybe two feet tall. When I lifted my foot to jump over it, my knee hit the top and stopped me. The air vacuumed from my lungs as I nearly dove over the edge of the building. I was looking down at the street—a good twenty stories below.

"What the hell?" I looked back at Greer and Rhom, trying to make sense of what was happening and how I ended up on the edge of a building. A minute ago I was running for my life, escaping an attack from . . . *Greer*? It was *Greer*?

I looked down at my throbbing hand, horrified by the sight of the wound and the memory of Greer dragging a knife through my flesh. Actually, it was more of a pink line, no longer bleeding and already starting to heal.

"It's your blood," he said.

His words rattled around my head like a foreign language, incomprehensible and useless. He walked up to me and took my wrist, running his finger over the blood caked down my arm, triggering a volatile reaction from the core of my stomach as his red-stained finger pulled away.

"It sets you off like a bomb."

I expected to feel a little drained the next morning due to the stunt Greer pulled the night before, but I felt just the opposite. My mind was clear and my energy level was through the roof.

The smell of food drew me down to the kitchen. Greer was eating breakfast when I walked into the dining room.

"I'm surprised you're still here." He was usually gone by the time I got up, but today he was eating and reading the paper like it was Sunday or a holiday. Apparently, it was me making him late for work, because last night wasn't finished.

With a fork, I speared a pancake from the platter on the table and a couple pieces of bacon. I figured that would do for starters, but with my appetite I could have finished it all. I waited for Greer to say something. He just sat there, drinking his coffee and looking at me suspiciously like I'd done something inappropriate.

"What?" I looked at the food on my plate. "I left some."

Sophia came into the dining room and placed a cup in front of me. "Thank you, ma'am," I said as she graciously poured my coffee.

She did a double take as she turned back toward the kitchen. A second later, the French press hit the table as her hands planted on her hips.

"What? Why is everyone looking at me like that?"

"You don't look so good." Sophia turned to Greer who was

still staring at me. "Mr. Sinclair, what you do to her last night?"

They both kept staring at me, so I finally got up and went into the living room to see for myself. I looked in the mirror and lost my breath. "Yeah!" I yelled back toward the dining room, "what *did* you do to me last night?"

My hand was sore and had a pink line running the length of my palm. I remembered the blood running down my fingers, and for some reason the image made my temper flare.

"Greer!" I stomped back to the dining room. "Library. Now!"

Sophia muttered something in Italian. "You better go, Mr. Sinclair. I don't think Miss Alex is kidding around."

Greer looked at his housekeeper and nodded. "You are correct, Sophia. Miss Alex is definitely not kidding around."

He placed his napkin on the table and followed me into the library. As soon as the door closed I confronted him. "What the hell happened last night?"

What I'd seen in the mirror scared and angered me at the same time. The whites of my eyes were pale blue, and my pupils were elongated. I looked like a freak.

"Explain this, please." I pointed to my eyes and opened my hand to expose the faded scar.

"Don't you remember?"

"I remember standing on the edge of a building." I looked at my palm. "Did you *stab* me?"

"Lesson one was a success," he declared with a casual tone that suggested there was nothing unusual about having blue cat eyes. "We now know what triggers you. And by the way, I'm a little disturbed by how easy it is for you to try to kill me."

I shook my head and began pacing the floor. "This is crazy. I don't know what's happening to me." The memory of quitting my job and walking out of Shakespeare's Library came rushing back, and I was overwhelmed with a sense of loss. "I feel sick."

"We've been through this, Alex. You're the one who decided it was time to face it head on, and I have to agree with that decision." He respected the space I'd put between us and stayed on the other side of the room. "We know exactly what brings out the devil in you, so now we can focus on controlling it."

"Control it?" I stopped pacing and looked at him like he'd just kicked me in the shin. "You mean control *me*?"

"Do you have any idea how lucky you are?" He shook his head. "You don't need a gun, and someday you won't need me. I'm going to make you into a badass, Alex."

I fought the grin spreading across my face. "Badass, huh? So, what exactly is my trigger?" I was still drawing a big blank about the previous night. I ran my fingers over the mark on my palm. "Blood? Is that it?"

Greer took a seat and told me to do the same. The details were short and to the point. Rhom administered the magic Kool-Aid on the way home from the shop yesterday, and I was more than willing to accompany him to the facility Greer referred to as CTC.

As he replayed the events of the evening, I could see bits and pieces of what had happened in that room. My hands were tied and the room was dark. Footsteps were moving back and forth across the floor, and then they stopped behind me.

"You sliced me open!" I remembered the knife moving down my arm before he plunged it into my palm.

I stood up. An uncomfortable wave of heat flashed through me as the memory of seeing my blood run down my arm turned my thoughts violent.

Greer must have sensed the shift taking place in my head, because he stood up and carefully slipped his hands around my tensed arms to pull me against him. "It's in your head, Alex," he whispered. "It's just a memory." He took my hand and showed me the closed wound. "No more blood. It's safe."

I looked at my hand with a strange fascination, and then

back at Greer. I sat back down, the rage subsiding. I didn't know it at the time, but it was Greer in that dark room dragging a knife through my skin, and I understood why he did it.

"I didn't know it was you, Greer. You smelled different. You smelled *awful*."

"I needed you on the defensive. I thought it wiser to make you feel isolated from the familiar." He snorted a short laugh. "Never underestimate the power of a bad cologne."

He sat back down and crossed his legs. "There's no doubt it's your blood. Your powers are triggered when you bleed." He shook his head. "You, my love, are a walking grenade."

Before last night, I'd shifted—seemed like an appropriate description—twice since coming back to New York, and both times involved the drawing of my blood. If Greer was right, I was a walking powder keg.

"Okay. Where do we go from here?"

The intensity in his eyes made me uneasy, but it was the length between my question and his answer that told me I wasn't going to like what he was about to say.

"I think we need to rule out if it's a compound effect."

"If what's a compound of what?"

"We know you're triggered when you bleed, but I'm questioning if it's that alone." He got up and looked out the window next to the desk. I could feel his discomfort as he worked out how to say what was on his mind. That made me even more nervous because Greer usually had no problem administering orders. They usually came swift and matter-of-fact.

"More testing," he finally said. "We need to run another test."

"You mean you need to cut me again."

"Possibly, but I think there's a simpler way." He headed for the door. "Stay here. I'll be right back."

I paced the room, examining the faded scar on my hand as the night in CTC came back to me. Rhom had been there, too, and possibly responsible for saving Greer's life. That's assuming I was strong enough to kill him.

Greer returned a few minutes later with Rhom. He dropped a small black bag on the desk and rifled through the top drawer. When he found what he was looking for, he asked me to sit.

"I'll sit after you tell me what's in your hand—and that bag."

He held up a pair of handcuffs. "Insurance."

I thought it strange that he needed to fetch Rhom, and even stranger that he had a pair of handcuffs in his desk drawer.

"You're kidding me, right?"

He shook his head and pointed to the chair.

"If I snap, you don't really think those will stop me, do you?"

"No, but they'll give me the advantage."

My eyes went to the black bag as I waited for him to show me what was inside. He unzipped it and pulled out a syringe.

"I thought we were clear on that, Greer." I made it clear a long time ago that I didn't like being drugged, and I wasn't planning to change my stance on that today. "You're not putting anything in my veins."

"You're right. I'm taking something out."

Reluctantly, I sat and waited for the experiment to begin.

"This will be easy," he assured me. "If I'm right, you won't hate me in the morning."

Greer cuffed me from the front. I watched as he swept an alcohol pad across the vein in the bend of my arm and then gently inserted the needle. The tube began to fill as he pulled the plunger toward him. "You're not afraid of me, are you?" he asked to rule out the variable of fear.

I shook my head. "Just do it."

My vision started to blur. I wasn't sure if it was the sight of my blood or the agitation building inside of me that caused my eyes to explode with light.

"Stay with me, Alex."

It came on so fast it was almost like he *had* shot me full of something. But there was nothing going into my vein. It was all coming out. The clear syringe transformed into a cylinder of dark crimson red.

"Are you okay?" he asked in the calm voice I knew so well. But it was beginning to sound different now. His voice was becoming the deep, hollow drone of a stranger.

"Alex? Stay with me. Almost done."

My head slowly cocked away from my arm to look at the man holding the syringe. "I . . . I *can't!*" I screamed as I shoved him sideways and yanked the syringe out with my teeth. "It's mine!"

He tackled me to the floor, grabbing the center of the cuff to wedge my arms over my head. I could hear his voice in the distance as he spoke to someone in the room, but the voices were muffled by the hurricane spinning in my head, energizing me like a high voltage wire.

A sharp pain radiated through my neck, and the storm went away.

FOUR

I stayed in bed for the next twenty-four hours, getting up every now and then but always finding myself right back under the covers. My reaction to Greer drawing my blood not only proved his theory, but put everyone in the house at risk. Thank God he was smart enough to bring backup, and Rhom managed to inject a sedative in my neck strong enough to put down an elephant—hence my lazy state.

He was right about my trigger being blood. But he wasn't convinced that fear had no part in it. I proved him wrong. It was just the blood, plain and simple, and I had a build-in defense mechanism against anyone or anything that tried to spill it.

Leda had been dispatched to babysit me while Greer went to the club for a few hours. She'd become an invaluable friend and one of Greer's most trusted associates—a former lover turned right-hand "man" who was just as formidable as any of the men on his team.

"Maybe we can play cards," she suggested with a blank look.

"Really, Leda? You want to play cards? Maybe we can start a quilting circle, too." In her Donna Karan dresses and Manolo Blahnik pumps, Leda wasn't the type to make small talk with her hands.

"Of course not, but we can't just sit here all day. We'll end up putting a bullet in our brains from boredom."

"That's it." I climbed out of bed and put on a pair of shorts. "You can't do this, Leda. You'll go crazy and end up hating me."

"Don't be ridiculous. I'll stay perfectly sane while I hate you."

I went downstairs to find Sophia. I think she was born with a chopping knife in her hand, so I went straight to the kitchen. She was stirring a large pot of sauce with one hand and checking the rise on a ball of bread dough with the other. "Oh, that smells good. Manicotti?"

"Cannelloni," she corrected.

"Right." I asked the next question cautiously. I'd never asked to have a guest for dinner before, and I didn't want to blindside her with a stranger at the table. "Would it bother you if I invited a friend for dinner?"

The spoon in her hand stopped for a second and then resumed stirring. "I love to cook for your friend, but Mr. Sinclair might not be so pleased." With a firm tap against the enameled pot, the excess sauce fell from the wooden spoon. She set it on a small plate next to the stove and turned around, running her eyes over my face. "You call Mr. Sinclair and tell him I make a nice dinner for you and your friend."

"You're the best, Sophia."

"Yeah, yeah, I know." She wiped her hands on her yellow apron and waved me out of the kitchen.

I hoped Katie had the day shift and would accept my invitation to dinner. I was desperate to spend some time with a normal person. But after dumping all my skeletons on her the other day and then quitting my job, I wasn't even sure we were still friends. Getting Greer on board was another hurdle. We hosted dinner parties all the time, but the faces around the table were Greer's friends, and I had no idea how he'd react to hosting one of mine.

Greer's cell phone rang once before he answered. "What's wrong?" he asked without a greeting.

"Nothing's wrong. I just wanted to ask you something." I don't know why I was so nervous about inviting a friend for dinner. Greer had always made it clear that his house was my house. "Sophia is making this fantastic cannelloni, and I'd like to invite my friend Katie to dinner."

There was silence on the other end. For a second I thought the connection dropped. "Is this the same friend who intercepted Lumen the other day?" he finally asked.

"Yes."

"Good. Invite her. I want to meet this girl."

Katie had been the subject of many conversations with Greer. I'd told him about her the day I got the job, but it was all white noise to him. He filtered out what he needed to hear and ignored the rest. I couldn't wait to see his reaction to the girl with the serpent tattoos and combat boots.

I called her cell phone. "Alex?" She sounded surprised to hear from me, and I wondered if she was about to give me the polite brushoff. I wouldn't blame her if she did. Even in her liberal world, I was a freak. "About time you called. I've been dying to talk to you. Your friend stopped by the shop this morning."

Besides Katie and Greer's posse, I didn't exactly have friends in New York. "Who?"

"Constantine. You know, that hot guy you've been hiding."

Constantine wasn't just some guy; he was a satyr with a perpetual hard-on, always looking for a new conquest. I hadn't seen him since he took me to Paris—or should I say abducted me. That was the day I discovered his neat little mode of transportation. One minute we were standing in New York, and the next we were in an apartment in Paris—via a stopover on top of the Brooklyn Bridge.

"Really? What did he want?"

"You, silly. He didn't seem very surprised when I told him you quit."

"He's got a really good poker face," I replied. "Did you tell him anything else?"

"Nope."

Constantine practically ravaged Katie with his eyes the first time he came to the shop, and I made sure he didn't come back. The vibe between the two of them was just too dangerous. The last thing Katie needed was a satyr in her bed. Getting her to come to dinner was even more important now, so I could find out what Constantine was up to.

"Are you working tonight?" I asked.

"I got off an hour ago. Why? Interested in a girl's night out?"

"I know it's short notice, but would you be interested in coming over for dinner? I need company, and Greer would like to meet you."

"Greer? The famous roommate who *isn't* a roommate?"

"Yep. That's the one."

"What time?" It was already a few minutes after six, so I gave her the address and told her to head over.

Leda was standing behind me when I ended the call. "A party?"

"I invited a friend for dinner. You should stay. I think you'd like her."

"I'd love to, but I don't want to be a third wheel." She dusted the imaginary lint from her skirt and smoothed her auburn hair away for her temples. "Is this appropriate?"

Leda always looked perfect. She could wear a paper sack and look perfect. Smart as a whip, too. She had that movie star quality that got men instantly hard and made women take notes. "You'll be the fourth wheel. Greer will be joining us, too."

"Well, all right, then. I'll stay." She headed for the kitchen to offer Sophia help with dinner, a polite gesture that would be politely rejected.

Katie didn't ask about the dress code. There wasn't one, but I didn't want her to feel underdressed next to Leda, so I went upstairs to put on a pair of jeans and a blouse. That way she'd be somewhere in the middle of feeling under or overdressed. Thomas was sitting in the living room when I came back downstairs.

"Hey there, handsome." I was used to seeing Thomas in uniform: black slacks, black shoes, black crew neck. The bartenders at Crusades could wear whatever they liked as long as it was black. Tonight he was dressed in fancy jeans and a pricey jacket. "You here for dinner?"

"Looks like it. Greer and I have some business tonight, so he offered to feed me first."

"Where is he?" It was getting late, and I wanted Greer to be here when Katie arrived. First impressions mattered, and for some reason I wanted her to like him.

"He was right behind me. Should be walking in any minute now."

"Honey, I'm home." Greer stepped off the elevator with a bunch of white tulips in his hand. He gave them to Sophia when she peeked into the foyer, and then kissed me on the cheek.

"What was that for?" I asked, my fingers feeling the spot where he'd pressed his lips.

"Just trying to play my part. Your significant other tonight, right?"

"Won't be necessary. She knows."

"Knows what?" His tone darkened, and I knew we were about to have one of our world class arguments . . . or should I say lectures.

"Just about everything. Well, almost everything."

"Really? And you don't see the problem with that?"

"Not at all." Katie was the kind of girl that took strange things to heart. She was an outsider herself, so the strange and unusual were appreciated. I think it made people like us feel normal. "At least wait until you meet her before you judge her. She was perfectly fine with everything. You know, she's the one who found my birthmark."

He threw his keys in the bowl on the table and headed up the stairs. "We'll continue this discussion after I change."

The doorbell rang as Greer was coming back down the steps. He'd exchanged his suit for a pair of casual slacks, but kept the shirt. Thomas made it to the door first. When he opened it, Katie was standing on the other side with a bottle of red wine in her hand. I'd never seen her in anything conservative, so the black sheath dress she was wearing made me question the identity of the woman standing on the threshold.

She glanced past Thomas and smiled at me. When she looked back at the man holding the door open, he was staring at her with intent. "I'm Katie." She extended her hand.

He took it and held it longer than was customary. "Thomas," he introduced himself. "You have extraordinary eyes."

Katie had that effect on both men and women because her eyes *were* extraordinary. The blue was striking in contrast with her jet black hair, creating an enhanced version of Elizabeth Taylor with photoshopped irises.

She didn't respond to Thomas' comment, but I could see a visual conversation taking place between them.

I moved in to break the spell, taking the bottle from her hand before grabbing her arm and leading her into the living room. "You have no idea how happy I am to see you."

"Me too. It sucks not having you at the shop. Apollo put a sign in the window right after you left and—"

My excitement faded as I realized how quickly I was being replaced. "Wow. It's final, isn't it? Just like that, I'm out."

"Alex, he's just doing his job. We're both pulling double shifts until we find someone. I'd be there right now if I hadn't worked twelve hours yesterday."

"I know. I'm sorry. No more downer talk." I mimicked zipping my mouth and gave her a hug.

"Are you going to introduce me to your friend?" Greer asked as he watched our reunion from the foyer.

"Oh, sorry. Katie Bishop, this is Greer Sinclair."

He came into the room and fixed his eyes on hers for a moment before extending his hand. "It's a pleasure to meet the girl with the guns."

Katie looked at me and then back at Greer. "Guns?"

"I hear you came to Alex's rescue the other day."

"Oh, you mean that creepy little witch that showed up at the shop the other morning. Just needed to establish some boundaries, that's all."

Greer released her hand but kept his eyes on her longer than I was comfortable with. Katie broke the connection first and then looked at me. "So, this is where you live, and this is your roommate?" she asked, looking back at Greer.

"Yes, and not exactly."

Leda entered the room. "Hello. Katie, right?"

"That's me."

She walked up and wrapped her arms around Katie, planting a cordial kiss on her cheek. "I hear you've been a good friend to our Alex." She stepped back to take Katie in. "My, you are lovely." Her eyes roamed along the tail that went down Katie's arm. It circled back up to her shoulder and then disappeared under the backside of her dress. "May I?"

"Be my guest," Katie responded, completely comfortable with the odd request.

I thought Leda was just going to take a closer look at Katie's exposed skin, but then Katie lifted her hair off of her neck as Leda circled around to her backside, slowly pulling her zipper down to reveal the ink creature embedded in Katie skin.

"It's magnificent. A real work of art." Leda ran a finger

along the intricate lines. She zipped the dress and came back around to Katie's front. "How rude of me. I'm Leda."

"Okay, that's enough butt sniffing," I said to break up the examination.

I was about to check on dinner when Sophia announced it was ready. Thomas wasted no time offering his arm to Katie as we went into the dining room. He had his eye on her, and from what I could see, she was receptive to the attention. I loved Thomas, but I wasn't sure it was a good idea for Katie to be loving him, too.

We sat around a mountain of the best Italian food this side of Campania placed in the center of the table. Sophia never went small when she cooked, creating a never-ending supply of leftovers in the fridge. It was a miracle I hadn't gained twenty pounds since moving in.

"Tell me, Katie," Leda began. "Why would a woman like you want to work in a used bookstore?"

I glared at Leda, because until a few days ago I worked in that same bookstore, and I would still be there if it was up to me.

"Well, I'm a student at Columbia." She placed her fork on the plate as she swallowed a bite of food. "Tuition isn't free, you know."

"I suppose not," Leda replied, spearing the tomato in her salad.

"I worked at Starbucks for a while. Then I spent a few weeks at this fancy boutique where rich women would drop thousands on dresses with price tags exceeding my weekly paycheck. But I found this hole-in-the-wall shop called Shakespeare's Library, and for the first time, that shitty little paycheck didn't seem so bad."

"Columbia?" Thomas seemed impressed. "Beautiful and smart."

"What are you studying up there?" Greer asked.

"Environmental engineering."

"So you want to clean up the world," he replied. "Make the water safer to drink."

"Something like that."

Despite Leda's off comment, the evening was perfect. For the first time in months, I was able to relax and not think about who might try to kill me next. Katie knew I was different and she didn't care. Greer seemed to like her, too. That was important because I planned to keep her around.

We finished off the pasta and drank several bottles of wine. After clearing the empty platters from the table, Sophia returned with one of her homemade Italian cheesecakes. Knowing it was Thomas' favorite, she placed it on the table in front of him. His eyes widened as he grabbed her around the waist and pulled her into his lap.

"Mr. Thomas!" she squealed. "You crazy man."

"You know I love you, woman. Keep bringing me these and I'll have to marry you."

She straightened her apron as he released her, a smile breaking over her face as she hurried out of the room.

Thomas offered a slice of cake to everyone at the table before cutting his own. Next came the coffee, marking the end of a perfect meal.

As the conversation bounced around the table, I noticed Leda watching Katie. I would have dismissed it as curiosity, but the look on her face wasn't curious—it was calculating.

Katie glanced at Leda now and then, but other than that she ignored the attention. The men picked up on it, too. Thomas looked at Greer, and then back at the two women who were having some sort of silent tête-à-tête.

"Where are your people from?" Leda eventually asked.

"You mean my parents?" replied Katie.

"Yes. The Bishop clan. Where are they from? What was their trade?"

Leda wasted no time dissecting Katie's history. Where she was born, her family's religious beliefs, *her* religious beliefs: I cringed at the thought of all the questions that were about to be hurled at my friend.

Without a word, Katie held Leda's stare. A polite standoff commenced, and everyone at the table felt the heat as the pot began to boil.

A nervous laugh peeped from my mouth as the absurdity reached a climax. *What the hell is Leda doing?*

"Have you heard of Crusades?" I asked Katie, trying to defuse the ticking bomb. "Greer owns the place. We should go some night."

Katie kept her eyes on Leda. "That's all right, Alex. I don't mind the questions." She took another bite of cake and slowly chewed as the rest of the table waited for her to continue.

The tension tightened, and I began to wonder if I was the only one at the table not privy to the real conversation.

"My family is from England," Katie continued. "My mother was actually born in Wales, but she was raised in England." She took a sip of coffee and looked back up at Leda. "Is that what you want to know?"

Leda maintained her flat expression without saying a word.

"I haven't been to Crusades, but I've heard of it," Katie said, picking up my hanging question. "Crusades is yours, Greer?"

"It is. You're welcome there anytime . . . as my guest."

"No, dear," Leda said, hijacking the conversation back to the original thread. "I mean your real parents. Russian?"

Katie put her cup down and glanced at her half-eaten slice of cake. Leda struck a nerve, and I was both embarrassed by the treatment of my friend, and curious as to how Leda knew such a personal detail about Katie's life. The look on Katie's face confirmed that Leda was right.

In a panic to fill the awkward silence, I blurted out the first thing that came to mind. "Russia? How interesting."

"How did you know?" Katie asked Leda.

"Know what?" Leda replied, acting like all was normal and she hadn't just called my friend a liar.

"That I was adopted."

FIVE

fter apologizing to Katie for the interrogation at dinner, I said good night and shut the door to her cab.

Obviously a bee had flown up Leda's ass, compelling my friend to defend herself unnecessarily. Katie never mentioned that she was adopted, and until she felt the need to share that information it was no one else's business to do it for her. Thank God Greer finally censured the inquisition before it reached the point of bullying, and we were able to salvage the rest of the evening.

I never did get to pick Katie's brain about Constantine's visit to the shop. Had it been eventful, I'm sure she would have said something before she left. It probably didn't matter anyway. I'd be lucky if I ever saw Katie again after what Leda just did.

As the cab pulled away from the curb, I just stood there under the streetlight, dismantling my plan to calmly walk back inside and murder Leda. It was getting late, but the clear sky gave off a soft light that made it appear earlier than it was. I considered the stupid idea of heading toward the park and walking until my legs gave out. Anything to avoid going back in there to face the Gestapo imposter in Leda's clothing.

A drop of rain hit my nose, reminding me that spring was here and the days were getting longer. It wouldn't be long now until it was still light at this time.

I turned to walk back to the house when I saw a shadow appear halfway between Greer's steps and the neighbor's. It seemed to mirror my movements, stopping when I did and continuing each time I took a step toward the stairs. Maybe if I ran I'd make it to the steps first. Maybe I was overreacting and it was just the neighbor taking out his garbage.

I took my chances and ran for it. As my foot hit the bottom step, an arm wrapped around my waist and a hand covered my mouth before I could scream.

"You're a difficult girl to find. Now that I have, we have things to discuss."

His voice was familiar, but I couldn't see his face.

I focused on the front door and considered how I could keep him from dragging me off the steps long enough for Greer to get suspicious and come looking for me.

He must have had the same thought, because he pulled me into the shaded corner behind the stairs, the glare of the streetlight revealing his face. It was Daemon, the man I met at Arthur Richmond's party last December. I was at the bar that night, and he mistook me for his missing date. He seemed perfectly harmless at the time, until I naively followed him to a room one floor up from the party and nearly found out just how wrong that first impression was. If it hadn't been for Constantine showing up and scaring him off, God knows what he would have done to me.

"It's nice to see you again, Alex." His face came closer, and the scent coming off his skin stirred an unpleasant memory. It was one of those scattered images that kept teasing me with fragments of a bigger picture.

I breathed his scent in again, and those scattered pieces began to come together, forming a face I vaguely remembered from the night I was held to the ground and nearly raped in Central Park. I was drugged that night—poisoned according to Greer—and barely made out the set of eyes staring down at me. But it was that faint scent of charred cedar coming off his skin that I'll never forget. The combination of that smell and those gripping brown eyes pulled all the pieces together. At Arthur Richmond's party the following month, his eyes had triggered something familiar, but the only thing I remembered smelling was his strong cologne.

That man was hunting, Constantine had warned. I thought he was overreacting, or just trying to block the competition.

Daemon must have been following me since that night in the park. All these months, he'd been watching me, patiently waiting for the right opportunity to finish what he started.

I closed my eyes and fought the sickness roiling up from my stomach. His hand was too tight on my mouth. I clawed at it frantically as my ability to breathe lessened and sent me into a panic.

"I don't want to hurt you," he whispered. "I just needed to see you for myself. I knew there was something different about you." He looked up at Greer's front door and then released my mouth with a visual warning not to scream.

"Is that why you attacked me in the park?" I choked out between gasps for air. "Because I'm so different?"

His expression sobered. "No. That's why I stopped."

I dug my fingers into his skin as he tightened his grip around my waist. "Get off of me, you sick bastard!"

"This isn't personal, Alex."

Right. There was nothing personal about it. In that moment, I realized he wasn't just one of the predators Greer had described to me the night he told me about the Rogues—he was delusional.

"I guess the amulet takes priority over *that*." I could feel the cool surface of the silver pressed against my bare skin under my shirt, and I wondered if he could, too.

He smiled as if reading my mind and ran his hand over my blouse. His fingers found it under the fabric but continued lower until they reached my chest. "The prophecy will give us control of the earth. But you, Alex," he cupped my breast and squeezed, "will make us kings."

We both looked up at the front door as it opened. Greer burst through it and took the steps four at a time. Daemon was gone the moment the light from the living room hit the outside threshold, and I was left standing alone on the sidewalk.

"Alex? What's taking so long?"

Greer was already smothering me, and telling him that a Rogue had been standing on his steps just before he came barreling through the door would set us back to lockdown status. I was surprised he even let me walk Katie to her cab without an escort.

"Easy, tiger. I'm just getting a little fresh air." I walked past him and prayed he wouldn't notice my hand trembling on the rail, or smell the adrenaline racing through my bloodstream. He studied me carefully as I ascended the steps, but said nothing. I guess the past few days warranted a little spike in my juices.

When I walked into the living room, Leda was sitting on the sofa with her head leaned back against the cushion. Ella Fitzgerald was singing "Someone to Watch Over Me." She hummed along, seemingly indifferent to the fact that she'd humiliated my friend at dinner.

"What was that all about?" I demanded.

She lifted her head and the volume instantly muted. "What? You mean our search for the truth?"

"Call it whatever you like, but it was wrong." Leda was a class act, but today I'd seen the mean girl who lived within. "That was just plain rude, Leda. I'll be surprised if Katie ever speaks to me again."

"Don't be so dramatic, Alex. If she's half the girl you say she is, she won't let a bitch like me break up a friendship." She stood up and walked over to me, fiddling with the collar of my blouse like an old mother hen. "But there's something I think you should know."

I swatted at her hands. "Would you stop."

"That girl is not who she says she is." She dropped her hands and took a step back.

I glared at Greer and then back at Leda. "Then who is she?"

"I haven't figured that out yet, but one thing I'm absolutely certain of—that girl is not English."

"Oh, well. There you go. I'm so glad you spared me from the big lie." I looked around the room at all the faces staring back at me. "God forbid someone around here is less than truthful about who they really are."

"Alex," Greer warned, playing arbiter.

"And you," I snapped at him. "You let it go on forever until you finally did something about it. You just sat there and let her humiliate my friend—in your own house."

Leda headed for the bar. She poured a drink and came back toward me.

"I don't want a damn drink, Leda."

"It's not for you, dear." She handed the glass to Greer. "He needs it more than you do."

"Leda's right," he agreed. "I don't know what it is, but there's definitely something not right about Katie. If it makes you feel any better, I don't think she knows she's lying."

"Which means technically she *isn't* lying," Leda added. "Very strong Slavic vibe."

"For God's sake, who cares where she's from!"

"We don't," Greer said. "We're more concerned about what she *is*."

It took a half hour of arguing, but I finally convinced Greer that his life would be immensely more peaceful if he allowed me to go to Shakespeare's Library long enough to try to patch my friendship with Katie. Allowing it would also eliminate my need to sneak out unchaperoned—an act he knew I was capable of. He agreed to give me an hour accompanied by Rhom.

Rhom was decent enough to wait outside the shop. When I walked inside, Katie was sitting at the library table with a man wearing chinos and a blazer in desperate need of ironing. She raised her index finger to let me know she'd be with me in a minute.

It was just past noon, and Katie was manning the shop alone, probably so Apollo could grab some lunch. I poked around the shelves while I waited and noticed a resume in her hand. The man sitting across the table from her seemed a bit nervous, shifting in his chair and playing with the ends of his tie. She was interviewing my replacement.

"Thanks for coming in, Kevin. Apollo will give you a call this afternoon." She closed the door as he left the shop and then turned to look at me.

"So . . . Kevin?"

"Looks like it," she sighed. "Nice guy, but it won't be the same around here."

"I can't begin to tell you how embarrassed I am about how Leda treated you at dinner. She usually isn't like that."

Katie laid the resume on the counter and crooked her finger, instructing me to follow her. We walked halfway down the sci-fi aisle before she stopped. "Didn't you ever wonder why I was so blasé about everything the night you asked me to comb through your hair? Why I never asked what that mark on the back of your head was all about?"

It was in this very room that we found the mark and I discovered that I was the Oracle.

"Well, I just figured you were being . . . you. You're not exactly mainstream, Katie."

"Come on, Alex. Who the hell would let something like that

go and never bring it up again?" She turned her back to me and began lifting the bottom of her shirt. "Take a look."

I'd never actually seen her entire tattoo. Even when she allowed Leda to unzip her dress at dinner, her back was away from me.

She pulled her tank top over her shoulders. "Undo my bra so you can get a better look."

I popped the clasp and the bra fell away from the canvas of her back. "Wow, that's some piece of art." I couldn't stop my finger from tracing the lines. "It must have taken months or years to complete." I'd always imagined some sort of serpent under her clothes, but now that it was right in front of me, it looked more like a dragon. "Did it hurt?" I asked as I refastened her bra.

"I don't know." She dropped her shirt and the ink disappeared back under the tank top. "I was born with it."

Either she was fucking with me as payback for our little fiasco at dinner, or she was a bigger freak than I was.

"You mean you don't remember getting it done?" I'd heard of people tattooing their children. They usually ended up in jail.

"No, I really don't. A woman came to visit me when I was a kid. She just showed up at my school and said she was my aunt. Made me show it to her, and then she showed me hers." She smirked nervously. "Looks like you're not the weirdest one in the room, after all."

"So . . . are you saying Leda was right?"

Her blue eyes sparkled as the morning light amplified through the window, the same color as the eyes of the creature on her back. "She was right about one thing—I'm adopted. I guess I should have mentioned that."

"It's none of my business, Katie."

"I just hate the way people look at me when I tell them I'm adopted. It's like I have some incurable disease."

"Then I guess we have more in common than we thought." I'd seen that same look a hundred times while I went from one foster home to the next. "Does this mean we're still friends?"

"Why wouldn't we be?" She looked genuinely surprised by the question. "What? You thought I'd dump you because of someone else's bad manners? Look, I don't know anything about Leda, but I bet she'd rip my throat out if I hurt you."

She was right about that. Leda was just trying to protect me from the conniving girl with the dragon tattoo.

"Can I ask you something, Alex?"

"Shoot."

"All that shit you told me the other day, the stuff about your eyes and this prophecy, is that everything?"

Here we go. I'd told her the meat of it but left out some of the worst parts, like my homicidal nature. Seeing how she probably had a few more secrets of her own, it seemed safe to share. "I left out a few things."

"I want all of it, Alex. I'm just dying to know more about those friends of yours."

"Me, too," I muttered.

"Thomas is hot." She bit her brightly painted lower lip. "And Greer! I don't know how you keep your hands off of him. Which one is Leda fucking?"

"Neither. Well, not anymore. She used to have a thing for Greer, but it's been over for a long time."

"So he's fair game?" she asked with an arched brow.

The question put me off balance. I guess he was fair game. I know I certainly had no claim.

She saw the look on my face and quickly clarified. "For *you*. Jesus, Alex. What kind of friend do you think I am?"

"Please." I rolled my eyes, waving my hand dismissively through the air.

"Come on. No more man talk." She motioned me over to the library table. "Let's start with why you really quit."

This wasn't going to be as tough as I thought. If Katie was actually born with that tattoo on her back, my lineage would seem tame in comparison.

The bell on the door chimed. We both looked up as an elderly woman walked into the shop. She had a pronounced hump on her upper back, forcing her to walk in a hunched manner. For a woman of her advanced age, she had a surprisingly dark head of hair. No gray, just a mane of jet black hair pulled back into a neat bun at the crown of her head. She went straight for the section on health and wellness but stopped at the end cap and looked back at the front door. Her right hand went up, and her finger began to tap against her thin lips.

"Can I help you find something?" Katie asked.

"No, dear. You go right back to what you were doing," she answered.

"You let us know if we can help you find something."

The woman disappeared down the aisle, and Katie turned back to our conversation. "You were saying?"

I was about to confess more sordid details about my messed up heritage. She already knew the highlights, so I was really just filling in the gaps.

Our conversation was interrupted by a thump coming from one of the aisles. It sounded like a heavy book hitting the floor. We both glanced in the direction of the noise, but when we heard nothing else I continued with my story.

"Remember when I told you about—"

Another sound came from the aisle, only this one sounded like a pile of books cascading from the shelf to the floor. Katie's eyes turned first. I hesitated before looking in the same direction.

"Everything all right in there?" she said loudly so the woman could hear. "Are you sure we can't help you find something?"

"No, dear. You go right back to what you were doing."

The woman was beginning to sound like a broken record. I could tell by the look on Katie's face that the same thought was going through her mind.

"Is the sky blue?" I said to the woman while looking at Katie.

"No, dear. You go right back to what you were doing."

The ruckus coming from inside the aisle got louder. I couldn't see the books flying off the shelves, but I could hear them hitting the floor in an avalanche of pulp and ink.

Katie got up and ran toward the aisle. I started to follow but stopped as a large shadow spread across the ceiling over the health and wellness section. It expanded and covered the entire side of the room as a long pole-shaped limb curled around the side of the shelf. Like giant pipe cleaners gripping the top, more appeared until there were four legs on each side. And then a pair of hooked fangs protruded over the end cap, followed by two rows of shiny black eyes.

"Katie!" I screamed as she disappeared into the stacks.

A loud hiss filled the room. The sound amplified, vibrating in my head until it felt like a knife slicing through my eardrum.

I stumbled backward as the massive black form emerged near the ceiling and started moving down the side of the shelf. My foot caught a pile of books left on the floor, and I hit the ground hard, struggling to right myself before the thing was on top of me.

One of its legs stepped over me and planted on my left side. Another did the same on my right, and I was caged by black furry bars as its fangs spread and lowered toward me.

They say your life flashes before your eyes just before you die, but all I could think about was all the unfinished business that would remain unfinished forever.

My eyes squeezed shut as I waited for the strike, but the blow never came. It was moving its back legs in a repetitive motion as it kept me caged beneath it. My arms pulled to my sides and my legs straighten as it lifted me off the floor and the room began to spin. But it wasn't the room spinning—it was me.

The pain intensified as I spun around like a piece of paper in the wind, its legs wrapping me like a baby swaddled in a tight blanket.

A tornado must have hit the shop, because the sound of a freight train suddenly rolled through it, and the black furry bars lifted off of me in one swift movement like a house coming off of its foundation.

As my vision cleared, I could see the new threat towering over me, its claws tossing black pipe cleaners through the air as they were ripped from the giant furry bulb.

"Katie!" I screamed. "Run!"

The creature making confetti out of the spider stopped and turned as if noticing me for the first time. It dropped the insect and came toward me. I pushed my way out of the thin blanket of silk and slid under the library table. A foot the size of a watermelon landed on the floor next to me, and then the room went completely still.

"What do you want?" I whispered. The stupid question slipped out of my mouth without a thought.

A giant claw hooked the fabric of my shirt and dragged me out from under the table. I dangled in the air, suspended by the massive scaled appendage and looked into the bright blue eyes of Katie Bishop.

SIX

The place looked different with the lights on. We were at the CTC—Central Training Center—where I almost dove twenty stories to my death. With its matching black ceiling, floor, and walls, the room looked like the inside of a black hole.

"That's the intention," said Greer. A psychological illusion meant to put the trainee off balance. "If you can't visually tell which side is up or down, you're more aware of your center of gravity."

We were about to start our first day of training. Now that we knew what my trigger was, it was vital that I learned how to control it. Until that happened, Greer wouldn't let me out of the house without an escort.

"You should have been able to kill that thing yourself," he said.

He was referring to the black widow that got past Rhom at the shop. Fortunately for me, Katie's dragon emerged to save the day. She didn't have a clue what she was. That all changed a week ago when she found herself faced with the dilemma of dying, or exposing her beast. She ended up saving both of our lives in exchange for being outed.

The widow wasn't actually trying to kill me, but Katie was excess baggage she didn't need. Too bad the spider didn't get the memo about the dragon.

As soon as her deadly claw lowered me back to the floor that day, Katie looked in the mirror and her dragon immediately shed its skin and returned to its home on her backside. Like an obedient dog, it submitted.

"Does that happen often?" I asked when it was over.

"Never. Well, I don't think so." She told me about an incident when some guy followed her out of a club and got a little too persistent. She blacked out, but in the back of her mind she knew he got what he deserved.

I considered not telling Greer about Katie's secret. It would just fuel an unpleasant argument whenever I wanted to see her. But Rhom took care of that. He heard the riot and came storming into the shop just in time to see the dragon retreat.

Greer took it better than I expected. He liked the idea of me having Katie as backup. "The dragon obviously knows you," he'd said, and that was the end of it.

I dropped my duffle bag on the floor. "Where do we start?"

He said nothing as he dropped his own bag next to mine, studying me to determine the best approach for taming my inner shrew.

The dark interior made the room look cozy, but the expanse of it became clear when he removed his shoes and took his time walking the perimeter.

He was wearing a pair of black warmup pants and a black T-shirt. "Another strategic illusion?" I asked, referring to the way he blended with the rest of the room, his exposed skin the only thing distinguishing him from the walls.

He watched me in silence. Maybe this was part of the training, a way of psyching the opponent. But as he moved around the room, I got the feeling he was looking for something underneath my skin, an entry point or some Achilles' heel.

"Penny for your thoughts." I smiled sweetly, anticipating the unpleasant dance we were about to engage in.

"This isn't a competition, Alex. You win, I win. You lose, I lose."

There was a medieval looking chair in the far corner of the room with metal cuffs chained to the arms and legs. "Is that for me?"

"If necessary." He stopped to face me as he said it, gauging my reaction to the possibility of restraints. The last time he cuffed me I ended up with a needle in my neck. The heaviness of the chair offered some additional insurance that this session wouldn't end the way that one did.

The door opened and Thomas walked in the room. He was wearing similar workout attire and had his hair pulled back in a stub of a ponytail.

"Good morning, Thomas. Tag team today?"

"You bet, sugar."

I looked back and forth between the two of them. "Haven't we been down this road before?" I was referring to the night I almost killed them both—with Greer's own knife. Arthur Richmond had locked me in a basement and tried to beat the whereabouts of the amulet out of me. At the time, no one knew I was a walking time bomb, and I almost killed everyone in the room when my little secret came out.

"There won't be any weapons in the room tonight," Greer informed me. "And I've arranged for a little extra reinforcement." He nodded to my rear. "Just in case."

I turned around and saw Rhom standing behind me. "Smart move."

As any good leader should, Greer had the power to give orders without words. He looked at Thomas and Rhom and the two men moved to the back wall.

He approached the center of the room and removed his shirt, exposing his lean waist and toned abdominal muscles. It wasn't the first time I'd seen him shirtless, and I knew exactly what that skin felt like against mine. But no matter how many times I saw his bare body, my breathing never failed to skip a beat.

Greer Sinclair was the prototype for what a man should look like.

"Are you trying to distract me?" I asked.

"Is it working?"

"This isn't exactly a fair fight, you know. I'm not coming out of the closet without a little bloodshed." As soon as the words left my mouth I regretted agreeing to any of this. "I don't suppose you have a hypodermic in that bag?"

He slowly shook his head. "I think we need to simulate a more realistic scenario. Wouldn't you agree, Thomas?" he asked without taking his eyes off of mine.

"Yes sir, boss," Thomas replied.

"I'm not getting in that chair."

Greer looked at the torturous contraption and then back at me. "I wouldn't think of putting you in that chair—yet."

He came forward and stopped within a foot of me. "Give me your hand."

"Are you going to cut me?"

"Yes."

I did what any obedient student would do. I stuck out my hand and whined pathetically. "Not too deep, now. Just nick me a little, Greer."

Greer didn't hesitate. He took his knife, sharpened enough to slice effortlessly through an alligator's skin, and drew a half-inch cut in the center of my palm. Then he tossed it to Rhom and told him to get rid of it.

Rhom opened the door and tossed the knife outside before locking us in.

At first I felt nothing, but a few seconds after the blade lifted from my skin, the latent pain kicked in. The cut expanded as my blood pushed through the edges like an eruption of pomegranate syrup.

My eyes burned and then cooled as my vision became crystal clear. *Who the hell is this fucker?*

"Alex?" I heard someone say. "Do you know me?"

I looked up and cocked my head at the two men standing against the wall. If I killed the one in front of me quickly, I'd have plenty of time to get to the other two before they made it to the door.

"What?" I craned my head back around to look at the one in front of me. "Do I know you?" I repeated back to him. "Yeah, I know you. You're the idiot who just cut me."

He took a few steps backward and turned around, giving me ample opportunity to strike. *Why is he doing that?* A large tattoo covered his skin and disappeared under the edge of his waistband. I studied the strange pattern as broken images teased my memory. I shook off the distraction and considered the best way to preserve the ink trophy once I carved it from his back.

I looked to my right as the men standing in the distance moved. Their leader was exposed and vulnerable, and that was making them nervous. He was their master, and a good warrior always protects his master.

The tattoo articulated like a complex mechanism as he walked away from me, each line flowing like a living breathing organism as his muscles rolled and contracted.

About ten feet out, he stopped. His shoulders expanded with each of his deep controlled breaths. "Shall we?" he offered without turning around.

I laughed—in a non-funny way. "You're a cocky bastard, aren't you?"

"So I've been told. And capable."

"Of?"

Now he turned to look at me. His grin faded as his hands

contracted into tight fists. "Of breaking you." His eyes never wavered as they stared into the blue light coming from mine.

Normally I'd let my opponent make the first move, but this one was getting under my skin with his cocky confidence, like he'd be the one walking away when it was over. "You need to learn some manners." I picked up speed as I moved toward him and reached for his throat.

He grabbed my wrist and my eyes turned into floodlights of blue. Partly from the shock that he'd managed to get his hands on me without me detecting his movement, and partly from the sight of the blood running down my arm. He pulled it to his mouth and pressed his lips over the trail of red. I could feel his tongue moving against my skin, his eyes never leaving mine as he tasted it.

His brow arched. "Salty."

The rage was beating against my chest, fighting to get out from under all the skin and bone so it could kill the man who'd just stolen my blood. *My blood!*

Part of me felt sorry for him because he was about to suffer a painful annihilation. But the part of me that wanted to see his own blood drain from his body overruled.

He started it, but I would end it.

"Say my name," he whispered with my wrist still gripped in his hand. And for reasons I couldn't comprehend, I allowed it. I closed my eyes and shook my head as the two voices in my mind reasoned with me in opposite directions.

The dangerous voice won and I threw myself backward, flipping in the air before landing about halfway between him and the other two men at the back of the room.

"Damn, Greer. The girl has moves," one of the men said. "Time for the shackles?"

I looked at the one they called *Greer*. He was the only real threat in the room. The others were just white noise. "No shackles today, Greer," I declared as I slowly shook my head.

I ran at him full speed, flipping my torso to extend my legs toward his chest. He absorbed the impact of the kick and slammed against the mat. I got back on my feet. So did he. I came at him again. This time he shifted sideways, causing me to sail past him and land hard against the padded wall. Over and over he took a defensive stance, never once attempting an offensive move.

"Why aren't you fighting?" His indifference was infuriating. "Are you stupid?"

He took a shallow breath and ordered his men out of the room. The two men looked at each other, and then left without questioning the logic of leaving him alone with a woman who was trying to kill him.

As soon as they were gone, I opened my mouth to antagonize him into striking. This time I wouldn't make the mistake of coming at him. That approach just wasn't working. But before I knew what hit me, my arms were tucked behind my back and my cheek was pressed against the cold rubberized pad lining the wall.

"Enough," he growled. "We end this here and now."

"Agreed. Now why don't you get off of me?"

He pushed me deeper into the wall. The heat coming off of him caused my already flushed skin to glisten with a thin film of moisture, and when his warm breath hit the side of my face, I thought I'd break out in a full sweat. His fingers circled my wrists and then I felt something cold slip around them.

He'd cuffed me.

"No," I protested. A fight on equal ground was one thing, but this was no fair fight.

"You were pretty effective the last time I put these on you." He flipped me around to face him. "Now, we're not leaving this room until we come to an understanding. Is that clear?"

His face was inches from mine, glowing from the light coming from my eyes that made his skin look silver. I looked in his eyes and calculated what it would take to get him to release me. Men are pretty easy creatures, after all. There are two kinds: the ones who lead with their heads and the ones who lead with their dicks. I wondered which kind he was.

I trailed my eyes down his face to the hollow of his neck, and then brought them back up to his. "Maybe we can come to some sort of arrangement," I coaxed. "You do like girls, don't you?"

His chest expanded, pushing me deeper into the wall. Then he leaned in even closer until I could feel the heat and moisture coming off of his lips. "I'm the other kind," he said.

The room began to spin as my wheels started coming off the tracks. The rage came on so fast I thought my eyes might explode from the intensity of the light.

"Look at me." He forced my eyes to stay on his as the convulsion of rage rolled through me. "You know who I am, Alex. I'm in there somewhere."

An image of a girl swirled around in my head. It was me, but it wasn't. I was sitting in a room, eating breakfast with the man who had me pinned to the wall. He was reading the newspaper. *Do I know him?*

My eyes flashed and the light dimmed as they began to cool down. I could feel my body softening as more images fragmented around his face, and the rage lessened to mild irritation.

"No, you don't," he warned. "I need you good and mad." He reached behind me and removed the cuffs. Then he took my hand and crushed it to release a fresh stream of blood from the cut. As the pain shot through me, he yanked my bloody palm up to my face and sent a fresh blaze of blue flooding from my eyes. "That's my girl."

"I'll kill you for that." It was an empty threat. The urge to kill him was replaced by a strange sense of betrayal, and an even stranger sense of . . . warmth.

He lowered my hand to my side but wouldn't let go of it. With his other, he cupped my face and ran his thumb across my lower lip. "Now, you see me."

My focus blurred, and for the first time I couldn't decide what to do with the man caging me against the wall. Rule number one: when cornered, make a *goddamn* decision. But as my namby-pamby brain made a recovery and my urge to kill returned, he blindsided me with a soft kiss.

It felt like an oncoming jet, the threat hurling straight for me as I pressed against the wall, suspended like a butterfly trapped in a web of brilliant blue. My brain had simply ceased to function, and all I could do was gaze at his parted lips as he pulled away and deepened his own gaze back at me.

My heartbeat accelerated as I panicked, and then the fear sailed right past me with a roar while the oxygen left my lungs in a heady rush.

"Greer?"

I knew him, and for the first time since he'd cut me, I had no impulse to hurt him.

He let go of my hand, and I glanced down at the blood that was now covering his palm. His eyes followed mine and then trailed back up to my face. "Still want me dead?" He opened his bloodstained hand to give me a better view. "Or have you figured out that I'm not the enemy?"

My head shook as the revelation made its way through my brain and I began to realize what was happening. I could slow my thoughts and logically piece together the scenario, separating him into the non-threat category of my mind, warming from the strange affection I felt for him. I recognized him completely for the first time.

A switch had been flipped like some muscle memory in my brain had finally kicked in.

"You *must* control this, Alex." He reached for my hand, squeezing it again before I could object.

"Ow! Jesus, Greer." My eyes flared but quickly dulled back down as I implemented my newly acquired self-control. "You know I could try to kill you for that."

"But you won't." He rested his forearm on the wall as he leaned over me. "Reason before revenge—yes?"

The trace of anger immediately melted away, a wide grin spreading across my face. For the first time in my life I felt real power. Not because I was cognizant of the devastating damage I was capable of, but because I knew I could control it instead of it controlling me.

Now *that* was power.

Greer held up his index finger as he backed away from me. He walked to the door on the other side of the room and motioned Rhom and Thomas back inside. The three of them threw me glances as they conferred, and when they seemed to agree that everything was under control, he walked back to me and delivered my fate.

"We'll have to work on that impulse management of yours a little more, but I think you're on your way to earning your concealed weapons permit."

He gazed at me a moment longer, considering his decision. "And your freedom."

SEVEN

I finished sorting the pile of books on the library table and headed for the register. Lucky for me Kevin quit after only a few days, and I got my job back after Greer certified me stable and in control of my powers.

Katie admitted that she'd gone out of her way to find a good reason not to hire anyone who applied after that, an unfair—not to mention illegal—tactic to stall the hiring process while I recovered from my "illness" and came back to work.

Greer's definition of freedom didn't include me getting my job back, but I reminded him that I wasn't the same girl who left Shakespeare's Library a couple of weeks earlier, and if he didn't give me some breathing room we'd both be miserable.

I'd been back at the shop for a week, and we quickly got back into the rhythm of working as a team.

"Afternoon, ladies." Apollo walked in with a box in his hands and headed straight for the library table. He pulled the top flap open and reached in to retrieve a tiny orange and white moving object.

"What is that?" Katie asked.

"What does it look like?" He held the kitten out so we could all get a good look.

I instinctively reached for it. Babies were fine, but puppies and kittens had a way of making my heart flutter.

"Oh. My. God!" I took it from Apollo's hand without asking, because there was no doubt in my mind that it belonged in mine.

"The guy said it's a male."

"Where did you get him?" The kitten purred as I rubbed the spot between his shoulder blades.

"Some guy on Seventy-Ninth Street had him in a box with a sign that said KITTENS FOR FOOD. I assumed he didn't mean I should take the kitten home and cook it."

"Was he homeless?" Katie asked.

"Looked like it. I gave him ten bucks for the last one."

I put the kitten on the floor so he could work off some energy. No telling how long he'd been in that box.

"What are you planning to do with it?" Katie asked. "You're never home, so I doubt you're going to keep it."

He grinned at her and then looked at me. "Alex will take him. Won't you?"

My smile faded as I looked up from the kitten pouncing around the floor. Even though I knew I was the only one in the room who was even remotely qualified to take care of him, convincing Greer to let me bring an animal home would be a stretch. And then there was Sophia. I doubt she'd be thrilled with a litter box in the house.

"Yeah, Alex," she smirked. "You can take it."

"Quit calling him *it*. He's a *he*." I watched him climb a pile of books left on the floor. "I'll talk to Greer, but Apollo will have to keep him temporarily."

"He can stay in the back room until you convince your daddy to let you have a kitty," he teased. "Everyone needs to pitch in with his care until then. Agreed?"

Katie frowned at the thought of scooping a litter box, but

she agreed to feed him as long as it only required dumping dry food in a bowl. Apollo and I agreed to do the dirty work.

"You're going to love this place, Katie. They've got all kinds of weird stuff."

It was her day off, and I had the early shift. She met me at the shop at five o'clock and we headed down to Den of Oddities and Antiquities. I figured if anyone could figure out what Katie was, it was Ava.

As soon as we walked through the door, Katie took a panoramic glance around the room. She stopped on the boar head with the third eye. "That's real, isn't it?"

"Yep. See all those drawers?" I pointed to the two-story wall lined with hundreds of small pulls. "Each one used to have a label. Isn't it amazing?"

Her face brightened as she looked up at all the tiny drawers. She walked over to the ladder that rolled along the length of the wall and climbed the first few steps to reach one of the bottom drawers.

"Um . . . maybe you shouldn't do that, Katie. I'll never hear the end of it if you break your neck."

She ignored my protest and reached for one of the small brass pulls. The wall was like a giant library index card cabinet. She opened the drawer and released the faded but permanently embedded smell of something earthy. Wrapped in several layers of tissue paper was a small petrified object.

"That's an oak handle from a peat bog in Ireland. Someone dropped it there around four thousand years ago."

We both looked at Patrick as he walked out from one of the aisles with a jar in his hand and a woman at his side.

"From a knife. Probably used for sacrifice," he added.

Katie respectfully returned the ancient handle to its drawer and stepped off the ladder.

"Alex," he nodded, stopping for a moment before continuing toward the register, "I'll be with you in a minute." His gaze shifted back to Katie and then to his customer as they proceeded to the counter.

He carefully wrapped the jar before putting it in a sturdy bag and escorting the woman to the door. "Good luck, Caroline. I hope it works for you." He closed the door behind her and came back to the counter.

"That wasn't an eyeball in that jar, was it?" Katie asked.

"Not just any eyeball." His voice deepened. "A wyvern."

I made a mental note to look up *wyvern* when I got home.

"I'm Patrick." He extended his hand.

"Katie," she replied, taking it.

With his bright hazel eyes and hybrid lilt, Patrick was almost as dangerous as Katie.

"Is Ava here?"

Patrick seemed to remember that I was in the room and pulled his eyes from Katie's. "Yes. She's in the back. I'll get her."

He disappeared toward the back room, and Katie looked at me with a blank face. "What?"

"Do you have to eye fuck every man you meet?"

Her eyes rolled. "It's not my fault if they all fantasize about getting a piece of the dragon girl."

She underestimated her beauty. Even Greer's eyes walked all over her face the night he met her.

"This is one weird place, Alex. I dig it." She browsed the items in the large glass display case. "No shit. Is that—"

"Yeah, it's real."

The vampire hunting kit was still there. With a price tag of twelve thousand dollars, I wasn't surprised.

"I know someone who could use that," she muttered.

Ava came out of the back room with a wide grin across her face. She wrapped her arms around me in a death grip. "It's so good to see you."

"I miss you, too." I had to admit it felt good to forgive. I spent months resenting her when I found out she was alive and well and had faked her own death. It took me a long time to accept that she had her reasons for doing what she did, but I knew they were good ones, and one day she would tell me the truth. I had to believe that because she was the closest thing I had to a mother.

"This is my friend Katie."

Ava ignored Katie's extended hand and gave her an unexpected hug instead. But as soon as Ava touched her, the friendly greeting changed to a rigid impasse. She recoiled and stepped back several feet, glancing at Katie from head to toe as her warm smile turned icy. "What are you?"

"That's why we're here," I explained. "We're not really sure."

Ava looked back and forth between us and then realized we weren't kidding. "Well then, let's find out."

She headed for the bookshelf behind the register—the one with the books that weren't for sale—and hauled one of the bigger ones onto the counter.

In my experience, all things mysterious and foreboding seemed to originate from very large and very old books. This one was almost as big as the book of magic that lived on the bottom shelf of the shop's huge display case, the one with the hidden compartment where we found the stolen amulet.

She opened it to the table of contents and ran her index finger down the list. "You're of Slavic blood, correct?"

Katie nodded. "I'm adopted, but my birth parents were from Russia. How does everyone know that?" she wondered aloud.

"Oh dear, it's written all over you," Ava replied. "Literally." Her eyes went back to the book.

"You mean my tattoo?"

"Well yes, that, too."

Ava's finger stopped on a chapter titled "Slovenia." She

skimmed the first few pages and looked at Katie. "What do you do for a living?"

"I work in a bookstore . . . with Alex." She looked back and forth between us. "Why? Is that important?"

"Possibly. Tell me more about yourself."

"Take a look at me." Katie spread her arms wide and smirked. "I kind of wear myself on my sleeve."

"Are you educated?" Ava asked.

"Depends on what you mean by 'educated.' I'm an engineering student at Columbia, so I guess you could say I'm educated." Her shoulders twisted awkwardly as her posture sank into a submissive slouch. "I'm a member of Mensa, if that means anything," she mumbled.

"Really? You never told me that." She just kept rolling out the surprises, impressing me more every time she opened her mouth.

"Well, I don't broadcast it. It was my father's idea. Thought it would look good on my college apps."

Ava went completely still as her mind worked. She resumed her breathing a moment later and began flipping through the book to the chapter on Slovenia. She combed through the pages, meticulously scanning the captions below each paragraph.

"My parents were from Russia, not Slovenia."

"I don't think so." Ava's eyes ran over Katie's face, examining her features for something. "If you were Russian you'd probably have three heads." She turned the book toward us and pointed to the illustration on the page. "I believe you are a dragon's child. The child of a Slavic zmaj, to be specific."

Katie and I looked at the drawing on the page. It was an image of a dragon flying over a city with fire coming from its mouth.

"I don't think I can do *that*," Katie said.

"Probably not. Zmaj are usually male, but a half-breed off-spring can be either. Most likely your mother was Russian and your father was . . . well, a zmaj. I guess you could say you're a demidragon."

"That is kind of what you looked like." I winced at the memory.

Ava gasped. "You've seen it?"

I summarized the encounter with the black widow, and told her how Katie had shifted into her dragon to protect me.

"Well, that eliminates any doubt," Ava declared. "Not only is a zmaj a brilliant creature—hence your academics—but it will do just about anything to protect its village. Alex, *you* are Katie's village."

"Huh, what do you know." Katie laughed and shoved my arm. "You're my village, Alex."

She looked at the illustration again, and the reality of what she was seeing kicked in. "Do I really look like that?"

"Close. Your eyes didn't change, though." The one thing I remembered as clear as day was the color of the dragon's eyes. It was how I knew I was looking at Katie Bishop when I was dragged out from under the table. "But you were kind of . . . green."

"Can I control it? I'd hate to turn into *that* at the grocery store."

"Oh, that's a tricky thing," Ava said. "I don't have any practical experience with dragon children, or zmaj for that matter. Are you aware of it when you change?"

Katie thought about the question for a minute. The only confirmed change was in the shop the day the black widow showed up. She had her suspicions about other incidents but couldn't be sure some of those blackouts weren't from too much drinking. At least she knew that on each of those occasions there was good reason for her inner dragon to emerge, and if there were casualties it hadn't put her on the front page of the *New York Times*. In other words, her dragon was discreet. "Not exactly."

"Well, now that you know what you are, you should become more in tune with it." Ava shut the book and rubbed Katie's arm. "You'll get used to your talents. We all do, in time," she added as her eyes shifted to mine.

It was nearly seven thirty when I got back to the house. Greer hadn't made it home yet and Sophia was at her usual spot over the stove. I looked around the house, trying to come up with a discreet place for a food bowl and a litter box before broaching the subject at dinner.

I heard the familiar sound of keys hitting the porcelain bowl as Greer got off the elevator. He was heading up the steps when I walked into the foyer. He usually stuck his head in the kitchen before going up to change, but not today.

"Rough day?" I asked.

He stopped mid-step but didn't turn. "Something like that." Then he disappeared up the stairs.

Twenty minutes later, he came back down wearing dark gray sweats and a pair of running shoes. "Going for a run?"

I thought he'd given it up, but it turned out that Greer liked running when other people slept. I discovered that when I came downstairs around three a.m. one morning as he was coming through the back door. I almost had a coronary. Good thing I didn't have a gun at the time because things might have gone very badly.

"No. I have business after dinner."

Greer normally didn't wear sweats for meetings, but I thought it wise to mind my own business and not dig for the details. He seemed a little tense and obviously wasn't in the mood to share.

"Dinner is ready. Sophia made chicken curry." As a native of Italy, Sophia made some of the best Italian food I'd ever eaten, but she also made a mean curry. In fact, there weren't many cuisines she hadn't mastered.

"Let's eat, then." He grabbed my hand as he strode past me toward the dining room.

Greer was unusually quiet as we sat across from each other, the only sound coming from the utensils hitting the china and an occasional creaking of our chairs.

"So," I began, "how was your day?"

"Fine, dear. How was yours?" he replied.

I chewed my food longer than necessary, avoiding as much actual conversation as possible. Usually I rambled when nervous, but tonight I wanted Greer to do the talking because he was obviously hiding something.

"And what did you do today?" he asked. "Besides work."

"I took Katie to see Ava."

He swallowed his food and placed his fork on the plate. "And?"

"Apparently, Katie's not a dragon after all." It was rare to surprise Greer, so I was eager to see that subtle but discernable shock when I said the next thing. "She's the child of one."

"Really? What kind?" he asked before picking his fork back up and resuming his meal.

I put my own fork down. "What kind? I tell you Katie is a dragon's child and you ask what kind?"

He ignored the sarcasm as his eyes rose to mine.

"A zmaj. Ava's pretty sure her father was a zmaj."

For a few seconds he remained perfectly still, taking in the information like it was the local weather report. The right side of his mouth twitched as he tried to suppress a growing smirk, and his shoulders shook from the wheezing under his breath that was growing louder by the second.

"What so damn funny?"

After a good laugh, he shook his head and leaned back in his chair. "If I had any doubt about your safety, that bit of information just alleviated it." The laughter returned for one final shindig before he sobered up. "Zmaj are very protective creatures. I'm afraid you might get a little tired of your friend now that she's adopted you."

"Adopted? That's just silly, Greer."

"See for yourself," he muttered.

This was as good a time as any to bring up the delicate subject of the kitten. "Speaking of adoption, do you have any objections to cats?"

"In general, no. Although I doubt there's anything general about your question." He expelled the contents from his lungs and leaned back. "Out with it, Alex."

"There's this kitten . . . at the bookstore . . . and it needs a home."

"Sounds like it already has one—the bookstore."

"The shop is temporary. He needs a real home." I could see I wasn't selling the idea. "He's this tiny orange ball of fur." My shoulders scrunched as I mimicked holding a delicate crystal ball with both hands.

"Why us?" he asked.

"Because someone's got to give a damn, that's why. He's just a baby."

Sophia interrupted our discussion to ask about dessert. "Why don't we see how Sophia feels about this new roommate you're proposing."

She looked back and forth between the two of us, her eyes narrowing when they reached mine. "Roommate?"

"Do *you* like cats, Sophia?"

As the word *cat* registered, her head began to shake back and forth and both hands went in the air. "Oh, no. I take care of no cat!" She nervously started collecting the plates before we'd finished our meal. "Cat litter and hair all over the place. And who's going to feed it? Me? Oh, no!"

"Calm down, Sophia," I said. "I'll do everything. I'll even keep it in my room. It's a *he*, by the way. I'll keep *him* in my room."

She grumbled as she headed back to the kitchen with an armful of dishes.

"I believe that's a concession." His breath rushed through his nose. "Please don't make us regret it."

I gave him a sincere smile. "Thank you. You won't even know he's here."

We finished our dinner before Sophia had a chance to come back in the room and take the rest of the dishes from under our forks. And there was still this business Greer hadn't yet divulged.

"You might as well tell me where you're going tonight," I said. "If it has anything to do with me, and I have a feeling it does, I'll badger the hell out of you until you tell me."

He didn't argue as I'd expected. Instead, he agreed. "You're right. It has everything to do with you."

EIGHT

I t had been such a long time since the last one that I foolishly thought they were gone. That, and the fact that the
last time the Vargr were in town, I'd killed two of their
pack mates—or whatever they called themselves. The mere
mention of them brought me right back to that room, with the
manacles on the wall and the smell of dog lingering in the air.
They were a race of wolves, looking more like Scandinavian
supermodels than dogs, with eyes as cold as glaciers. I shuddered at the thought of staring into those eyes again. But since
they'd left another marker—a severed animal head with their
mark written in blood on its forehead—the odds of that happening were high.

It was the third one. The first one showed up months ago
on 128th Street, followed by a second marker found on the
Lower East Side. The markers were their official calling cards,
putting everyone on notice that the wolves were in town.

"Where did you find it?"

"Lincoln Center. They left the damn thing on the ring of
the Revson Fountain."

"That's bold." I imagined a severed stag head lying on the
granite ring as the patrons of the arts gawked in horror.

Greer grunted in agreement. "I guess we should consider ourselves lucky that we found it before half of Manhattan did."

His people had a way of finding these things. The markers were usually left with something else, a small sacrificial artifact guaranteed to attract the attention of Greer and his men, leading them straight to the bloody message.

"So, what do we do now?" I asked.

"We do absolutely nothing."

If there's one thing I learned from my brief encounter with the Vargr, it's that they're bona fide egomaniacs. "Won't that piss them off?"

"Let's hope so. Agitated equals careless."

"That's all good and nice, but I'll be the target of all the agitation." I was the one they wanted. The more we stirred them up, the worse it would be for me when we met, and I had no doubt we would.

"Then you better make sure you bleed."

My jaw dropped. I don't know why, because it was exactly the response I expected from him. He was right. A drop of blood was all it took to make visceral confetti out of the last two dogs that held me in that dungeon.

"I don't think we have to worry about them yet," he said. "They're up to something, but they're lying low."

The door to the library swung open, and Rhom and Loden walked in.

Rhom looked back and forth between us. "What's up, boss?"

Loden was the youngest gun on Greer's team—at least he looked to be the youngest. He was wearing a pair of black leather pants with a black silk shirt, signifying that he hadn't gotten the message that the eighties were dead. On him it actually worked, and based on the cocky grin he was sporting, he knew his style—good or bad—stood out.

"There's my girl." Loden greeted me with one of his flirtatious winks that were always laced with innuendo. "Long time, love."

Greer handled him with a single look. Loden's grin rose higher for a defiant instant, then flattened.

Rhom looked at me and then back at Greer. "Did you tell her?"

"She knows about the marker, but we have more immediate issues to address." He stared at Rhom while they had some silent debriefing. "What do we have?"

"What we have is a situation." Rhom circled the room before taking a seat in one of the big leather chairs. "Isabetta wants to have a sit-down."

"And why would I want to do that?"

"Who's Isabetta?" The room went quiet as everyone waited for Greer to answer my question.

"Isabetta Falcone." Greer's expression soured as her name left his mouth. "She's one of those people you'd prefer not to sit down with."

Rhom snorted. "Yeah. Unless you like getting your balls busted."

"A real man-eater," Loden added. "I hear she likes chicks, too."

Greer reined the conversation back in with a loaded stare pointed at Rhom.

"Says she's got some information we might be interested in. Says it's about the vessel."

The vessel Rhom was referring to contained the ultimate grand prize—the third prophecy, the ability to control space and time. The amulet was the key that opened it. Now that we had the amulet, all we needed was the vessel, and voila, the world would be safe from its own self-destruction.

"Set up the meeting," Greer said.

Rhom glanced at Greer's attire. "Lose the sweats, boss. We're late."

*   *   *

Being late for a meeting with Isabetta Falcone was not a good idea, so we were going into it without taking the time to formulate a plan. Greer described her as some sort of syndicate head.

"She controls lower Manhattan. Everything south of Houston Street."

"You mean mafia?" I prayed he'd correct me with something a little less criminal sounding.

"Something like that."

"And you need me there because . . . "

"You're collateral. If Isabetta has a lead on the vessel and she's willing to share that information with us, it's because she wants us to do the dirty work and find it for her. She sees you, she has more incentive to share."

He took his right hand off the steering wheel and held it out. "Give it to me."

I clutched the amulet hanging under my shirt. "Why?"

"Because if I'm wrong, you're the target. Now, let me have it—please."

I pulled the chain over my head and handed it to him. The separation was painful as I watched it disappear in his fist.

We parked just north of Little Italy. "Keep an eye on the door," Greer told Rhom as we got out of the car and approached the restaurant. He tossed the amulet to Loden. "You know what to do with this."

The place was packed, but the noise level was subdued, giving the illusion of privacy. The waiters were dressed in uniform black suits, good enough for any Park Avenue eatery.

When we entered, a man motioned for us to follow without having to tell him whom we were meeting. He led us toward the far end of the room to a tall booth lined with leather dyed the shade of ripe cherries.

"Isabetta." Greer greeted the Italian princess as an arm

extended from behind the wall of leather. He kissed the hand at the end of it.

I walked around him to get a better look at Isabetta Falcone, but I was blocked by a man standing at the edge of the booth. Obviously, he was her linebacker.

"No, Demitri. Leave her alone." Isabetta sank deeper into the leather booth and examined me. Her eyes walked from my face down to the lowest point the inconvenient table would allow. "So this is the golden child."

I waited uncomfortably for an introduction as she pinned me with her stare.

"Is she yours?" she asked Greer without looking at him.

"No, I'm not," I informed her before Greer had a chance to chime in. "Are you his?" I nodded toward Demitri.

"That's quite a set of testicles you have, baby." Her grin widened. "I like it."

"Isabetta Falcone, this is Alex Kelley." He glanced at the seat opposite hers. "May we?"

"Where are my manners? Please, sit." She motioned for the waiter. "What would you like to drink?"

We both ordered scotch.

Isabetta Falcone was a good-looking woman, but under all that makeup, I imagined there'd be an ordinary face. She appeared to be in her late thirties, though she could have been younger. Certain lifestyles can do that to a woman. Her lavender blonde hair was swept up in the back and teased to give it volume at the crown. Nobody had eyelashes that long, and her pale, frosted lips were enhanced with a thick line at the outside edges to give them pout. But what stood out the most were her sharp hazel eyes.

"Why are we here?" Greer asked.

Isabetta seemed surprised by the abrupt question. "Where I come from, pleasure precedes business—within reason."

Two waiters approached, one carrying a large tray while the

other unfolded a small portable serving table. Waiter number one placed the tray on the server and waited for his instructions. "Just make room and leave it," she ordered as she swept the back of her hand over the tabletop. Waiter number two carefully placed the large platters and basket of bread in the middle of the table.

"I hope you like pasta. I was in the mood for a good steak, but I didn't know how you liked your meat. We can still order some, if you'd like." Her eyes flipped up to mine. "Unless you don't eat meat."

"I like meat just fine," I retorted.

She reached for the bottle of wine. As she poured it into our glasses, her long fingernails revealed a tiny diamond embedded in the center of each. There wasn't a mark on her skin. The combination of pampering and bling gave away the fact that she wasn't a fan of manual labor. And why should she be?

She looked at the two of us just sitting there. "Eat."

Still stuffed from chicken curry, we loaded up on pasta out of courtesy, because the real reason for the meeting wasn't going to be revealed until we showed some respect.

I tried to relax as she watched me eat, occasionally glancing at Greer but never taking her attention away from me for more than a few seconds. Something touched my knee and I realized it was hers. I looked up and she was still staring at me, running her middle finger over the pout of her lower lip.

The waiter replaced the empty bottle of wine on the table, disrupting the awkward moment.

Greer looked at the two of us. Picking up on the situation, he diverted Isabetta's attention by repeating his earlier question. "Why are we here, Isabetta?"

She ignored him and continued with the visual conversation she was having with me. "I ask out of courtesy, Alex. I usually just take what I want."

A response escaped me. The idea of Isabetta Falcone using

me as her plaything wasn't pleasant, and even Greer might not be able to get me out of this corner.

She lingered on me for a few more seconds and then turned to address Greer's question. "We have a mutual interest."

"In what?" he asked.

"In the prophecy."

"Half of New York City has an interest in the prophecy. What makes yours any different?"

She straightened in her seat and lost the grin. "I own this part of town." Her voice dropped an octave, and I had a feeling we were about to see the other side of her—the authentic side. "Do you think I plan to give that up for some little *fuck* who finds it before we do?"

Something deep and hollow sounded around the table, and I realized it was Greer. "You'd be wise to remember whom you're talking to, Isabetta," he warned. It was the scary Greer I hadn't seen in months.

Demitri stepped forward. Isabetta put her hand up, stopping him before Greer did. The room went still as every ear in the place was on our table. The sudden absence of noise almost made me forget we were in a crowded restaurant.

"You're right." She smiled cockily back at Greer. "It was rude of me to lose my temper."

He nodded once, acknowledging the concession. "Now, stop wasting my time and get to the point."

She took a deep drink of wine. "Have you heard of a man named David Oxford?"

"No. Who is he?"

"Dr. Oxford has developed something that could be quite useful to us. Rumor has it that the vessel containing the prophecy has been so elusive because we can't see it." Her cocky grin returned as she saw the interest fire up on Greer's face. "It could be sitting right on top of this table and we wouldn't know it."

My eyes shot to Greer for confirmation that what she was saying might be true.

"Where did you get your information?" he asked.

"I have my sources, and they're bulletproof. Apparently it's made up of colors we can't see."

"Ultraviolet?" His interest piqued.

"Oh, it's beyond that. From what I've been told, the spectrum has never been documented. David Oxford has figured out a way to detect it."

Greer saw the question in my eyes. He had the ultrasonic hearing of a moth, so I assumed his eyes were just as powerful. He moved his head slightly, warning me not to speak as he asked the question himself.

"The obvious question is why you haven't gone after this Dr. Oxford yourself. What do you need us for?"

She looked back and forth between the two of us. "Well, I don't want it for myself. Like I said, I just don't want some piece of shit getting his hands on it and fucking up the whole damn world." She let out a throaty laugh. "I mean, could you imagine some guido from Staten Island getting his hands on the prophecy?"

"That's not a very nice way to refer to your relatives," he said.

Isabetta's face went as still as a stone. Her pale coloring flushed to a bright shade of pink as the blood rushed to her head. A second later the table jolted as she lurched forward, practically knocking over the bottle of wine. "I'll feed you your balls if you ever say something like that to me again!" Her eyes darted to mine, and her temper lowered to a simmer. "Don't you ever call me that again, Sinclair."

He hadn't actually called her anything, but a nerve had been struck. He knew just which button to push, and I wondered how.

Greer showed no reaction to the outburst. I, on the other hand, was plastered to the back of the booth from the force of her threat. I knew a cat when I saw one, and Isabetta Falcone had some pretty nasty claws.

"I assume you're going to tell me where I can find this Dr. Oxford?" he continued, calmly taking a sip of whiskey.

She sat back down, moving a strand of hair from her eyes and taking a forced bite of pasta. "Now I'm not so sure I want to. You really are a bastard, Greer." She glanced at me. "*You* know what I'm saying."

I'd been quiet through most of the exchange but felt the urge to cut the rubber band tightening around the table. I expected Demitri to get in on the action, too, but he just stood against the wall looking bored.

"All right, I'll tell you," she finally conceded. "This is business, and I'm not going to let a prick like you stop me from taking care of business."

I wanted to defend him. Greer may be a prick, but he was *my* prick. If anyone was going to call him one, it was going to be me, not some mafia princess with a diamond manicure.

"He's a professor at Cornell. Physics or something like that. He's been working on some kind of telescope. You know, the kind NASA uses to see what's out there." She leaned into the table and lowered her voice. "My sources tell me he stumbled across some anomaly, whatever the fuck that is."

"What are we supposed to do with a thousand-pound telescope?" I asked, no longer able to stay quiet.

Greer looked at me and then back at Isabetta, because it was a valid question.

She shook her head. "See, that's the thing—he's working on something else. He's got some kind of glasses or goggles that can see shit."

"And this 'shit' is . . . ?"

"Look, I'm no scientist, but I know we can't see ultraviolet light with the human eye—learned that in high school. We can use a black light to make ultraviolet things glow, but this invention of his can see even beyond that. We're talking *beyond* ultraviolet."

"Interesting." He nodded as the notion rolled around his head. "So these glasses are in some lab at Cornell?"

"Most likely. He knows about the prophecy, Greer."

That was all he needed to hear. It was one thing for a professor to be working on the next great discovery in electromagnetic spectrums, but another for that same professor to use that technology for the purpose of finding the vessel.

"He lives in Binghamton." She handed Greer a slip of paper with David Oxford's home address as we got up to leave.

We grabbed Rhom on the way out and headed for the car. Loden gave me back the amulet, and we filled the two of them in on what Isabetta Falcone had told us.

"If she's telling us the truth, and I think she is, we're taking a road trip," Greer informed me without opening it up for discussion.

Rhom looked unconvinced. "I don't trust the bitch. Excuse my language, Alex."

"It's okay, Rhom. She is one."

"She's as greedy as the next one," he muttered. "Why the hell isn't she sending her own guys up there?"

Greer smirked as he considered the question. This wasn't his first rodeo with Isabetta Falcone, and I had a feeling he knew her better than he let on. "Because she doesn't think her idiots can get the job done, and she knows we can."

Rhom wasn't buying it. "I still don't trust her. And she's full of it if she says she doesn't want to get her hands on the vessel. Wants us to safely contain it—bullshit."

Greer nodded in agreement. "She wants it all right, but she wants us to do all the work. As soon as we get our hands on whatever this thing is up at Cornell, she'll come for it."

"Then let's do it," Loden said.

Greer gave it about two seconds of thought and then looked at me. "Want to take a drive?"

NINE

Cornell University was located a little more than two hundred miles northwest of Manhattan in the city of Ithaca. That meant I was about to spend a minimum of three hours in a car with Greer—depending on how well he obeyed the speed limit.

There were faster ways for him to get to Ithaca without the use of a car, but those methods would require a tremendous expense of energy. With me in tow, it would be worse. The benefits of saving a few hours would be outweighed by the time it took for him to rejuvenate after manipulating matter—for both of us. And Greer liked his fleet of toys. A trip upstate gave him an excuse to let loose on the road without the restrictions of city driving.

"Respectfully, boss, I have to disagree with you on this one." Rhom shook his head as we prepared for the trip.

"I second that," agreed Thomas. "Nothing good will come from the two of you up there without backup."

"That may be true, but I need you here." Greer looked at his men and then at me. "I think we can handle a Ph.D. and some campus security."

I trusted his judgment, but I was still a shaky mess when it came to controlling my powers. Our session at CTC had opened up the door between my two selves. But even though I was now supposedly capable of recognizing friend from foe, it hadn't been tested in an actual combat situation. In other words, I had no idea if the next time someone cut me, I would politely ask for a Band-Aid or blindly try to kill everyone in the room.

"It's going to suck if I kill a security guard or a student. And what about Dr. Oxford? What if I end up offing *him*?"

Rhom looked from me to Greer and nodded. "*Yeah.*"

"No one's killing anyone," Greer said. "We're going up there for due diligence. If what Isabetta said turns out to be true and we find something, then we'll take it. Peacefully."

Rhom shook his head and sighed. "How many times have I heard that before?"

"Okay, look," Thomas interrupted. "No point arguing. They're going, so let's move on to something we can all actually agree on." He walked over to me and lifted the amulet from where it rested on my shirt. "We all agree that the amulet has to be protected."

I knew where he was going with this, but I didn't like it. Giving it up for a meeting with Isabetta Falcone was one thing, but leaving it hundreds of miles away for a day or two was not okay.

"It comes with us," Greer decided. "You never know, we might get lucky. We might put on those magic glasses and see it in the middle of the damn road."

Thomas sneered but then realized Greer was serious.

"Stranger things have happened," Greer said, shrugging. "We know it's in New York, but it is possible it's been moved somewhere outside of the city. Not likely, but possible."

The faces of the three men standing in front of us went ashen, like children being informed that Santa Claus was a lie.

"You fucking with us?" Thomas asked.

Greer took a deep breath. "Forget I said that, but the amulet stays with us."

We took the elevator to the garage and headed for the big black Yukon, a vehicle I'd never seen him drive before.

"I guess you're not worried about the price of gas." Not that it mattered to someone with Greer's bank account.

He nearly cracked a smile. "I like a little extra cargo space when I travel. Never know what you might pick up on the road."

We crossed the George Washington Bridge heading west, and I enjoyed my first trip outside of the city since arriving the previous fall—if I didn't count the night in Paris with Constantine a couple of months back.

That's the thing about living in New York; you can go for months or even years without leaving the perimeter of the five boroughs, because there's no need to. If you can't find what you need within those borders, it probably doesn't exist.

It was my day off from work, but I made it clear I had to be back in the city by nightfall to get some sleep for my shift the next day.

We drove for a little over an hour when my stomach started to growl. Greer had given Sophia the day off, and instead of fending for myself and cooking a proper breakfast, I settled for a banana. The fuel from that banana had just run out.

"Can we—"

"Hungry?"

"I'm going to eat my purse if I don't get some food very soon."

We pulled off the interstate and followed the signs toward the main street of a small village. As we drove down the center of town, I felt a bit of déjà vu because it reminded me of some of the buried little towns in Indiana I'd passed through. Not the dead kind with the CLOSED signs in the windows in the middle of the day, but the kind that lived at a slower pace by choice. These shops looked cared for, and they were open for business.

"Look at that." I pointed at a dog with a paper bag in its mouth. Its jowls were wrapped around the folded top like someone had carefully placed it there to be taken to its master.

We drove past a few antique shops and an old-fashioned pharmacy. The town looked like a snapshot from another time.

"That place looks popular." Greer nodded toward a packed diner that probably served as the town's social nucleus. People lined the booths along the front window, and there were more seated on the benches outside waiting to get in.

"Yeah, but there's a long wait. Let's drive a little farther."

On the next block, I spotted a place with an interesting façade and a sign in bold chartreuse letters. The Trillium Café's windows were draped in fuchsia fabric—on the outside of the building—and the front door was painted a bold shade of turquoise, the kind of color you see on the front doors of old English cottages. The box running along the length of the window spilled over with violas and moonflower vines.

"A little early for annuals," I muttered.

"What?"

"Nothing. Just thinking out loud." I pointed to the café. "Let's eat there."

We found an empty space directly in front of the place and headed for the boldly colored door. In comparison to the diner a block back, this place was much more relaxed. There were a few people sitting at the tables scattered around the room and a couple leaving as we walked in, but it was clear who did the bulk of the business in town.

"Take any seat you like," a waitress said as she balanced three plates of food and a bowl of soup. "I'll be over in a minute."

We took one of the tables by the front window. The room felt warm and cozy with the smell of coffee and baked pie moving through the air. The walls were covered with old paint-by-number paintings and photographs of people who were probably repeat customers or local celebrities: the mayor, a local kid who landed a part in a film, the harvest queen.

My eyes were drawn to the weathered green paint on the floor, and the wide gaps that would disappear as the heat and humidity of summer moved in. "My kind of place."

Greer looked around the room. "It does have its charm."

The waitress hurried over to our table to take our order. She was wearing one of those retro uniforms, but instead of pink or blue pastel under the white apron, her dress was fire-engine red with a neckline that plunged to the center of her cleavage. Her brown eyes reminded me of a doe's, the color so deep it blended seamlessly with her pupils.

"You folks just passing through our little town?"

"Is it that obvious?" I asked.

She glanced out the front window at the shiny black Yukon. "I know everyone within a thirty-mile radius of this town. Unless you're someone's kid back from school, I'm guessing you're either coming from or heading to the city."

"We're on our way to Ithaca."

"What's good here?" Greer cut off the conversation before I could divulge our full itinerary.

The waitress turned her eyes to Greer. "Can't think of a bad thing. You just let me know what looks good on the menu, and I'll warn you if it's a bad idea."

"Perfect. Can we have one?" he asked. "A menu."

The waitress glanced at the bare table. "Well, I guess that would help, wouldn't it?" She grabbed two menus from the vacant table next to ours.

Greer ordered a burger, and I ordered a grilled cheese with

a cup of vegetable soup. The waitress nodded her approval to both our choices, then disappeared through the door leading to the kitchen.

"What's the matter, Greer? Worried she might be a spy?"

"Right now, everyone's a spy until I know otherwise." He motioned to the golden retriever trotting past the window with the bag still wedged between its jowls. "Even that dog out there."

Two tables over, a group of teenage girls glanced at us between huddled whispers. It was Greer they were interested in. One of them kept dropping her napkin on the floor so she could get a better look as she bent down. He ignored the attention, and I wondered if he was even aware of the effect he was having on them.

"I think you have some fans."

He said nothing as he turned and made eye contact with each of them. One by one their faces sobered, and a rash of heat crawled over their skin. They squirmed in their seats as it passed through them. When the waitress brought their check, they paid it immediately and took the long way around the room, avoiding our table. They wouldn't even look at us as they hurried down the sidewalk in front of the window.

"What did you just do to those girls, Greer? I think you scared the hell out of them."

"That was the point. I just taught them a valuable lesson about men."

"That's a little creepy, don't you think?"

"Creepy is the fact that the one with the short brown hair is already pregnant."

"How—"

"Here you go." The waitress set our food down on the table. "I'll check back on you in a few minutes."

We thanked her and dove in. The food was good, dripping with fat and calories just like diner food should. Even a salad in a place like this was mainly a pool of ranch dressing with a few vegetables taking a swim.

Greer must have been hungrier than I was, because he polished off his burger before I finished the first half of my grilled cheese. He pushed his fries toward the center of the table to share.

"You know," I began, "this Oxford guy could turn out to be fake. Maybe Isabetta Falcone just wanted to get us out of the city for a day or two. Maybe she's got a different lead and wanted to act on it without any interference from you. Did you think about that, Greer?"

He tossed his napkin on the table and sank back in his seat. "Such little faith, Alex. Why do you think I left the others behind? You don't think I'm that stupid, do you?"

I didn't think there was a stupid bone in his body, but it was a valid question.

"Finish your food. We need to get back on the road or we'll be finding a hotel tonight."

The waitress came back and placed a cup of tea on the table in front of me. She looked at Greer. "Would you like one, too?"

"No, thank you," he said, eyeing the cup suspiciously.

"I didn't order this."

"That's okay, hon. Someone did." She patted me on the shoulder and walked away.

I looked at the tea leaves floating to the top of the brew. "I think you forgot to strain it," I called out, but she was already heading down the aisle.

She turned to look back at me, and my breath caught at the sight of her emerald green eyes. "That's the good part," she said before disappearing through the kitchen door.

The tea leaves floated to the top of the liquid like donuts rising to the surface of a fryer full of oil. As they moved around the perimeter of the cup, they picked up speed, circling as if an invisible spoon had stirred them into motion. The leaves spun faster, creating a mini cyclone in the center of the delicate china, and then they abruptly stopped and took their places to form a perfect circle. A line formed on one side of the circle, and then two more grew from each end to form an equally perfect triangle.

As I stared at the replication of my birthmark in a cup of tea, the leaves collapsed into a solid black mass that filled the top surface of the water. I looked closer and the leaves were moving in a clockwise direction, forming another cyclone in the center of the cup.

I closed my eyes as the room began to spin. I could hear Greer in the background calling my name, his voice fading as if we were moving apart. When my eyes reopened, I was in a circle with grass under my feet and soft glowing light illuminating the space. The light was coming from a wall of candles placed along a stone ledge around the outer edge of the circle. There was something else around the perimeter. As my eyes adjusted, I saw a row of black figures creating a second circle between me and the stones. The figures remained perfectly still, like sentinels guarding a sacred tomb, their faces hidden by the long hoods veiled over their heads.

A brief laugh slipped from my lips as I recognized the monuments marking the four quarters of the circle. I don't know how I knew, but the meaning and the directions of the stones came to me just like breathing.

At the north end of the circle was a massive table made of stone. I stepped closer and reached for the smooth surface with my left hand, but my right hand seemed to dominate and ended up on the table first. A pair of tall candles marked each side, surrounded by various objects made of metal and wood. They were tools for the honoring and worship of the gods, and

I recognized every one of them as my own. I was standing before an altar.

My eyes trailed up to the dark wings spreading beyond the edges of the stone, following the lines of the black feathers until I was looking into the eyes of a stone raven.

I bent down to touch the carpet of lush grass, feeling each blade through my fingers, through the leather soles of my shoes. The circle was alive and I was its beating heart.

A hand slipped over my shoulder as I stood back up. The waitress with the bright red uniform, and the brown eyes that now looked like shining emeralds, was smiling back at me when I turned around. This was her temple, and it was my temple. I was looking into the eyes of my mother.

The light from the wall of candles flared, and in a swift symphony of movement, the figures around the circle removed their hoods. One by one I looked into the eyes of my people, recognizing only Lumen but still knowing each face.

I tried to speak, but when I opened my mouth my vocal cords wouldn't move. My mother raised her finger to her lips and instructed me to remain silent. "They're coming," she whispered. "The Rogues are coming."

She went to the altar and reached for a wooden box carved with symbols on each side. A small object reflected the light from the candles as she lifted it from the velvet lining and enveloped it in her hand. "Find the prophecy before they come." She opened her hand and revealed a piece of glass in the shape of a long triangle.

I took it. "What is it?"

Her lips were moving, but there was no sound as the light around her face darkened. Her mouth stretched wide, and her eyes rolled in a strange flowing motion. It was like a drug had kicked in and everything was starting to gel together.

I stumbled back and looked at the robed figures circled around us. They were moving, too, morphing like blobs of black wax in a giant lava lamp.

The ground shook. I fell to the cold grass and looked up at the sky. Not a single star or cloud floated in its orbit. All I could see was a black hole getting wider until everything was gone. My mother was gone.

My eyes fluttered as they adjusted to the bright light. I looked back up at the sky and took in the blue canvas of billowy clouds. I was on fire, and then Greer's face came into view and I realized I was pressed against his furnace of a chest.

I panicked and pushed him away.

"Whoa." He pulled me tighter as I squirmed.

"You're smothering me!"

His grip loosened, and I catapulted from his lap and landed on the ground. When he bent down to help me up, I shoved his hand away and burst into tears.

"Alex, what the hell just happened?" My protests were ignored as he lifted me off the ground and sat me down on the bench next to him. His arm wrapped around my shaking shoulders, and the tears streamed down my face as the image of my mother stuck in my mind like a brand.

"I . . . I saw her," I managed between choking breaths.

"Her?"

"My mother."

Greer let up on my shoulders. He took my face in his other hand and forced me to look at him. My vision cleared as he wiped the tears from my eyes with his thumb. "Tell me."

"I don't know. I was looking at the cup of tea, and then I was in a circle surrounded by candles and an altar. She was there, Greer. My mother was right there."

I gasped. "The waitress!"

He lost the worried expression and stiffened. "What about her?"

"She was there, but she was my mother!"

Greer was up and running before I could blink. We were in

a small park somewhere in town, and my guess was he was heading back to the café. I ran after him.

When we got there, he looked around the room for our waitress. He spotted her waiting on a customer at the back of the room and headed for the table. She reacted the way you'd expect from being grabbed from behind and turned sharply— she swung at him. He caught her wrist and looked her in the face.

"I'll ask you nicely to take your hand off of me," she warned in an even tone.

The customer sitting at the table started to get up. "Dude, let go of the lady."

Greer outweighed him substantially, and by the look on the guy's face, he was regretting the chivalry.

Greer looked in her eyes for a few more seconds, and then gently lowered her wrist to her side, keeping his hand on it for a moment longer. "My apologies. I thought you were someone else."

The waitress looked at him with a confused expression. Then she looked at me. I thought I saw a slight grin cross her face before she turned back to Greer.

He grabbed my hand and led me out of the café. When we climbed into the Yukon, we sat in silence while he waited for me to say something.

I reached into my pocket, wondering if it had all been some wild hallucination, a side effect of all the stress I was under. When I pulled my hand back out, I was holding the piece of glass.

"Where did you get that?" he asked as his eyes went to the object.

"She gave it to me. My mother. I don't know what it is."

He studied it for a few more seconds. "It's a prism."

TEN

We arrived in Ithaca a few hours later. On the way, I told Greer what I remembered about the strange vision. But seeing how I had physical proof in my pocket, I guess it was more than just a vision.

He took his eyes off of the road to look at me, which wasn't the safest thing to do. "Considering who and what you are, it really isn't that unusual for her to manifest and speak to you."

"Yeah, well . . . I wish she would have shown up all those times when I really needed her."

"Are you so sure she didn't?"

I stared at his profile as we drove through the campus entrance, not really knowing how to respond to that. I'd survived some strange and unpleasant things between the time Ava disappeared and I came back to this place. Maybe he was right.

We parked in one of the metered spaces and headed out to the campus. A couple of students directed us to the physics department. Our only plan was to find Dr. David Oxford. After that, we'd wing it.

When we arrived at Clark Hall, we were stopped by a security guard who offered to call Dr. Oxford's office. "Your name, sir?"

"It doesn't matter," Greer replied. "It might as well be Albert Einstein."

The guard and I both looked at him like he'd lost a few screws.

"Just tell me where his office is."

I practically choked when he leaned over the desk and stared the guard down.

The guard's face went blank as he wrote a room number on a piece of paper and directed us to a set of elevators.

"Thank you." Greer leaned in to inspect the man's name tag. "Ted."

"You're welcome, Mr. Sinclair," the guard said in a monotone voice.

We got on the elevator and headed for the fifth floor. "How'd you pull that off? And how did he know your name?"

"Talent, Alex. Persuasive talent."

The elevator opened at the fifth floor, and we made a random guess on the direction of Dr. Oxford's office. When we found it, the door was open and the doctor was standing at a whiteboard, feverishly scribbling numbers and symbols, stepping back every few seconds to examine what he'd written. He mumbled and nodded his head in agreement with his own thoughts.

Greer tapped his knuckle against the doorframe and David Oxford turned around. His eyes flashed a brilliant blue—or maybe it was green—and then dulled to a normal radiance. "Yes? Can I help you?"

"I hope so," Greer answered, flashing the doctor a friendly smile to put him at ease.

Oxford cocked his head. "Well, all right then, come in." He put his marker down. "Made it past Ted. Clever."

His face was clean-shaven, but a plume of wiry hairs stuck out from each ear cavity. Other than a thin spot on his crown, his hair was thick and looked like a grenade had gone off in the center of it. He kind of reminded me of a mad scientist without the bushy mustache.

"Sit, please." He looked at the marked-up board and then at the two of us. "Do you know what this is?"

I studied the random numbers, barely recognizing a few of the symbols from high school math class. "No. Can't say that I do."

Greer shook his head as well. "Over my head, too."

"Good," nodded Oxford. "Then I won't have to kill you." He chuckled at the cliché and took a seat on the other side of the desk. "So?"

Greer got right to the point. "We believe you have something that might be of considerable value to us."

"Oh? And what might that be?"

I don't know what came over me, but I just blurted it out. "Beyond ultraviolet glasses."

Greer glared at me and I sank into my chair. If we were planning on a sneak attack, I'd just ruined it.

"A pair of what?" Oxford stood up and went to the window. "Who did you say you are? I don't believe you introduced yourselves."

Greer met him at the window and extended his hand. "Apologies for our rudeness. My name is Greer Sinclair. My friend with the overzealous nature is Alex Kelley."

I watched his reaction to hearing my name, because everyone seemed to know it. Either he had a damn good poker face or had no idea who I was. Considering that Isabetta said he knew about the prophecy, I found that hard to believe.

"I can see you're a busy man, so I'll get to the point." Greer began to pace in a short line. "Do you know a woman by the name of Isabetta Falcone?"

Oxford stroked his hand down the sides of his chin, bringing his fingers together at the tip as if smoothing an imaginary beard—a nervous habit. "You're from the city?"

"I'll take that as a yes," Greer said, waiting for the doctor to come clean. When Oxford remained mute, he continued. "Ms. Kelley and I had an interesting conversation with Isabetta last night."

"About?"

"About you, Dr. Oxford."

"The prophecy," I clarified. "We know you're looking for it."

I glared at Greer before he had a chance to admonish me. I was the one responsible for the prophecy so I had every right to speak my mind, and he was doing a poor job of cutting to the chase. I was just moving the conversation along.

"I don't suppose you'd believe me if I told you I wanted no part of it," the doctor said.

"No, we wouldn't," Greer shot back. "And you'd be wise to consider whom you're working for."

"Working for? I'm not working for anyone." Oxford crossed the room and pulled a letter-sized envelope from the desk drawer. "See for yourself." He handed it to Greer. The letter was addressed to Isabetta. He opened it and removed its contents. A check floated to the floor as he unfolded the sheet of paper encasing it. It was made out to David Oxford in the amount of fifty thousand dollars.

"Cheap," I mumbled.

The piece of paper had two words written in large capital letters—KEEP IT.

"I have no desire to get into bed with that woman," Oxford said with a touch of disgust. "Figuratively speaking, of course."

"That may be true, Doctor, but why haven't you mailed it?" I asked.

He looked at me like I'd just asked him why the earth was round. "Because I didn't have a stamp, Ms. Kelley." He scratched his head and looked at the ground. "Need to get to the post office," he muttered as an afterthought. "The market, too. I have to pick up toothpaste."

He mumbled off a list of mundane items he needed to purchase, and I realized we were losing the brilliant doctor. "Dr. Oxford . . . the prophecy." That seemed to bring him back from the distraction of his grocery list.

"Yes, the prophecy. Fantastic discovery, isn't it?"

"Isabetta Falcone thinks she's getting a fifty-thousand-dollar pair of superman glasses. Why would she think that?" I asked.

"Well, I believe she's right."

"Right about what?"

"About the vessel being invisible to the human eye."

I looked at Greer who was being unusually quiet for a man who liked to dominate the conversation, but he just listened as Oxford spoke.

"Are you saying you *have* developed a pair of glasses that can see it?"

He laughed at my question. "Ms. Kelley, are you familiar with cone cells?"

I had no idea what he was talking about, and I hoped he wasn't about to go off on another tangent.

Greer finally piped up. "You mean the color sensitivity of the eye?"

"Exactly. The human eye has three types. Most of us are trichromats, meaning we have three types of color receptors in our eyes. To simplify, think of them as the three primary color receptors. It also means our perception of the world around us is limited to a specific range within that electromagnetic spectrum. But we still have to be able to see those wavelengths of color in order to identify an object. Isabetta is correct that I've been working on something that can see certain wavelengths that otherwise might not be detectable."

"I'm curious, Dr. Oxford." Greer wasn't buying the whole story. "Would you like to tell us how you even know about the prophecy? Isabetta is a smart woman, but I doubt she made the connection between your work and the vessel and just looked you up to see if you wanted a little freelance work. I also doubt she told you the real reason she was interested in your research."

"I'd heard rumors about the vessel—or vessels—for years," Oxford said. "The spectral research community is very tight. Our ears are always up, so something as exciting as a prophetic vessel does not remain underground for long. When Isabetta approached me and said she was looking for some kind of invisible container, I made the connection myself. I was point blank with her about my suspicions, so she talked." His face took on a more serious note. "But let me assure you, Mr. Sinclair, my research was started for very different reasons. Once it's complete, however, it can easily be applied to the hunt for the vessel."

"Then you *do* have something she wants?"

"Oh, I have something she wants, Mr. Sinclair. She's just not going to get it." He took a deep breath and looked at the two of us. "The question is, will you?"

I wasn't worried about that part because Greer had a way of making people do anything he wanted. But before he could compel the good doctor to give up his invention, we needed to know what it was.

"Have you ever heard of a place called Lochaber?" Dr. Oxford asked.

"In the Scottish Highlands?" Greer seemed to be less clueless than I was.

"There's a village there called Glenfinnan. You may be familiar with their famous monument to the Jacobite clansmen. But there's a little secret they aren't quite as public about."

"I've heard of the place," Greer said. "Continue."

"For centuries, the villagers stood at the shores of Loch Shiel and never knew they had a visitor. Then one day, there was a storm and all hell broke loose in the glen. It's a beautiful place, but on that particular day it must have been terrifying." He stopped talking and wandered off again.

"Dr. Oxford." I managed to corral his attention back to the story.

"Yes, sorry. As I was saying, a storm rolled in. But this wasn't just any storm. Lightning flashed through the glen for hours, and the thunder it created—" He shook his head and paused as if he'd been there to see it for himself. "Witnesses say it was like the hand of God was cracking a whip through the valley. They could see a giant figure appear on the shore each time the lightning struck. Some sort of statue about thirty feet tall. It would appear and then simply vanish with the lightning."

"This is all very interesting, Dr. Oxford, but what's the relevance?"

"The relevance, Mr. Sinclair, is that it keeps happening. Every time lightning strikes, the statue appears. No one has been able to pinpoint it, but I believe the lightning is being reflected off of a natural prism hidden somewhere in the glen. That prism is taking the source light and separating it into the usual wavelengths—primary colors the human eye can see—but it's also separating out a new one—a hybrid that has never been documented. A hybrid that the human eye can see."

My gaze shot to Greer's. He was already thinking what I was. The prism in my pocket was a tool to find the vessel.

"Pardon me, Dr. Oxford," I interrupted. "Science and math weren't my strong points in school. Can you dumb it down just a hair?"

"Of course. Sunlight, or white light, is a composition of all the colors of the spectrum. When light hits an object, say . . . a lemon, the lemon will absorb some but not all of that light. What doesn't get absorbed gets reflected to the human eye. In the case of our lemon, the color yellow is not absorbed and gets reflected. Our brain translates those reflected wavelengths as color. Hence, we see the object and our brain knows that it's yellow."

He studied my face for signs that I was getting it. "Does that make sense, Ms. Kelley?"

"Yes, thank you. But I still don't understand what makes the statue invisible."

"Ah, that's the good part. I believe the statue is capable of absorbing one hundred percent of the light hitting it. There simply is nothing reflected for the eye to see, so it's invisible. That is, until the lightning hits this mysterious prism which separates and creates this new wavelength of light that the statue can't absorb."

"And this 'hybrid' light that isn't absorbed is reflected for the whole world to see," Greer added.

"Exactly, Mr. Sinclair. But it's only visible for a few seconds as the lightning strikes, and then it's gone again. I'm convinced that the vessel is made up of the same particles as the mysterious statue of Loch Shiel. My research has been to replicate this mysterious anomaly in the form of a lens containing a prism––a very unusual prism. Can you imagine how many things are out there just waiting to be seen with the right lens?"

"Is your research complete?" Greer asked.

"Not yet, but I'm getting very close. Isabetta Falcone contacted me and offered me money for the technology. I have to say, it took some convincing to get her to tell me why she wanted it." He lowered his voice. "I mean no offense, but I doubt Ms. Falcone was capable of making the connection between my work and the vessel. As you said, Mr. Sinclair, she's smart but not that smart. I suspect she's working with someone who is."

"We agree on that." Greer glanced at me while I replayed the science lesson in my head. "And I intend to find out who that is."

"May I ask, Dr. Oxford, where are these magic lenses?" Even if they weren't finished yet, I was a little worried about the glasses sitting in a university lab just waiting to be stolen.

He appeared benign enough, but the question seemed to invoke a man much more cunning in nature. "Ms. Kelley. The technology for filtering out a new wavelength of light that has never been documented before is not as simple as throwing on a generic pair of prism-imbedded glasses. It's true that we all share a common range of sight, but something of this sensitivity would require the finest tuning of the individual wearing them."

He leaned in closer and looked me in the eye. "Do you really think all that power can be put into a one-size-fits-all lens?"

I gasped as the color of his irises shifted from blue to green, and then to red. "They're in your eyes."

"Clever girl, Ms. Kelley."

"Oxford!" Greer commanded, compelling the doctor to look at him, confirming for himself that the lenses were indeed in the man's eyes.

"Surgically implanted. No one's getting their hands on these."

"Why are you telling us all this?" I was surprised Greer hadn't already asked the question.

Dr. Oxford smiled. "Because I know who you are, Ms. Kelley. Everyone knows who you are."

We left Cornell University knowing two things: the true nature of Dr. David Oxford's work, and that Isabetta Falcone had an accomplice.

Dr. Oxford agreed to let us know if Isabetta contacted him for anything else. In the meantime, Greer was planning to find out who her accomplice was as soon as we got back to the city.

I pulled the prism from my pocket and examined it closely. It was about two inches tall and long, nothing unusual as far as prisms go, I supposed.

"Careful with your new toy," Greer warned.

I played with it for a moment longer before putting it back in my pocket. "She's watching me."

"Who?"

"My mother. It's not a coincidence that she gave it to me now. She knew we were on our way to see Dr. Oxford."

The doctor had inadvertently filled in the blanks where my mother left off. The object in my pocket would allow my mere human eyes to see the vessel. Now I just needed to walk from the Battery to Harlem and point it at every square inch in between. If that turned up nothing, I'd start on the five boroughs. Should only take about a hundred years.

"Greer," I began hesitantly, dreading telling him the small thing I left out earlier. "She said something else to me. She said the Rogues are coming."

I woke up as we were driving down our street. I was happy to see the familiar buildings and green awnings. Even the sound of traffic and car horns was music to my ears.

The clock on the console said 9:08 p.m. I had the day shift the next morning, which meant I had an hour or two before I had to hit the sack.

Greer showed little reaction when I told him about my mother's warning. I supposed it was because he already knew. Lumen said the same thing the day she showed up at the shop, and Greer, I suspected, took her warning as gospel. He didn't want her anywhere near me, but her words clearly carried a lot of weight with him.

Sophia greeted us as we got off the elevator. Greer had given her the day off, but true to her hardworking Italian nature and her loyalty, she came to work anyway to make sure food was in the oven when we got home.

"That was really thoughtful, Sophia." As usual, I was starving and grateful for her cooking.

Greer offered to drive her home, but he'd been behind the wheel for more than three hours, so she insisted he let her take the car service.

We served ourselves straight from the pan on the stovetop and sat at the kitchen counter to eat Sophia's eggplant Parmesan.

"You don't think Oxford is full of shit, do you?"

Greer shook his head. "I think he knows exactly what he's doing and told us everything he knows. He has no reason to lie to us. In fact, I think he's betting on us as his second line of defense."

"Against what?"

"Against Isabetta Falcone. When he does mail that letter, and I have a feeling it'll be tomorrow, she'll send someone else up there. No stamp, my ass. He was scared to send it."

"Do you really think she'd hurt him?"

"If she finds out where his research is, I wouldn't put it past her to try to dig his eyes out herself."

The image of David Oxford lying in a pool of blood with two butchered eye sockets jarred me. "Greer, we can't let her do that to him."

"I already made a call. She won't get anywhere near him."

We were cleaning up from dinner when Greer's cell phone went off. He walked out of the kitchen to take the call. When he returned, he had a box in his hand.

"That was Sophia. She forgot to mention the package that was delivered today." He handed it to me. "It's for you."

The box was about a foot long and half as thick. There was no return address and no reason for anyone to send it to me. "What should I do?"

"I think you should open it."

I stared at the plain brown package and thought about all the bad things that could be inside. I hadn't ordered anything. Packages didn't just show up on your doorstep without a reason, and that reason was making my imagination run wild.

I pulled a knife from the drawer and ran it along the packing tape. The top flaps released, and I waited to see if anything moved inside. It wouldn't be the first time I handled a live package. The last time I opened a mysterious package—or envelope—it contained the missing amulet.

"I'm not going to find David Oxford's eyeballs in there, am I?"

He smirked. "I doubt it."

Inside the packing box was a smaller cardboard box that looked about the right size for a pair of ballerina slippers. A piece of silver tissue paper unfolded as I pulled the lid off. Under that was a bundle wrapped in black velvet. I pulled it out of the box and set it on the kitchen counter. Whatever was inside was heavier than it looked.

Before unwrapping the mystery present, I glanced at Greer one last time. "Here goes nothing."

I peeled the fabric back and stared at the double-sided blade. It was marked with symbols and looked like it could use a good polish. The handle was made of wood or bone, painted black and intricately carved into the shape of a bird's wing.

"It's beautiful, but why would someone sent me a dagger?"

Greer nodded toward the box. A strange expression crossed his face, and I could tell he knew the answer. At the bottom of the box was a piece of paper with a hand-written note. The note simply said, *Come home*, with the initials *A. T.* written underneath.

I looked up at Greer for help in understanding what was happening. His tired blue eyes walked over mine as the energy drained from his face.

"You know I hate when you do that," I whispered. "You don't get to look defeated."

"Pick it up," he said.

I took it and molded my hand around the intricate handle. It fit in my palm like it had been carved just for me, and I knew it was mine.

His face went cold. "I know who Isabetta Falcone is working with."

ELEVEN

I t's your birthright." Greer grabbed my wrist as I raised my hand to throw the dagger at the wall.

"It's also my right to say I don't want it."

I lowered my arm and put the dagger back in the box. If there had been a return address, I would have handed it back to the UPS man the next morning.

Greer immediately recognized the initials as those of Alasdair Templeton, the man who I saw in the picture in Arthur Richmond's office the night of his party, and the man who presided as high priest of my mother coven in Ireland.

"That blade is not just a knife, Alex. It's an athame." He warned me with his eyes not to do anything stupid as he began his trademark pace across the kitchen floor.

"Would you stop doing that, Greer? You make me nervous when you act like a caged leopard."

He stopped and faced me. "It was Maeve's."

My eyes went to the box as the instinct to reach back in and touch it overwhelmed me. The fact that my mother's hand once held it made me rethink the gift, regardless of the price to be paid for accepting it.

"Do you even know what an athame is?"

"No. Why don't you educate me?" I relented and pulled the dagger back out of the box to examine it. The symbols along the blade were half hidden under years of tarnish, but the handle was perfect. When I looked closer I could see that it was actually green, a shade so deep that it appeared to be black.

Greer moved his hand closer but wouldn't allow his fingers to actually touch it. "It's black jade."

"You'd think they'd take better care of it." I ran the tip of my own finger along the dull blade. "Looks like it hasn't been polished in years."

"I doubt it has. An athame is a witch's most powerful tool. It should never be handled by anyone else."

I nearly dropped it. "Then why did you let me touch it? Damn it, Greer! You told me to pick it up."

"Because it belongs to you now."

"And if I don't want it?" Of course I wanted it. It belonged to my mother, but I had a feeling there were some pretty hefty strings attached to accepting it, and I wasn't about to give Alasdair Templeton the opportunity to tangle me up in old family business.

"You are a Raven—Fitheach. That is something you can't change, Alex."

My heart skipped when he came toward me and took my face in his hands. "They want you back. They plan to *take* you back."

We were living in the twenty-first century. You couldn't just take people against their will. But by the look on Greer's face, he thought otherwise.

His expression sank as if his own words had triggered an unpleasant epiphany. I followed him as he headed for the library muttering something about a box.

"What are you looking for?" I asked as he rifled through the shelves, seemingly oblivious to the books crashing to the ground.

He found the book he was looking for and opened it. "If Templeton wants a war, he's got one." He pulled something from its pages and tossed the book on the floor next to the others. It was one of those fake books with a hollow compartment in the center.

The object passed through his fingers for a few seconds while the wheels in his head turned. Then he held it between his thumb and index fingers for me to see. It was a key.

The doorbell rang an hour after Greer ransacked his own library. When he opened it, Ava was standing on the other side with a metal box in her hands. Melanie Harris stood behind her looking timid as a scared rabbit.

"Thank you both for coming. I know it's late." He shut the door and led everyone into the living room.

"Are you kidding?" Ava laughed softly. "I've been waiting for this call since the day she stepped off that plane."

I eyed the two of them, waiting to be let in on the secret. It was me, after all, that they were talking about. I was the one the Lord of Darkness was after.

Ava handed the box to Greer and hugged me like it might be the last time. I let go first and took a step back. "Which one of you is going to tell me what's in the box?"

"Leverage," Ava said with a sly grin. "Always take out insurance for priceless possessions."

"Are you sure we should do this?" Melanie seemed to be the only one with reservations about what they were about to do.

"Stop being such a coward," Ava scolded. "You agreed to this a long time ago, and this box has afforded you your freedom."

Melanie shrunk back into a shorter version of herself, and I thought she might bolt for the door. Instead, her neck elongated as her shoulders squared. "A coward wouldn't have done what I did."

Ava gave her a hug. "You were very brave, but you need to be just as brave now." She turned to Greer and told him to open the box.

The four of us gathered around the coffee table and watched as Greer fumbled with the small key. His hands were usually as steady as a surgeon's, but today they seemed a little shaky. The lock disengaged. He paused for a moment before reaching for the lid, while the three of them seemed to debate the rationality of what they were about to do. The newly confident Melanie beat him to it and slowly lifted the lid on its hinges. The inside of the metal box was padded thickly on all sides, securing a smaller silver box with a removable lid. Like a bomb specialist, she lifted the four-inch box from the larger one and placed it gingerly on the table.

"Alex, why don't you do the honors?" Ava motioned to the box with her eyes. "Just lift the lid. *Carefully*."

Butterflies circled around my ribcage as I reached for the box, half expecting Tinker Bell to fly out of it. My hand seemed to have a mind of its own and refused to move as if the box was a mousetrap waiting to snap at my fingers.

Ava gave me a weak smile. "It's all right, Alex. Open it."

I removed the lid, and the four sides of the box collapsed outward, leaving the contents completely exposed. In the center was a moving mass of light and metal that looked like a three-dimensional hologram. A trio of gold rings orbited around a ball of light that alternated between blue and white. The rings moved in a perfectly timed pattern, sending audible waves into the air that sounded like a singing bowl or a fingertip circling the edge of a crystal glass.

"What is it?" I asked without taking my eyes off of it.

"It's the golden egg," Ava explained. "You're looking at a life force."

"A life force? Of what?"

A nervous giggle escape Melanie's mouth. When I looked

at her, I thought she was about to burst into either laughter or tears.

"It's the life force of the circle. To be more specific, Alasdair Templeton's circle." Ava placed her hand over the rings and the light intensified, illuminating straight through her muscles and bones. "The force exists as long as the rings move. If they stop spinning, the coven stops. The power dies." She bent her finger in a mock attempt to knock them over. "It would be as simple as flipping a light switch."

I could see the anxiety on her face, mingled with the fascination of the what-if scenario.

Greer was smirking when I glanced at him. "We've got him by his balls."

"That we do," Ava agreed. "We've been waiting twenty-seven years to play this card, and now we have a good reason to."

"It's been in this box for twenty-seven years?" That meant it was put in there just before I was born.

"Almost twenty-eight," Melanie added.

"The coven wasn't happy when your mother decided to leave. They thought they could force her to stay, and they would have if it wasn't for a very brave soul." Ava put her hand on Melanie's arm. "Maeve just needed a little insurance, and Melanie was a loyal friend."

"Why haven't they come after it?"

Ava focused on the fragile mix of light and metal dancing on the table, and the silver walls re-erected around it. "Because it would be suicide. It's a delicate decision to approach something teetering on the edge of a cliff. One poorly placed foot, and poof!"

"Don't get me wrong, I think my mother was the best thing since sliced bread, but what made her so irreplaceable to the coven? Couldn't they find someone else to do her job? It just seems like a lot of trouble to force her to stay."

With her meek nature and lack of self-confidence, Melanie was the last person I expected to look at me like I didn't have a brain in my head. "Do her job?" she repeated indignantly.

Ava glared at Melanie. "Let's all just simmer down. Alex doesn't know her entire family history."

"There's more?" Didn't I have enough to digest? Could I handle more?

"I'm afraid so."

"Easy, Ava," Greer said. "Take it slow."

"Destruction of what's in that box isn't the only way to destroy the circle. There's another surefire way."

She placed the silver lid back on the small box and secured it inside the larger one. "Alex, you have to remember what you are. You are the Oracle. For decades the Fitheach thought it was your mother, and her mother before that. It seems the family has been chasing false prophets for generations."

"You mean, they thought my grandmother was the Oracle?"

"That's exactly what I'm saying. She had the mark, and so did your mother. But it wasn't quite right, was it?"

I'd discovered that little secret after finding an old book at the shop. It was my mother who led me to it. She knew she wasn't the Oracle and kept that fact hidden to protect me, but it was looking like the secret was out, because my pseudo-family wanted me back in a desperate way.

"It started a long time ago." Melanie began to tell the backstory of how we went from ordinary peasants to keepers of the most notorious artifact known to the world. "We were a small clan. Nothing particularly special about the Fitheach. We worshipped our gods, honoring them with the appropriate gifts. Then one day they decided to speak. Your grandmother—" She stopped and looked at me. "Did Maeve ever tell you her name?"

"No. She never told me about any of our family."

She took a calming breath and continued. "Your grandmother's name was Isla Kelley. She was a fierce witch. Not one for letting the inwards take control."

"The inwards?"

"The visitors. It's appropriate to invite them in and let them have a stroll through the soul."

"It's called invocation," Ava clarified when Melanie started to lose me. "It's when the gods are invited to enter your body."

"Yes." Melanie continued with the story. "Isla was respectful about the whole thing, but she didn't like to give them control. Most priestesses just let the gods steer the boat, but Isla preferred to have a private conversation with them and then interpret their words for the clan. The gods were respectful of her wishes, but then one night, the words sprang from her mouth like Danu herself. The gods spoke of three prophecies and the vessels that contained them, and then declared to the clan that the blood of Isla Kelley would be the keeper of those prophecies. The storm hit a second later, and a bolt of lightning came from the sky, striking Isla on the side of her head. Burned the mark right into her skin."

Ava watched me like a hawk while Melanie gave me the condensed version of the events leading up to the revelation of the prophecies.

"Where did my mother get the amulet?"

Ava completed the puzzle by revealing the last piece. "Isla went to her grave with a secret. The gods had given her the amulet, but she told no one about its existence. You see, Alex, ignorance and greed are a dangerous combination. She could have been killed for it. Isla spent the rest of her days looking over her shoulder."

"So how did the amulet get exposed?"

"When Maeve was born, she bore a mark almost identical to the mark the gods had burned into Isla's skin. That's when

Isla realized she wasn't the Oracle, and she did what needed to be done to protect her child. It was on her deathbed that she finally gave Maeve the amulet and told her everything. Maeve wasn't as afraid as Isla, though. But she should have been."

Ava sighed heavily and shook her head. "The secret got out, and like a bad rumor the whole damn world got wind of it."

"Is that why my mother left Ireland and came here? To hide?"

Ava hesitated, choosing her words carefully before answering. "Maeve had her reasons for coming to New York. She was pregnant with you at the time. When you were born—"

"She did the same thing Isla did." When she saw my birthmark and realized the triangle had been completed, she knew I was the real Oracle. It was an evolution of the original mark left by the gods, and my mother was smart enough to know it. The amulet was passed to me as it had been passed to her, only I never got the family history because I was only five years old. My mother was killed before she could prepare me for the truth.

"Alex," Ava put her hand over mine, "*you* are the blood of Isla Kelley."

"We were given a task by the gods," Melanie said. "In exchange, the coven was blessed with great power. If the coven fails, they'll take it away."

"So you see, Alex," Ava continued, "you are non-negotiable. In the eyes of the coven, you and that life force sitting on the table are one and the same."

I had a dream that night that I was kneeling in a large sea of blue-green grass. The blades were tiny fans of silk, alive and restless against my bare skin.

On the ground in front of me was a polished stone, small enough to fit in the palm of my hand. I reached for it, and as I tumbled its smooth surface through my fingers, it began to grow. Soon it was bigger than my hand, and the stone leapt from my fingers and landed a few feet away in the grass. I watched it grow. As it got bigger, it began to take a different shape.

A bird flew over my head, and my eyes moved from the stone to the sky. When I looked back down, the round stone with the soft curves had become a large structure with hard edges and flat surfaces. The stone had become an altar.

The darkness suddenly lifted as candles lit up in a circle around me. I'd been in this place before, only this time there were no dark figures with hoods separating me from the wall. There was no sense of my mother, and if I turned around I knew I'd find nothing but an empty space. I was alone.

One by one, the altar filled with objects. A pair of tall candles in ornately carved holders ignited, and then a plume of gentle smoke circled up from a silver bowl, releasing the smell of spice and something sweet into the night air. It was the same scent I'd smelled a hundred times before. It was the scent embedded in the drawers lining the two-story wall of Ava's shop, and the incense that burned atop the mantel in our home. It was the scent of my childhood. It used to cling to my mother's skin and clothes, and it was as familiar and comforting as the memory of her face.

I heard a flutter, and my eyes were pulled to the looming black shadow that filled the space above the altar. As my eyes adjusted, I could see the wings spanning past the edges of the stone. The statue was carved from the same black jade as the handle of my mother's athame.

The bird's head was angled slightly to the right, but the eyes were looking down at me—two black circles reflecting the light from the sky, inanimate but alive.

A scraping sound drew me away from the statue, and I saw the tip of my mother's athame protrude over the edge of the altar. The light from the candles reflected off the metal, illuminating the liquid coating the edge. And then a single drop fell from the blade. As the blood descended toward the ground, it slowed. The crimson drop became a long black feather that floated playfully in the air. It swung back and forth like a pendulum as it continued down, catching the breeze each time it came within an inch of the grass, swooping back into the wind to start the dance again. On the fifth swing, it sailed straight toward me and jetted over my head, disappearing into the sky.

I tried to stand but felt something rub against the skin of my foot. A thin silver chain was wrapped around my ankle, and though it looked delicate enough to snap with a light tug, it felt as heavy as the steel of a ship's anchor.

My eyes followed the length of chain as the other end disappeared into the earth.

"What is this?" No one was there to answer, but I knew they were all listening. Under the sea of grass and behind the veil concealing their forms, I knew they were all standing there, witnessing my epiphany as I realized they were the ones holding the other end.

They would never let me go.

I reached for the chain and tried to pull it from the earth. Each time I grabbed hold of the thin silver, it seemed to slip through my fingers as if I were grasping air.

I turned to look at my hands which had become inept tools of uselessness, but all I could see were the shiny black feathers of my wings.

TWELVE

When I got to the shop the next morning, Katie had already straightened the mess pile from the night before. It was inventory day, and that meant hours of plowing through the shelves and the endless task of recording book titles.

"You're here early." I picked up a book that was left on the end of the counter. "Fishing for a raise?"

"Ooh, do you think it'll work?"

"I think you'll have to sleep with the boss for that."

"Yeah, well . . ." She trailed off and dropped the banter, not quite her usual witty self.

"What's the matter, Katie? You're awfully quiet this morning."

She was holding back. I could feel it. After all we'd been through, it bothered me a little. I knew her biggest secret, and she knew most of mine. But something had her buttoned up tight today.

I glanced around the shop in preparation for our monumental task. When I looked back at Katie, I noticed her dreamy expression and the way she was twirling her fingertips along the edge of the book in her hand. She was completely distracted by a thought that put a coy smile on her face. Katie Bishop had the euphoric look of a woman who was sleeping with someone new.

"Anyone I know?" I casually asked.

She kept her eyes on the book in her hand and ignored my question.

"Come on, Katie. Tell Momma about your new toy."

She exhaled the breath she was holding. "Well . . . he's tall and very hot. That's all I'm saying."

Of course he was tall and hot. Katie was gorgeous. A little overboard with her piercings, but none of it could camouflage the goddess underneath her plaid miniskirt and weathered combat boots.

She had her own unique style, but sometimes I wondered if it was just her way of weeding out all the noise—the frat boys and all the other dicks trying to get into her pants. If you could see past the costume, you stood a chance of getting her attention.

"Fine. I'll let it go—for now."

We had the whole day to chat, so I decided to let the conversation happen organically. A few mindless hours of clipboards and scribbling down book titles, and we'd both be giving up secrets.

"Where's Bear?"

"Who?"

"My kitty. His name is Bear. Where is he?"

"Ah, the kitten. I guess that means you got Daddy's permission to keep him?"

"*Daddy* didn't have a choice. If he said no, I was going to bring his home anyway."

I headed for the back room to make sure he'd been properly cared for while I was away.

When I opened the door, I heard a tiny meow and felt the tug of a small claw at the bottom of my pants. I swooped him off my leg and held him up to my face. "Did you miss me, boo?

Mommy missed you." I planted a kiss on top of his head and inspected the room for food, water, and something that served as a litter box.

"Oh, don't worry about him," Katie snorted. "He's getting the *Lion King* treatment. I think Apollo is getting attached, so you better get him out of here soon or he's going to end up in someone else's house."

"He's coming home with me today." I put Bear back down and shut the door.

"So, where do we start?" I looked at the shelves on each side of the shop and wondered how three people could possibly drudge through the thousands of books crammed from floor to ceiling. Lucky for us we had a lot of copies—unusual for a used bookstore—which would make the job go a little faster.

Katie handed me a clipboard and a pen and pointed to the first aisle of the romance section. "I'll start on that side and you can start on the other. We'll chat our way around."

"This is going to take days," I groaned.

Apollo had failed to mention that inventory day actually meant inventory week. Katie had worked at Shakespeare's Library for about a year. The gods must have been looking out for her, because she started a few days after inventory ended last year. This would be a first for both of us.

A few minutes into the mind-numbing task, I heard Katie's clipboard hit the floor. "Oh, God. This one brings back memories. Have you read it?" She stuck the book through a gap in the shelf.

Savage Dance was written in bold gothic letters across the top. The woman on the cover was slumped in a man's arms, and her long red dress plunged to the center of her breasts. He looked like he was planning to crawl inside of her.

"Can't say that I have."

The book disappeared back through the hole. "Hey, don't judge. This was the book that introduced me to the fabulous world of soft porn." She started flipping through the pages. "See, someone else liked it, too. All the best pages are dog-eared."

"We'll be here for a month if you don't pick that clipboard back up," I said.

She started reading one of those marked pages, and I got a visual of the fingers that had been on that book. "'He hesitated, heightening her wild desire before he plunged into her soft, wet core, claiming her with the forceful strokes of his eager *cock*.'"

"Gross, Katie! Are you actually touching those pages?"

"'She moaned as he held her in place to shove his cock deeper, stroking his tongue inside her mouth with each *thrust*.'"

"Jeez, would you stop!"

"Oh come on, Alex. This is good stuff. Nothing *soft* about it, though. Can't wait to read *hard*," she snorted.

"My, you're in funny form today."

"You know, Alex, the guy on the cover kind of looks like that boyfriend of yours."

"He's not my boyfriend," I reminded her for the hundredth time.

"Yeah, right."

We kept plowing through the shelves, picking through the endless mountain of books at a steady clip. Even so, it would take more than a week to get through them all.

"Isn't there a more efficient way of doing this, Katie? I mean, this is the twenty-first century. There's software that does this kind of stuff, you know."

"Yeah, no shit. The owner is too cheap to invest in an inventory system, and why should he when he's got cheap labor? I don't think anyone has ever actually finished. Apollo says they just start at the opposite end of the store every year and work back around."

"I like this place, Katie, but let's just hope we're both gone before next year's inventory."

It was midafternoon before we finished the romance

section. We'd had few interruptions, and the laborious process had actually been a pleasant distraction from an otherwise boring day.

Katie finished the last book on her side and came around to work back-to-back with me on the metaphysics and occult aisle.

I picked up a copy of a book titled *Here There Be Witches.* "I know this book." On the cover was the face of a jagged old witch with a tiny snake wrapped around her ring finger. "My mother had a copy. Used to scare the heck out of me until we read it together." I tossed in on the floor. "It's in the wrong section. It's really a children's book."

"You know, if you really delved into all the fairy tales we read to children, they'd scare the crap out of you," Katie mused. "The old ones, anyway. The new ones are too PC."

"Speaking of fairy tales, how's that dragon of yours been lately? Charred anyone?"

"Now who's the funny one?"

"You know, you still haven't told me about this new guy. Has *he* seen the dragon?"

"You're asking me if my dragon likes to fuck?"

I shrugged. "I hadn't thought about it like that, but since you brought it up . . ."

"To be honest, I don't know. But with this new guy—"

We both looked up as the door chimed. A short guy wearing a pair of dark sunglasses walked inside. He took a strategically placed step in each direction as he bobbed his head and scanned the room. His leather jacket squeaked when he moved, and his black shoes looked like they'd been polished with oil.

Satisfied with the surroundings, his nostrils flared as he took a deep breath and looked at the two of us from across the room. His mouth moved and I thought he was going to speak, but it was just to resume chewing the gum he had tucked in his cheek.

"You Kelley?" he eventually asked.

Katie and I glanced at each other, and then looked back at

the guy. "Who wants to know?" we both asked in Scorsese scripted unison.

He resumed that annoying bobbing of his head as he pursed his lips and reached for the door. He opened it, and the bob turned into a firm nod.

Demitri entered the shop and smiled at me like a lion greeting his dinner. The other guy looked like a child next to him. Demitri was twice his size, but their shoe size looked to be about the same. What is it about guys and their feet?

"Someone would like to have a word with you." It was the first time I'd actually heard Demitri speak, and his voice matched his appearance perfectly.

Isabetta Falcone walked through the door and surveyed the room, much the same way as the short guy had. She had a relaxed stride and a half-cocked look on her face that made you wonder what was so amusing. The casual smile on her face radiated pure confidence, and the tailored pant suit she wore made me forget for a moment that she was second or third generation Staten Island "family." Without the two men standing next to her, you'd think she was a socialite or a rich housewife slumming it from the Upper East Side.

Her eyes reached around the room one last time, stopping on Katie for a moment before continuing to me. "So, this is where you work." She walked toward me, triggering the two leather-clad puppets to catch up.

I took a step back as she approached, the memory of her knee stroking mine sending a traitorous flutter around my gut. "What are you doing here?"

Her hazel eyes leveled on mine as the smell of Chanel emitted from her skin. I would have thought her more of a Giorgio BH girl. Isabetta could wear all the expensive suits she wanted and load up on the perfume, but she was what she was, and nothing could mask her affinity for bejeweled fingertips and a good catfight.

Her lips rose slightly as her gaze shifted to Katie. "Aren't you going to introduce me to your friend?"

"Isabetta Falcone," I nodded to my right, "Katie Bishop."

Katie extended her hand. "It's nice to meet you."

Isabetta took it, and I felt like karate chopping the shake. Apparently I was Isabetta's type, but Katie was everyone's type.

I got an image of the dragon in my head, and my concern for Katie disappeared. *Go ahead, Isabetta. Try it.*

Katie pulled away first, glancing at me for confirmation that she wasn't imagining the vibe she was getting from Isabetta.

"Why are you here?" I asked again, providing needed interference between the two women.

"I thought I'd stop by and see how your trip to Cornell went."

"Shouldn't you be having this conversation with Greer?" It was his audience she'd requested, not mine. If she wanted an update on the meeting with Dr. David Oxford, she needed to pick up the phone and call Greer.

She huffed at my audacity. "Displaying those big balls of yours again. You remind me of . . . me." Her eyes moved around the room again and stopped on a poster that read *Life begins when you find your fit.* She panned back to me and lost her smile. "Is this what you want out of life, Alex? Is this," she waved her hand around the room, "your fit?"

"I'm sorry." Katie slumped her shoulders and cocked her head to the side. "Did we forget to show you our fine collection of diamond-studded panties at the front counter?"

"Let it go, Katie," I mumbled.

Isabetta ignored the remark because she was too fixated on my chest. Her eyes roamed over my blouse, and then her hand reached for the silver chain disappearing under it.

"Uh-uh. Hands off." I caught her wrist before she could touch it.

She looked seriously pissed off by my lack of subservience,

and then she grabbed my arm with her other hand and practically dragged me to the other side of the room. "If you know what's good for you, you'll cooperate." Her Staten Island was peeking through as she slipped into her own bad Scorsese part. "What happened with Oxford? Tell me!"

I yanked my arm out of her clingy little fingers. "If you know what's good for *you*, you'll back off. I know what you're doing. You think you can bypass the middleman and go straight to the source." Why deal with Greer when all she needed was me, the amulet, and those non-existent glasses Dr. Oxford was working on? "Not going to happen, Isabetta. Greer and I are a team."

It wasn't that I felt an overwhelming sense of duty to bring Greer in on everything I did. We were partners, but no one made decisions for me. The truth was, Isabetta Falcone scared me. She didn't have to be a Gambino or a Bonanno to break my legs, and her guys could do a lot of damage before a drop of blood was shed to turn the tables.

Isabetta suddenly looked a little less confident. The cocky smile on her face went flat as she stepped back a few feet.

"And here I thought we had a deal," someone said from behind me.

I turned around, and the first thing that came into focus was the birthmark on Alasdair Templeton's forehead. He was standing near the front door by himself. No backup, no guns; just a man in a well-tailored suit and a presence that demanded respect.

Isabetta was speechless. By the look on her face, it was from fear that she'd been caught red-handed trying to circumvent the man she was in cahoots with.

She glared at Demitri and the short guy, but they were already moving toward the other end of the room.

"I don't pay you two to be pussies!" she snarled.

Demitri stepped forward first. "Mr. Templeton, we were—"

Alasdair Templeton put his hand in the air. "No, no," he said. "We were doing just fine a moment ago. And then you had to go and ruin it by opening your mouth."

He stared at Isabetta and her men for a few more uncomfortable seconds, and then he turned his attention back to me. He then looked at Katie and offered his hand. "Alasdair Templeton. And you are?"

She glanced at me before taking it. "Katie Bishop."

He drew her hand to his lips and kissed it. "Katie," he murmured. "It's a pleasure to meet you. Now, would you mind giving Alex and me a moment of privacy?" He looked at Isabetta and her men and silently told them to get the hell out. "We have family business to discuss."

THIRTEEN

e hadn't changed at all. The man I remembered seeing in my living room when I was a child was the same man from the photo in Arthur Richmond's office. And he'd apparently discovered the fountain of youth. Other than a slight graying around the temples, he looked the same.

I'd never been this close to Alasdair Templeton before. As a child, I'd only seen him from the crack under my bedroom door. But it was the mark on his forehead that distinguished him from every other human being on the planet. Who else would have a mark in the shape of a candle flame perfectly centered just above their eyes?

"I've waited a long time to see you again," he said. "Your entire family has been waiting for a very long time."

"I guess that depends on your definition of family."

A broad smile crossed his face. "Do you remember her? You were very young when your mother died. Except for the eye color, you look just like her."

He took a step closer and reached out his hand. When he opened it, a silver chain fell from his palm and dangled from his index finger. At the end of it was a small silver pendant in the shape of a bird. "It was Maeve's. Now it belongs to you."

"A raven. How original."

He smiled at my sarcasm. "Oh, it's so much more than that. And now," he held it closer to me, "it's yours."

"And if I take it?"

He caught the pendant in his other hand and ran his thumb over the bird. "It isn't a matter of *if* you take it—it's a matter of *when*. You see, Alex, this is not a choice. Although, nothing would make me happier than you choosing to come back to your family willingly."

"You do realize you can't force me to do anything."

His smile faded as an underlying emotion edged its way to the surface. I could feel him losing patience when I refused to cave to his absurd suggestion that I should just drop everything and come back to Ireland with him. Alasdair Templeton was the high priest of my mother's former coven, but she chose to walk away when I was conceived, and that meant I walked away, too.

"Take the necklace!" he snapped, his temper flaring.

The raven swung like a pendulum from the force of his thrust. My impulse was to grab it, but my instincts told me that would be a mistake.

"No. And while you're here, why don't you give me an address so I can return the athame as well. I don't want *it* either."

I turned toward the back room to collect my kitten and let Katie know my conversation with Templeton was over. Something flew over my head, and the silver chain hung in the air like a carrot being dangled in front of a horse. The silver bird at the end of it swung back and forth like it had in Templeton's hand. Then I realized it wasn't swinging at all, it was trying to fly off the chain. It thrashed wildly, spreading its silver wings as black feathers sprouted from its sides and opened into giant fans that filled half the room. The wings lifted me off the ground and spun me into a dark cyclone.

When it stopped, I was suspended in the black void with Templeton's face all around me.

"Take it!" he demanded again.

A light appeared behind him. It grew until another face came into view. I could see her, floating like a transparent veil in the distance, shaking her head as her image faded in the mist. Her face dissolved in and out of the light, but her bright green eyes remained fully corporeal as they warned me not to take the bait.

The room shook from a single thunderous blow to the ground, and a gust of wind sent me backward, slamming my head against the floor. I fought back the black fuzzy frame filling my peripheral vision, threatening to knock me out while a freight train roared through the room. I rolled to my side and covered my ears to block the deafening sound. And then as fast as it came, it was gone.

"Jesus, Alex! Are you okay?" Katie grabbed my arm to help me up. "Who the hell was that?"

A heavy rock crashed against the inside walls of my head as I sat up and looked around the room.

She shook her head. "He's gone."

"What did you do to him?" I looked her up and down, but her dragon was already gone.

"I scared the shit out of the old bastard." Her concern was replaced with a wicked smile. "I don't think he's coming back."

I gave her the condensed version of who and what Templeton was. Then I looked around the room and estimated the amount of books left to inventory. "I'm all right. We can knock this out today."

"Don't be an idiot, Alex. You might have a concussion. Take your cat and go home."

I hadn't thought about how to actually transport Bear to the house, so I placed him in my satchel bag and zipped it partially shut.

"Be a good boy and stay in there, or you'll end up back on the street I some guy's box."

The short trip home was uneventful. I got a few strange looks when my bag started to bounce around my hip, but I was thankful not to be chasing a tiny kitten through the streets of New York.

Sophia was in the kitchen pantry with a notepad and pen when I walked in. "You need anything from the market?" She glanced at my moving bag while he jotted her list. "You got that poor thing in there?"

I unzipped the bag and pulled out my new best friend. "Bear, this is Sophia." His tail flopped back and forth as his ears flattened.

"He don't look too happy right now," she noted. "You better put him down before he eats your hand."

I put him on the floor and looked at Sophia's list. "Sophia," I said sweetly.

"We already talk about this." She shook her head and wagged her finger in the air. "The *gatto* is your responsibility."

All I wanted to do was add a few items to her shopping list. I would have been happy to stop myself for a litter box and food, but seeing how I had a cat in my bag, I thought it wiser to get him home first and worry about necessities later.

She pointed to a large box in the corner of the foyer. I looked inside and found an assortment of supplies: a litter box, a bag of litter, kitten food, and two bowls painted with paw prints—one for water and one for food.

"Did you do this?" I asked.

"Mr. Sinclair."

I imagined Greer scouring a pet store, trying to decide between the paw prints or little fish decorated bowls.

"Really?"

"Yes, really. Now, you better get that box fixed up before he pees on the floor."

The rest of the afternoon was spent getting Bear settled in. He made himself right at home like he knew the place. Like he was born to live in the big house.

I went upstairs for a minute, and when I came back down Sophia was carrying on a conversation with him about house rules. "You scratch the sofa, I kill you. You jump up on my kitchen counter, I kill you."

She crumpled a piece of foil into a tight ball and tossed it on the floor.

"I thought you didn't like cats," I commented as Bear chased the shiny ball around the edges of the kitchen island.

"I like cats. I just don't like cat poop."

"I told you I'd take care of him." I scooped up my drowsy kitten and placed him on a chair where he curled up and went to sleep.

Sophia finished making her list and headed for the door. "I be back in an hour to start dinner. Mr. Sinclair say he be home around seven."

That gave me a few hours to rest before the pyrotechnics took place when I told Greer about my visit from Isabetta Falcone and Alasdair Templeton. Isabetta's visit was bad enough, but Templeton's boldness would send him through the roof. That meant the walls of my free zone were about to start closing in again. Greer wasn't about to let me handle Templeton on my own, and rightly so. I could handle Isabetta, but Templeton was in another league. He was a window to my birthright, and that gave him power.

Greer walked through the door at seven o'clock. He looked at Bear who was still sleeping in the chair, and then at me. He said nothing for a few uncomfortable seconds, and by the look on his face I could tell he knew I had something important to say.

He glanced over his shoulder as he headed up the stairs. "We'll discuss it over dinner."

Twenty minutes later we were sitting at the table with a roasted chicken in front of us. Greer sat silent as he watched me fill my plate. Each second seemed like an hour as he refused to let up on the mind fucking. He was an expert at that, letting you stew in your own thoughts while he just sat back and waited for you to cave.

"You know, Greer, you should work for the CIA. You could make anyone talk just to get you to stop looking at them like that."

"In my experience, only those with something to hide have a problem with scrutiny. Do *you* have something to hide, Alex?"

I opened my mouth to let the party begin. "Isabetta Falcone came by the shop this afternoon," I mentioned as I scooped a spoonful of glazed carrots onto my plate. "Apparently, she thought it more beneficial to bypass you and speak to me directly."

He placed a bite of food in his mouth and took his time chewing it before responding. "What did she want?"

"I think you know what she wanted." I could feel the room heating up as his temper subtly flared. "She's greedy. Why bother with you when she can go straight to the source?"

"Did she threaten you?" he asked in a controlled, even voice. Greer didn't like being circumvented, and he was doing a good job of concealing his anger.

"She didn't have a chance. We were interrupted." Greer's face hardened as I spoke, because some invisible hand had thumped him on the head. In that way that only Greer had, he knew I was about to tell him something far worse than the story of a mafia princess trying to shake me down. "Alasdair Templeton also decided to drop by."

"What?" Greer was standing over the table before I could blink. The room shook and Bear shot from the cushion of the chair. "You didn't think that was important enough to pick up the phone?"

"It wasn't like I had a chance. And by the way, he did send Isabetta and her cronies running for the hills." I shook my head and picked at my plate. "What was I supposed to do? Tell him to hold that thought while I conferred with you?"

His eyes shut as he steadied himself with a calming breath. "You need to tell me everything he said. Every word, every syllable. I don't care if he asked you about the *fucking* weather."

"Fine. Every word. But you have *got* to lighten up. Jesus, Greer. I'm not exactly helpless."

To be completely honest, I don't know if I could have gotten myself out of the situation if Katie hadn't been there to go all dragon on Templeton. Maybe I would have taken the necklace. And if I had, what would that mean?

Greer came around the table and motioned toward the library. "Let's go."

"What? Now? Can't I at least eat my dinner first?"

"Are you actually hungry?"

My appetite suddenly ceased. "You scared Bear." I got up to retrieve him from behind the door.

Sophia was standing in the doorway watching the fireworks. She was used to the strange things that went on in her employer's house, but she didn't approve of him raising his voice to me, even if I wasn't the actual target of his anger.

"I watch Bear for you," she offered, shooting Greer one of her looks.

"Everything's fine, Sophia. Alex and I are just having a discussion."

I nodded to put her at ease. Greer may act like a Neanderthal at times, but he would never hurt me. I knew that as strongly as I knew that time never stopped ticking by.

He shut the library door and waited for me to begin.

I started with Isabetta. "She was trying to find out if we had David Oxford's invention."

"You mean the one that doesn't exist?"

"I didn't mention that part. And then Templeton showed up right about the time she started manhandling me."

His expression went cold as I told him how Isabetta dragged me across the room and threatened me, and I knew he'd make her pay for it. Then I told him about Alasdair Templeton and the necklace, and how my mother showed up again and warned me not to take it.

"I'm relieved that you chose not to take that necklace."

"What would have happened if I did?"

"You would have signed your life away." His eyebrows cocked as he matter-of-factly told me how accepting that necklace would have been the equivalent of signing a contract in blood.

"Jesus, Greer. Why didn't you tell me about the necklace before?"

"I didn't know about it until now."

I suddenly felt sick as the image of the package came to mind. "The athame! I need to send it back!"

He leaned in and looked closely at my panicked face. "No. The necklace belongs to the coven, but the athame belongs to the witch."

"But not this witch."

"You still don't get it, do you? What was hers is yours, Alex. To the coven, you and your mother are the same."

"I thought you were going to use that life force thing to make him go away."

"That 'life force thing' is our ace card. We may need it in the future, so we'll try to do this nicely first. But if he persists, we'll knock his fucking house down. Just promise me one thing. If Templeton shows up again, you'll pick up the damn phone."

FOURTEEN

I woke the next morning with a burning headache. The day before had been a real shitstorm, and if today was going to be a repeat, I preferred to stay in bed. But there was inventory to take, and Katie didn't deserve to have all that fun by herself.

My feet hit the floor as I dragged myself up and headed for the shower. I just stood under the water like a statue for a good ten minutes, reconsidering the sanity of going into work when I was so clearly a target anywhere outside of this house.

Having been so rudely interrupted by Alasdair Templeton, I wondered if Isabetta would be stupid enough to come back and make good on her threat. I'm sure she was curious about my conversation with him. At least I knew Templeton wasn't coming back to the shop, but he *would* be back. Now that I knew what he wanted, I knew he'd never stop coming unless Greer threatened him with that small silver box.

I stepped out of the shower and wrapped myself in a robe. Bear padded his little feet after me as I grabbed my hairbrush and headed back into the bedroom.

"Come up here you little monster." Stupid of me to think a tiny kitten could leap on top of the bed when my own feet barely touched the ground as I sat on the edge.

Bear made a chirping sound, and then a sharp pain radiated across the top of my shin as he obeyed my command and demonstrated his climbing skills. He was just a baby. He didn't know that the scratch he'd just gouged into my leg could turn me into something dangerous.

I started to panic as a tiny line of blood oozed from the scratch. "Everything's okay. Bear is not the enemy," I repeated several times, staring at the innocent kitten sitting at the foot of the bed.

Greer and I had worked on my half-cocked reaction to shedding blood, but since that day at CTC I hadn't had the opportunity to test my control of it with anyone—or anything—other than him. But based on how my eyes were burning and the way the rage was building in my head, I wasn't sure I'd made much progress at all.

"Get out of here, Bear! Now!" I yelled, trying to scare him away before I could hurt him. He just sat there at the foot of the bed with his eyes fixed on mine and his tail sweeping back and forth across the comforter.

My head snapped in the direction of the window as a bird hit the glass and landed on the narrow ledge. Its stunned body quickly recovered, and it hopped back to its feet and cocked its head to inspect the interior of the room.

"Not another fucking bird," I muttered. I used to like birds, but they'd become a real liability lately.

I'd never noticed a discernable expression on a bird's face before, all beak and eyes permanently fixed in place. Expression or not, this one seemed awfully determined. It flew back into the air but kept aiming for the window and bouncing off the glass.

Bear craned his head to look at it. A staccato-like clicking came from his throat, and the bird settled back on the ledge for a moment before flying away.

When he looked back at me, his eyes were different. No longer green but a midnight blue that nearly matched his arched black brows, and the symbols framing them. His face was covered with fluid black lines that knotted and swirled like a mask around his eyes, nose, and mouth—his very human mouth.

I shut my eyes to clear the hallucination. When they reopened, his blue eyes were back to green and his tiny face was covered with orange fur.

"Bear?" I whispered, the image of that face still vivid in my mind. "What are you?"

His paw rose to his mouth so he could lick the small spot of blood from the white fur on the underside. When he was finished, he bobbed his head and murmured a sound into the air.

"What did you say?"

I knew the question was absurd the second it left my lips. But then my eyes rolled back in my head as a wave of fantastic light came at me and slammed into the center of my chest. It moved straight through me, leaving something behind as it exited through my back just as quickly as it had entered.

"Whoa." I tried to stand but plopped back down as my head spun in a light, euphoric swirl, like I'd had too much wine or half a Valium to take the edge off.

A tiny flame flickered at the stem of my navel, spreading through my stomach and limbs like a blanket of ermine or a shot of smooth whiskey. It spread deeper and deeper until every drop of rage vanished, and the heat in my belly lowered to a warm glow.

I shook my head to clear the fuzzy haze that was clouding my thoughts, and a familiar voice whispered something in my head reminding me that it was time to go downstairs and start breakfast.

Taking care not to catch my heels on the wooden treads, I hurried down the steps to the kitchen. How I'd managed to do it every day without taking a nasty fall astonished me. But it was getting late, and if I didn't hurry I'd never get breakfast ready.

"Good morning, Sophia." She was pushing down on the coffee press, releasing the aroma of freshly brewed Sumatran beans.

I grabbed the loaf of bread from the counter and opened the fridge to get the eggs and milk. I could feel her eyes on my backside as I scurried to catch up on lost time, disappointed that I'd interfered with her plans to prepare breakfast herself.

She stopped pressing the coffee and stared at me with her mouth open.

"Is he up yet?" I asked as I pulled the whisk from the drawer. I cracked the eggs into a bowl and whisked them into a light foam with the milk.

"You feeling okay, Miss Alex?"

I stopped whisking and turned to look at her. "I feel fine. Why would you ask me that?"

It must have been the late start that had her questioning my mood.

"I just got up a little late this morning. I think I had a headache when I went to bed last night. Took something for it and it just knocked me out."

Her eyes ran from my shoes to my neckline, and then continued up to my face. "Why you dressed like that?"

"Like what?" I looked down at my floral print dress and beige pumps. "Oh, I know. The yellow is a little bright, but it is spring. When in Rome . . . "

She reached for the bowl I was mixing, but I pushed her aside with my hip. "Now Sophia, I know you like to cook breakfast, but I've got this. Why don't you just pour yourself a cup of coffee and relax for a moment."

"Huh?" Her face twisted into a tight knot as she released the metal bowl and stepped back.

"Is the master up?" I asked for the second time. "Do I need to go upstairs and get that man out of bed myself?"

"Mr. Sinclair!" Sophia yelled.

I dropped a couple of slices into the egg mixture and then plopped the soaked bread onto the griddle. The French toast sizzled as it hit the buttered surface, filling the room with the delicious smell of fried custard.

"Where is my brain?" I headed back to the refrigerator and rummaged through the shelves. "Are we out of bacon? French toast without bacon?"

Sophia reached around me and pulled a pack from the bottom drawer. She handed it to me without a word and called out for Greer again. "Mr. Sinclair! I think you need to come down here."

As I snipped the end of the package open, Greer came into the kitchen. I turned around and caught my breath when I saw him leaning against the wall. No matter how many times I looked at my husband, he still took my breath away.

"There's my lazy man."

A butterfly dipped into the lower region of my stomach as he looked back at me with his beautiful blue eyes. The scissors slipped from my hand as I crossed the kitchen floor and kissed him, the perfume on my skin mixing with the faint scent of his aftershave. "Good morning, baby. Did you sleep well?"

When he didn't respond and the returned kiss was cooler than I'd expected from the man I loved, I took a step back and studied his face. "Is everything all right?"

His eyes roamed over mine. "I was about to ask you the same question."

"Everything's fine. Why does everyone keep asking me that?"

I went back to the stove and placed the bacon on the griddle. "Breakfast is almost ready. Why don't you sit down with the paper and I'll bring it in."

Greer glanced at Sophia who was standing at the other end of the island looking back and forth between the two of us. She shrugged her shoulders as if he'd asked a question.

"Sophia, would you mind changing the sheets on my bed?" he asked.

My mouth dropped. "Greer, that can wait until after we eat. I'm sure Sophia is hungry, aren't you?" I asked as my eyes went to hers.

She shook her head and threw her hands in the air as she walked out of the kitchen, something Italian muttering from her mouth as she headed for the stairs.

"That wasn't very nice, Greer." I flipped the bacon and began piling the French toast on a plate. "The woman hasn't even had her breakfast yet."

His arm came from behind me as he took the spatula from my hand and turned off the burner. I could feel his breath against my skin as he turned me around and caged me against the counter, inspecting my eyes again and then the rest of my face.

"Alex, did something happen this morning?"

"What a vague question, Greer. You and Sophia are acting so strange, and it's beginning to make me nervous."

"*We're* acting strange?"

"Yes!" My arms reached around his waist as I buried my face in the warmth of his chest. "I just want to go back to bed and start the morning over." I pulled away and trailed my eyes up to his neck. "Why are you wearing a tie? You hate ties." I reached for it to adjust the over-tightened knot. "I don't think I've seen you wear one since our wedding."

His body stiffened, and then he took me by the shoulders and held me at arm's length. The expression on his face was as awkward as I'd ever seen, and I could feel the tension balling up in the space between us.

I'd heard of this happening. I'd been warned that newlyweds could go through rough patches where they doubted what they'd just done, and second guessed their decision to get married. It was a normal part of a newlywed's roller coaster of emotions, but the rejection still hurt.

"Please don't do that." I pulled on his tie, drawing him back to me, snuggling back into the crook of his neck. "Tell me that you don't regret marrying me."

Greer Sinclair was the only man I ever loved. If he left me, I swear I'd dive off the Brooklyn Bridge.

My entire body breathed with his as his lungs filled and the heat of his skin radiated into mine. His arms reached around me for the first time since pinning me against the counter, and his lips met the top of my head. "No. No regrets," he promised. "Now, let's enjoy this beautiful breakfast you've made."

I reluctantly pushed him away, and we filled our plates and ate our breakfast on the kitchen island. He watched me silently as I chewed my food and sipped my coffee. It was one of those moments where words would just be clutter, and the silence served as foreplay for things to come, either after breakfast or the moment he returned home from work.

Newlyweds were like that, always needing to touch each other and never feeling full.

A little loving after breakfast wasn't an option. Greer was on his way to a meeting, hence the formality of a tie, so I would have to wait out the long day until he returned.

Before leaving, he went upstairs to talk to Sophia. I could hear the muffled conversation that I assumed was an apology for acting like an ass earlier that morning.

Sophia's voice occasionally rose and then lowered, and it seemed they'd come to a truce as they came back down the stairs together with matching wide grins on their faces.

"I'll be home by seven o'clock." He glanced at Sophia and nodded.

As he went to kiss me on the cheek, I turned and caught his lips with mine, a sly smile forming on my face as he pulled away. "I don't know if I can wait that long."

The elevator door opened. Greer's eyes lingered on mine for a moment before he stepped inside. As the door closed, Sophia announced that we were going shopping.

When Sophia said we were going shopping, I thought she meant grocery shopping. But instead of shopping for cheeses and breads and meats, we ended up at a store I'd only seen from the outside.

When I was a child, my mother and I used to stroll along Fifth Avenue every December to see the amazing windows of Lord and Taylor, Saks Fifth Avenue, and of course, Bergdorf Goodman.

As we walked through the elaborate entrance, I felt that familiar sense of being an impostor, a stranger in a strange land, a flea on an inoculated dog. Even with Greer's line of credit, I couldn't imagine being able to buy anything my heart desired within the walls of Bergdorf Goodman.

"Mr. Sinclair say I need to keep you busy today."

"Now, why would you need to do that? Honestly, Sophia, the two of you are acting so weird today."

Sophia rolled her eyes and headed for the escalator. "You want shoes?"

We got off on the second floor and headed for the shoe department. I hadn't met a girl yet who didn't appreciate a beautiful pair of shoes, and since I intended to buy something special for this evening, a new pair of shoes was justified. It was difficult to think of Greer's money as our money, but we were married now.

The shoe salon was an Alice in Wonderland trip through the world of luxury foot adornments. An organized search was simply impossible. Each time I headed toward a pair I liked, I was detoured by another. I must have tried on fifteen pairs just to say I'd had my foot in the shoe of every designer on Fifth Avenue.

"Do you like these?" I asked Sophia, holding up a pair for her approval.

"Hmm," she said, looking bored and impatient. "Is just a shoe."

Despite her lack of enthusiasm, I thought they were fabulous. But I was hoping to find a pair that wasn't as expensive. I tried to like the less expensive Jimmy Choos, but the cute little heel of the Valentinos in my hand kept calling my name. I figured if I was going to spend that much money, I might as well get the pair I really wanted. Seemed like a waste to buy a pair I didn't absolutely love just because they were five hundred dollars less.

Sophia frowned as the sales person presented the total for the shoes. "Mr. Sinclair is going to kill you," she mumbled as I signed the credit card slip.

"Not when he sees what I plan to wear with them."

We headed for the sixth floor where I picked out a very sexy, but tasteful, lacy black bra with matching panties.

Sophia's brow arched as her mouth puckered like she'd just eaten a lemon.

"What? Too much?"

"No. Is fine if you don't want a man to respect you." Her Catholic ways were showing.

"He's my husband, Sophia. A girl has to keep it fresh."

"If he's your husband, where's your wedding ring?" She quickly covered her mouth after the words spilled out, but it was too late.

The smile left my face as I looked down at my left hand and began twisting the imaginary ring on my finger. "It was too big. I'm having it resized."

"I know, Miss Alex," she answered quickly. "I'm getting old. My memory is—"

"It's okay, Sophia." I waved the thought away with the back of my hand and suggested we get some lunch.

In all the months I'd eaten her delicious meals and worked

so hard to gain her approval, I'd never taken the time to ask the simple questions that would give me a window into who she was. I knew nothing about her, really. Was she married? Did she have children? Lunch was the perfect opportunity to get to know the woman I'd practically lived with for the better part of a year.

An Italian restaurant wasn't the best place to take a native who could probably outcook the chef, but the restaurant we chose was less crowded than the others, and my goal was to have a real conversation and not just eat over the noise of a hundred voices.

"Sophia, are you sure? We can do Mexican or Chinese if you'd like."

Her shoulders shrugged. "I'm not the only Italian cook in New York City. Maybe I send a note to the chef with a little advice."

"You're kidding, right?"

She ignored me and walked inside. Sophia was a bold woman, so I wouldn't put it past her to head to the kitchen for a private cooking lesson with the chef—her being the instructor. I prayed the food was up to her standards.

We were seated at a table near the window and handed a pair of menus. Sophia's brow did a series of acrobatics as she grunted her way through the list and then declared the menu adequate. She ordered the sardine and artichoke pie, while I stuck with pasta with broad beans and ricotta.

In all the time I'd live in Greer's house, I'd never seen Sophia drink, so I was surprised when she ordered a glass of red wine.

"So tell me, Sophia, what do you like to do when you're not working?" The question was general enough. My goal was not to pry but to open the door for voluntary disclosure of things like children and marital status. "Do you live in Manhattan?"

Her dull stare suggested I was a fool. "Brooklyn." She sipped her wine and picked at a piece of lint on the tablecloth. "Is stupid to serve Italian food on a white tablecloth."

"That's a long commute, isn't it?" I was stricken with a case of nerves as I realized the conversation was fizzling. I hated small talk, but Sophia wasn't contributing, and I'd be damned if I'd let the lunch go down in flames because I couldn't engage her in a real conversation.

Our food arrived just as the awkwardness reached its peak. Sophia examined both of our plates before picking up her fork. She took a bite of the sardines rolled in breadcrumbs and artichokes and nodded her head. After washing it down with a generous gulp of wine, her eyes softened, and I could tell she was beginning to loosen up.

"Mr. Sinclair sends a car for me. Big black car comes to my house every morning and drops me off every night. My neighbors are jealous." A rare grin spread across her face as she chewed another mouthful. "They think I have a rich boyfriend."

"That's why I love him." The thought of his generosity and attention to Sophia's needs brought a smile to my face. "He's such a thoughtful man."

Her grin vanished as that same strange look fell over her face again. "Miss Alex, what kind of pills you take for that headache last night?"

"So," I replied as if her question hadn't been asked, "do you live with anyone?"

Her fork paused on its way to her mouth, and for a second the room seemed to pause with it. When the noise resumed, she put the fork back down and started moving the sardines around her plate. "You want to know if I have a husband?"

"Well, sure. Or children?"

"I have a daughter, Adrianna. She lives in London. Met a

fancy Wall Street guy and moved across the ocean." She muttered something under her breath. "No more husband, either."

"Divorced?"

She smirked. "Catholic. We don't get divorced."

"Sorry. I wasn't trying to pry."

"Yes, you were, but don't be sorry. He was an asshole."

She looked at my barely touched plate and then back at my face. "What? You not hungry? You invite me to lunch, you eat. Is a sin to waste good food."

I twirled the pasta around my fork and took a large bite. I would never say it, but it was as good as hers. In fact, I had to restrain myself from stuffing the pasta into my famished mouth for fear of her knowing. At least I was certain she wouldn't be interrupting the chef.

"My husband was a drunk. I cook and I clean for him every day, but it was never enough." The waiter brought her another glass of wine, and she continued to loosen up and reveal her life. "When he didn't like my food, you know what he did?" She drank half the glass in one gulp and leaned into the table on her sturdy forearms. "He gave it right back to me—with the skillet."

I stared at her in disbelief. Sophia was a formidable woman, and the thought of someone hitting her and getting away with it was incomprehensible. Was this the same woman who scared the hell out of me the first time I stepped foot in Greer's house?

"Sometimes you convince yourself you deserve it," she continued. "Sometimes I throw it back at him, sometimes he miss and I run, sometimes I wake up on the floor." She put her fork down and pushed her plate away. "But when he touch my baby—" She shook her head and looked out the window. "She don't deserve that."

"What did you do?"

She sat back in her chair but kept her eyes on the window, and for a moment she was somewhere else. When she looked back at me, her eyes were present, lucid as a hawk. "I got rid of him."

I had a delayed reaction to her words, but as soon as they registered, a large lump formed at the back of my throat. I laughed nervously and waited for her to laugh with me and tell me the truth about what happened to her husband. But she just sat there with a stone-cold stare.

"How . . . how'd you do that?" I finally got out, trying to sound casual about asking Greer's Italian housekeeper how she got rid of her abusive husband. But the words trembled as they left my mouth.

"I called Mr. Sinclair."

FIFTEEN

There are many ways to make someone disappear, and not all of those ways include murder. Sophia tightened up like a wire-corked bottle of champagne when I pressed for more. Maybe Greer paid him off, or maybe he'd threatened Sophia's husband into leaving and never coming back. Either way, I knew Greer wasn't a murderer, and that man walked out of Sophia's house still breathing.

Bear bounced off of his chair and demanded to be picked up the minute we came through the front door.

"Mommy missed you." I planted half a dozen kisses on his face and dropped him in the shopping bag on top of the shoe-box. "Come on. Let's go unpack."

He was too little to climb the wooden stair treads, which made me wonder how he'd gotten down to the first floor. Visions of him somersaulting all the way down made me cringe.

"Poor baby. That will teach you to stay put in your room until you're big enough to climb the stairs."

"What you want for dinner?" asked Sophia.

"Are you kidding? I'm still stuffed from lunch. Why don't you just throw something simple together for Greer and go home early." I had plans for my husband that evening and wanted the house to ourselves. "Oh, go on, Sophia. Enjoy an evening off for a change."

I took my bags and started up the stairs. When I looked back down, Sophia was standing at the bottom with her hands planted on her hips. "You know what?" I mused, feeling domestic in my new role as wife. "I think I'll cook."

"Mr. Sinclair will not like me leaving without telling him."

"Now Sophia, this is my home, too." I was careful to tread lightly and not sound like I was giving orders. She'd worked for Greer for God knows how many years, and the introduction of a wife was sure to upset the power structure in the house.

"I don't feel so good about this. Mr. Sinclair told me not to leave you alone."

"Nonsense, Sophia. I'll tell Greer you *resisted* and I *insisted*."

Twenty minutes later I was walking Sophia to her car. She reluctantly climbed in and looked at me with that same strange expression she'd had on her face all day.

Bear was sitting in the foyer when I walked back inside. "Not again?" I eyed the long staircase suspiciously, swooping him up to go back upstairs to get ready.

I unpacked my new lingerie and shoes. Then I picked out the perfect dress, something I could slide out of easily.

Leda had stocked my closet months ago with her own clothes. Partly because she was tired of schlepping them over every time I needed a last minute outfit, and partly because she rarely wore the same outfit twice and hated to see such beautiful things go to waste. I was happy to take them off her hands.

I took a shower and smoothed my favorite scented lotion over my skin. Perfection was the goal, because after a long day at the club, Greer deserved to come home to the perfect, attentive wife. I practiced untying the pretty little wrap dress and letting it slide to the floor, leaving me in just the lingerie and shoes standing before him. If that didn't get him juiced, I'd question the man I married.

*   *   *

Greer stepped off the elevator just before seven and tossed his keys in the bowl. The smell of tomatoes and basil filled the air from the pot simmering on the stove. I'd decided on a light sauce with angel hair pasta just in case we actually made it to the dining room.

We didn't.

I stood in the foyer looking at the man I loved, and before I could get a word out, I was leaping into his arms and wrapping my legs around his hips. The smell of his body triggered something primal in me, and the sight of him sent my own body into a kaleidoscope of emotions that jumbled my brain and extended to the lowest regions of my stomach. I was a living, breathing mass of arousal that needed to be sated.

"Easy now." He tamed my assault as my lips traveled over his face and stopped at his.

"Why aren't you kissing me, Greer?" My legs dropped back down to the floor, and I took a step back. He had that same annoying expression that seemed to be afflicting everyone in the house but me, and it was killing the moment.

"Damn it, Greer. You're scaring me. I had this wonderful evening planned for us, but now it's ruined."

Without a word, he pulled me into his arms and gave me a proper kiss—the kind a man gives a woman when he's been looking at the clock all day in anticipation of feeling her naked body under his. The heat of his chest intensified, and for a moment I thought I might burst into flames. Then he picked me up and took the stairs two at a time.

"What about dinner?" A playful smile fell over my face as I feigned Martha Stewart.

"What about it?"

He carried me to the bedroom and dropped me on the mattress, leaving my skirt hiked to the top of my thighs. He stepped back a good five feet and gave me a warning look as if something dangerous was about to happen.

I squirmed to slide the skirt higher and parted my legs a few more inches before looking back at him, letting him know I was ready and willing to take on that danger.

"Come here," I breathed.

He shook his head slowly as his fists clenched and his eyes lowered. "Forgive me," he whispered in a voice so quiet I wasn't sure if it was meant to be heard.

"Forgive you? Whatever for?"

He ignored my question and began unbuttoning his shirt. His jacket hit the chair, and then he slid his crisp cotton shirt over his shoulders and tossed it next to the jacket. His fingers went for his belt but stopped after disengaging the buckle and releasing the button, leaving his pants hanging at the crease of his hips.

"Stop teasing me, baby," I whispered as I spread my knees wider and rolled my head back.

Greer crooked his finger, instructing me to come to him. I obeyed because it meant I'd get him inside of me faster.

I stopped just within arm's reach and we locked eyes. We stood like that, wordless for a good minute before he reached his hand around the small of my back and pulled me into him. His breath warmed my cheek as he ran his hand down the back of my thigh and inched my dress higher.

"Tell me to stop, Alex. Do it now, because a minute from now I won't be able to."

I shook my head as I buried my face in his naked chest and bit gently on his muscle. My nipples hardened as they rubbed against the fabric of my dress and pressed into his hot skin.

The carefully practiced escape from my dress wasn't necessary after all, because his hand was already working the sash loose around my waist. It fell away from my hips and slipped over my shoulders, falling to the floor in a fluttering pool of vivid blue around my feet.

He raised my chin to bring my eyes to his as his other hand slipped past the silk and moved between my legs. I moaned as he pushed his fingers deeper, and before I could catch my breath, he was on his knees moving my legs apart.

"Oh, God," I breathed, trying not to fall as his hands gripped my hips and pulled me closer. And then his tongue replaced his fingers, and my legs went completely boneless.

My back was against the bed before I could open my eyes. Greer gazed down at me while he unzipped his pants halfway. But just when I thought I couldn't take another second of waiting, his fingers went still and he walked back toward the chair with his hands dragging across his face.

"I can't do this," he gritted out, reaching for his shirt.

I jumped off the bed and wrapped my arms around his waist, pressing my cheek into his back, squeezing him so hard I was afraid I'd cut off the air to both of us. "I want you so bad I can't breathe. If you leave, I'll die. I'll just die, Greer."

A moment later, I was back on the bed. Greer worked his pants off in a matter of seconds and stood next to the bed naked, gazing at me like he wanted to eat me alive, his breathing so labored, it alarmed me.

"Are you all right, Greer?"

He swallowed hard. "No. I'm not all right."

I propped myself up on the bed with my elbows, watching the man I loved refuse his own bride. And then I collapsed into a weeping, vulnerable mess. Tears burst from my eyes as I realized it was over. Our relationship was over before it even began.

Greer's face sobered. He sat on the edge of the bed and pulled me into him. "Stop." His fingers swept the tears from my face. "I can't stand it."

"But you don't want me," I sobbed.

He stiffened against me, and then he turned my face to his and kissed me softly on the forehead.

I thought I'd break apart when he rose from the bed and

walked to the other end of the room, standing in deep consideration, trying to come up with an amiable way to say goodbye to the girl he'd foolishly taken as his bride. Then he took a fortifying breath and came back toward the bed. His eyes flashed a brilliant blue as his lips parted and words came out of his mouth in poetic verse. They were beautiful, Latin or some other language I wasn't fluent in. The words floated through the air like a soothing love song, elevating my desire and the need to have him inside of me.

"Lie back," he said. "I'm going to show you just how much I want you."

A swarm of bees circled through me as I did what he asked. I pushed myself higher on the bed and dropped my head to the pillow.

He moved his hand up my stomach and released the front clasp of my bra. My breasts bloomed as the delicate lace fell away. Then he moved down my torso and pulled the panties over my thighs and past my calves, leaving me completely exposed and open on the bed.

My modesty got the best of me, as I shyly pulled my legs up and covered the tips of my breasts with my elbows.

Greer slowly shook his head and reached for my wrists, gently pulling them away from my firm and erect nipples, revealing me to anything that might wander through the room. "Don't ever do that," he whispered. "Don't ever hide from me."

I blinked and shook my head in answer, letting him know I would never hide from him again. His body responded by growing harder, his erection straining toward the muscles of his stomach.

He climbed onto the bed and crawled over my body, moving my legs apart with his knee as he settled between them. I opened them wider to accommodate his long, muscular thighs, and he pushed deep inside of me.

"Greer," I gasped from the sensation and the intense emotion flashing through every conceivable part of me. I dug my fingers into the rounds of his biceps and wrapped my legs tighter around his waist. He moved higher and pushed deeper, and all I could hear was the pounding of our hearts and the blood racing through our veins.

I promised never to hide from him again, but the heat in his eyes humbled and weakened me. It was too much, like being split open by the sword of God and letting every secret fly free, both breathtaking and terrifying as I met his raw gaze.

The tension broke as my face turned into the pillow. "No, no," he whispered as he pulled my eyes back to his and the verse spilled from his mouth in an unintelligible river of sound. And then nothing mattered but our breathing and our rhythm, and the steady friction and pleasure as our bodies entwined into a single moving force. The sky seemed to explode as stars filled the room and I could feel him in my head, caressing my mind with the thought of never wanting anything but him.

A roar echoed off the walls as he strained against me and sent a quake through my body. Then he dropped to the bed beside me, panting like an animal after a long, zealous hunt.

"*Fuck*, Alex." He turned to look at me as his face heated up again.

I reached for his Rolex, teetering on the edge of the nightstand from the force of the bed shaking the floor. "Leave it," he said as his arms wrapped around my waist and pulled me on top of him, lowering me onto his hips until he was deep inside of me again. I moved against him as he met my body with equal force, his eyes beautiful and wild, while mine lit up the room with a soft glow that got brighter as we reached our second shattering climax.

We spent the rest of the night working each other to the point of exhaustion, and when neither of us could move another inch, he circled me and kissed the damp skin of my belly before laying his head on it and falling into a deep and satisfied coma.

We spent the rest of the night working each other to the point of exhaustion, and when neither of us could move another inch, he circled his arms around me and kissed the damp skin of my belly before laying his head on it and falling into a deep and satisfied coma.

I woke to the feeling of sandpaper running across my nose. Bear had managed to climb up the bedspread and was eager for me to get up.

"That, my friend, hurts." I pushed him under the covers before he could lick my face again because cat tongues weren't made for sensitive facial skin.

My head was pounding from the miniature marching band trapped inside my skull, and every muscle from my thighs to my waist ached as I swung my legs over the side of the bed. "Jesus, Bear. What did we do last night? Run a damn marathon?"

Either I was coming down with the flu, or I had a monster hangover. I don't know which was worse.

One of Leda's dresses was draped over the chair, and a pair of amazing shoes sat on the floor next to it. Leda must have left them. The black bra and panties tossed in the corner were a little more difficult to explain.

"Did I go out last night?" I mumbled.

The smell of bacon and eggs floating down the hallway perked me up. At that moment, I couldn't think of anything I wanted more than one of Sophia's breakfast spreads and a very large cup of coffee. For the first time, I actually considered blowing off work. But it was inventory week so I didn't dare. At least I had the late shift, which gave me all morning to recover from whatever it was making me feel like hell.

I took a long shower, and then got dressed and followed the

smell to the kitchen. I grabbed a bagel from the counter before joining Sophia at the stove. A pot of tomato sauce sat on the back burner. "I love your sauces, Sophia, but I'm not putting that on my eggs."

She took the pan of bacon off the burner and turned to look at me. Her hand went to that place on her hip that usually meant she was about to give me some Italian momma tongue, but before she could speak, her eyes moved over my shoulder to her approaching employer.

Greer walked into the kitchen and stopped when he saw me standing at the stove. He and Sophia glanced at each other and had one of those silent conversations I was never privy to.

"What?" I looked back and forth between the two of them, and then glanced down at my T-shirt to see if something was out of place. By the way they were both gawking at me, I figured I'd either done or said something the night before that I needed desperately to remember.

Sophia's eyes went sideways to the cold sauce on the stove, and then back to mine. Her brow raised, and I could tell by her expression that she wasn't the one who left it there. "Don't look at me," I shrugged, glancing at Greer, wondering if he was a closet cook.

Someone had to break the ice, so I grabbed a plate and piled it full of bacon and eggs and headed for the dining room. Greer followed with a cup of coffee. He sat across the table and stared at me without saying a word.

"You know, I really wish you would just say what's on your mind, Greer."

He was looking at me far too seriously. "Are you okay?"

"Why wouldn't I be?" I mumbled around a mouthful of eggs.

Without answering, he continued watching me closely while I chewed my bacon. "Okay, you need to stop staring at me like that. If I did something stupid last night, just tell me."

"I was just wondering—" He hesitated, his face twisting

slightly before continuing. "I was wondering if you enjoyed your afternoon yesterday?"

"My afternoon?" I was about to make some comment about his obsessive interest in every mundane move I made, but I stopped when I realized I had no idea how my afternoon had gone. Then I remembered Isabetta Falcone showing up at the shop and Alasdair Templeton shoving a necklace in my face. Was that yesterday or the day before?

Sophia came into the dining room, placed a cup of espresso in front of me, and then glanced at Greer. "Drink," she ordered. I preferred my coffee on the lighter side but took a sip of the powerful black brew to appease her.

"Sophia, did we have lunch yesterday?" I was beginning to remember fragments of an interesting conversation with the woman standing next to me. I shot my own glance at Greer as the conversation about her husband started to come back. "You were telling me about your daughter—and your husband."

Greer's eyes darted to Sophia. I detected a slight shake of her head as she looked back at him.

"We went shopping and we ate." She made a sweeping motion with both hands as she headed back toward the kitchen. "I come in this morning and find uneaten food all over the place. Is a sin to waste good food."

When I turned back to Greer, he was gazing at me intently, sending an uncomfortable flutter through me like he was about to drop a bombshell.

"Is that all you remember about yesterday?" he asked.

I glared back suspiciously. "Why?" He didn't answer, and I knew there was a reason for that enormous headache I woke up with. "*Should* I remember something?"

He held my stare for a minute before his eyes dropped to the newspaper in his left hand. I noticed he was wearing a pair of warmup pants and a T-shirt. "Aren't you going to the club today?"

"I was planning to take the morning off." He scanned the front page of the paper as he spoke. "But I've changed my mind." The paper landed on the table as he got up. "I'll be at the club if there's anything you need . . . or would like to discuss."

An article in the lower left corner of the page caught my eye: THIRD WOMAN ATTACKED IN CENTRAL PARK.

The memory of the night I was attacked in the park came rushing back. It had been an entire season since it happened, but the headline made it all feel like it had happened just yesterday.

Number three. I wondered how many others hadn't come forward because of the strange circumstances around how the Rogues handled their victims, poisoning them from a distance and scrambling their thoughts until they dropped to the ground willingly in some sort of hypnotic obedience. How do you convince yourself that it wasn't your fault? How do you explain *that* to the NYPD?

Greer came back down the stairs dressed in a dark navy suit. He hesitated for a few seconds as he reached the bottom of the stairs, and I could feel him looking at me as I considered my half-eaten breakfast.

"What?" I asked when I caught him staring at me.

He just stood there mute like something was burning a hole in his tongue, something he considered carefully but chose not to say. A moment later, he stepped into the elevator and pushed the button.

As the elevator door shut, Constantine's face popped into my head. The question had never been asked because it hadn't occurred to me until that very moment to ask it. On that day in November when I was attacked, where was Constantine? If he was the self-proclaimed "King of Central Park" and he knew who I was, why didn't *he* defend me?

That was just one of the many questions I had for him, but

I was more interested in finding out how much he knew about Alasdair Templeton. Of course, the ultimate prize was the vessel, and even though he would never admit it, he knew where it was. I'd stake my life on that. If I could get him to talk about Templeton, I might be able to convince him to drop a hint about the vessel's location without compromising his self-imposed code of ethics. It was a long shot, but worth a trip to Central Park.

SIXTEEN

Central Park was the one place I preferred to avoid because nothing good ever happened when I set foot over its threshold, but it was the most likely place I'd find Constantine.

I had the morning and part of the afternoon to find him and convince him to tell me what he knew about Templeton.

I stopped at the corner store to grab a cup of green tea. "On the house." The man behind the counter smiled and waved my money away. I shopped there just about every day, so I guess a free cup of tea to a regular was just good customer relations.

"Thank you." I smiled and put my money away.

My mood was unusually good today, light and euphoric for no particular reason other than the fact that I was alive and free to explore without a babysitter. I sipped my tea as I crossed the street and headed south.

The sound of a low flying bird broke my calm, ruining that rare moment of peace when I didn't feel like every stranger on the street was gunning for me. I was back to my old suspicious self, where the buildings had eyes and the pigeons were messengers of doom.

I glanced up at the stone face glaring down at me. The buildings really did have eyes. The creature's face shifted toward me as its mouth twisted in a grotesque grin that looked like an expression of pain. Its hands cupped the sides of its face in an agonizing grip. There was another one on the next building, only that one had wings and a lapping tongue protruding from a row of jagged teeth.

My eyes dropped back to the sidewalk as I moved faster. *One, two, three.* I counted the seams in the cement as a distraction from all the noise taking over my head. And then I saw the shadow creeping up from my rear, growing wider and taller until it was almost as long as my own.

I wanted to turn around and see who or what was behind me, but my face refused to move from the sidewalk. Eventually I just stopped walking and let the shadow catch up.

"If I didn't like you so much, I'd kill you," I muttered to Rhom as he stepped from behind me.

"Where are you going, Alex?"

"To find someone."

He glanced at my chest before looking at my face. Rhom was too much of a gentleman to blatantly rake a woman's breasts, so I knew it wasn't to assess my cleavage. "Mind if I tag along?" he asked.

"Do I have a choice? I thought we were done with the babysitting."

His job was to hover, smother, and protect me, so what I wanted was irrelevant. "I won't interfere," he assured me. "But I will be joining you."

He gave my chest another glance, and the dynamic between us suddenly shifted. In all the time I'd known him, it was the first time he'd ever made me uncomfortable.

We walked in silence for several blocks. Rhom and I had spent many days and nights walking side by side without saying a word, never feeling the need to force a conversation. But there was something different about the way he occupied the space next to me today, and I wondered if it was because of his unease or mine.

He was staring at me intently when I glanced at him. "Is something wrong, Rhom?"

I was just noting the way you smell."

"Smell? You were noting how I *smell?*"

His nostrils flared and the corners of his mouth dropped. Rhom's features were chiseled and hard, but there was always intelligence and kindness cutting through the toughness of his face. Today I was looking at a stone.

His eyes locked on mine, and then he abruptly turned away as something slithered past his lips. He pulled something from his pocket, and when he turned back to face me he was wearing a pair of dark sunglasses.

I stiffened as a chill raced through me. The hair on my arms stood on end when his jaw tensed and I heard a cracking sound coming from his teeth. He caught my shift as I moved a few inches away, his glasses turning slightly toward me to watch my next move.

"So, Greer decided to take the day off," I baited.

He hesitated before nodding his head.

Actually, Greer had changed his mind and decided to go to Crusades after all. For a man who usually knew his boss's every move, I thought it careless of him to not know Greer's current whereabouts. I didn't believe it for a second.

The lenses of his glasses changed from black to dark ruby red as the eyes behind them glowed. I'd caught the lie and he knew it.

"Thank you for keeping me company last night." I added more bait. I may not have remembered what I did the night before, but I was pretty sure Rhom wasn't anywhere near me. "I really needed someone to bounce some shit off of."

"It was my pleasure, Alex."

I forced a smile as we walked the last half of the block toward the intersection. When we reached Seventy-Second Street, I bolted left and ran toward the park, trying not to look back at what was behind me. My impulse won, and I glanced over my shoulder at the imposter masquerading as my friend and bodyguard. He looked like Rhom, but the cold expression on his face and the guttural noises coming from his throat confirmed that it wasn't Rhom.

I managed to stay alive as I ran across a busy Central Park West and through the entrance of the park, turning down every path I came across in a useless attempt to lose him. I ran until my legs were numb, conjuring Constantine in my mind as I realized I was losing the race. And then it was over. Something jammed in my knee. A sharp pain shot through my leg as I went airborne. I hit the ground hard and slid a good five feet. When I looked up, my hunter was standing over me.

He pulled the sunglasses from his face, and the red glow was replaced by black sockets. There was nothing there but two holes in the front of his face.

"Very rude of you not to wait for me, Ms. Kelley."

I searched my hands for a cut or even a scrape. All that commotion and not a single drop of blood to get me out of this.

His face went pale the second his hand touched my arm. Then he was moving backward like a parasailer catching a violent gust of wind, his voice fading and his body getting smaller. Smaller and smaller he shrunk until he was nothing more than a black speck in the distance, fluttering in the air like a piece of ash escaping a bonfire. And then he was gone.

"Why is it that every time we meet, you bring baggage with you?"

Constantine was standing behind me. He was right about baggage. I seemed to bring calamity to his doorstep every time we met, and he had become one of my personal saviors.

"I have to admit, Constantine, I've never been happier to see you."

"Well, it's about time you admitted your attraction to me."

"I never said I was att—"

"What brings you to my neighborhood?" He extended his hand. I took it, and he pulled me off the ground effortlessly. "You look exceptionally vibrant today, considering the circumstances."

I looked back at the spot where the imposter had vaporized. "What was that?"

"Just another minion trying to catch the brass ring," he replied nonchalantly. "Only this one was smart enough to get inside your head. He knew exactly what you needed to see."

Constantine nailed it. When I saw that shadow on the sidewalk, I was hoping it was Rhom following me and not another stalker. Apparently my thoughts were pretty transparent.

"Enough of this small talk. Walk with me and tell me why you've come. Although the reason for your visit is irrelevant." He motioned toward the path and I followed.

I felt completely safe and at ease walking next to him. Our relationship had become reciprocal. Constantine filled in the gaps where Greer and his men fell short—like just now—and in return, I amused him. For reasons I wasn't quite sure of, he genuinely liked me, and for that I held a get-out-of-jail-card in perpetuity.

"Well . . . I've been thinking about you lately, and my friend mentioned you'd dropped by Shakespeare's Library looking for me. So I thought I'd check in on you."

He seemed unusually light today. Compared to his usual intensity, the difference stood out like a beacon. He even smelled different—but familiar.

"Your hair is all ruffled up." I looked at the shiny black locks hanging loosely around his face. Constantine was a real stickler when it came to his appearance. I'd never seen a hair out of place. "What have you been up to?"

He stopped in the middle of the path and smoothed his disheveled hair. Then he turned to look at me, clasping his hands behind his back as he waited for me to come clean about what *I* was up to. But as I opened my mouth to tell him the real reason for the visit, his face softened into a curious gaze. His hand met the underside of my chin as his thumb traced the swollen center of my lower lip. "You've been kissed."

"What?" I shoved his hand away.

He examined my face a little too closely as his own heated up. "And fucked."

The absurdity of the comment floored me, and then those two words danced around in my head while an odd warmth cradled my stomach.

"Who?" he asked. The tone of his voice was as heated as his face. Constantine had an uncanny ability to make every syllable an erotic slither up and down a woman's auditory organs.

I snapped out of it and met his stare. "Are you serious? I think I'd remember being kissed, and—"

"Can't say the word?"

"Really, Constantine." He was baiting me. Trying to elicit some sort of sexual game. You'd think I'd be used to it by now considering that was our normal course of exchange. I'd never spend more than a few minutes with him when he didn't try to get a rise out of me. He was a satyr, after all. Sex and lust were his specialty, as he reminded me repeatedly.

He took my arm and we began to walk again. It was a rare act of intimacy, because he usually didn't touch, preferring to parade his eroticism just out of reach.

"There was another attack," I announced bluntly. "Here in the park." Of course he already knew that. Why he allowed it was the real mystery. Out of the corner of my eye I could see the controlled anger on his face. This was his territory, and to hear him speak of it, he was in control of everything that went on within the walls of Central Park. "It made me think about the night I was attacked."

He stopped walking and waited for me to ask my question.

"Where were you that night, Constantine?"

"Ah, so you want to know why I didn't come riding in on a white horse to save you?"

"Don't be such an ass." I pulled my arm away from his and got right to the point. "But you're right. I would like to know why you lurked in the background and let that creep put his hands on me." It was a bold move to practically call him a coward, and he could easily make me regret it.

The look on his face made me uneasy as I considered how I'd react if he told me he just didn't care, that I got what I deserved for walking in the park after dark. Even Greer had made a comment about my arrogance for doing that.

"I may not have ridden up on a white horse, but are you so sure I didn't come to your rescue? You offend me with your assessment of my lack of benevolence."

"Then prove me wrong."

He resumed walking and took a panoramic look around the park. "This is all mine. Not a leaf drops from a tree that I am not aware of. But you must understand that unpleasant things happen for a reason, and it's not my place to change the course of events."

He pointed to a young couple standing under a tree, embroiled in a heated conversation. "Do you see those two? He's telling her that he isn't in love with her anymore. She'll go through the usual round of human emotions. She'll cry until her eyes are swollen and convince herself that she's ugly and unworthy of love. Her apartment will be littered with the sacrificed trees she'll wipe her nose with. And when the sun goes down and the pain of loss and rejection have settled into a dull ache, she'll wash down a bottle of Vicodin with whiskey and never wake up."

I stopped and stared at the couple like an interloper witnessing something I had no right to see.

"Now, I could go over there and change the course of what will happened to both of them, because it isn't only her life that will be changed forever. I could make him love her again, or seal their destiny with a marriage and two children. I could make her leave him. I might even remove the cancer from her bones before it's diagnosed. But that would steer the world in a direction it isn't meant to take."

I gawked at him in disbelief, wondering if any of it was true or if he was just being a master of tall tales.

"The woman's sister will continue down a path toward a career that leaves her numb, instead of taking inspiration from the loss and writing the first of many novels," he continued. "The man will conveniently move on to another woman who will become his wife, and he will treat her like an indentured servant as he fucks his mistress. He'll never be humbled by the knowledge that he had an indirect hand in the ending of a life, and subsequently become a real man."

"Is there a point to all this?"

"The point, Alex, is that if you're going to fuck with the grand path of the universe, it better be for a damn good reason. There is no turning back." He stepped closer and pummeled me with one of his smart looks. "You, my love, are a damn good reason."

I shook my head in exasperation. Getting a straight answer out of him was an exercise in futility.

"If I'm such a good reason, why didn't you try to change *my* outcome?"

"What makes you think I didn't? How do you think that man of yours knew where to find you?"

My mouth dropped. "I thought Patrick—"

"Patrick merely told Greer you were back in New York."

I still didn't understand why he didn't just swoop down himself and get me out of there. He'd done it before.

"Because you needed to be found," he explained before I could ask the question. "And not by me."

SEVENTEEN

Constantine once told me that he knew everything, but that some secrets weren't his to tell. I thought he was puffing, but I learned very quickly that even when he sounded like he was full of himself, you could bet on his words. He was always truthful, often to the point of rudeness. He knew where the amulet was from the moment it disappeared last year, and I was sure he knew exactly where the vessel was, too. The trick was in getting him to talk.

"Greer and I went to see a man at Cornell University the other day." I thought it best to offer a little information of my own. Although it probably wasn't news, seeing how he knew everything. I bet he knew all about our trip to see Dr. Oxford and our dealings with Isabetta Falcone, but at least it showed good faith and a willingness to participate in a little give and take.

A sly grin spread across his face as he focused straight ahead and said nothing.

"But I guess you already knew about that," I said.

"And you thought it wise to tell me a secret I already knew?"

"I just thought—"

"No, Alex. Don't spoil the generosity with a mundane

explanation. It shows thoughtfulness and trust. I can't think of anything more soul-baring than trust."

Is that what I was doing? Baring my soul? Constantine had a way of extracting things from me that I preferred to keep hidden. But like it or not, he'd become a trusted ally, and I knew it was to my advantage to have him on my side of the fence. I pitied the person who stood on the other.

"I guess you know about Alasdair Templeton, too." I glanced at him and detected a slight jar in his expression. Was it possible that he didn't know about Templeton? Maybe I did have a few cards left in my hand, after all. "You know who he is, right?"

"Don't be obtuse, Alex."

"That's a mighty big word," I said as I stopped walking. "Kind of insulting, don't you think?"

"My apologies. The name incites a bit of abhorrence in me." He examined the fingertips of his right hand before casually asking me to expound.

"You mean you don't know about him trying to get me to come back to Ireland? He tried to bait me with a necklace that's supposed to have some kind of binding powers." I could see his body go rigid when I mentioned the necklace. "You know about the necklace, don't you? Then how is it you don't know about him coming to see me?"

"Because he's a walking ward," he said with contempt. "That man has discovered a very effective way of choosing whom he lets in, and whom he shuts out."

"Really? You mean a mere mortal has found a way to outsmart you?"

"There is nothing mere or mortal about Alasdair Templeton." He examined me out of the corner of his eye. "Since you're strolling through the park with me, I assume you didn't accept his gift. That would have been tragic. I would have missed our chats."

"Aww. You really do like me, don't you?" There was something both comforting and terrifying about having such a powerful creature casting a protective shadow over my head.

"I suppose I do."

"Well, I think we scared him off for a while. My friend Katie—" I caught myself before the words slipped out.

"You mean your dragon friend? Yes, she is something, isn't she?"

Of course he knew what she was. "Can't hide anything from you, can I."

"Not if I can help it." His face took on a more serious note. "He'll be back, Alex. Get used to dealing with that parasite because he won't stop until he gets what he came for. You may not be biologically connected, but you are his blood in a much deeper way—through the bonds of power. In his eyes, that makes you his property. Much like a man who thinks he owns his spouse and offspring."

He turned into me on the path to punctuate his next words. "He'll dangle that carrot in front of you in other ways. Be very discriminating about what you reach for."

A woman came down the path wearing a pair of leggings and a tank top that showed off her perfectly sculpted figure. Her blonde ponytail swung back and forth as each foot made contact with the ground.

Constantine seemed oblivious as she passed us, but his eyes suddenly broke from mine and followed her as she moved down the path behind me. "Be very careful, Alex."

I turned just in time to see her head do a one-eighty and look back at me from an unnatural angle. Her eyes turned as black as Constantine's, and her ponytail lengthened and ran down her back before protruding from her tailbone like a whip.

He looked back at me and held my gaze with uncomfortable intensity until I broke eye contact. "Point taken," I conceded.

I contemplated a delicate way to raise the subject of why I was really here. He deplored small talk, but manipulation was even more offensive, especially when he wasn't the one doing it. "Is it obvious why I'm here?"

"I know why you've come to see me. I was hoping you actually felt the urge to be in my presence, but I'll take your company any way I can get it." He took my right hand in his and gently stroked his thumb over my knuckles. "Your skin is so soft, like a layer of silk stretched over clay. I cannot imagine anything else covering your bones." His hand slipped away. "You are too light to be so dark."

He shifted and continued down the path, gesturing for me to follow. My instincts told me not to. But no risk meant no reward, and the stakes were just too high.

We walked in silence for what seemed like an hour. When I looked to my left, he was gone. But the smell of pine, musk, and lavender emitting from his skin still filled the air, putting to rest any doubt that he'd been standing next to me a moment earlier.

"Constantine," I whispered as my eyes closed and a rush of cold wind hit my skin. The sounds of the city faded, mingling into a single note until all I could hear was the vague droning of a distant machine. The ground beneath my feet fell away. I opened my eyes as the wind grew stronger, and I was moving through a black hole with tiny flecks of light glimmering against the dark walls.

Constantine was somewhere in the background, watching me, laughing from the other side of a veil. And then his face went cold as he nodded once before fading farther away, like a specter.

I spotted something in the distance, something I knew but couldn't quite place. I'd been there before. I kept moving toward it, glancing down at my feet and wondering where they'd gone. The closer I got, the more familiar it looked. As soon as I reached the spectacle of billboards at Seventh and Broadway,

I knew what it was. It was the tiered line of lights leading up to the observation deck of the Empire State Building. I gazed in fascination as the lights grew brighter, and in an instant I was breezing past the trail of bulbs illuminating the tip of the antenna.

I gasped as I circled around the structure and headed west toward the Hudson River. The sky went from black to deep blue as the water reflected and mixed with the glow of the city. The lights sprinkled through it like sequins on a blanket of blue velvet, and all I could do was marvel at the sheer beauty of the sea in front of me.

I was flying.

My arms felt like the wings of a bird. When I looked at them, they were as black and polished as the day I first saw them in my dream. I commanded the right one to flap as if it were my own arm. It obeyed because it was my arm, and I knew if I looked at my reflection in the mirrors of the skyscrapers, I would see the shiny black head of a raven looking back.

I sailed over the water and dipped from the sky to see my image reflect across the waves. They shot into the air and nearly took me as I teased the surface with my wings. I was magnificent, and for the first time since finding out who and what I was, I understood it and welcomed it.

The lure of the city pulled me back toward land. I flew over the crowds moving like tiny marching ants along the trails of New York streets, toward the park where I'd found my wings and left Constantine standing below.

I spotted a man walking along the reservoir, not far from where I'd walked the night I was attacked. Didn't he know the danger of walking the park at night?

An oak tree served as a vantage point while I spied on the man pacing back and forth. He seemed to be debating the sanity of continuing across the park in the dark, as I had done. He was wearing a pair of jeans and a T-shirt with the words SHIVA POSSE in bold letters across the front. Shiva the destroyer, the ultimate outlaw of the god kingdom. Either he knew that, or it was a really cool name for a band.

An odd sense of urgency nagged at me, ruffling my feathers like an itch that couldn't be reached. It kept nipping at me until it propelled me back into the sky. I reached a spot high above the park as the itch grew stronger and then stunned me. My wings failed in mid-flight, and I descended toward the ground, gazing in horror as my feathers began to disappear into the pores of my skin, turning my wings back into flesh and bone arms. My feet flailed as they untucked from the underside of my tail feathers and went from talons back to toes. But I saw no images of my life flashing before me, or the Grim Reaper waiting below. My descent just slowed, and then my feet gently touched the ground.

The man looked at me with his mouth slack as if he'd seen an archangel descend from the sky. But I was no angel, and based on the thoughts that were running through my head, the decent part of me wanted to scream *run*! He just stood there, mute, paralyzed with fear as I reached for him and pressed my palm against his chest. His heart beat like a terrified rabbit about to be fed to a wolf.

The smell of his fear incited the strangest instinct. I tried to shake the thought, but the ground lit up in a blaze of blue light, bringing him to his knees. I wanted to straddle him and squeeze him between my legs until he disappeared inside of me, filling me with his flesh and his memories. I wanted to suck the life right out of him.

I heard my name. Someone was calling me, and it was like a light had been switched on. I looked at the silhouette of the trees and the ground under my feet, and I recognized the exact spot where Daemon had held me down. Suddenly I couldn't breathe. Something was squeezing the air from my lungs. I flew back into the sky, wingless and powerless, into the black hole from which I'd come.

*   *   *

My eyes opened and stung from the brightness of the late morning sun. Constantine was looking at me with a bare smile that seemed to commiserate with my horrified eyes.

"Are you all right?" he asked. It seemed less a question of concern than a confirmation that the catharsis was over.

"What did you just do to me, Constantine? Did you see?"

"It is yours to see. Anyone else is merely trespassing." He reached down to pluck a blade of grass from the side of the path and placed it in my palm. "Do not allow trespassers to judge who you are, Alex. You'll judge yourself harshly enough."

He closed my fingers over the blade and then shifted back into his aloof self. "So, you were telling me about this man you've been fucking." He continued as if he hadn't just planted a nightmare in my head.

"What?" I'd barely stopped shaking from the hallucination and he was asking me about my sex life? "I wasn't telling you anything."

"Well then, out with it."

"I don't know where all this is coming from, Constantine, but it won't work." It was a strategic move. He knew I was here to convince him to tell me where the vessel was hidden, and sending me on some head-trip vision quest was the perfect way to divert the conversation.

"No, no, Alex. Always in such a rush." He sighed heavily. "You are one of the most impatient creatures I have ever known. Don't you think you have enough to explore before we get to that?"

I stopped walking and waited for him to turn around. "There is nothing more important," I said as he faced me. "I'll keep asking, so why not just tell me where it is?"

He came within an inch of my face. "You are an extraordinarily special girl. The problem is you don't know how special. Go home to your man, Alex. Dig deep and find that door. It won't be pleasant, but when we all gather to play out our little game, you will thank me for my guidance."

"Guidance? Horse shit, Constantine! Quit playing *your* game."

He glanced at his Cartier. "I have thoroughly enjoyed our visit, but I'm afraid I have no more time to chat. I must be off."

"Off? You must be off? I went to a lot of trouble to get here this morning, and you can't spare a little more of your precious time?" I glanced at my cell phone. "It's not even noon."

"Alex." His index figure found the tip of my chin as he raised my face back to his. "You've been here since yesterday morning."

I tried to reconcile the date on my phone. The days were all starting to run together. When I looked back up, he was gone.

My hand—still clutching the blade of grass—opened. In the center of my palm was a tiny black feather.

EIGHTEEN

Greer was going to murder me. I mean, literally end my life for pulling the disappearing act. It didn't matter that I had no idea how much time I'd lost, and if he found out whom I was with, my retribution would be far worse.

The domains of Greer and Constantine were off limits to each other, which meant as long as I was with one, the other couldn't see me. As far as Greer knew, I'd fallen off the planet for the past twenty-four hours.

I debated whether to go straight to the club, because at noon on a weekday that's where he'd usually be. But since he was probably going ballistic, home was a more likely place to find him.

As I turned the corner and approached the steps leading up to the front door, I wondered what he'd do to me this time. The last time I disappeared, he threatened to glue himself to my side and make sure my whereabouts were never in question again. Visions of a tracking device implanted under my skin came to mind. We were past all that, though. Greer would have to accept that I was no longer that helpless girl that stepped off a plane the year before.

I was Fitheach. I was a Raven.

Why I bothered I don't know, but I quietly turned the key in the lock and listened as the deadbolt disengaged and receded from the doorjamb. No matter how discreet my attempt to get past him, if he was in the house, he'd smell me before I made it past the foyer.

I slipped inside. The faint sound of a spoon or a knife came from the kitchen, and I assumed Sophia was busy prepping for dinner. She normally didn't cook lunch for Greer because he usually wasn't home during the day. But I guess today was as good a day as any to break that routine, an idea that proved correct as I slowly turned my head toward the living room and looked into his face.

"Jesus, Greer." He didn't move as I jolted from the surprise of seeing him standing a few feet away. "You're like a ghost sometimes."

He covered the space between us in two steps and reached for me. Before I could react, he wrapped his hand around my head and pulled me into him. The heat of his chest enveloped me as my cheek rested against his crisp shirt. I could feel his heartbeat accelerate as he gripped me tighter, and just when I thought he might cut off my air supply and put an end to all this nonsense about amulets and scavenger hunts to save the world, he pressed his lips to my head and asked, "Are you hungry?"

I hadn't eaten in over twenty-four hours, so a piece of cardboard would have been appetizing.

"Starving." I pushed away and scrutinized his face. "Why did you do that?"

As if I hadn't just asked a perfectly valid question, he took my hand and led me into the kitchen.

"Sophia has made us a beautiful lunch."

It was more than lunch—it was a feast. I scanned the excessive amount of food spread across the kitchen island and glanced at Greer, wondering what all the fuss was for. "How did you know?"

"Know what?"

"That I'd walk through the door just now?"

I glanced at Sophia, who was finishing off a ripe strawberry and watching our exchange. Her usual aloofness was replaced with genuine interest as she hung on Greer's next words.

He gazed at me for a moment, like I'd asked him a difficult question. "I could feel you. Now, I feed you."

The strawberry slipped from Sophia's mouth as she expelled her captive breath. A smile breached her lips but quickly disappeared when I didn't respond.

Greer's face went cold. The gesture deserved a response. But all I could do was stare at the enormous meal on the counter, thinking about the juxtaposition between the girl who stepped off a plane last fall and the one standing over a man in the park, meaning to do him harm. Dream or not, it felt real enough to make me wonder who I was becoming.

"Thank you," I glanced back and forth between the two of them, "but I'm not hungry anymore."

Sophia gasped as a cold veil fell over the room. Greer didn't react at all, and I knew if I touched his face it would feel like a hard, lifeless stone.

I opened my mouth to take it back, but before I could speak, the sting of Sophia's words stopped me.

"You ungrateful girl!"

"Sophia!" Greer's eyes shot to his housekeeper.

"Sophia, I didn't mean to—"

"You got no heart, Miss Alex." Her head slowly shook as she wiggled her index finger in front of my face. "You better be careful. Life don't give you too many of these." She motioned toward Greer.

"That's enough, Sophia." He laid his hand on her wrist to

put an end to it, and with a firm nod and a bitter glare, she punctuated her point and walked out of the kitchen.

"What the hell was that all about, Greer?"

He glanced at the mountain of food on the counter and then back at me. The look on his face triggered a swelling in my chest. As I recovered from the humbling, he headed for the elevator. I considered asking him to stay, but the growing feeling of shame wrapped around me like a dirty blanket, severing my right to ask him for anything. I'd managed to offend them both and wasn't quite sure how. But I knew one thing: it was the first and last time I'd ever refuse one of Sophia's meals.

I went upstairs and changed into fresh clothes. I came back down, hoping Greer had decided to go to the club after all. It was bad enough that I had to face Sophia, but the thought of facing them both was overwhelming. Besides, there was no time to try to make things right. If I got to Shakespeare's Library before half the day was over, I might be able to salvage my job with some fabricated story about why I'd been MIA.

Greer's distinctive scent hit my nose before I made it to the bottom step. Sophia was working over the stove when I walked past the kitchen. She turned her head slightly but wouldn't look at me, not quite ready for pleasantries or forgiveness for whatever I'd done.

He was looking directly at me as I walked into the dining room and took my usual seat at the table.

"I'm sorry." Inconsiderate and rude I was not, so the idea that I'd been both of those things sat on my heart like a brick. "Will you let me explain?"

He shook his head. "You've done nothing wrong. You're a grown woman. You can come and go as you please. No more smothering." He got up from the table. "I have to take care of some business at Crusades, but I'll be home in a few hours. We can get back to business then."

The last few days had been scattered, and we were losing precious time to find the vessel before someone else did. Constantine was a dead end. Even though I was convinced he knew where it was, getting the information out of him had proven futile because of some stupid sense of loyalty to keep cosmic secrets.

Some things are not mine to tell. That was Constantine's perennial response to everything.

"Balance, my ass," I muttered as I recalled my conversation with him in an apartment in Paris a few months back. He'd been referring to the code of ethics he lived by; some mumbo jumbo about universal balance.

"What?"

"Nothing. Just thinking out loud."

His eyes kept lingering on me until I felt uncomfortably exposed, like I was standing in front of him naked.

"I have the late shift. I won't be home until after nine."

He looked disappointed. My pesky job was getting in the way again.

He grabbed his jacket from the back of the chair and cupped my cheek with his other hand. "So much unfinished business. You exhaust me, Alex." He caught me off guard with a kiss to my cheek, and an image flashed in my mind. I was standing in front of him, and he was on his knees. I pulled away sharply as the image vanished.

He straightened and pulled his hand back. "I'm sorry."

"No. It's not that."

"Then what is it, Alex? Have we gotten to the point where we avoid each other in our own home?"

Our home. He'd never said that before, and neither had I. It was all too much for one day, and I could barely catch my breath.

"I've got to get out of here." I stood up and walked out of

the room without looking back. "I'm probably already fired."

I'd lost an entire day, and Apollo probably already called that temp back to take my job.

The sign for Shakespeare's Library came into view. I'd disappeared for an entire day without so much as a phone call to feign an illness, and if Apollo hadn't already fired me, I was prepared to grovel and make up an elaborate lie to justify my carelessness. What was I going to do, tell him the truth? *I'm sorry Apollo, I was sent on a vision quest by an arrogant satyr with a penchant for tough love.*

My stomach knotted as I pushed the door open. The shop was empty except for a girl on a stepladder with a pen in her mouth.

"Inventory. Shit." I'd forgotten about that. I hadn't just disappeared for a day; I'd disappeared for a day during inventory week.

The girl turned to look at me when she heard the door chime. She hopped off the ladder and laid her clipboard down. "Sorry for the mess. We're in the middle of inventory."

I was about to introduce myself when Apollo came out of the back room. His shoulders sagged when he saw me. "Alex, what the fuck?"

I'd never heard Apollo swear before. His head shook as he held his palms up in a what-gives motion. His overgrown head of curls looked messier than usual, and he looked as tired as a student during final exam week.

"God, I'm sorry, Apollo. I can't even begin to tell you how sorry." I had no idea what to say. The truth wasn't an option, and I'd failed miserably on the way over to come up with a plausible lie.

"A death," I blurted. "I had a death in the family. My . . . uncle. I had to go upstate for the funeral."

Unlike Katie, Apollo knew very little about my background, so a dead relative in upstate New York wasn't completely out of left field.

"And you didn't think it was necessary to let me know?"

"Didn't I?" I looked around the room for Katie. She'd back me up on the lie and ask me for the real story later. It would be her ass for not relaying the information to Apollo, and God knows I felt like shit for that.

"No. I don't believe you did." There was just a hint of sarcasm in his voice, another side of him I'd never seen.

"I told Katie. Is she here?"

Apollo squeezed his eyes shut and rubbed the sockets. "Well, you see that's the problem. Katie's not here either. Apparently, she's been ill for the past three days."

"Um . . . should I go back and . . ." The girl grabbed her clipboard and pointed to the ladder.

"Yes, Erica. I would appreciate it if you could finish sci-fi before you leave this afternoon."

I waited for her to climb back on the ladder and then continued with the lie. "Three days? That doesn't make sense, Apollo. She was here the day before I left."

"Yes. That was Tuesday—three days ago. And you were supposed to open this morning."

The date on my phone confirmed that it was Friday. I did the math. We came back from Cornell Monday night. Isabetta Falcone and Templeton showed up at the shop the next day. It was the day after that—yesterday—that I went to the park to find Constantine and ended up staying until this afternoon. Today should be Thursday.

I flipped through my incoming call log and found four missed calls from the shop, three on Wednesday and one yesterday.

My conversation with Sophia yesterday morning suddenly came back to me. She said we went shopping and had lunch.

That must have been Wednesday. I was so confused with my days, I was afraid I'd bungle my own lie. At least Katie's absence bought me time to get my story straight. Now I just needed to talk to her before Apollo did.

"Give me two minutes, Apollo. I'll have a clipboard in my hand and we'll get this done."

When I got to the back room, I dialed Katie's number. On top of all the lying that made me sick to my stomach, I worried about what illness could keep the unsinkable Katie Bishop home in bed for three days—*three* days. The message on her voicemail said her inbox was full.

"Alex. Please!"

I shoved the phone in my pocket and grabbed a clipboard. "Coming."

We spent the next seven hours counting books, recording each one until our fingers burned. "This is nuts, Apollo."

"Agreed, but it's better than flipping burgers until two in the morning."

He looked exhausted, and I had a feeling he hadn't had much sleep with two people out and one temp to pick up the slack.

"Alex," he began with a serious face, "I need you to tell me you'll never disappear like that again. If you're sick, you call me, not Katie. Understood?"

"Completely."

I apologized like a broken record about twenty more times until we finally flipped the sign on the door to CLOSED. I'd tried Katie's number several more times throughout the day, but each time I was sent straight to a full mailbox.

"I'm worried about Katie," I said. "She isn't answering her phone, and it's not like her to be out for three days in a row."

"Or one, for that matter," Apollo noted. "In the year that we've worked together, I've seen her walk through that door with everything from a broken wrist to the flu. She just doesn't know how to do sick. I don't think she's ever taken a single day."

I stopped straightening the books and stared at my frazzled boss, who looked like he was about to drop from exhaustion. "If you don't get out of here, you'll be sick, too. Take that girl with you." I nodded toward Erica who was half asleep on top of the books piled up on the floor.

"You sure? I can stay and help close."

"Positive." I pointed to the door. "Oh, and if Katie isn't here in the morning, one of us is going to her apartment."

I think taking a physical inventory cost more in manpower than a cheap software system. The store was littered with books that had come off the shelves as we fingered through them, and my estimate was that I'd be stuck at the shop for an extra hour just to clean up the mess.

It was just after ten when I looked at my phone. Greer was used to seeing me walk through the door by now, so I expected to see Rhom—the real Rhom—at the door to fetch me home. That never happened.

At ten thirty, I locked the shop door and headed north. Columbus Avenue was always crowded, but being Friday night it was busier than usual.

The sidewalk tables were full as the spring air enticed people outdoors to sip beer and salty margaritas under the stars. There was something about eating under the night sky that seemed to make the food taste better, and the company sitting across the table more likable.

A sea of heads bobbed up and down the sidewalk. Some stared straight ahead with blank expressions, while others tapped away on the keyboards of their phones in the all-consuming need to stay on top of social media. They had a name for that: Obsessive Compulsive Social Media Disorder or OCSMD.

My head panned to the left as I felt one of those faces

looking back at me. His eyes zeroed in on mine, mocking me like a predator stalking prey. My first instinct was to run, but I'd done that too many times, and I was tired of running. I made the decision in the middle of the sidewalk to face him head on.

Daemon stopped as I began to work my way through the crowd toward him. With each step, his expression grew less cocky and more surprised at my audacity; a mere woman having the balls to challenge his threat and approach within two feet.

"I guess it's not so easy to grab me in the middle of hundreds of witnesses. I'm not afraid of you anymore. I know exactly what you are."

Rogues were nothing more than rapists and child abductors, building an army of stolen half-breed children they sired with their victims.

He cocked his head and a small grin returned to his face. "You think you know what I am? I bet you don't know why I'm here."

I said nothing and glanced at the mob of pedestrians moving past us, confident that he didn't have the upper hand this time.

"Just get to the point and tell me what you want? Is it the amulet? Well, get in line."

His eyes walked over my face and then ran down the length of my body. "Does it hurt when sunlight hits your skin?" he asked in a distracted way. "You're so fair. It never used to hurt mine, but I find it more uncomfortable these days. Makes me wonder if we'll all end up underground someday." He caught himself and amended his statement. "We're not vampire, Alex. I wouldn't want to mislead you based on my candor, but the light does seem to cause discomfort lately."

"May I touch your skin?" His hand moved toward my arm.

I snorted and glared at him incredulously. "Why would I let you do that?"

His mouth was against my ear before I even saw him move. "Because you belong to me, and I asked you nicely." He pulled back, lingering within a few inches of me as his eyes explored my face. "I don't think I like the smell of other men on you."

His breath crawled over my skin. I tried to step back but froze, unable to move as he crossed that boundary he no longer respected.

"You're in my space," I said through clenched teeth. "I don't think I like the smell of *you*."

His eyes darted to my right, and his grin widened as he began moving backward into the crowd. "I'll be back for you, Alex."

Rhom came out of nowhere a moment after Daemon disappeared into the ocean of moving bodies.

He rubbed his forehead and looked at me. "It's almost eleven. What the fuck, Alex?"

"Why does everyone keep saying that to me?"

NINETEEN

Constantine thought about the first time he'd felt the sting of passion intertwined with unrequited love. It was a hard lesson in wanting and devotion, and the all too common one-sidedness that so often came with it.

He was a yearling when it happened, that constriction of the heart, and the blind faith of trusting the one at the other end of that constricting rope. He was in love, and about to learn the lessons that could only be gleaned through unconditional trust and the complete opening of the heart.

His mother had died in childbirth, alone in the forest where no one would hear her screams as he pushed from her body with his soft but powerful hooves. She took her last breath under a three-hundred-year-old oak, leaving her child to be raised by the woods: trees that grew at will and cascaded over his moss-lined cradle; streams that flowed to his lips and then receded so not to drown him; birds with gifts of berries and insects.

At the age of three, the forest booted him to the fields where he was found and brought to the Queen.

Desiree watched him grow for fourteen years before taking him as her companion, warning the other young maidens that any indiscretions would be judged as the crime of thievery. Constantine was hers, and as Desiree was the Queen, theft of her property would result in a punishment worse than any death.

She took Constantine's innocence on his seventeenth birthday, quickly schooling him in the art of pleasure. It was a late age for a young satyr to experience his rite of passage, but she'd grown expert in spotting the perfect time to release the lust and passion satyrs were legendary for.

He loved her and fantasized about becoming her king when the reigning king took his last breath. No matter if it took ten or twenty years, he would wait for her. But as smart and devoted as he was, he was also blinded by the very passion his kind were known for.

It was Imbolc, the start of the spring festivals. Under the thick layer of snow, the crepe-paper orange and yellow fringe fell from the witch hazel, and purple cups of hellebore sprang from underneath the naked trees. It was the beginning of the new in the middle of frost and winter and symbolized the rebirth of the young King from his long winter sleep.

Constantine had been called by the Queen and wondered if tonight would be the night he became her young king. He picked a sprig of bright red berries from the holly tree at the crossroads, and walked through the thick carpet of white snow that led to the entrance of the Queen's chambers. He'd walked through that door and shared her bed for a total of one-hundred and sixty-seven nights since the last Beltane when she claimed him, but never had he seen another face when he entered her walls.

Tonight the room was filled with faces. Their eyes followed Constantine as he approached the bed where Desiree lay, with her exposed legs spread wide and her knees pulled toward the sky.

He stood at the foot of the bed and waited for her instructions. As the room fell silent and all eyes remained on him, he took it as a sign and shed his own clothes, standing naked while the audience watched and murmured quietly behind the veil of dim light in the room.

As the minutes passed and the crowd continued to stare, his discomfort and shame began to cloud his thoughts. He fought the urge to cover his exposed genitals from their eyes, but then he lifted his leg to climb onto the bed. She was his Queen and he would not question her motives for sharing their lovemaking with a room full of strangers. And then it occurred to him that it was the rite of Imbolc, and he was honored.

Desiree pushed up on her elbows and gave him a warning look as he climbed higher on the bed, ready to play his part in the rite of fertility.

"Not you," she said. "You disappoint me. You've grown too old."

Her eyes remained on his as her finger crooked at someone on the other side of the room. A young man, barely a season less than Constantine, appeared from the dark corner and climbed onto the bed. Her legs widened as the man's head dropped between them. And when she'd had enough of his tongue, she rolled him on his back and mounted him.

"Fuck," she commanded, her eyes still locked on Constantine's as she rode the younger man's hips.

Constantine watched as the man worked his Queen for some time. She moaned as she had with Constantine inside of her for so many days and nights.

As the sex grew frenzied and the man brought her to a climax, a single tear rolled from Constantine's eye. But just one, because in that small moment of teaching, his soul had hardened.

Desiree rose from the bed and walked naked to Constantine, meeting his eyes with a sympathetic but cold stare. He had suffered the additional shame of an erection throughout the entire display. She took his cock in her hand and stroked. "As witnessed this night, I release you."

She turned to the crowd assembled around her bed and offered Constantine to anyone in the room, man or woman, without discretion.

It was the first and last taste of humiliation he would ever suffer. And he swore to himself he would never inflict that feeling on another soul as long as he existed—not even the Queen.

Constantine came back to the here and now, shedding the memory of the betrayal as far back in his mind as it would go. It was a constant reminder to tread the soul with care.

Fucking was fucking, but the woman beside him was something more. He would not cheapen her or make her feel anything but cared for and wanted.

She'd slipped into a deep sleep, well deserved from all the energy expended during their hours of battle under the damp sheets.

Constantine hadn't slept in a century. There was too much to miss in those fleeting moments of altered state. But what he feared most was letting down his guard for any trespasser to come in and wreak havoc with the existence he'd crafted so intently. He would never let anyone tinker with his sphere of existence ever again.

"Are you hungry?" she asked as she woke from her sleep and rolled over to look at him.

"I have never been so hungry." His eyes filled with heat. "But I doubt there is anything that could sate my appetite."

She smiled in that way a woman does when she's ready to show a man how wrong he is.

"Not again. I'm raw, woman." He sat up and pulled the sheet back to show her. "See what you've done to me." Constantine's parts looked a bit tender, but despite the wear of excessive lovemaking, he was growing again.

"Ah, now see?" she purred. "I think we need to do something about that."

He hopped off the bed and stretched his magnificent form like a tiger waking from a lazy nap, his erection taming from the separation. She followed and wrapped her arms around his waist, burying her cheek in the muscles of his back. "Where did you come from and how do I keep you here?"

"You can let me feed *you*," he growled playfully as he turned to kiss her and engulf her naked body with his. The feel of her breasts against his skin ignited his need to be inside of her again. He broke the embrace and reasoned with his desire. "You need to eat, and then we can take a shower."

"And after that?" She looked at him for reassurance that he'd stay.

He led her to the kitchen and opened the refrigerator. "God, woman. How do you survive?" Except for an expired container of yogurt and a limp head of lettuce, it was empty.

"I think there's some cereal in the cabinet."

Constantine grabbed the box of Cheerios and found a bag of raisins. "Remind me to bring you some food."

"Does that mean you'll be coming back?" She had that look again, the one that said *more*. Her eyelids fell and her mouth appeared fuller as the lust washed through her again. "Will this ever stop?" she asked. "Wanting you?"

"Ah, *fuck*." Constantine threw the food on the counter and descended on her like a starving dog. A minute later, he had her against the wall of the shower, moving into her as the water ran down their bodies and washed the stains of lovemaking from their skin.

It had been days since they entered that bed, and if they didn't take hold of their crippling need, it would be days more before they were forced to tread into the bright glare of the world.

When they finally emerged from the shower, clean and ready for yet another round under the sheets, he knew it would have to end. But not until he had one last taste of her.

Constantine laid her on the bed and gently slid his hand up

and down the skin of her freshly bathed calf, stopping to kiss the inside of her knee. Then he wrapped his fingers around her ankles and placed them on his tightly muscled shoulders. With a single stroke, he pushed inside of her, holding firmly against her as he reached full penetration and watched her face contort and twist into a picture of ecstasy. He pulled out of her and then pushed back inside with the same determination, taking note of each detail of her face.

He would use these memories as foreplay for the next time they made love, and the next, and the next. He would remember every nuance of her pleasured expression and do whatever it took to produce that same look over and over again.

She tightened around him, and he lowered his body on top of hers, his forearms leveraged as he rocked inside of her and looked in her eyes. The release came as intensely as the first one had, and the second, and the tenth. How many days had they been like this, lost in the powerful lust that gripped them and refused to let them leave this place?

She rolled to her side in a slack, boneless laze of sated flesh, and he ran his fingers over the black lines as if he could feel the edges of her tattoo. He stroked them and followed them down to where they intersected with the dimple of her back. And then they began to move and expand. Constantine had marveled the first time he'd seen it and felt the strange sensation slide across his skin.

He waited for the shadow to grow and take up the better part of the room, and then he lay back on the bed with his hands tucked behind his head, and let his dragon have her turn.

Saturdays were the busiest days at Shakespeare's Library. I liked working weekends because time flew by, and everyone's mood was brighter knowing they had one more day of freedom before returning to the jobs that chained them.

I got to the shop at eight a.m., an hour early to make sure the place was shipshape for the Saturday rush. I also wanted to catch Katie before Apollo did so I could coach her on my big fat lie.

When the doors opened at nine, it was clear that Katie was a no-show for day number four.

"Are you going, or am I?" I asked Apollo. Visions of Katie lying on the floor of her apartment—dead or dying—filled my head.

Apollo looked at the paperwork in his hands and asked if I could go. I was relieved, because I was going regardless of his decision.

Katie lived in a small apartment on the *uppe*r Upper West Side, conveniently located about halfway between Columbia University and the shop. I'd never actually been to her place, but Apollo had no problem breaking the law and giving me her address, considering the unusual and concerning circumstances.

The front door of her building was open, but the door past the mailboxes was locked. I hit the buzzer to apartment 6B. Considering she was probably lying comatose on the floor, I didn't expect to get an answer. I buzzed a second time and heard her sleepy voice over the intercom.

"Katie?"

There was brief silence on the other end and then muffled sounds of a male voice in the background.

"Alex?"

"Let me in, Katie!"

The door buzzed and I hit the stairs to climb the six flights. Was she with a guy all this time? "I'll kill her," I growled under my breath.

I reached her apartment, huffing from the six-story sprint, and rang the doorbell. A minute later, the door swung open. Constantine stood in the middle of the frame wearing nothing but a pair of half-zipped pants. He leaned back against the frame with his tousled hair and intense stare, and motioned me in.

The distinct smell of sex hit my nose as I took a step inside. "Are you kidding me?" I snapped as I stepped back into the hall.

Katie appeared behind him and wrapped her arms around his waist. She couldn't contain her smile as her face peered around his back. "Alex—"

"Don't *Alex* me. We thought you were dead!"

Through it all, Constantine kept his eyes on mine but said nothing.

"I don't believe this." I turned and marched back toward the stairs.

"Alex, wait." She trailed down the hall after me in her T-shirt and underwear and grabbed my arm as I started down the steps. "I think I love him."

I went completely still. Greer had warned me months earlier about letting a satyr in my head. Constantine and I had developed a clear understanding in that department, but Katie had no such understanding with him.

Before you know what's happening, he'll have you so enthralled you'll be permanently repulsed by the touch of any other man.

"It's not you talking," I said as I turned to look at my brainwashed friend. "He has you entranced. God, Katie! You're ruined!"

I glanced at Constantine who was leaning against the wall, listening to the entire exchange. He seemed passive about the whole thing, and I wondered if it meant anything that he'd done this to my friend. Not Katie. Not the girl who was fearless and let no man dictate her life.

He must have seen the disappointment in my face, because he stepped back inside the apartment and reappeared a minute later fully dressed.

"Katie," he called in a tone that was much too subdued for him.

Fearing he would leave, she ran back to him and shook her head. He dragged her to his chest and kissed her thoroughly, and then he vanished. He just disappeared in the middle of the hall.

"Get dressed," I said. "You're going to work."

Katie refused to speak or even look at me during the cab ride back to the shop, so I started the conversation. She needed to know what he'd done to her, and I needed to know how despite my attempts to keep Constantine away from her for this very reason, he'd managed to circumvent those efforts.

"How did this happen, Katie?"

She kept her eyes on the window as she spoke. "I told you he stopped by the shop last week. He was looking for you." Her face softened as she continued. "He has this hold on me. I can't explain it, Alex. He does things to me."

"I bet he does," I muttered. "Do you even know what he is?"

She was looking at me now, staring at me as if I'd asked the most preposterous question she'd ever heard. "He's a god, Alex."

"He's a lecherous, conniving, egotistical satyr. *That's* what he is."

"And I'm a weak, senseless dragon."

"Katie, there's something you need to know." She needed to understand why she'd never get him out of her head.

Just a kiss. That's all it takes, Greer and Leda had both warned.

Judging by the looks of her, and the fact that they'd been sequestered in that apartment for the better part of a week, I was pretty sure they'd done a lot more than kiss. God, if a kiss had that much power, *fucking* could make spaghetti out of her brains.

"I do know. He warned me."

She told me everything about the night Constantine showed up at her apartment. "He was just standing there in front of my door. We went inside and stared at each other for an hour without saying a word."

Relaying the details seemed to surprise even her. "He caged me against the wall and said, 'No going back, Katie. I'll never let you go, and you'll never want me to.' "

"And you didn't think that was a red flag?"

She just shook her head. "Lock, stock, and barrel. He owns me, and I love it."

I was distracted from the whole Constantine-Katie cluster-fuck by thoughts of my alibi. I was also perplexed by the fact that Constantine had apparently been in two places at the same time. He was with me in the park at the same time he was supposedly shacked up with Katie. How the hell did he pull that one off?

"Has he been with you the entire time—since Wednesday?"

"Yes."

He must have slipped away from her to meet me. Although I'd apparently been in the park for an entire day, I'd only seen Constantine for a total of thirty or forty minutes. That explained his rush to get out of there. It also explained his disheveled hair. And his smell. I knew there was something familiar about it—he had Katie splashed all over him.

I coached her on my story, and we agreed to back each other up. We'd corroborate each other's lie and feel like shit about it. Apollo deserved better, but the truth wasn't an option.

"Katie? Can I ask you a strange question?"

"Is there any other kind?" she snorted.

I was still missing an entire day. "Did you see me at all on Wednesday?"

TWENTY

pollo took one look at Katie and told her she should have stayed home for one more day. She was sick, all right—lovesick. Constantine hadn't just slept with her, he'd mind fucked her good and hard, and I planned to find out if he intended to rip her heart out, too.

We spent the remainder of the morning counting books. By noon, we'd finished the grueling weeklong task of recording every title in the stop. The only thing missing was a bottle of champagne to celebrate.

I vowed to never take inventory of anything ever again.

Constantine walked through the front door as I was about to head out and grab some lunch. I held my breath as he surveyed the room. He spotted me and nodded, but it wasn't me he was looking for. His eyes continued around the room, stopping on Katie as she emerged from one of the aisles.

Her gasp was audible from across the room as she looked up and saw him standing near the door. In his hand was a shiny metal box with a bright pink handle. He made a beeline across the room and met her halfway. "You need to eat. Or you'll die," he said in his usual pert voice, handing her the box.

She took the lunch box with the Batgirl decals and gazed at

it as if he'd just handed her a beautiful Birkin bag. She turned it sideways and balanced it on the palm of her left hand, opening the top with her right. Inside was a parchment-wrapped sandwich secured with a silver ribbon and a frilled cellophane toothpick speared through the center. Next to the sandwich was a shiny red apple, a package of raisins, and a single-serve box of Cheerios.

"Oh, Constantine." Her eyes raised back to his as a demure smile crept across her face. "I'll eat every bite. I promise."

They gazed at each other without a word for some time, and then he glanced at his Cartier. "I must leave. I'm late for an appointment."

Katie's smile vanished. Then she put her thumb and pinkie to the side of her head and mouthed the words *call me*.

As he was leaving, Leda walked through the door. Her tan riding pants and perfectly tailored cream shirt conjured images of what Rita Hayworth might look like if she walked through that door, fresh off a country ride with Gene Kelly.

"Con," she blurted, startled to see the man who once proclaimed his love for her, and swore that she was his one and only true mate. "What on earth are you doing here?"

"Leda." Constantine looked just as startled. I could see a slight expansion of his chest, similar to the reaction he'd elicited from Katie a few minutes earlier. His cheeks deflated as his nostrils flared slightly. And as he stiffened, he grew a couple of inches taller, betraying the impact that only Leda had on him.

"God, here we go," I muttered. Leda was that old habit Constantine never could quite shake, and I cringed at the thought of him parading that weakness in front of the entire shop. If he embarrassed Katie, I'd rip his privates off.

"It's good to see you, Leda." He took her hand as if it were a delicate bird and raised it to his lips. He kissed her pale skin and winked discreetly at Katie, reassuring her that the kiss was merely cordial. "I would love to stay and chat, but I'm afraid I'm late for an appointment."

A second later, he was gone. I was shocked by his care and consideration. Constantine had once again surprised me.

Katie was smiling to herself when I looked back at her. She stared at the shiny black lunch box with its pink trim, and I knew that something much deeper had transpired between the two of them over the course of those days holed up in her tiny apartment.

"Well—" Leda had utter confusion stamped across her face. "Alex?"

"I'll tell you about it later. Is everything okay? Is Greer okay?"

"Greer's fine. I just thought I'd stop by and see where you worked and take you to lunch."

Leda didn't do lunch. She was a good friend, but my guess was that Greer sent her.

"I'd love to have lunch, but you're going to have to tell me the real reason you're here."

It was a beautiful afternoon, and what I really wanted to do was grab a slice of pizza and sit outside. Leda, on the other hand, had different plans.

We turned down a side street that looked more residential than commercial and entered a small restaurant with no signage. If you didn't know it was there, you'd pass right by without thinking twice about the green door leading into the small room with white linen tablecloths and vintage chandeliers.

As soon as we entered, the smell of fine food hit my nose, and the noise of Manhattan was replaced by the steady hum of civilized conversation and forks meeting china. There was no takeout here. The rushed diners trying to get back to their jobs seemed to have gone to a different restaurant. Here, you took your time and enjoyed the experience, not just the food.

"Ms. Westbrook." An older gentleman dressed in a starched white shirt and black pants greeted us as we entered the room.

Leda extended her hand. "William." Her face lit up as he took it and kissed the back of her fingers. "I thought you retired."

"Ah, there's that *R* word again. I'm trying. Maybe at the end of the year."

"Well, I'll have to stop in over the holidays to say goodbye." She glanced around the crowded room. "I'm afraid we don't have a reservation."

He smiled conservatively. "I think we can manage."

Leda pointed to a table in the back corner of the room, positioned in a small nook behind a half wall. The kitchen door swung in and out about six feet to the left of it.

William's brow furrowed as the smile left his face. "Back there? Are you sure?"

"It'll be fine, really. We'd like the privacy."

"As you wish," he complied, reluctant to put a woman like Leda in a back corner next to the kitchen. abide

We followed William to the most undesirable table in the room and allowed him to seat us properly.

"Can I bring you and your guest something to drink?"

"A glass of red wine?" She looked to me for confirmation.

"Water with lemon for me, please." Wine would make going back to work for the rest of the afternoon unbearable.

"I'll send your waiter right over. It's so good to see you again, Ms. Westbrook."

In all the months I'd known Leda, I never bothered to ask her last name. Westbrook fit her. Had a proper ring to it. Smith or Jones would disappear against her vibrant personality, but Westbrook . . . that was a name that held its own.

"This is quite a place. I hope you're paying," I joked playfully. I was used to places with days of the week for names, or neon signs in the window—anything that didn't require two types of forks to consume a meal.

"Stop that, Alex. You fit in just fine here." She was doing that annoying mind reading thing that I hated.

I got right to it. "Look, I know Greer is going through one of his Alex-needs-a-babysitter phases, but—"

Her index finger went up to hush me. "First of all, Greer didn't ask me to come." She opened her napkin and spread it over her lap. "My God, Alex. What are you doing to that man? And what was Con doing at Shakespeare's Den . . . or Shop . . . or whatever?"

"Well, apparently Constantine is sleeping with Katie."

"Really?" she replied as she rearranged her fork and knife. "I didn't think he cared for reptiles."

"You're not jealous, are you?"

"Just feeling the sting of no longer being worshipped. I guess it had to happen eventually. At least it wasn't for a waitress or some mundane debutante." She flexed a forced smile. "A *dragon*. Now that's competition."

"Oh, come on, Leda. You never wanted him anyway."

"True, but it's nice to know you're on someone's mind." She leaned into the table on folded arms. "Now, what's going on with Greer?"

"I have no idea what you're talking about. Can you be a little less cryptic?"

Our waiter approached the table and handed us a pair of menus. "Good afternoon, ladies. My name is Peter and I'll be serving you today."

Peter was a tall brunette with blue eyes and a beautiful set of pouty lips. I imagined he wasn't a career waiter but a fledgling actor or model supplementing his income while he waited for his big break.

He looked at me first, and then turned his chiseled jaw

toward Leda who was looking at him like *he* was on the menu. His eyes heated as the moment turned into a long stretch of innuendo. It took the sound of my chair shifting to break up our awkward threesome.

Leda pulled her eyes from the young man and plucked the menu from my hand. She handed them both back to the distracted waiter and ordered two grilled salmon salads, exactly what I would have chosen.

"I think you just ruined him for the rest of the day," I pointed out.

"Actually, I think I just *made* his day," she countered. "We shall see."

"A little young for you, isn't he?"

Her head cocked slightly as she fired back. "That's a bit of a double standard, don't you think? What, he's around your age? And I'm around Greer's age?"

"Yes, but Greer and I aren't doing . . . *that*."

"Don't you dare judge me, Alex. And don't treat me like I'm stupid."

I threw my hands up in surrender. "You're right. I apologize."

"Speaking of Greer," she steered the conversation back, "that man has been walking around all week like he's been medicated. The man can't remember his own name half the time. I've never seen him so distracted and subdued."

Subdued was not a word I'd ever use to describe Greer, and he was the most focused person I'd ever met. But the look on her face confirmed her concern. Leda was the type who never worried. You could tell her she had two weeks to live, and I doubt you'd get more than a sly smile and some comment about living it up for the next fourteen days.

"He was fine when I left him last night." Rhom had escorted me home the night before, showing up seconds after Daemon disappeared. When we got to the house, Greer was in the library and barely acknowledged us over the documents he was reviewing at his desk. He was already gone when I came down for breakfast.

"And nothing unusual happened this week between you two?"

That was a silly question. Unusual was the norm. She should have asked if anything *normal* happened this week. Now that would throw up some red flags.

She muttered something under her breath before reaching for her compact to apply more lipstick to her already perfectly painted lips. "There's something you need to know," she said as she examined her reflection in the small mirror.

Those words usually preceded something I *didn't* want to know. Why is it that people always put the fear of God in you before delivering bad news, like the preamble will somehow make the news a little less bitter?

"God, now what?"

She snapped the compact shut and looked back at me. "There's something you need to know about us. Well, about our men."

By *us,* I assumed she meant *her* people—*Greer's* people.

"What? That they're alphas with control issues? I'm well aware of that, Leda."

"This is serious, Alex." She reached across the table and covered my hand with hers. "Now, I'd like you to keep an open mind and hear me out before going all panicky on me. Sometimes the boys get a little attached to their women."

"And this is news?"

Anyone with eyes knew that Greer had a bad habit of smothering me like I was some breakable vase. Had I been a weaker person I wouldn't have a job, or friends, or the freedom to come and go as I pleased. So yes, I was well aware of his attachment issues.

"Maybe *attached* isn't the right word." She thought about it for a minute and came up with a more fitting description. "They imprint," she stated matter-of-factly. "For . . . ever. Well, in most cases."

"Leda, why are we having this conversation?"

Peter returned with a basket of warm bread. He placed it in the middle of the table and gave Leda another one of those looks before retreating back through the kitchen door. I stuffed a piece into my dry mouth. Maybe if I chewed hard enough I could appease the sick feeling welling up from my gut.

"Because I know that look, Alex. I've seen it a thousand times, and it's been walking around the club for the past few days."

My chest hurt from the sharp pain stabbing me behind my ribcage, and I could hear what sounded like tiny feet crunching through snow as the blood raced back and forth in my ears. I reached for another piece of bread with a shaky hand, but I knew it would never make it into my mouth because I couldn't even swallow the piece that was already in there.

"Alex? Are you okay?"

"I don't understand what you're saying, Leda."

"I'm saying that I think Greer has imprinted on you."

Any normal woman would feel like she'd just won the lottery. Except for his controlling, stubborn demeanor, he was perfect. Gorgeous, rich, smart: what else could a girl possibly ask for? That's the problem—I'm not a normal girl.

A few months ago I would have entertained the thought. But the closer I got to Greer, the more I realized I wasn't his girl. We were in different leagues, and I preferred to stay where I wouldn't have my heart ripped out.

"Did you hear what I said, Alex?"

I envisioned a duckling following a human who'd raised it from a hatchling. "People don't imprint, Leda."

"You're right, Alex. *People* don't."

It was a stark reminder that I'd been straddling two worlds.

Somehow I always thought I'd wake up one day and it would be over. I'd be in my own bed, back in my shitty mundane world, with an equally shitty job and nothing to look forward to. Never once did I think this fantasy was permanent, and I'd end up with my own happy ending.

"It's different for us. We imprint sexually."

"What the hell does that mean?" I squealed, bringing all eyes in the room to our table.

"Calm down, Alex. Take a breath and relax." She took a breath of her own and continued to explain the preposterous. "Think of it as . . . mating."

Oh, well, that made it *much* better. We'd gone from imprinting sexually to mating, all in the span of five minutes.

"There's only one way for that to happen, Alex. Imprinting is triggered by copulation." She looked at me with a modest smile as the clinical description left her mouth. "You know how much I hate sticking my nose in other people's business, but in this case I have to ask. There's just too much at stake, and I need to know where Greer's head is at."

I swallowed the lump of bread in my mouth and waited for the punchline.

"Don't be shy, Alex. Every one of those boys will end up going through it at some point. If it isn't reciprocated, they may even go through it more than once. It's nothing to be ashamed of. It's as natural as breathing."

Natural if you're a bird or an elephant.

"Leda, Greer and I haven't done *that*." I shook my head. "I swear." There was an awkward encounter a few months earlier, the night I found out Ava was still alive. Greer and I came about as close as two people could to consummating our relationship, but we stopped before it went too far. *If we cross that line, the choice to stay or go will no longer be yours to make.* That's what he said to me that night before he walked out the door and disappeared for a week.

"What makes you think it's me? Greer's a real catch. I'm sure he has women crawling all over him at the club. Ever think about that?"

The cocky smile on her face was beginning to annoy me. "We're not blind, Alex. It's going to takes a pretty special female to hook Greer Sinclair. Even I couldn't trigger him."

"Maybe it's like the Immaculate Conception," I offered weakly. "Without the baby."

Her smile faded. I was seeing a hint of the Leda who only came out when provoked, the scary Leda who could send thoughts and images through your mind that should never be seen.

"Look, Alex, I really don't care who you're fucking. I just need to know if it's Greer."

I shook my head as the emotions began to swell behind my eyes. Something was happening to me, and I had no idea what it was or how to manage it. I'd already lost an entire day, gone on a strange vision quest where I was apparently a predator, and now the woman I thought was my friend was looking at me like she wanted to torture a lie out of me.

"Oh, honey." She leaned in and touched my arm. "You're telling me the truth, aren't you?"

I thought it best to nod since words would probably turn me into a sobbing mess.

"Are you sure you haven't forgotten something?"

"Are you kidding me? You think I could forget about sleeping with someone . . . while I'm sober? With *Greer*?"

"I don't know, Alex. There would be signs, though. Has he been overly attentive toward you? Is he trying to shove food in your mouth all the time? Or take care of you in other smothering ways? Jealously toward other men?"

I thought about the enormous lunch I came home to yesterday. It was a little over the top, but Sophia seemed more upset than he was when I refused to eat it. And as far as being protective, well, that was normal for Greer. It was a constant battle between us.

I shook my head. "No. Nothing out of the ordinary."

She leaned back in her chair and folded her arms. "I guess I need to have a conversation with Mr. Sinclair."

TWENTY-ONE

Leda ate her lunch while I pushed chunks of king salmon around my plate. It looked appealing enough, but the conversation had dulled my usually insatiable appetite.

We said our goodbyes to William and left the restaurant, Leda heading back to wherever it was she spent her days, while I made my way back to work. Seeing how I'd already come close to losing my job, I had no choice but to go back to Shakespeare's Library and finish out the day.

Katie was on the floor huddled over a pile of books with her back to me. She was wearing a see-through blouse over a tank top. As she breathed, her tattoo seemed to come alive like a stirring animal shifting in its sleep. It looked alive because it was alive. I'd seen it with my own two eyes morph into a formidable creature, and then recede back into a canvas of black ink with a girl under it.

"Are you going to ask or just stare?" She continued sorting without turning around.

"Ask what?"

She stood up and dropped a stack of books on the library table. "If I'm planning to buy a box of razor blades on my way home from work."

"Don't be absurd," I scoffed. "There's a perfectly good bridge across town."

We stared at each other in consideration of whether the exchange was humorous or tragic, and then we both began to laugh uncontrollably. Katie snorted while I nearly cried. We let the laughter run its course, and then we both sat on the floor and finished sorting through the books.

"I just don't want you to get hurt."

She absently thumbed the edge of the book in her hand, pinning me with her unreal blue eyes. "I'm a fucking dragon, Alex. We have pretty thick skin."

"And if he walks away but refuses to release you? Then what?"

"He wouldn't do that to me."

I said nothing as the delusion fortified behind her eyes. The delusion that after a grand total of four days, the two of them had developed a bond that included diplomacy upon breakup.

"He wouldn't," she repeated with a resolute shake of her head.

I let it go and decide to take it up with the man himself. Constantine wasn't your average guy, but Katie wasn't exactly average either. Perhaps his skills weren't as effective on her dragon, and she'd come out of this unscathed.

We heard something fall from the shelf a couple of aisles down. When we got there, Erica was on the floor with the stepladder lying sideways next to her.

"Are you okay?" I asked, helping her off the floor.

Erica looked at the two of us as if she'd just committed a cardinal sin, a flush of red spreading across her face from embarrassment. "I'm such a *klutz*."

"No, you're just a girl who fell off a lad—"

Katie looked at me as my face went still. "Alex? What's wrong?"

I inhaled through my nose and waited for the distinct scent to return. "Can you smell that?"

Katie sniffed the air. "Incense?"

"Yeah, I thought it was an interesting cologne when I smelled him," Erica added.

"Him?" I practically pressed the poor girl against the opposite shelf. "Who's *him*?"

"The guy who came in this afternoon. Said he was just looking." A demure smile crept across her face. "He was good-looking."

"Sandalwood . . . or cedar." Katie sniffed the air again. "Yep, that's what it smells like."

"Did he tell you his name?"

Erica shook her head as the smile vanished from her face. "Was I supposed to ask?"

"Of course not," Katie sniped. "Alex, give the girl some space."

"Sorry." I stepped back and gave Erica some breathing room. "What did he look like?"

Her smile returned. "Like I said, he was good-looking. *Hot.* Tall with brown hair and eyes. There was something really confident about him."

"Did he buy anything?"

She shook her head. "I kind of got the impression he was looking for someone. He kept walking around the room and looking down each aisle."

"Then what?"

"He left. I got busy with another customer. When I looked back up, he was gone."

Katie's brow went up. "You know this guy, Alex?"

The morning Lumen came into the shop, I told Katie about the attack in Central Park, minus the part about him being a demented minion of an organized group of rapists who stole children. I figured those details were a little too much, too soon. But that was before I knew her secret. Erica—on the other hand—would not be privy to any of it.

"I think he's a guy who's been stalking me."

Erica's eyes widened. "Should we call the police?"

"No. He seems harmless. Just creeps me out a little bit."

Katie eyed me suspiciously. "I told you about him," I reminded her. "He's the guy from the park."

It took her a minute, but she eventually connected the dots. Her eyes widened, too. "Jesus, Alex. Maybe we should call the cops."

"You met him in the park?" Erica's face brightened with some romantic notion.

"Something like that." I shook my head. "I don't want to talk about it anymore."

Katie reluctantly dropped the subject and we spent the next few hours staring at the clock. She couldn't wait to get home to see Constantine, while I prepared to face the man who may have imprinted on me like a newly hatched duckling.

I walked out the door at five o'clock. Greer rarely sent an escort on my early days, but today Rhom was waiting for me at the curb.

"I'd say it's nice to see you, Rhom, but every time you show up unexpectedly I get bad news."

"Such a pessimist, Alex." He tucked his copy of the *New York Post* under his arm and lifted off the side of the building. "Greer's just a little jumpy today. He's worried about you. Is that so hard to believe?"

"Fine. Thanks for the backup."

We took our time walking home. The weather was near perfect, and Rhom was wearing a pair of shades to block the late afternoon sun. I lifted them from his face to check his eyes. After my encounter with his imposter, I had a feeling I'd be doing that every time he wore them.

"What's this all about?" he questioned as I lowered them back to the bridge of his nose.

I told him about his imposter, and I thought I saw steam piping from his ears like some cartoon character.

"I'll rip the bastard in half *when* I find him," he promised.

"It's okay, Rhom. I chased the bad man away. You'll just have to get used to me doing that for a while."

"I'm still going to track him down and make him regret it."

If I'd had Greer or Thomas in my head at the time, it would have been one of them the imposter embodied, and their homicidal reaction would be the same.

"Thanks, Rhom. I feel much safer now."

"No problem."

"Is Greer at the house?"

"Yeah. He's at the house, Alex." His head bobbed up and down like it usually did when his softer side came out. "But you got nothing to worry about. The boss is right as rain today."

It was an odd comment, like he was delivering me somewhere unpleasant, but for my own good. I felt like a five-year-old getting dropped off for my first day at kindergarten, and Rhom would be waiting at the end of the day with a lollipop and a hug when it was over.

When we got to the foot of the steps, my stomach felt like a hornet's nest. The closer I got to Greer, the bigger the swarm grew, until my hand shook on the stair rail.

"Are you okay, Alex?" His voice was sweet now. "You got nothing to fear up there." He motioned toward the front door with a flick of his head as a grin spread across his face.

"Aren't you coming in?" I asked when he stopped at the foot of the stairs.

"I'll be up in a minute. I'll let you and the boss have a little privacy first." His grin widened, and I realized he knew. They all did. Every last one of Greer's people must have noticed the change that Leda had seen.

I walked up the steps feeling like some sacrificial lamb being offered up to a hungry lion. The smell of tomatoes and basil filled the foyer as I walked inside. *Sophia*. I was thankful to have her there as a buffer.

The sound of water running, and the clanking of metal on metal, melded with the quiet singing coming from the kitchen. I peeked inside and watched Sophia battle with a head of garlic on the cutting board. Her palm came down hard on the bulb, and it split into a dozen small cloves.

Something soft brushed my legs, distracting me from the lesson in garlic execution. Bear wound his small body around my ankles and then jumped. He was too little to make it past my thighs, so I caught him in mid-flight and nuzzled him against my chest as he purred like a miniature motorboat.

"You're growing too fast." I was surprised at how big he'd gotten in just a week. "Stop doing that."

I put him back down and looked at Sophia who was watching me now. She grabbed a large knife from the magnetic strip on the wall and whacked one of the cloves, sending the husky skin flying across the kitchen. "You going to be nice to Mr. Sinclair today?"

"Sophia!"

"Don't you *Sophia* me, Miss Alex." She pointed the tip of the knife in my direction. "That man put a beautiful roof over your head and feeds you. A lot of women come through this house, and he don't do that for any of them." She nodded firmly before continuing her assault on the garlic.

"Alex." Greer was standing behind me when I turned. He was still wearing his suit, so I assumed he'd gotten home just before me. "Are you staying for dinner?"

"Of course. Why wouldn't I be?"

I turned to Rhom, who had come inside and was sitting in the living room. "Rhom, would you like to join us? I'm sure Sophia is making enough to feed a small army."

He looked to Greer for approval. Sophia's Italian food was

a religious experience, and like most men, Rhom never refused an offer for good grub.

"He'll be staying," Greer announced. "We're having a little dinner party tonight."

By seven thirty, the house was buzzing with people, mediating the awkward tension between Greer and me. Thomas and Loden arrived first, and Leda showed up a few minutes later.

Greer described the impromptu gathering as a "working dinner" and reminded everyone that we still had a monster of a job to do in finding the vessel. Even Morgan—the faerie wannabe—walked through the door. I hadn't seen her in months since she worked so hard to assert her claim on Greer, and I'd hoped to never see her again.

At eight o'clock sharp the doorbell rang. I looked at Greer who seemed unsurprised by the sound.

"Now that our final guest has arrived, we can eat." He opened the door and Dr. David Oxford stood on the other side.

"I wasn't sure what we were having, so I gambled on a red." Oxford handed Greer a bottle of Bordeaux and walked into the room.

"Dr. Oxford!" I was surprised and a little wary to see him standing in front of me. His hair had been trimmed since we'd met, but the wiry curls jetting from his ears remained untamed. "What brings you to the city?"

Greer headed for the dining room before the doctor could answer. "Let's eat, folks," he announced as he led the way. He waited for his guests to be seated, and then took his place at the table, watching me unabashedly as I squirmed under his intense stare.

Sophia entered the room with a large roasting pan and

placed it in the middle of the table. "Mangia! Mangia!" she beamed with a look of pride stamped over her face. The room erupted in celebratory praise for the beautiful rows of eggplant and pasta stuffed with cheese and topped with fresh tomatoes and basil.

Thomas stood and grabbed her around the waist, placing his usual flirty kiss on her cheek as she swatted him away.

Greer motioned for my plate, piling it with more food than I could possibly eat. Then he proceeded to serve the rest of his guests before serving himself.

Thomas was the first to ask. "So, boss. I'm assuming there's a motive behind the invite."

Greer finished chewing the bite of food in his mouth, then chased it with a sip of wine. "Dr. Oxford, would you like to tell everyone why you're here?"

All eyes turned to David Oxford. A flush of pink crawled across his face as he cleared his throat, and it dawned on me that the doctor was shy. Scientists were often introverts, and he was obviously caught off guard when Greer asked him to lead the discussion.

"Well, as I explained to Mr. Sinclair, I received an interesting call yesterday afternoon." He took another bite of pasta and held his finger up while he quickly chewed and swallowed it. "Apparently, Ms. Falcone has become privy to some information and needs my help."

"What kind of help?" I asked warily.

"She claims to have a lead on the approximate location of the vessel. The problem is she can't see it. She needs the lenses I've been working on."

"I guess you never sent that letter. The one where you clearly told her to keep her money."

"Oh, I sent it all right. I can thank you for that, Ms. Kelley. It was you who motivated me to go to the market and buy stamps the next day."

Greer leaned into the table to focus the conversation before the doctor veered off on a tangent. "Tell me exactly what Isabetta said."

"Yes, of course. She said, 'Dr. Oxford. This is Isabetta Falcone.' And I said 'I know who you are because your name is showing up on my phone.' You see, I have her entered in my phone contacts and—"

"Maybe you should just summarize what was discussed," Greer interjected.

"The bottom line is that Ms. Falcone claims to know where the vessel is, and she wants me to meet her tomorrow night to see if we can locate it with the lenses."

"You didn't tell her they're in your eyes, did you?" I asked with concern.

"What the hell?" Thomas, who was sitting next to Oxford, took the man's chin and looked into his eyes. "No shit." He shook his head in disbelief. "You're a smart motherfucker."

Oxford gave Thomas a puzzled look. "Is that a compliment?"

"I assume you told her you've changed your mind about the offer and agreed to meet her?" Greer asked.

Oxford went mute as he looked around the room at the seven faces staring back at him. Even Sophia stood in the doorway hanging on his words.

"Dr. Oxford? What did you tell her?" Greer asked again.

I sensed the panic rolling over the doctor's face as he contemplated his answer. "There's no right or wrong answer, David," I coaxed, hoping the informal use of his first name would help put him at ease. "We can fix this."

He took a deep sip of wine. "I asked her where and what time."

The entire table—except for me—took a collective sigh of relief as the million-dollar question was answered. A meeting with Isabetta Falcone meant a meeting with Alasdair Templeton.

Vessel or not, I feared that letting him near me again was the gateway to my deportation to the Emerald Isle.

Greer was studying me when I looked at him. He knew what was going through my head, and it must have been the catalyst for his next words.

"Alex, you're not going. We can always bring the mountain to Mohammed, if necessary."

I shook my head. "No. I'm going." It was a thoughtful gesture, but who were we kidding? Aside from David Oxford, I was the one person who needed to be there if the vessel was found. "If Templeton is there—"

"He won't be. Templeton is an asshole, but he's brilliant. He knows I'll knock his fucking house down if he pushes me. As long as he plays nice, his kingdom is safe inside that box."

He looked at Dr. Oxford again. "Continue, please."

"Nine o'clock. Battery Park." Dr. Oxford whipped out a pair of black glasses with a thick, awkward frame. "These will have to serve as props. They're 3D, so if Ms. Falcone insists on seeing for herself, she'll at least get a little play on color—or a slight headache."

Rhom stood up and towered over the table. "Am I the only one here who smells a load of shit? Seems too damn convenient that Isabetta just picked up the phone and laid the prophecy right in our hands." He looked at me, and then slowly panned over to Greer. "With all due respect, boss, I think your judgment is a little clouded right now."

You could hear a feather hit the floor. Loden and Thomas averted their eyes to their plates while Morgan—always the instigator—let a short laugh escape her throat. Leda was the only one with the balls to put the boys in their places.

"All right, you two." She glanced at Greer. "You and I are going to have a chat later." Her eyes went to Rhom next. "And you, a little discretion, please."

"Look," Rhom countered, "all I'm saying is we have no

proof if this is legit. Since when did we stop vetting situations that could get us killed?"

"Since the situation involves the vessel!" Greer shot back.

Rhom backed down and took his seat.

The room went quiet again, and everyone turned to the doctor who was sitting catatonic in his chair. I imagined he was used to faculty socials and the company of fellow scientists, so the testosterone flooding the room must have sent the fear of God through him.

"My apologies, Dr. Oxford." Leda put her hand on his arm to reassure him that a brawl wasn't imminent. "I think these boys need a good dose of manners. But don't you worry about them. I think the tantrum has passed."

"I was out of line, boss. You can kick my ass later."

Greer ran his hand through his hair as he began pacing the dining room. "I think we're all a little wired." He reached inside the sideboard cabinet and pulled out a bottle of scotch. "Anyone else need a drink?"

We resumed our dinner and civilly discussed Rhom's concerns about the validity of the lead. If Isabetta's motives were to get her hands on the fictitious glasses she thought Oxford was working on, Greer's posse would be there for backup. The pros and cons were weighed, and the pros won.

A hand slipped around my shoulder. Loden was a natural flirt, and tonight was no different than any other. He winked at me with his brilliant sky-blue eyes and grinned. "Don't you worry, love. I've got you tomorrow night."

I bumped him with my shoulder, reciprocating with the harmless flirting. "I think I might have to keep *you* safe," I grinned back.

We both laughed, and a second later the room shook. Greer stood up and nearly took the table with him. His chest heaved as he leaned across it and gave Loden a warning look that would have given an ordinary man a reason to piss his pants.

Greer turned his eyes on me for a few uncomfortable seconds, and then he glared back at Loden. The message was clear—*hands off.*

TWENTY-TWO

Greer's actions the night before added weight to Leda's suspicions. No matter how innocent my bantering with Loden had been, we were still flirting, and Greer's instinct to cockblock any male that came within ten feet of me, with even the slightest amorous intent, had come out like a lion.

It was times like these that I missed my mother the most. Maeve Kelley would have known how to handle such situations. Maeve Kelley would know what to do with a man who confused partnership with ownership.

I decided to seek out the next best thing.

The front door of Den of Oddities and Antiquities was different. The color had gone from a deep blue to a warm red. I had to check the name on the window to make sure I hadn't walked up the wrong flight of steps.

I went for the handle, but the door opened before I reached it. Ava stood on the other side and beckoned me in. "I was wondering when you'd show up."

"You painted the door."

"Yes. Next spring it will be painted again. A door's color symbolizes what's behind it. Historically, a red door signaled to weary travelers that they were welcome—and safe. Anyone who walks through that door is safe, Alex. Remember that."

Melanie was rummaging through a cardboard box on the counter. "Good morning, Alex. Nice to see you again." She pulled her hand out of the box and opened it. The flat object resting on her palm began to move. It looked like a piece of paper folded several times over, freed to unfold and return to its original shape. Or one of those magic sponges that expanded when you added water. It flew into the air and zoomed around the two-story room. As it buzzed past my head, it sounded like the flapping wings of a hummingbird or the propeller of a toy helicopter.

My eyes followed it around the room. "What is that?"

Melanie snapped her fingers three times and the object stopped in mid-flight near the ceiling of the second story. It spiraled toward the floor but slowed as it caught the air and fluttered like a leaf riding a breeze.

"It's a pseudo wren," Ava said.

Melanie retrieved it and held up the flat, inanimate cutout. I examined it, looking for some sort of hidden motor. But it was just a thin piece of paper in the silhouette of a bird. "How——"

The two of them laughed softly as the illusion did its magic on me. "It's a trick, isn't it?"

Melanie snapped her fingers and the paper began to move again.

"*Melanie,*" Ava scolded gently.

She stopped short of a third snap, and the paper died back down to what it was—a lifeless piece of pulp.

Ave wrapped her arm around my shoulder and steered me to the sofa in the reading nook. It was the same spot where we'd found the missing amulet stuffed inside the big book of magic.

"So, what's got these shoulders of yours tensed so tight? Tell me what's bothering you. And don't lie, because I'll know."

"Why do you think something is bothering me?"

She smiled in that way people did when they knew your motives better than you knew them yourself. Ava raised me for three years after my mother died, and even before then I'd seen her every day for the first five years of my life. She was the next best thing to my mother.

"Would you like something to drink? I just made a pot of gyokuro tea. Expensive as hell, but damn is it good."

"That sounds great."

She returned with the pot and poured us both a cup. "Okay. Out with it. What's got you so wound up?"

"Ava, what do you know about imprinting?"

She considered the question for a moment. "You mean like an animal imprinting on its parents?"

"No. Like mating."

Her eyelids dropped as her brow and mouth flattened. "Oh, *that* kind. Can be a real nuisance if you're not receptive to the attention." She took a sip of tea and froze. Then she looked at me and waited for me to confirm the question written all over her face.

"Leda thinks Greer has imprinted on me."

She took her time processing what I'd just said, and then she smiled and cupped my cheek in her right hand. "Maeve would be very happy for you."

"What?" My tea went flying as I jerked back. "I didn't come here for your blessing, Ava. I need to wrap my head around it, and I was hoping you could shed some unbiased light on how this works. God, Ava. Greer and I fight all the time. I don't know how he can even stand me."

She laughed softly and sighed before sinking into the cushion. "My sweet, naive child. Do you have any idea how special you are?" The smile disappeared from her face as her eyes scrunched together. "Wait . . . imprinting is triggered by—"

"Yeah, yeah, yeah. Leda already told me. See, that's the problem. We haven't done *that*."

"Well, I'm fairly certain there is no other way."

She got up from the sofa and started rifling through the shop's private bookshelf, the one with the books on dragons and who knows what else.

She found the one she was looking for and flipped through its pages. "It's right here."

I got up and went to see for myself. I looked over her shoulder at the book titled *Rituals of the Gods*. "What does this book have to do with Greer?"

Ava looked at me oddly. "What do you mean? *This* is their Bible."

"Their Bible?"

"Technically, yes."

Ava took one look at my face and moved into action. "Alex? Sit down!" She grabbed me around the waist. "Melanie!" The two of them managed to get me to the sofa before I fainted. "Alex, what on earth just happened?"

I was speechless. I knew Greer was different, but I never knew *how* different. I opened my mouth to speak, but all that came out was a garble of words even I couldn't make out. I guess it shouldn't have been that much of a surprise.

Ava grabbed the book and dropped it on the coffee table. "Show me, Alex. What scared you like that?"

I pointed to the title of the book in the top margin of the page. Ava followed my finger, and after a brief moment of confusion, her eyes went wide. "You mean you didn't know?"

I shook my head. "Not exactly."

"Well, what did you think he was?"

"Oh, I don't know . . . maybe your garden variety immortal. *Hell*, Ava, not a freaking god!"

"Technically, he's a demigod. They all are—Leda, Thomas, Loden, Rhom. And that cat who calls herself Morgan."

Her concerned expression was replaced by a grin. "So, how does it feel to be worshipped by a god?"

"Terrifying."

"Well, if it's true and you haven't been intimate with him, I guess we need to figure out how you did it."

We decided to try a little free-form regression. Ava would get me to a state where my mind could wander and address whatever my soul deemed most important. If bonding with a demigod wasn't at the top of that list, then what was?

Ava opened two bags of loose herbs and released the smell through the small kitchen at the back of the shop. It was the smell of rosemary mixed with something pungent and sharp. The scent triggered an image of my mother climbing the two-story ladder, searching the hundreds of drawers that lined the wall for the ingredients of whatever concoction she was cooking up.

"Rosemary will help with your memory once the agrimony has cleared the blockage." She mixed the two bags into a pot on the stove and let the water be its own spoon as the slurry began to swirl.

I looked closer at the sludge I was expected to drink. "What's that nasty smell?"

"It's best you don't know," she smirked.

She saw the growing anxiety on my face and consoled me. "You trust me, don't you? Because if you don't, this is all for nothing. Trust is the most important ingredient in any psyche working."

My mother trusted Ava with her most important possession—me. And for that reason alone, there was no one I trusted more.

I nodded and sat at the table to wait for the soul-searching experiment to begin. At best, I'd find some answers to how I'd managed to manipulate a god into thinking I was his chosen one; at worst, I'd have to suffer swallowing a vile concoction and deal with the aftereffects of indigestion.

Ava handed me a cup of warm liquid. "Now, I need you to take this down quickly. The whole cup."

I did as she said. I drank the liquid faster than my taste buds could react. "Oh, that's *disgusting*," I managed between gags.

"Eat this. It will help."

The peppermint candy masked the horrible aftertaste of the potion.

"Better?"

"Much." I leaned back in the chair as the light dimmed and my head began to spin. The room was becoming a faint backdrop to the tunnel I was suddenly walking down. At the end, I could see the light getting brighter again.

A voice was calling to me in the distance, and I recognized it as Ava's. She was telling me to follow the path and let her know when I reached the end.

"Keep walking, Alex. Don't you even think about that monster at the other end of the tunnel." The voice wasn't Ava's anymore—it was mine. It wasn't the first time I'd run up against my alter ego, and I knew better than to argue with myself.

I kept moving, but the sphere of light moved in the same direction, staying the same dime-sized mirage in the distance. It was like I was on a treadmill, or the light was a carrot dangling over my head.

As I grew frustrated and questioned the useless experiment, I was suddenly thrown headfirst into it. I fell through billowing fans of evergreen fronds that bent deeply as I tumbled toward the ground. They snapped back up toward the sky and swallowed the glimpse of light from the hole I'd fallen through. The limbs slowed me down, and a thick layer of leaves and moss cushioned my fall.

I sat up and looked at the forest, the one I knew like the back of my hand, the one place where I held the power. He couldn't outrun me here.

My legs extended in front of me like two dirty sticks, covered with scratches from briars, and bruises from colliding with anything that got in my way. I was too small to fight, but I could run.

Blood began to flow in the center of my palm as I watched my skin slice open. An image of Ava filled my head. She took my hand in her own bloodstained palm as her soul seemed to enter mine. A million lights exploded like a sparkler in my chest, and for an instant, I felt as if the entire universe had filled me.

"Show me," she said.

I scanned the tree line, marveling as a blue filter covered the green canopy and every leaf and blade of grass as far as I could see. The forest had become an aquamarine sea.

Something was moving toward me from the edge of the trees, crushing sticks and pinecones on the forest floor. My head snapped in the direction of the sound, but I knew what was coming. I knew those boots as if I'd been running from them just a moment ago.

A figure appeared at the edge of the trees, his white shirt smeared with the blood of chickens, and his rubber boots covered with their shit. I stood up to face him. He reeked of death and cruelty, and I could still smell the sickening fear that rose from my gut every day of that summer.

He stepped from the trees and waited for me to run, because that's what made it fun for him. He was a predator. He took pleasure in hunting children who had already lost everything in their short little lives.

But on that day, I didn't run.

Ava's invisible hand squeezed harder as he moved toward me. He sneered with his tobacco-stained teeth and his cracked lips, and the smell of whiskey mixed with blood and dirt hit my nose.

His hand reached out as he took a step closer, and then he walked right through me.

A bird distracted me, flapping its noisy wings and calling out from the trees. When I looked behind me, I saw a young girl with flame-red hair lying on the ground. She wiped the blood from the cut on her knee as she climbed back to her feet. The farmer stood paralyzed as the blue light coming from her eyes held him in place like a moth pinned to a board.

"I can't," I whispered.

You have to see. It was Ava's voice coming from inside of me.

The bird kept flapping its noisy wings and interjecting its presence with a throaty call. The deep vibrato of the *kraa kraa* grew louder as more birds filled the upper canopy. I looked up and saw their black feathers protruding through the dense fronds of hemlock and pine. One by one they appeared, and within a minute the trees were more black than green.

The girl screamed as the light coming from her eyes grew into a blowtorch of deadly blue fire.

A handful of birds descended from the trees, diving toward the ground, smashing into the farmer with the force of downed fighter planes. Their wings cut through his skin like knives and filled the air with bright ribbons of blood. A dozen birds became hundreds. They tore at his clothes and skin with their curved beaks, pulling the flesh from his bones as they ate him.

He never screamed, not once, the only sound coming from the rapid flapping of wings.

I stumbled backward when the flock took up the surrounding space and grew into a giant ball of red and black feathers. The farmer's body began to disappear as they consumed it. The commotion of wings compressed into a tight sphere that dwindled until the remaining round mass of feathers unfolded into a single black bird.

My eyes closed. When they reopened, I was on the floor with my head in Ava's lap. Her hand was still wrapped around mine. She let go, and the bright blood between our palms gave off the smell of dirt and copper.

Ava got up to wash the blood from her hand. She returned with a basin of water and a couple of towels. It appeared we both needed bandaging from the deep cuts.

"I'm sorry if that hurt," she said. "I had to do it fast so you wouldn't stop me. You'd never let me draw your blood if you saw it coming."

"I bet it was more painful for you." I examined the deep cut on her palm. "It can't be easy slicing your own hand open like that."

Her eyes flashed wide as she nodded in agreement.

The whole vision—or whatever it was—flashed through my head again, and the tears welled up like a dam behind my eyes.

"Go ahead, sweetheart. Let it all out."

I crumbled under the weight of it and cried like a baby. "I thought it was me."

"Thought what was you?"

"All this time, I thought I killed him." I wiped my face dry and sat up on the floor. "For years, I've had these sick visions about it. I remember him coming after me, and then the birds were in the trees and . . . " I looked at Ava and shook my head. "I thought there'd be fire. I remember a fire."

Ava, who'd held it together until this point, wrapped her arm around me and began to sob into my shoulder. "My poor baby. I didn't know." She heaved against me a few more times and then stopped and pulled back to look at me with her wet eyes. "*This* was what happened, Alex. It was the power of the coven that killed him. Most likely a manifestation of it. The mind sees what it needs to see to protect it. All those other memories were just your mind's way of coping with that monster."

I was relieved to finally know what really happened all those years ago, and to know that I wasn't some murderous child.

"It's a good thing he's dead, Alex. Because if he wasn't, I'd buy a plane ticket today and kill him myself."

"I need something to drink, Ava."

"Would you like some more tea?"

I sighed. "Nothing would make me happier right now than a shot of single malt."

"I think we can manage that. We have a Scot in the house, after all."

Ava raided Patrick's stash and slid down the wall with two glasses of the good stuff. We sat on the floor with our backs against the wall and discussed what we had and hadn't learned from the working.

"Weren't you afraid to cut me?"

"Not really," she shrugged. "I knew my blood would neutralize that killer quality you apparently possess. I have some pretty powerful stuff running through my veins, too, you know."

"How did you do that? How did you talk to me . . . like you were in my head?"

"Through the blood, of course. You were my guide. The mixing of our blood made your eyes, my eyes. I felt the whole thing right alongside you." She shook her head. "That man was pure evil. I could feel it. I hate to say this about another human being, but he deserved to die, and no one would have blamed you if you'd done it yourself."

The wound was already starting to heal when I took Ava's hand and pulled her bandage back.

"Your blood is healing me," she observed. "I'm sure yours is almost gone by now."

There was still a very big unanswered question that I asked next with trepidation because I wasn't up for any more psyche workings. "We did this whole thing to find out how I triggered Greer's *mating* instincts."

Mating. Stupid damn word. Every time it came up, I pictured a dog in heat.

"Yes. That's still a mystery. I guess your mind had more important things to unblock and resolve, don't you think, darling?"

She polished off her drink. "That was a pretty powerful potion, obviously. The herbs will stay with you for days and could easily kick in again. In fact, I know they will. Other things will surface, Alex, and I don't like the idea of leaving you alone when they do."

"Don't worry. I'll be with Greer."

"That's what I'm afraid of."

TWENTY-THREE

When I left Den of Oddities and Antiquities, my brain was spinning from all the things I'd learned in the span of a couple of hours. Not only did I now know what Greer was, I also knew what *I* wasn't.

To calm the turbulent sea inside my head, I decided to forgo the train and walk the distance from Greenwich Village to the Upper West Side. Seventy plus blocks was ambitious, but there were dozens of subway entrances along the way if my feet gave out.

Seven hours from now, Dr. Oxford was scheduled to meet Isabetta Falcone at Battery Park. The plan was for Greer and me to go with him. It didn't take a brain surgeon to figure out that Isabetta was banking on Oxford bringing us along. What she wasn't banking on was the others tagging along, too.

I was about to cross Thirty-Fourth Street when I heard his voice behind me. "Would it make you feel better if I brought you a lunch box, too?"

"A little far south for you, isn't it?"

Constantine hitched his arm around mine and escorted me across the busy intersection. "I have a wide range, as you know. Would you like to chat here, or would you prefer to sit down somewhere more private?"

I knew better than to take him up on his offer of privacy. I had no time nor the desire to across the ocean today. The streets of New York would do just fine.

"Do you love her?" I saw no reason to beat around the bush.

He released my arm as if it suddenly felt uncomfortable against his. "Why must a good battle between the sheets always rest on the morals of love?"

I stopped and faced him. "Seriously, Constantine? Have you *seen* the way she looks at you? I don't understand men." My head shook at the callousness that usually accompanied the interpretation of hasty sexual encounters.

"You question my integrity, and yet here you are, orchestrating the love life of Katie Bishop while your own hangs on a very thin thread."

He was right about me having no business sticking my nose in their relationship. Katie was my friend, but she was also a grown woman with a rock-solid brain. But he was way off base about my love life. Just because Greer had the misguided idea that I was his soul mate, didn't make it so. In fact, I had a feeling that little delusion would eventually resolve itself.

"You're right. It's none of my business," I agreed. "But if you rip her heart out, I'll rip yours out. Got that?"

He ran his index finger from the intersection of my brows down to the bridge of my nose. "You are much too young and pretty to have these worry lines."

"I'm serious, Constantine," I warned as I grabbed his wrist.

"Of course you are. You're a smart, powerful woman who just hasn't figured it all out yet." His gaze deepened, and his eyes went black and vacant as a shark's. "But when you do . . ."

"You scare me when you do that."

"As I should." The humanity returned to his face as he straightened up and sucked a lungful of air through his nose. "Now, go home. Eat. Sleep. Fuck. Do whatever you need to do to figure it out."

I ignored his cryptic comments. I was used to Constantine representing my life as a riddle. I also knew from experience that questioning those riddles would get me nowhere, because he would just blather on and on about how they were mine to figure out.

"Alex," he said as he turned to leave, "if it's Greer you're fucking, good for you. The big fish."

When I got home, the house was unusually quiet. I heard no noise in the kitchen, and then I remembered it was Sunday, Sophia's day off.

Bear was lying on his chair in the living room. I was almost past the room when I did a double take. He was still a kitten, but today he looked more like a cat.

"Bear?" He sat in his chair looking very proud of himself. Proud, because he'd managed to double his size overnight.

I looked around the room to see if we'd acquired a second cat while I was gone. I grabbed him off the chair and checked for the one oddly shaped patch of white on his underbelly—it was definitely Bear.

I don't know why it surprised me so much. A kitten growing into a cat overnight seemed mild in comparison to everything else going on.

A noise came from the library. I put Bear back on his chair and went to see who was in the other room. Greer was standing by the one wall in the room that wasn't lined with bookcases. He was pinning photographs to it, punching tiny holes in the original wood paneling that would be impossible to replace.

"You'll ruin that beautiful surface," I sadly commented as I sat in a chair and witnessed his destruction of the past.

He glanced at me before resuming construction of the makeshift bulletin board.

Most of the pictures were of me. They were the ones I'd

found months ago hidden under the desktop panel, the ones he felt compelled to hide until now.

"Why are you doing that?"

He said nothing as he took another photo from the pile. It was a picture of me when I was around six or seven. After pinning it to the wall, he stepped back to get a better view of what he was creating.

"I know what you are." I continued with our one-sided conversation. "Ava told me, so you can stop lying."

He paused without looking at me. "I told you once that I'd never lie to you, and I haven't."

"Okay. Then you can stop omitting the facts."

He kept pinning the damn snapshots to the wall, stepping back after each one to examine his work. When there were none left, he sat in the chair next to mine and stared at the giant collage.

I saw it differently now. It wasn't just a random tacking of memories floating on the wall. It was a timeline of my life from when I was still in my mother's womb until I disappeared just after my ninth birthday. It began with pictures of my mother, pregnant and smiling at the face behind the camera. The rest of them were of me at various ages. The collage ended with the last photo Ava ever took of me.

Greer had assembled my early life on the wall, all the way up to the point when it was shattered.

"I'm trying to understand where it all derailed," he began. "I was supposed to be your guardian. Nothing more."

My mother was pregnant with me when she came here from Ireland. "You were waiting for her, weren't you?"

He nodded. "Maeve was my charge, my responsibility. When you were born, you became my responsibility as well."

He rolled a brass thumbtack between his fingers and then threw it into the trash. "Maeve trusted me with the most important thing in her life, and I failed you both."

I couldn't stand to see him looking at me like that, like I was being pitied all over again. I was the girl with the dead mother, and now I was the girl who Greer failed.

His face went still as he pulled the thoughts from my head. "Pity? Is that what you think this is?" He got up and walked to the wall. The pictures flew through the air as he ripped them from the thumbtacks. "This is wrong!" he growled.

"What's wrong with *you*, Greer?" I growled back.

He glared at me like I'd just popped him in the head. And then he stalked toward me and stopped when his knees touched mine. "Get out of my head!"

"*Your* head? I'm the one being mind-raped here!"

His breathing went from zero to sixty as he moved backward and hit the edge of the desk. "No more make-believe, Alex. You don't get to hide anymore." He stood taller and ran a hand over the top of his head. "We settle this now."

"Settle what?" I stood up because sitting seemed inappropriate for the discussion we were about to have.

He composed himself and steadied his breathing. I could feel the energy coming off of him like a live wire discharging from a snipped end. Then he came toward me and stopped an arm's length away.

"Look at me, Alex." It was a command, not a request. "Now, I want you to think about something." His eyes softened, and that fluttering in my belly went all haywire again. "I want you to think about yellow dresses, and wedding rings, and . . . Bergdorf Goodman."

"Bergdorf Goodman?"

It seemed like a silly request, but then it wasn't so silly anymore. I stared at the lenses of his eyes and began to see a tiny story play out on the shiny surface. I was standing at the stove flipping bacon—in a yellow dress.

I looked away to shake the hallucination. I didn't own a

yellow dress, and I couldn't recall ever cooking bacon in Sophia's kitchen.

"You want the truth, don't you?" He pulled my face back to his. "Because we're just getting started."

I forced myself to look at his eyes again, to remember. I was walking over a bright, shiny floor. The tips of my high heels hit the surface with a metered clacking sound as Sophia and I walked toward the escalator. We'd gone shopping, something we'd never done before.

My eyes closed again as the images broke up and then flashed around my head in a scattered order. I was trying on shoes and Sophia was looking at me with her usual disciplinarian expression.

"What is this, Greer?"

He said nothing as I slipped back into the memory. Sophia and I were eating lunch and she was telling me about her family. An image of her with a skillet in her hand came to mind, and I remembered her telling me about her husband.

"I don't want to see this." I turned my back to him. There was much more behind his eyes, and I knew if I continued to recall that missing day, our relationship would change forever.

He placed his hand on my shoulder and ran it down the side of my arm. "We haven't gotten to the important part yet," he whispered. "We haven't gotten to the part where you'll begin to hate me."

I could never hate him, and the mere suggestion that something so awful could still be waiting behind his eyes, waiting for me to remember, sent a shudder through me. I thought about whether or not I really needed to know, because the slush pile that was my life was already brimming with garbage. If it was that bad, I figured I would remember on my own, and Greer did have a bad habit of sweating the small things where I was concerned.

"All right." I turned back around to look in his eyes and a shot of lust slammed through me. It wasn't the first time he'd had that effect on me, but it was the first time it nearly sent me to my knees.

"Alex!" He grabbed me around the waist as my legs gave out and I started to go down.

As he held me against his chest, I looked back in his eyes. I saw his body moving over mine. He was on top of me and inside of me, and my body was moving with his. Then I was on top of him, thrusting against his rocking hips. I was making love to my . . . *husband.*

My eyes flew wide and the air left my lungs. I shoved him away as the memory grew more vivid. "Greer?" I whispered, thinking I'd gotten it wrong, and he would lend a perspective that might make the reality seem like less of a betrayal. "I thought you were my . . . and you let me believe it."

He stood silent as I backed away, and the entire farce of a day came roaring back to me. I remembered waking up that morning and Bear climbing my leg. There was blood running down my shin. But instead of turning into an unpredictable assassin, I fell into some absurd fantasy that Greer and I were married. He played right along. Even Sophia went along with the charade.

I got up and headed for the library door.

"Don't walk away, Alex."

Without responding, I went to the kitchen and grabbed a bottle of wine. I struggled to uncork it as my fingers trembled with rage. Greer took it from my hands and uncorked it himself. Then he poured us both a glass.

"God, I thought you were more of a man than that."

"You see, Alex, that's the problem. You keep comparing me to a man."

"Well, I won't make that mistake again."

He polished off his wine, excusing himself to retrieve the bottle of scotch from the dining room cabinet.

"You know," he said angrily as he walked back in, "there's a small detail you need to remember." He swigged the liquor straight from the bottle and offered it to me.

"No. I want nothing from you."

The whiskey sloshed as he pointed at me with his other fingers wrapped around the bottle. "You came on to me. *You* wouldn't take no for an answer. Jesus, Alex, you were all over me. Sophia couldn't even shake it off you."

"Yeah, remind me to thank her for having my back."

At least the mystery was solved about how he'd managed to imprint on me, though at the moment he wasn't acting very attentive. If I didn't know better, I'd swear I was the last person he wanted to see. That was just fine with me.

"So, it's true," I confirmed.

"*What?*"

"That you've imprinted on me like some animal."

He stepped back and looked mildly stunned. "Where did you hear that?"

"Leda. I thought she was out of her mind. But given the circumstances and the way you almost ripped Loden's head off last night, I assume there's some truth to it."

He put the bottle down and leaned back against the counter, burying his face in his hands as he rubbed his forehead. "That's just *fucking* fantastic," he growled.

"What? Is it supposed to be a secret? Because everyone seems to know. And what happens now? Am I supposed to just go around blindly worshipping you while you go out and provide for me like a caveman? Feed me—is that what you do?"

He laughed bitterly. "No. Actually, I'm supposed to blindly worship *you*."

I felt my cheeks grow hot at the idea of him stumbling over himself to please me. No man had ever shown me that kind of attention, let alone a god like Greer Sinclair. But the heat passed through me as I felt my freedom slipping away. The air in the room seemed to evaporate as the beginnings of panic spread through me.

"Can't you just control it?" I blurted out.

"Control it?" He was laughing again, sarcastically punctuating my naïve understanding of what it meant to be an obsessed god. "We don't control this. It fucking controls us! You don't get it, do you? I didn't choose you, Alex."

I'd been slapped in the face before, and it left less of a sting than his words. Underneath all my layers of aloof disregard for him, if I ever allowed myself the luxury of being loved, there was no one else I wanted more.

"I don't want you either," I threw back at him, my defenses up and my heart bruised.

The look on his face was incredulous. "I never said I didn't want you."

"Oh, I think you just did."

My hand went up as he reached for my face. "Don't you dare touch me, Greer."

He ignored my warning and kept coming. "I may not have chosen you, but this little coupling has been in play for a long time, Alex. I felt it the moment I touched you in the park last year, like a *fucking* lightning rod. And you can bet I've been fighting it ever since."

My back hit the edge of the counter as he trapped me in the corner where they intersected. He moved a loose strand of hair out of my eyes with his index finger and continued with his confession. "It felt wrong for a long time. Still does, a little. I was supposed to be your guardian, not your lover."

My heart felt like it was ready to beat out of my chest. I mean literally crack my bones and burst through my skin. It was the fear of what I'd have to give up if I opened my heart. I'd been alone too long, and I had no idea how to embrace what he was offering.

"Back the fuck off, Greer," I warned as I shoved past him.

He remained still, staring at the corner where I'd just been standing before escaping his cage. "You're acting like a woman who's never had a man in her bed," he said without turning around.

"And you were a frat boy rapist that night with a drunk girl in *your* bed."

I didn't mean it. I swear I didn't. But the fear had turned me into a real bitch, and the words just spilled from my mouth. There was no taking them back. The best I could do was downplay the suggestion that I thought he was a predator. But when he turned around, the look on his face told me I'd crossed a line. I'd hit a nerve so deep we might never recover from it. Was it possible to worship and hate at the same time, because I was afraid that might be his next dilemma.

We both turned when Thomas walked into the kitchen. It was late afternoon and we had an appointment that evening in Battery Park.

"So, you folks ready to rock and roll?" He took one look at the two of us and shook his head. "Well, fuck."

TWENTY-FOUR

Greer and I managed to put our very strained relationship on the shelf for one night, for the sake of possibly finding the vessel. Tomorrow was a new day, and we'd have plenty of time to carry on with our differences in the morning.

The plan was to meet Isabetta Falcone at the East Coast Memorial at the southern tip of Battery Park. Dr. Oxford, Greer, and I would go to the center of the memorial while Thomas, Rhom, and Loden watched from a distance.

There were more direct routes, but we decided to take the long way and walk the promenade along the Hudson River. With the others heading in from the top end, it gave us the advantage of scoping out both ends of the park to make sure we weren't being set up for an ambush.

It was dark by the time we arrived, and the black water rolled against the promenade seawall as Lady Liberty held her torch high in the middle of New York Harbor. It was a magnificent sight, opening up my memories of seeing her for the first time from the World Trade Center. My mother had a friend who worked in one of the towers. It was the Fourth of July and we were invited to come up to the fifty-eighth floor for a private viewing of what a real fireworks display looked like. I remember pressing my face against the floor-to-ceiling windows, looking out over the harbor at the explosion of color filling the sky, reflecting against the sheet of black water below.

"There it is." Greer's voice broke the spell of the memory. "There's no one there."

We walked down the plaza, past the giant granite pylons engraved with the names of thousands of servicemen lost at sea during World War II. Looking over the pylons was a massive bronze eagle gripping a wreath.

The eight pylons stood around twenty feet tall, with four on each side of the plaza.

"We're sitting ducks with all these obstructions," I pointed out.

Dr. Oxford looked jumpy. "One would think Isabetta would be on time for such an important meeting."

"Yes, one *would* think," Greer agreed. "Considering she has door-to-door transportation straight from home." He nodded toward the east. "The Staten Island Ferry Terminal is just a couple blocks from here."

I glared at him. "Don't piss her off, Greer."

"I just like fucking with her. If she's on the defense, it means we're on the offense. That's exactly where we want to be."

The doctor hummed nervously as his head scanned back and forth, looking for something only he might be able to see.

My eyes caught something in the distance. All three of us turned and looked down the long plaza toward the Statue of Liberty as three figures approached. The three dots got bigger, and then Isabetta Falcone stepped out of the shadows. Demitri was with her, and the short guy with the big feet.

"Alex Kelley," she said without even glancing at Oxford or Greer. "I didn't expect to see you here."

"Come on, Isabetta. You knew I'd tag along." I turned to walk away. "But I can leave if you'd like."

A short burst of air expelled from her nostrils. "Enough games." She finally looked at Dr. Oxford and then at Greer. "*You*, on the other hand—"

Greer glanced at his watch. "You're late. What's the matter? Ferry running a little behind tonight?"

I thought her head was going to explode as she fought to keep her pointed fingernails at her side. I could just feel the catfight itching to surface, and I had no doubt that if they were confined to a room together, he'd have some gouges to show for it.

Demitri must have sensed it, too. He took a step toward Greer and sneered.

"Not now." Isabetta's face relaxed, and like an obedient pit bull, Demitri stepped back in line. "I'm sure Greer meant no disrespect."

I didn't trust her. She was being a little bit too tolerant. I watched her like a hawk as her eyes roamed discreetly around the plaza before landing on Oxford's hand.

"Are those the glasses?"

Oxford flipped the frames shut and slipped them into his shirt pocket. "Yes. A prototype."

"May I?" She extended her hand.

"I mean no disrespect, but no, you may not. No one touches the specs but me."

She didn't look happy about being snubbed. In her eyes, I'm sure she took Oxford's letter telling her to politely fuck off as a negotiation. "I thought we had a deal."

"What part of my letter didn't you understand?"

She glanced at Demitri, and he moved toward the doctor. Greer made a move, too. He gave Demitri a warning look that clarified who had the upper hand. It seemed both Isabetta and her goons had forgotten whom they were dealing with, and Greer's past tolerances gave them a false sense of power.

"I've given you the wrong impression, Isabetta," Greer cautioned. "You'd be wise to know your place." He looked at

Demitri again, and I watched the big man begin to shrink as his shoulders lowered into a submissive posture.

"Now, shall we begin? Where does your 'source' suggest we start looking?"

She was beginning to look as jumpy as the doctor, and I detected a telltale twitch around the corner of her mouth. Her eyes were doing that roaming thing again, only now she wasn't as discreet about it.

I looked at Greer who seemed as suspicious as I was.

"*Fuck.*" He dove at me, but he was a half second too late.

My feet left the ground. Before I could process what was happening, I landed on top of one of the pylons. I twisted sideways to get a look at who or what was dragging me along the granite ledge, twenty feet above the ground. The eyes staring back at me were brown.

"You look surprised to see me, Alex. I told you I'd be back for you. Did you think I was bluffing?" Daemon's arm wrapped around my waist tighter. His cheek slid down the side of mine, grazing my sensitive skin with the roughness of a day-old beard.

The pylon began to shake, and I imagined falling to the ground as a couple tons of granite buried me alive.

"Let her go, and I'll consider killing you quickly." Greer was staring at Daemon with a blackness in his eyes I'd never seen before.

Daemon laughed. "Now, you know what they say about possession and the law. Looks like I win."

The granite began to shift again. Daemon grabbed my chin and forced me to look at Greer. I could see a small bottle in his other hand. A clear liquid splashed around the sides as I struggled against him. He tilted it toward my face. "Such beautiful skin. It would be unfortunate to destroy it. Don't make me do that, Sinclair."

I felt sick when I realized what was in the bottle. All Daemon cared about was taking me alive, because in the grander scheme of things, it really didn't matter what I looked like.

Greer fell on his left knee, his eyes shutting tight from some invisible pain driving through him. Rhom came out of nowhere and pulled his boss to his feet, but Greer pushed him away and glared at Daemon with a hatred that would have incinerated an ordinary man.

Daemon moved the bottle away from my face but kept it in his hand, ready to use it if Greer made a move. He let go of my chin and moved his hand down to my neck, forcing a strangled gag from my throat as he squeezed my airway shut.

Greer took the bait. I could feel a shift happening around me, a vibration in the air. The waves crashed against the promenade with such force, I thought the walls might break and allow the sea to swallow us.

"So the rumors are true," Daemon murmured against my ear. "The mighty Greer Sinclair has his cock tied to the end of a very short string." The muscles of his chest contracted with sharp jerks as a mocking laugh wheezed from his throat. "I'll have to scrub his smell off of you."

The battle was over without a fight. Greer would never let that liquid touch my skin. He would stand there, while the man who nearly raped me carried me away. The lesser of two evils.

Ironically, Daemon was the one who set everything in motion, my introduction to Greer Sinclair. He was the one who'd started it all, and now he would be the one to end it.

I felt refreshed and alive when I woke up, like I'd been sprinkled with stardust, or pixie powder and rainbows. Not once did I feel like I'd been abducted and dragged off by a monster who may have done terrible things to me while I slept.

The feeling disappeared the second I remembered how I got there, in a strange room with an even stranger smell of freshly baked bread filling the air.

The space was bright, but the light was coming from the lamps in the room. There were no windows.

Through a door on the right side of the room, I spotted a toilet and a sink. Other than the bed and a couple of small tables to hold the lamps, the rest of the room was empty.

I pushed the comforter back and looked at the oversized T-shirt I was wearing. It wasn't mine.

"I took the liberty of dressing you in something more appropriate for sleeping."

My head snapped toward the voice. Daemon was sitting in a chair behind me, in the corner on the other side of the bed.

"Don't worry. I was very respectful about it. Although I did peek."

I grabbed the sheet and pulled it back. "Have you been sitting there leering at me all night? That's what perverts do, isn't it?"

He looked at me with amusement. "Why do women always do that—clutch the sheet?"

"Are you speaking from experience?"

A subtle smile appeared. "Did you know that you curl up in a tight ball when you sleep? It must stem from some insecurity."

"What do you want from me?" Other than the obvious, I had a sick feeling I wasn't there just for the amulet and vessel. They could have come for me months ago, like all the rest. But there was something more going on. Daemon seemed to take a personal interest in me.

He lifted out of the chair and took his time walking around the bed. His hand fell, and his index finger ran along the blanket until it reached the outline of my leg. I nearly jerked my thigh out of its path, but he anticipated my response and retracted his hand before I could react. He liked control.

He reached into his pocket and pulled out a small object. Before laying it on the table next to the bed, he examined it, running his finger over the slightly yellowed surface and giving it a good sniff. It was the good luck charm I'd carried with me all my life. My mother told me it was a gift from the faeries on my fourth birthday. But I learned the truth the night Greer placed my hand on the scar at the dimple of his back where the bone had been cut. It was a piece of him, meant to serve as a powerful connection between us.

"It fell out of your pocket when I was making you more comfortable." He picked it back up and rolled it between his fingers. "Is it bone?"

I suppressed my reaction to seeing it in his hand. "Ivory." I lied, not wanting him to explore the source and possibly take it from me.

He flicked his eyes from the charm to my face. "It's bone."

"Is it?"

He swallowed it in his hand but then reconsidered and let it roll back onto the table.

I released the air trapped in my chest as my only connection to the outside world settled on the small table. I figured it had a few favors left in it, and if the magic was still there, I might be able to get Greer's attentions.

"Are you hungry?"

Now that he brought it up, I was starving. And if he was fetching food, he wasn't in the room. "I could use something to eat."

He reached for my chin and lifted my eyes to his. "Then I shall feed you."

The look of pleasure on his face made me uneasy. What was it about feeding me that gave men such a hard-on?

"Thank you," I forced myself to say, following the false gratitude with a sweet smile. "And coffee."

He smiled back with satisfaction. "You're in luck. A fresh batch of cornetti should be coming out of the oven right about now." His eyes drifted to the ceiling. "There's a bakery above us."

He noticed the flicker in my eyes. "Ah, you think I've just

slipped up and given away a clue to our location. There are hundreds if not thousands of bakeries in New York. I could have just as easily said there's a coffee shop above us. But I'm afraid you'll be staying with us for a while, so it really wouldn't matter if I gave you the exact address."

"Us?"

"Ah, my manners. I haven't explained anything, have I?"

I inched back as he sat on the edge of the bed. His eyes moved to the spot where the amulet rested under my shirt. "It's still there. The amulet is useless without its keeper, so we saw no reason to remove it from your neck."

"Was this all just a hoax to get your hands on me?" I couldn't understand why they'd bothered jumping through all the hoops when they could have just snatched me from Shakespeare's Library. Especially since he'd been there. He knew exactly where I worked.

"You *and* the doctor. It appears that Greer and his colleagues have made it very difficult to get to David Oxford, so we decided to bring the doctor to us. You see, it's true. We believe the vessel is hiding in plain sight—invisible. It's very clever of the gods, don't you think?"

Clever, all right. If he only knew how clever Dr. Oxford was. For the sake of the doctor's eyes, I hoped he never figured it out.

"Dr. Oxford has become almost as valuable as you, and Ms. Falcone was more than happy to reevaluate her loyalties and switch sides. Greed is quite useful. We simply asked her to make a call. As we expected, Dr. Oxford took care of the rest."

"So you'll use us to find it, and then we're dead? Is that the plan? You've got what you want. Don't I at least deserve to know my fate?"

His head slowly craned to look at me. "That's the beauty of all this. It's such a win-win for us—for me. We get the prophecy, and—" His smile shut down as he realized he'd spoken too freely. "In time, Alex. It will all make sense very soon."

"You keep saying *we* and *us*, but all I see is you."

"You mean Greer hasn't told you what we are?"

"You're a Rogue," I answered, choosing to leave out the colorful expletives that described their nature so thoroughly.

He let my words sink in. "That's a very dramatic label we've been given. We prefer to think of ourselves as warriors."

"And *warrior* isn't?"

He showed no reaction to my snark. Instead, he stood up with his back to me. "You're a guest in our castle." When I gave no further response, he headed for the door. "I'll get that food now."

I heard the lock on the door engage, and then his footsteps disappeared down the hall. I grabbed the bone off the table and rubbed it between my fingers. "Come on, Greer. Don't fail me now," I whispered, suspecting the room was bugged.

I knew Greer could sense the bone, but it had a poor track record as an actual GPS. Maybe now that we were in the same city it would be more reliable, and he'd come through that door to take me home.

My clothes were draped over a chair in the corner. While I was getting dressed, I heard a faint whimper coming from somewhere in the room. I followed the sound to a vent at the base of the wall. "Dr. Oxford?"

The whimpering stopped. I held my breath, thinking I'd imagined it.

"Ms. Kelley? Is that you?"

"Yes. I'm here. Are you all right?"

"I'm afraid I've had better days." His voice stuttered and hitched around a stifled sob.

Fear was getting the best of him, and he sounded like he was cracking under the pressure. David Oxford was a scientist, unaccustomed to life outside his box of what could be controlled and proven. Even the vessel was within that box because its invisible properties could be explained and measured with science. On the other hand, its contents could not. I imagined he'd struggle with that if we ever found it.

"Dr. Oxford, did they hurt you?" I shuddered as I thought about his secret—his eyes. "Do they have the glasses?" I asked, referring to the 3D fakes he'd brought with him.

Pulling one over on Isabetta wasn't brain surgery, but deceiving the Rogues was a different ball game.

Damn things are smart, Greer said to me when he first told me about them, and I'd seen Daemon's intelligence firsthand.

"I don't know what happened to them. I was rendered unconscious for a time. When I woke up, they were gone."

He cleared his throat as a crack grasped his vocal chords. "I fear, Ms. Kelley, that the gift of sight may not be in my future. Can you imagine a scientist who studies the spectrum of light, without eyes? My life's work is over."

"Don't even think about that, Doctor. And keep your voice down." I whispered. "For all they know, the glasses work."

He sighed heavily into the vent on the other side of the wall. "I'm afraid they may have figured it out."

"Why do you say that?"

"One of them was looking at me oddly. He was staring into my eyes—smirking."

I heard a noise in the background of Oxford's room. It was the door opening. "They've come for me, Ms. Kelley," he whispered in a small, defeated voice.

The muffled sounds of a struggle penetrated the thin drywall. I stood up and smashed my fists into the wall as the helpless man screamed. "Don't you touch him!" I yelled.

I imagined Dr. Oxford had never used his hands for more than a handshake or the construction of a science project, so the thought of a couple of thugs dragging him out of the room made me sick to my stomach.

The struggle was over in less than a minute. The door to my room opened as the sounds from Oxford's room went silent.

Daemon entered and carried a tray of food toward the nightstand.

"You son of a bitch!" I screamed as I flew at him and knocked the tray out of his hands. "What are they doing to him?"

He took a step back and caught my arms, nearly stumbling over the dropped tray. Two more men came through the door. One was huge and made Greer and his men seem small in comparison. The other had a nasty expression on his face as he leered at me and sniffed the air.

Daemon shoved me behind him, nearly sending me to the floor. He put his hand up to stop the two steamrollers who were coming straight at us. "Get. Out!" he roared at them.

They stopped cold and began to back their way out of the room. When they crossed the threshold, the door shut on its own with a loud slam.

Daemon turned and delivered a blow to me next. Not to my head, to my mind.

TWENTY-FIVE

I'm one of those people with an internal clock that can usually predict the time of day with reasonable accuracy. Mine was telling me it was early evening, but since there were no windows in the room to confirm that, it could have just as easily been morning or the middle of the night.

I checked to make sure I still had the amulet and the bone charm. Both were where they belonged. I'd triggered Daemon's anger, and he'd rewarded me with some kind of mind assault that knocked me out cold. Confiscating the two things that meant the most to me would have been clever payback. And though he chose not to, I had no doubt he would take them the minute it served his purpose to do so.

My brain felt like a lump of fruit in a blender, spinning wildly when I tried to get up. I rolled back on the bed, my throat and stomach throbbing with hunger, dreaming of that food I'd knocked out of his hands.

As if on cue, the door opened and in walked my captor with a freshly prepared tray of something fragrant and amazing. I think a loaf of stale bread slathered with rancid butter would have tasted like a three-star Michelin meal.

He set the tray on the table next to the bed and waited for me to dig in, but I kept my eyes on him instead.

"I know you're hungry. Two days without food will make you weak, and we can't have you weak when Maelcolm arrives. He'll think we've been mistreating you."

"Two days?"

"Yes. You've been here for two days. Who knows how long it's been since you've actually eaten."

The last thing I put in my mouth was a shot of whiskey when I went to see Ava. The subsequent fight with Greer had killed my appetite, so I refused dinner before we left for Battery Park.

He brought me a plate of stuffed pasta with cream sauce, a salad, and a basket of warm bread. There was even a glass of red wine.

I swung my legs over the mattress and attempted to eat without looking like a pig. "Who is this Maelcolm?" I asked as I caved in to my hunger and stuffed a huge bite of pasta in my mouth.

"This *Maelcolm* is the Chairman of the Board."

"So you've organized the exploitation of women and children," I stated without looking up from my plate, without sarcasm.

He continued with his half-formed grin and humorless eyes. "He's my chief. And he will be yours, too. I mean no disrespect, Alex, but I'd suggest you lose the smug attitude and learn to curtsy."

Having suddenly lost my appetite, I pushed the tray away. "You're kidding, right?"

"I think we can do without the curtsy, but that mouth of yours might get you killed." He leaned down and looked me square in the eye. "When your usefulness has worn off, you'll want Maelcolm to enjoy your company enough to keep you around."

The fork balancing on the edge of the plate fell and drew Daemon's attention to the uneaten food. "Finish your dinner. I'll be back for the tray later." His eyes roamed over the shirt I'd worn for days. "There are towels in the bath and some fresh clothes on the chair."

"Wait," I blurted as he turned to leave. "Where is Dr. Oxford?" He hesitated as he reached for the doorknob, but then he continued out of the room without answering my question.

It's surprising how effective four white walls and utter silence can be at torturing you into submission. The isolation was making me batshit. Even a dungeon or a jail cell had sounds, but with the absence of Dr. Oxford's sobs on the other side of the wall, the room was a torturous void. Even the smell of baking flour and yeast had ceased.

The uneaten food was still on the table. It was cold now, but that's when Italian food tasted best, when all the flavors had time to relax and marry into perfection.

There was a parchment paper bag on the tray with the word ADELINA'S stamped in small capital letters. I opened it, and the smell of citrus and ricotta cheese filled my nose. I'd eaten sfogliatelle before but forgot how special they were. An Italian classic—golden seashells of paper-thin pastry, filled with sweetened ricotta and semolina—hard to find outside of an authentic Italian bakery. The one above me, I assumed.

I ate the rest of the pasta and bread, and then devoured the pastry, running my finger along the inside of the bag to capture the sugar trapped in the creases. When I was finished, I folded the paper into a small square, framing the letters, more out of boredom than anything else.

I tossed the paper on the tray when I heard the doorknob turn. A man I hadn't seen before walked in the room. No knock, no request to enter, he just barreled his way in and looked around the room. His eyes landed on the target, and he headed for the tray on the table.

"I could have been naked, you know." He ignored my comment. With his shaved head and tattooed limbs, he looked like a typical skinhead. "Sure, I'm done," I said as he rudely reached over me. I got the feeling he was avoiding eye contact, like I was beneath him and not worth his acknowledgement. He leaned closer to lift the tray and went completely still except for the deep contractions of his chest. His lungs inflated sharply as his eyes went from brown to black.

My warning bells went off when his head twisted in a mechanical motion, and those void eyes zeroed in on mine. Only a few inches separated us, and I was overwhelmed by the discomfort of my own heartbeat throbbing painfully against the walls of my chest.

He straightened back up, and the tray began to shake. I realized it was his trembling hand causing the cutlery to jump and rattle against the china. I moved as far back on the mattress as my seated legs would allow, and then I did what a predator usually doesn't expect—I met his eyes. It was all bluff.

"Where's Daemon?" I mustered underneath all the adrenaline threatening to give me away.

His mouth spread into a wicked grin, and then it collapsed and his jaw went slack. I could hear his breath quicken and rush through his parted lips.

The tray hit the floor. My arms flattened above my head as he wrestled me to the mattress. "Get off of me!" I jabbed him with my knee, but the fight seemed to excite him even more. He came down on me harder and started pulling on the edge of my jeans, and I let out a piercing scream loud enough to get the attention of the whole damn building.

He lifted off of me and flew back against the wall as Daemon took his place in front of me. "Get up," he snarled.

I jump off the bed as two more men came through the door.

"You'll be learning to share," said my attacker. "Maelcolm will see to that."

Daemon pulled something from his pocket and threw it in the air with a broad stroke. The substance seemed to take on a life of its own as it swirled and darkened into a ball of black mist in the center of the room, cutting off my view of the three men on the other side.

When all I could see was the dark cloud snaking around my body like a dense fog, Daemon wrapped himself around me and closed my eyelids with his fingertips.

When I opened my eyes, I expected to see the black fog still filling the room. But I wasn't in the windowless room with the monotonous white walls; I was sitting on a black leather sofa with my head leaning against the cushion. My shoes were gone, but I was still wearing the same clothes.

The room was sparse and clean, modern and monochrome with a view to die for. I approached the floor-to-ceiling windows spanning the wall and looked out at the millions of lights dappling the city. The familiar shapes of landmarks confirmed we were definitely in New York, an important detail to note considering my history of finding myself in swank rooms overlooking strange cities.

It could have been worse. I could have been looking at all those lights from a dirty, abandoned warehouse somewhere across the river, with my hands bound and my mouth taped shut. Abducted women usually didn't find themselves in places like this.

The amulet was still around my neck, but when I reached in my pocket and felt for the bone charm, it was gone. I felt around the sofa cushions to see if it had slipped out. I found a nickel and a few pennies, but no charm.

I walked back to the window, scanning the surrounding buildings to get an idea of what part of town I was in.

"Do you like it?"

Daemon was standing on the other side of the room when I turned around.

"What?" I asked, not entirely sure what he meant.

"The view."

I ignored the question, refusing to make small talk with him. He'd attacked me, stalked me, kidnapped me, and now he was asking me how I liked the view? *How the fuck do you like it?*

The shine left his eyes as my thoughts bled into his. He took a few steps but stopped when I began to move back toward the window. I tried to pull my eyes from his, but he wouldn't let up on that damn hold he had on me. I couldn't manage the simple task of averting my eyes, even though all my instincts told me to look away.

He came closer and extended his hand.

I looked at his open palm in disbelief. "Are you kidding me?"

"Our dinner is getting cold." The trace of warmth in his face disappeared when I refused his hand.

"Take it," he said in a deceptively calm voice.

"Or what?"

"Or I'll drag you into that dining room and sit you down myself."

I followed his eyes as he glanced toward the right side of the room. The open space contained an elegant table and chairs, complete with a meal on top of it.

Continuing to ignore his outstretched hand, I walked past him and seated myself.

"You need food." He sat at the opposite end, looking pleased with the spread on top of the table.

I had no idea how long I'd been sleeping on that sofa or when I ate that plate of cold pasta, but the sight of the food triggered my hunger.

I'd given up on trying to track time, and my internal clock had failed me. It could have been a few days or a week since Daemon took me. I was banking on the former because the longer he had me, the less confident I was that Greer was coming.

Daemon leaned back in his chair and waited for me to commence eating. "What is this place?" I asked without touching the platter of roasted chicken sitting in the center of the table.

"This is my home."

"You mean you don't live in your . . . what did you call it? Your *castle*?"

Maybe he was a successful entrepreneur outside of his nasty double life, or had some high-powered benefactors like Greer. Apartments like this were for the filthy rich, so a boatload of money was coming from somewhere.

"Distraction won't work, Alex. Now be a good girl and eat."

I held his stare and refused to move. I would not eat another bite of his food or drink another drop of liquid. Dead, I wouldn't be of much use to him or his people. Maybe he'd get that message and bargain with something useful.

"Where's the piece of bone I had in my pocket? The one you were thinking about taking from me the other day."

I noticed a slight hitch in his expression, a momentary tensing of his jaw and a contraction of his nose. "I have no idea what you're talking about."

"It was in my pocket before you brought me here, and now it's gone."

"Then I guess you lost it."

I glared at the thief and made a vow to myself to get it back as soon as this was over.

He stood up and towered over the table. "I am many things, but I am not a liar or a thief."

"You stole me," I retorted with a sort of satisfaction for getting the last word. "Didn't you?"

He sat back down and eased into his chair. "I cannot steal what is mine."

I was speechless. Was that why he'd been stalking me? Because he thought he owned me?

Greer had told me in very blunt terms what they were; males like him, who had gone Rogue, raping human women and then stealing their offspring to build their own Rogue army. When I asked Greer why they didn't breed with their own kind, he said they weren't capable of producing female offspring. They needed human women, and what could be more powerful than the offspring of a demigod and a Fitheach witch who also happened to be the Oracle?

I looked back up at Daemon who was feasting on my thoughts.

You can't work for the gods if you want to be the gods. Those were Greer's words when he described the Rogues to me. That statement made perfect sense now.

Daemon was a demigod with an identity crisis—a very dangerous one.

He straightened in his chair and reached for his plate, topping it with a chicken breast, a dinner roll, and a generous portion of caramelized carrots and potatoes. Then he stood up and placed the full plate on top of my empty one. "*Eat,*" he barked.

My own temper was beginning to flare—a very Irish temper—and I stared back at him with a defiant go-to-hell look stamped across my face.

I wasn't a dog, and I was getting tired of men telling me where and when to eat.

"Eat the fucking food or I'll force it down your throat!"

The plate hit the wall so hard it sent bits of chicken ricocheting back at the table. I looked at my hand in disbelief that I'd actually done it.

"Eat it yourself!" I growled back. My entire body shook from the adrenaline raging through it.

Daemon came around the table and grabbed the empty plate under the one I'd just hurled across the room. He piled it with just as much food as the previous one and shoved it in front of me. "We can do this all night, if you'd like."

He stepped behind my chair and placed his hands on my shoulders, spreading his fingers across my tensed muscles until they reached my clavicle. Then he bent down and spoke in my ear. "But I must warn you. All this foreplay gets me very excited. I'd like to save that for later, but if you'd like to play now, we can—"

"I'll eat," I said.

His hands softened around the cuffs of my shoulders. Then he removed them and walked leisurely back to his chair, resuming his seat with a thick intake of air. The ball was in my court.

I gave him a last defiant look and then reached for my fork. The chicken pulled away from the bone effortlessly as I forced myself to assemble a bite and place it in my mouth. I chewed mechanically, and despite the bitter taste of adrenaline mixing with the small amount of saliva left in my mouth, it was delicious.

Thick like a lump of dry clay in the back of my throat, but delicious.

TWENTY-SIX

Greer paced the long stretch of room under the watchful eyes of the mounted boar head. He'd gone down to Den of Oddities and Antiquities to see if Ava had picked up anything on the astral grapevine, because his sense of Alex was fading, and they were running out of time.

Isabetta Falcone had turned out to be nothing but a backstabbing power junkie, working every angle to get a piece of the pie. First with Alasdair Templeton, but when Greer's threats to destroy his house sent him back into the shadows, she wasted no time forming an idiot's alliance with the Rogues. And they played her like the fool she was.

"She's gone, Ava. She's just fucking gone!"

Ava reached for his arm as he made his hundredth pass in front of her. "We'll find her, Greer. I know that with absolute certainty."

"How could I just stand there and let him take her?"

"You had no choice, Greer."

He turned to look at her like she'd rattled off some ridiculous rhetoric. "Don't patronize me, Ava. There's always a choice. You know that as well as anyone."

The comment stung. He was referring to the choice she'd

made eighteen years earlier when she sent her car off a bridge into the Wabash River to fake her own death, leaving Alex an orphan with an assumed name.

Alex kept her promise and never revealed her real identity, and it wasn't until she stepped foot back on New York soil that she became Alex Kelley again.

"You're right. I did have a choice." She owned that choice, knowing she would be judged for what seemed like selfishness. She could have stayed the course, given up her own existence for the sake of a child. But no one knew what she knew. She made a promise, and if she had to take all that judgment to the grave, she gladly would. "But I made the right choice, Greer. Had I gone with the alternative, we wouldn't be here right now."

"Exactly," he relied sharply.

"Because she'd already be dead—or worse!"

"Something worse than death?" He eyed her suspiciously. "What could possibly be worse?"

Ava headed for the counter and began rearranging objects around the thick glass top: a cardholder containing the shop's business cards went from the left side of the cash register to the right, a vase with a few spring flowers took its place, and an old book moved a few inches to the left.

His hand grasped her wrist. "Stop."

"You did the right thing, Greer." She continued nervously searching for distractions on the countertop. "She would have never forgiven you if that monster had destroyed her face."

She noted the sense of loss in his eyes and the fury buried just below the surface of his skin. "You love her, don't you?"

Greer seemed surprised by the frankness of her question. It was his turn to look for distractions. He looked around the shop, taking it all in as if the magic solution to their problem could be found on one of the shelves filled with the strange accouterments of the past.

"Look at me," she ordered.

A shimmer of mercury rimmed his blue irises. "You've chosen her. You've bonded with her, haven't you?"

He released his resignation with a chest-hollowing rush of air, the exhaustion from the denial finally sending up a white flag. "*This* was not a choice."

"I'm still trying to figure out how all this happened in the first place. This *imprinting*. That's what we're talking about, right?"

His eyes leveled on hers. "The old-fashioned way."

The conversation lulled for a moment as Ava wrapped her head around "the old-fashioned way" meaning. Then she reached for the same book she'd referenced the morning Alex came to see her.

"Alex says otherwise. I don't mean to give you a lesson on the birds and the bees, Greer, but it's all right here in the book." She pointed to the section in *Rituals of the Gods* that detailed—with clinical precision—the method required to trigger imprinting. "Are you telling me you've found a different way?"

Greer said nothing as the truth snaked its way into Ava's head. Her lower lip dropped a bit as her mouth formed an unintelligible word. Half a word, really. "Wel—" Her head twisted as a scenario ran through her mind, and then she gave him a look that could melt the skin off of a crocodile's back like butter. "What did you do, Greer? You didn't—"

"No, damn it! I didn't force myself on her!" His hands raked over his head with a sound similar to a foot blowing through a pile of dried leaves. "Why does everyone keep pointing a finger at me like I'm some sort of . . . deviant?"

"Everyone?"

"Alex practically called me a rapist. In fact, she did. And you're over there handing me my lunch with those eyes."

"Well, Greer—"

"And Leda." His head shook back and forth. "I can just see the inquisition coming."

Ava held her tongue and waited for the drama to pass. She knew Greer would never hurt Alex, but things of this nature where just that—nature—and nature wasn't always democratic or sensible where the power of instinct was concerned. People often made bad decisions where instinct came into play, and if that were the case here, he'd made a very bad one.

"She came to me," he said. "I knew there was something . . . *wrong* with her that day. Even Sophia knew it. At first I pushed her away. But then I saw what I wanted to see. I let it happen, Ava. God help me, I let it happen."

"I'll ask you again, Greer. Do you love her?"

He looked at her with a resolute gaze. "She is my breath. My annoying, stubborn, infuriating oxygen."

"Well, I guess that's as good a description of love as any," declared Ava.

"That's not the point, is it? We both know I can't give her what she needs. There's a shelf life on this relationship."

"Because she'll grow old and you won't?"

He looked genuinely surprised by the comment and wondered if he seemed so shallow that Ava would think him capable of such callousness.

"I don't give a damn about that, but I doubt she'll feel the same way. She's more than earned her right to a family—a normal one."

"Oh, I think it's a little premature to determine what Alex's future should look like. We don't even know what she's capable of. She's not exactly *normal*, is she?"

He thought about what to do next. Where to start. Right now he just needed her back. They'd figure the rest out later, one daunting task at a time. For all he knew, she'd never let him near her again and the dilemma would be resolved.

"Maeve would sever my cock if she were alive to see this." He glanced at her apologetically. "Pardon my candor."

"Maeve would approve, Greer."

The bell on the door rang as Patrick strode in with a paper bag tucked under his arm. "GS, good to see you." He flashed the bright smile of a young man without a care in the world. "How's that little firecracker doing?"

Ava shot Patrick a warning look to stifle any further reference to Alex. He didn't know that Alex's life hung in the balance, and any indirect flirtation—remote or otherwise—might get his ass handed back to him, due to Greer's instinctual urge to oust any competition.

"Now that's a boy Maeve might approve of," Greer muttered.

Patrick pulled a six pack of Guinness from the bag and headed for the kitchen in the back room. "Anyone up for a draft?" he asked, followed by a rambunctious grin. "Don't worry, Auntie, just keeping them cold until we close up."

She shook her head. "That boy has another ten years of carousing to get out of his system before he earns any mother's approval."

Greer headed for the door. "Thomas and the others will be at my place soon. I told them to pack their toothbrushes. No one's going home until we find her."

"Greer," Ava called out as he reached for the door, "you'll get our girl back, won't you?"

"If I don't, you'll never see me again," he replied as he walked out.

Greer stepped off the elevator and looked around his quiet house. Except for the barely audible ticking coming from the clock on the fireplace mantel and the sound of muffled traffic beyond the exterior walls, the place was as quiet as a morgue. He felt utterly alone for the first time in years, and exhausted from lack of sleep. Not that he needed sleep to survive, but rest was a universal requirement for just about any species, human or otherwise, and he'd had none for the past two days.

Even before the events at Battery Park, his rest had been sporadic as he reconciled with his new state of perpetual desire, and his responsibility to the woman who'd made him that way. His men were also in need of a well-deserved break. They were loyal, and every one of them would drive themselves into the ground before conceding defeat or giving up.

They loved her, too.

Sophia was standing at the kitchen counter when he looked through the doorway. Her wrist began to rotate mechanically as she whisked a bowl of oil and herbs into an emulsified foam. The whirling stopped when he approached and looked over her shoulder. He was usually considerate in giving her advance notice when guests were coming for dinner, but his mind had been elsewhere, and he'd failed to tell her that morning that the dinner table would be full for one more night.

His hand found the center of her back as he gently gave her the news. "We'll order pizza," he said after apologizing for wasting her time cooking whatever she had in the oven, assuming it wouldn't be enough for all his men. "We can have it tomorrow night." Leftovers were always better the next day.

Her expression remained neutral as she let go of the whisk and opened the oven door. With a thick pair of oven mitts, she bent down and removed a large cherry-red pan from the center rack.

"I know you," she muttered. The word *pizza* rolled off her tongue with a touch of contempt. "I make enough for ten. You got more guests than that, then you order pizza."

He glanced at the large wooden bowl on the counter filled with enough salad to feed an army of rabbits. He kissed her on the cheek and left the kitchen so she could continue preparing the meal she'd foretold. Sometimes he wondered if she knew him better than he knew himself.

Although she'd said nothing over the course of the last two days, the abduction had taken a toll on her, too. Sophia wasn't one to interfere in her employer's business, especially when it concerned matters that were not of this world. But she wasn't a stupid woman, and nothing went on in Greer's house that she didn't have some degree of knowledge about. A missing woman was no small thing, and Sophia had grown to love Alex just like the rest of them.

Greer went to the library and knelt next to the pictures that still littered the floor. Sophia had known better than to disturb them, because this wasn't just a pile of randomly thrown trash on the floor. This was a discarded heap of emotions that needed to be tended to by the discarder.

He bent down to clean up the creased and torn images. The door opened and Sophia poked her head through the crack. "Come in, Sophia."

Her feet stopped next to his legs, and he could hear the creak in her knees as she descended to the floor next to him. "Thank you, Sophia, but I've got this."

She picked up one of the photographs and studied the young girl with the bright red curls. "Miss Alex?"

"They are all of Miss Alex," he replied.

She ignored his protests, and the two of them collected the pictures and put them in the envelope he pulled from the desktop.

"What you going to do with that girl when you find her?"

He looked at her strangely. Partly because the question was asked with such a definitive assumption that she would be found, and partly because he had no idea. He was so focused on just getting her back that he had no idea where the two of them were headed after she *was* back. "That's a good question, Sophia."

Her lips tightened into a flat line, and he could see her Catholic wheels turning as she nodded her head.

"Do not judge me, Sophia."

She said nothing more as she gripped the edge of the desk to stand back up.

"We're living in the twenty-first century," he reminded her, rising to help her back to her feet.

She headed for the door to finish preparing dinner. "I been with you for a long time, Mr. Sinclair, and I see a lot of women come and go from this house. They walk out that door with moons in their eyes." She turned to look at him before leaving the room. "Alex isn't like them, but she got moons in her eyes, too."

He threw the envelope on the desk and collapsed into the leather chair, Sophia's words still ringing with truth in his head. She was right about Alex being different. She was also right to disapprove of the way he was handling the whole situation. For a change, he was the one who needed to pick a side and jump.

Sophia came back into the room. "I forget to tell you. That girl came by this afternoon."

He waited for her to expound on "that girl", but she just stood there with a flat expression.

"Can you be more specific, Sophia?"

"The one with the big blue eyes. Alex's friend. Kathy or—"

"Katie?"

"That's the girl. She was worried because Alex didn't show up for work today."

"*Fuck.*" He glanced at Sophia with a silent apology for his sailor's tongue. "What did you tell her?"

"I told her Alex wasn't home. Is true, yes?"

He hadn't even thought about Shakespeare's Library, or the fact that Alex would probably be fired. The truth was, he hated the idea of her working for minimum wage when it was so damned unnecessary. But he also knew she didn't do it for the money. She needed the independence and the sense of normalcy.

"Sophia," he said, his eyes apologetic for what he was about to ask. "I would never ask you for this if it wasn't important. I need a favor—a big one."

The four men assembled in the dining room, settling in for another long night of trying to locate their missing girl. Considering the circumstances, Sophia's beautiful spread of food went barely touched.

It wasn't just fatigue that kept their appetites low; it was the underlying thought running through each of their heads that Alex was probably cold and hungry in some dingy cellar or basement. How could they indulge in a beautiful meal with that at the forefront of their minds?

Sophia stuck her head in the room now and then and noted the ignored food. She didn't take it personally, because she understood that it had nothing to do with the quality of the meal.

The one thing they didn't ignore was the bottle of wine in the center of the table.

She replaced the empty bottle with a full one. "Drunks are useless," she grumbled, shaking her head, speaking from the experience of spending years living under the same roof with one.

Greer reached behind him and opened the cabinet door. "You're right, Sophia." He pulled the bottle of scotch from the cabinet and set it on the table next to the wine. "This will keep us sufficiently sober." He handed the wine back to her.

She muttered something in Italian as she went back to the kitchen with the unopened bottle.

Greer poured himself a glass and slid the bottle across the table to Thomas. "What did you get out of him?"

The *him* he was referring to was the short bodyguard Isabetta Falcone never left home without. Demitri disappeared with his boss in the middle of all the mayhem at Battery Park, but the men managed to get their hands on the one who called himself Vito.

"Pussy cried like a baby when I gave him a little trailer of what we were about to do to him," Thomas sneered, pouring his own glass of whiskey. "Too bad he doesn't know shit. Looks like Isabetta keeps her boys stupid."

"Probably the only smart thing she ever did," Rhom added. "Unfortunately, it leaves us with nothing."

"We got one thing out of him," Thomas said. "Isabetta has been spending a lot of time down on Mulberry Street. Little Italy. The idiot said Demitri has been escorting her down there. Says he doesn't know why, but she's been real hush hush about it."

"And you believed him?" Greer asked.

"I think he's too stupid to be trusted with anything significant. So yeah, I believed him."

Greer polished off the remainder of his glass. "*Fuck.*"

Bear stuck his head around the corner and vocalized something between a purr and a meow. He brushed against the molding as he strolled into the dining room with his tail pointed to the ceiling.

"Is that the same cat?" Loden asked.

Greer glanced at the orange tabby. "Yeah, that is interesting, isn't it?"

Bear had grown at a record rate. But considering the company in the room, a kitten with a robust growth spurt wasn't that unusual.

He hopped on top of the sideboard cabinet and began licking his paw. He groomed himself for another minute and then looked at each of the men sitting at the table. The intelligence behind his bright green eyes was unsettling, not because it was unusual for a cat to show some real smarts, but because Bear seemed to be contemplating each one of them individually.

He started with Rhom and then moved his eyes around the

table to Thomas. Then he methodically looked at Loden. When he reached Greer, he stopped and released something between a word and a purr through his closed mouth. A half meow escaped his throat as his head lurched and began to pump back and forth like the piston of a machine.

"Shit," Loden said as he pushed back in his chair. "That cat's getting ready to hurl."

The pumping of his head got faster, and a clucking sound came up from his throat. Bear's mouth stretched into a wide cat grin, revealing his snow-white incisors as his tongue jetted out of his mouth and strained toward his feet.

Something pushed its way up his throat and over the top of his tongue. The object landed on the smooth mirror-like finish of the mahogany sideboard.

"What the fuck is that?" Thomas asked.

Greer looked shaken, trying to resolve what he was seeing on the cabinet. It was a piece of bone, the one he'd cut from his own back twenty years earlier. "It's Alex's charm." He looked at the cat and then back at the bone. "She never lets it out of her sight."

"I guess she left it home this time," Thomas pointed out. "The cat must have liked it, too."

Before Greer could disagree and explain why he knew that wasn't true, Bear started to lurch again.

Loden winced. "Shit, he's doing it again."

Another object hurled out of Bear's mouth and Rhom got up to look at it.

"Ah, man," Thomas groaned, "don't touch that shit."

"I'm not picking it up. Jeez." Rhom looked closer and examined the dry, neatly-folded piece of parchment paper without a drop of cat saliva on it, and read the word stamped on the front. "Adelina's."

Greer was standing now. "What the hell is that?"

"Best damn cannoli in the city." The men turned to look at

Loden who seemed to be the only one in the know. "Adelina's. What? You never been there?"

The four men went still, and Thomas, Rhom, and Loden each turned to look at Greer. In unison, all four men said the two words that glued the pieces together.

"Little Italy."

TWENTY-SEVEN

The bed I woke up in was considerably more comfortable than the last one. The sheets smelled of real lavender buds, and the thick comforter reminded me of a giant marshmallow painted with irises and periwinkle.

I lay there with my back to the mattress, staring at the ceiling while the memory of the past few days crept back inside my head. I was in Daemon's apartment. We were eating chicken but I couldn't remember what happened next. *This* was the next, me waking up in this strange bed with these strange smells, and no memory past the taste of chicken in my mouth.

There was an open door to my right, and I could see a countertop and a veined floor that looked like marble. The bathroom.

I pulled the bedding back. I was wearing a long nightshirt and underwear but no bra. The thought of him undressing me made me sick. I examined myself hesitantly for any marks or tenderness, anything that might tell me he'd finally finished what he'd started.

There were none.

A sliver of light slipped through either side of the accordion shade covering the window. Based on the intensity of the glow, it was either morning or early evening just before dusk.

The marble in the bathroom was cold against my feet as I stepped up to the counter and looked in the mirror. The girl looking back through the reflection was barely recognizable. She had the same auburn hair, and the blue eyes with the faint speck of brown in the middle of the left iris. But her cheeks seemed shallower, and the brightness of her eyes had dulled. The face staring back at me had aged years in a few short months, a steep price for peeling back all the layers hiding the real woman underneath.

The reflection of the shower caught my eye. The inside wall was lined with bottles of shampoo and conditioner. I reached inside for the bar of soap. It smelled of lemon and verbena and was embossed with a French name. The bottles were just as haute.

A cabinet mounted on the wall next to the mirror was filled with more extravagant things: perfume, body lotion, bath salts. There were thick towels—far too plush for my skin—neatly folded on a small table next to the shower, and a pair of slippers pushed underneath.

I walked past the dress hanging on the bathroom door and headed for the closet. A sick feeling began to roil up in my stomach as I walked inside.

The closet was big enough to fit a bed, and the walls were lined with clothes. On my right were dresses in every color and style conceivable. The left side was stuffed with pants and shirts and an entire section reserved for designer jeans and T-shirts. But the most outrageous part was the wall in front of me. From the floor to the ceiling was a series of slanted shelves displaying shoes. There must have been a hundred pairs: sandals, pumps, flats, stilettos, wedges. There was even a shelf for sneakers and running shoes.

It was obscene.

That feeling was coming back—the one that felt like a cat fighting with my intestines. I stepped back from the glow of the closet light and steadied myself against the dresser just outside the door.

"I believe the sizes are correct." Daemon was standing behind me. "Anything that doesn't fit will be replaced."

I turned around slowly to keep my balance. The clothes, the scent of lavender, the ostentatious bath paraphernalia—it was all for me. He intended to keep me.

"I don't want any of it." My head shook as I took a step back.

"Don't be silly, Alex. This is your home, now." The smile left his face. "Would you prefer I stock the closet with rags and buy your toiletries from a dollar store?"

He didn't get it. "You can stock this jail cell with anything you like, but I'm not wearing any of it. I won't be bathing either. Maybe you should think about that."

He prolonged his stare, as did I. When it was clear I had no intention of backing down, he puffed up like a ruffled rooster. "This is for your own good," he said between slightly clenched teeth. "Do I need to remind you of what happened the last time I left you alone? Would you like to go back there? What do you think will happen if you do?"

Before I could answer with an I'll-take-my-chances kind of response, he elaborated. "You'd be on your back in that other room with those animals crawling on top of you."

"You know that Greer will kill you when he finds this place, and he will." I had to believe that or I'd fall apart. I could never let Daemon see that weak spot.

He glanced at the dress hanging on the bathroom door. "Get dressed," he instructed as he left the room.

The living room was empty when I came out of the bedroom. The light was obscured by the blinds covering the windows. I remembered the night Daemon showed up on Columbus Avenue, telling me that the light made him uncomfortable, asking me if he could touch my skin.

The smell of bacon and freshly brewed coffee made my mouth water. There was enough food on the dining room table to feed half a dozen people. But as hungry as I was and as much as I wanted a cup of that coffee, the thought of accepting it felt like a betrayal. He'd have to force me to eat it like he'd done the night before.

Daemon came out of the kitchen and assessed the dress he'd chosen for me. His eyes ran down my body, and then back up to my face. "You look lovely."

He motioned to the table. "Sit. Please." When I didn't move, he came toward me and took my arm with just enough tenderness to mask the aggression my defiance had stirred. "I don't like raising my voice to you, Alex. Please don't make me do it again."

I jerked my arm from his hand and looked him in the eye before walking to the table and sitting down. "I'd be more cooperative if I knew what you had planned for me."

He reached over my shoulder and poured coffee into my cup. "Cream and sugar?"

"I've got it." I grabbed the creamer before he could.

"Did you sleep well?" He sat across from me and poured his own cup. "I took the liberty of giving you something."

"You drugged me?"

"I wouldn't call it a drug. Just something to take the edge off. You were a difficult girl last night."

That edge was coming back in droves. I had no memory of the last evening past the part where I'd forced myself to eat the food he'd threatened to shove down my throat. He could have done anything to me. Such an easy mark I must have been, with all my humanness.

He sat and stared at me, waiting for me to serve myself before taking his first bite. Well, what do you know, a predator with manners. I thought about antagonizing the situation by refusing again, but that tactic seemed to backfire. And I was really hungry. Fighting my way out of this nightmare would be difficult enough without a raging hunger in my throat.

I leaned across the table and spooned some scrambled eggs, bacon, and an English muffin on my plate. When I was done assembling my breakfast, I sat back and looked at him, giving him the green light to dig in. He continued to wait until I finally put a forkful of food in my mouth.

He began to eat as I chewed, and I wondered how many more of these meals I'd have to suffer through before he finally lost the manners and showed his true colors.

"Why don't you just tell me why I'm here." I reached for the muffin in a show of good faith that I was willing to cooperate. "If it's the vessel—"

I stopped myself from saying the words that might get Dr. Oxford killed, or at best maimed when they ripped the lenses from his eyes. If I told him those ridiculous glasses were nothing but a ruse and we needed Oxford in the flesh to find the vessel, I would seal that poor man's fate. I couldn't live with that.

A fleeting smile crossed his face as he tore at a piece of bacon and chased it with a glass of orange juice. When he'd sufficiently chewed and swallowed, he wiped his mouth with the cloth napkin and laid it next to his plate. "Yes, the vessel. There is that," he said with enough curiosity to make me question the crux of this whole abduction.

Something unpleasant settled in my gut and gnawed at my intestines, like a tiny rat chewing on the wires inside my walls. It was that old intuition that a girl should never ignore.

The sound of my fork meeting the tabletop resonated through the air as I looked at Daemon's still face, his eyes resting on mine as if he were waiting for a bright, shiny lightbulb to appear above my head.

"I'll keep asking the same questions over and over until you can't take it anymore," I promised.

He released a heavy sigh and looked at me exasperatedly. "You frustrate me so . . . completely. Don't you trust me?"

I had to remember that he was deluded, capable of convincing himself of whatever he needed to in order to justify the fantasy he'd created in this apartment.

"I will tell you one last time, and then the subject will be closed. This," his eyes traveled around the room before settling back on mine, "is your home now."

The chair made a rough scraping sound as I stood up and nearly toppled it over. I made it to the bedroom and slammed the door. There was no lock, but I imagined it wouldn't matter if it had a deadbolt. A man—or should I say *male*—like Daemon wouldn't let a little contraption made of metal keep him out of the room.

The door swung open. He leaned into the frame as I took the lamp from the nightstand and hurled it at the wall.

"There's another one over there." He gestured to another lamp on the dresser.

I ran to the closet and started pulling the clothes from the hangers, throwing dresses and shoes and blouses through the door into a pile on the bedroom floor. "I don't want any of this!" I screamed.

He watched what he must have thought equivalent to a childish tantrum, with his face expressionless and sober. Then the clothes started flying back at me. Each garment flew back on its hanger, and each shoe landed right back in its place on the shelf. The shards of the shattered lamp began to move, and then they reassembled as if a giant magnet had called them back together.

"Are you done?" he asked calmly.

My blood felt like it was on fire. It raced through my veins, causing my heart to thump wildly and pulse in my ears. I ran into the bathroom. A moment later, I was running at him with a razor in my hand. He caught my arm and held it at a distance, looking at the thin shielded blade as if trying to make sense of how I intended to use it.

"Don't be ridiculous, Alex." He lowered my arm and smiled in that condescending way a parent confronts an insufferable child.

And then I did it. I lifted my other arm and swiftly shoved my wrist along the edge of the blade. Just a drop would do it. An intense pain radiated from my arm and shot through my body as I managed to slice a small gash along the vein of my wrist.

Daemon dropped his hold on me and stepped back as I inhaled sharply and gasped. His eyes went to the blood running down my wrist, and then they slowly reached back up to my face. "What have you done?"

I waited for the monster inside of me to emerge and prayed that it would know what to do. Greer had trained me to control it, but only with him, not with someone my monster had never met.

As I stood there bracing myself, Daemon took my hand and raised my wrist to his lips. I watched in horror as his tongue slipped from his mouth and pressed against the dark red fluid that was draining down the inside of my arm. He covered the surface of my wrist with his mouth and sucked. Then he raised his head and licked the blood clean from the rim of his lips. "It is as perfect as I imagined."

The cut stopped bleeding, and I watched as the wound healed itself into a thin pink line. And then it was over. Just like that. Nothing happened.

I looked back up at Daemon whose eyes had turn an intense black. His lips parted to accommodate the acceleration of his breath, and for the second time, I was staring into the eyes that almost detonated my life so many months ago in the park.

I knew that look like I'd seen it just yesterday, and I knew what would happen if I didn't run.

His fingers slid around the edge of my jaw while his thumb skimmed my lower lip. "You understand that this has to happen, don't you?" His look bordered on incredulous as he scanned my face for acceptance. "If it was one of the others, I'm afraid you wouldn't be treated with the respect you deserve."

That doubtful expression began to change and turn agitated. His eyes moved back and forth between mine as if one might be saying something different from the other, and I could sense his growing anger as his grip on my jaw tightened.

"You ungrateful girl," he whispered.

Sophia's face flashed in my mind as the word *ungrateful* rang through my ears. Everyone seemed to have an opinion on my proclivity for gratitude.

Run, my brain kept saying. But there was nowhere to go. I was in a room with my attacker between me and the only way out, and there was nowhere to run.

He let go of my face, but only to shut the door. We were alone in the apartment, but some things are too reprehensible even for an empty house to see.

There's a time for curling into a tight ball and shutting the world out. And then there are times like these when that kind of weakness can get you killed.

I was alive, more so than ever because a deep and festering wound had been gouged straight through my soul, and I could feel every bit of its torn edges with acute awareness.

I know I should have felt sickened and violated by what he'd done to me, but all I felt was rage for what he'd taken, for the future he'd just ruined. All I could think about was Greer's face. All I could see were his eyes looking back at mine and knowing that this girl wasn't the same one he'd walk through fire for.

I'd lost everything. He'd stolen everything.

The bed moved as Daemon shifted next to me. The heat from his skin crawled over mine, inciting a mild panic at the thought of it suffocating me.

My eyes closed and I went completely still, hoping he wouldn't wake and force me to look at him again. That moment was the most significant of my life, as I waited to see if he'd turn to me or continue to sleep. The latter was my fate, and when I was sure I wasn't about to suffer another round of his twisted form of love, I quietly rolled my back to his.

I would survive this, and then I would kill him.

TWENTY-EIGHT

A thunderstorm cracked the sky and rumbled the tail end of its whip through the room, waking me from a dead sleep. But when I turned toward the window I saw a beam of sunlight, with all its particles of floating, white dust, cast across the wood floor. For a few beautiful seconds I was at home in my bed, with thoughts of Sophia's French toast and freshly pressed coffee.

And then I wasn't.

My memory of what happened was as clear as sparkling water, but I still tried to manipulate the images like a collage or a storyboard, reconstructing the events leading up to this very moment.

I turned around, careful not to disturb the mattress. The other side was empty. Maybe it had all been a vivid nightmare. Or maybe my monster had come through for me after all, and I'd feel Daemon's slaughtered body under my feet when I swung my legs over the side of the bed.

My head craned in the direction of the door as it opened. A man walked in and looked at me like he had the right to inspect my naked body.

He must have been six foot six, but moved as if maneuvering

in and out of standard door frames wasn't a challenge at all. His blond hair had the slightest hint of orange, and it was pulled back in one of those man buns that seemed to be all the rage with the hipsters. Or maybe he was rocking Buddha.

Either way, I doubted he cared what anyone thought about his choice of style, because he was wearing a kilt of deeply hued blue and green tartan. His heavy black boots laced up to the middle of his shins, and for a moment I thought I heard bag-pipes skirling up from the bright green knoll I visualized around him.

"Maelcolm?" I asked. Who else would it be?

He walked around the perimeter of the bed, examining me from every angle. Then he raised his head as only a *Maelcolm* could, and turned it toward the bedroom door.

My eyes followed his. Daemon was standing in the doorway with a man at each side. The man on his left was holding a metal chain that led to a thick cuff circling Daemon's neck. He took an involuntary step toward me and the chain snapped with a violent jerk that pulled him back outside the room.

Maelcolm turned his attention back on me. "Did this man force himself on you?" He pointed in the direction of the door.

Why did it matter? I wondered. Wasn't that what they did? Didn't they make sport of preying on women? Had protocol been broken, turning their neat little system into undisciplined predation?

I turned to look Daemon in the eye. I knew they'd do something horrible to him if I testified in that room. And though I wanted to kill him myself, the humanity in me suffered a small pang of compassion as I delivered my answer.

"Yes."

Maelcolm nodded once and the two men hauled Daemon away. Not a single protest left his mouth as he disappeared from the doorway. The chain rattled as they led him down the hall, and then the sound abruptly stopped.

"Put some clothes on." His heavy boots hit the floor with an unexpected grace as he headed for the door.

"I need to take a shower," I uttered in a voice that was barely a whisper. I knew that wasn't what I was supposed to do, but Daemon was already being dealt with. There would be no report, no need for evidence. That's not how it worked in this world.

"Very well," he allowed. "Ten minutes."

"Twenty," I replied boldly.

He conceded by saying nothing as he walked out of the room.

I walked into the ridiculous closet and found my own T-shirt and jeans, newly washed and hung neatly along with all the new clothes that were meant for me.

What a waste, I thought. *What a fucking waste.* I wanted to set the closet on fire, destroy any evidence I'd ever been in that room.

My hands shook as I laid the clothes on the countertop and stepped into the stream of water. It wasn't hot enough. But any hotter and my skin would boil and slide off of my flesh. The contrast of the cold stone tiling the shower wall soothed my back as I slipped down to the floor and took every second of my twenty minutes.

Maelcolm was staring out the window when I walked into the living room. The light seemed to have no effect on him, and I wondered if the aversion to it was all in Daemon's twisted imagination. In his delusion, had he convinced himself that he was some sort of night crawler?

From his profile, I could tell it was an east-facing window. The bright light made his pale skin look almost white from the intense glare. He had a deep furrow running across his forehead, softened by the exaggeration of his thick arched brow.

He ran his hand over the length of his beard and turned to

looked at me. I averted my eyes to the man standing guard near the front door. There were two more nosing around in the kitchen.

"What will happen to him?" I asked.

His expression was neutral as he examined my wet hair and the clothes that seemed to hang on me like old rags. They used to fit me perfectly, but I was beginning to shrink under the weight of everything happening around me. I hadn't even noticed I'd lost a full size over the past few weeks.

It's funny how that happens. You're dieting and anxiously checking the scale every morning for that half-pound loss, stripping naked before stepping on because your underwear obviously yielded that half pound that wasn't going away. Then all of a sudden you're wearing a size six instead of an eight.

"Daemon's fate is not your concern."

I recognized the man coming out of the kitchen. He was one of the men who tried to attack me the day Daemon brought me here.

"He said this place was for my own good." I looked around the room, stopping to glare at the man by the kitchen, feeling a false sense of security now that the big kahuna had arrived. If Daemon had committed a major faux pas by touching me, surely no one else would be stupid enough to try anything now.

That safety net began to wither as it occurred to me that maybe the offense was in daring to touch what Maelcolm wanted for himself. Maybe I was meant for him.

Maelcolm was watching me intently when I looked back at him. "Was he right?" I asked, referring to Daemon's warped reasons for bringing me here, taking his own liberties instead of letting the whole dungeon have a turn.

"Yes," he murmured as he came toward me. He extended his hand over my face just like Daemon had done, and with that same smooth flick of his fingers, his hand swept over my eyes and the world faded away.

The room was different, but I knew I was back in that same place where this started. I was in a bed, fully clothed with my hair still damp and molded into a messy knot against the pillow.

"Fuck," I muttered. My eyes burned, and my head throbbed from the intense contractions taking place under my skull.

I heard sounds echoing from the vent at the base of the wall, and I jumped off the bed to crouch and listen for the voice of Dr. Oxford. Maybe they'd taken him back to the same room and I was just on the other side of it. Maybe he still had his eyes. But the sounds I heard were not made by Dr. Oxford: silverware tapping the edges of plates, the muffled voices of a crowd, the hum of machinery. But it was the smell of bread and sugar and coffee that told me I wasn't listening to the sounds from Oxford's room.

A light tap came from the door. "Come in," I said hesitantly as if I might actually have a choice. *Go away.* I wondered what would happen if I simply ignored the tap.

The door opened and Maelcolm walked into the room. He was wearing the same brightly colored kilt, but his beard had been trimmed close to his face and he'd changed into a fresh shirt.

The room seemed to shrink with him in it. Each step sent a vibration through the old pine planks like a large animal was being paraded across the floor. There would be no element of surprise with this one. This man couldn't hide from anyone.

His eyes turned, and I nearly gasped at the brightness of the blue staring back at me.

As hard and dangerous as I knew he was, there was something noble or even kind in the way he prepared me for the impending interrogation. With a single look he said, *this is going to hurt, but it is necessary.*

Still, I took an involuntary step backward as he moved closer. Picking up on my caution, he detoured toward the chair.

He glanced at the edge of the bed. "Sit."

"I've done enough of that," I replied. "I'd prefer to stand."

He nodded and remained standing, too. "You must be wondering," he began.

"Wondering what?"

"What will happen next."

I gave no response, choosing instead to let him do all the talking. Maybe the awkward silence would ignite a little small talk. People say too much with small talk. They can't stand the excruciating silence and fill it with things that should never leave their mouths. Maybe some awkward babbling would get me answers. But I doubted a man like Maelcolm would ever waste his time with unnecessary words.

"May I see it?" he eventually asked.

I played dumb, hoping for some stroke of genius in those few precious seconds that would prevent him from taking the amulet from me.

"I'm not accustomed to asking for things, Alex. I'm even less accustomed to non-compliance."

The look on his face told me my time was up and that stroke of genius wasn't coming. I reached for the chain and pulled the amulet out from under my shirt. I figured he could see it just fine from where he was standing, and I had no intention of removing it from around my neck and just handing it over.

He stepped closer and reached for it. "I won't take it from you," he assured me as my hand went up to stop him.

He was so close to me now that I could feel that telltale heat, reminding me that he and Greer were cut from the same mold, despite the million ways they were so very different.

"You have my word." He leaned in for a better look at the

plain silver necklace in the unassuming shape of a dog tag. "Quite an ordinary looking thing, isn't it?" he remarked. "Who would think that the young woman standing in front of me, with this unimpressive piece of jewelry hanging from her neck, is the key to everything."

"Yeah, who would have thought?" I agreed. "I guess the gods had a good time with that one, didn't they?"

"I am sorry about all this, Alex."

I wasn't sure if he meant my immediate predicament, or if he was referring to my role as the reluctant messiah.

"Here you are," he went on. "Home at last. And now you're forced to suffer fools who can't seem to think their way out of a paper bag. Had I known what was happening, I would have come sooner." He leaned forward as if to tell me something in confidence, in that way that intimate friends do. "I want you to know that Daemon has been dealt with."

Okay. Well, at least you're discriminating about how and when you ruin lives.

I know I should have felt more than I did, more violated or enraged by what Daemon did to me. Isn't that how it's supposed to work? The expectation of grief seems just as profane as the tragedy that causes it. Maybe I'd feel something if we were back in the park again, and my attacker didn't have a face or a name. But I was never good at being a victim, and I felt nothing, surprisingly blank and numb. I'd already put Daemon in a dark closet in the back of my mind, and I simply couldn't afford the luxury of feeling the wound. I couldn't afford to be a victim while my life hung in the hands of the Highlander standing in front of me.

"You're working with Isabetta Falcone?" I asked, wondering if Maelcolm was the source she'd referred to when she dumped Dr. Oxford's secrets on the table in that Italian restaurant.

He scoffed at the suggestion. "She was useful."

"Alasdair Templeton? Has he been useful, too?"

At the mention of the name, his body stiffened. His cheeks drew in as his jaw tightened, and I could feel the storm brewing behind his icy blue eyes. Apparently, there was no love lost between the two of them, and I'd found a potentially useful trigger.

"That old . . . *fuck*." His nostrils flared as a deep breath brought him back down to a simmer. "I wouldn't let that relic clean my toilet."

That ruled out an alliance between the two of them, which was a good thing, because I'd be on my way to Ireland if they were washing each other's backs.

He took a stroll around the small space. There was a thought perched on the tip of his tongue as he looked around the room, glancing at the walls and the floor and the rumpled bed linens, a distraction to keep him from speaking prematurely or saying something less than perfect. Everything about him seemed calculated.

Premeditated. That was the word that popped into my head.

"Do you have a last name?" I asked.

He stopped his meditative survey of the room. "Does it matter?"

In the broader perspective of things, it probably didn't. But I was imprisoned in this place at his will, and it seemed like a reasonable request to know the full name of the person who might be responsible for eventually ending my life.

He waited for further useless questions with a touch of annoyance on his face. I decided that keeping the peace between us was more important than a name, and let it go.

It seemed like days were passing as we stood a few yards apart, staring at each other in silence, playing out a game of who will crack first. He just stood there, expressionless with his hands clasped behind his back. I was like a bug under a magnifying glass with a laser of light burning a hole in the center of my forehead, waiting to combust into flames if I didn't get out from under his intense, wordless stare.

"Say something!" I finally blurted.

His brow arched quizzically. "Does silence make you uncomfortable?"

"*You* make me uncomfortable."

"No. It's not me, Alex. You're beginning to wake up, and *that* makes you uncomfortable. In fact, I suspect you're more awake now than you've ever been. You're not used to taking what you want—what you need." He cracked a condescending smile. "Tell me . . . that young man in the park, the one with the distasteful T-shirt who almost cost you your humanity, did *he* have something you needed?"

"How do you—"

His head cocked slightly as he read my reaction. "There's nothing wrong with taking what you need."

The vision I had in the park the day I went to see Constantine wasn't real, but the memory of it still shamed me. "How do you know about that?"

He ignored my question and continued. "Poor little girl vanishes and then returns twenty-one years later, only to find out she's destined for something unimaginable."

He stepped closer and leaned into the void between us. The room seemed to disappear as his presence swallowed the space. His warm breath pooled over my skin as he reached toward my face and took a lock of my hair in his hand. "You remind me of her," he murmured, rolling the ends between his fingers.

I jerked back and tugged my hair out of his hand. It was like he'd slapped me in the face.

"My mother? You knew her?"

I don't know why that surprised me. Everyone seemed to know Maeve Kelley, the famous witch of New York, the original golden child.

A subtle laugh came from his throat as he stood taller and moved back a step. The brightness in his eyes dulled, and I noticed for the first time the thin rings of brown around the blue. The mutation was barely detectable, but I could see the soft brown outer edges feather and disappear into the overwhelming blue of his irises.

"She was perfect in every way, except one," he said. I flinched but didn't stop him as he caressed the side of my face with the palm of his massive hand. "She was a little too smart."

He sensed my repulsion and pulled his hand away. "Well, we have many things to discuss, but let's get you fed first."

I decided on a different approach to make me feel like less of a sellout for accepting his food—I would dictate the meal and let him worry about how to get it.

"I want French toast," I demanded. "And don't forget the maple syrup."

TWENTY-NINE

Sophia stood on the sidewalk, looking up at the green house with the red shutters, and thought about how endearing and inviting the façade looked. But there were things in that house that were not so endearing, things she thought she was done with, things long buried.

Mr. Sinclair had asked for a favor, although he would never call it payback. She could do him a thousand favors and still never call it even.

For approximately one hour every morning and one every evening, she traveled between Manhattan and Bensonhurst, Brooklyn in the fancy car service Greer paid for. But on this particular day, the drive home seemed to take only a minute.

The ticking of the clock in the living room echoed through the empty house as she walked through the front door and headed straight for the kitchen. She took a glass from the cabinet above the sink and filled it from the tap. As she sipped the water, she gazed out the window at the neglected garden in her tiny backyard. The basil would be coming back from seed soon, and the thyme and rosemary would be waking up with new growth. She promised to be more attentive this season.

She washed the glass and placed it upside down on the towel

next to the sink. Then she headed for the pantry to get on with the business of the past.

Her eyes moved around the small space, distracted by all the boxes and cans, and the jars of preserved tomatoes she would never get around to eating. She spotted the box of tools on the lower shelf and rummaged through the rarely used screwdrivers, hammers, and wrenches until she found what she was looking for.

The stairs seemed to breathe as she ascended them to the second floor. When she reached the top step, she thought again about all the reasons she'd walked away from a life that had filled her with so much purpose, completed her like a conjoined twin. But no matter how far she ran from it, that life would always be patiently waiting for her return, because she didn't choose it—she was born of it.

On her way to the door at the end of the hall, she stopped at her bedroom and walked inside. She picked up the picture of her daughter from the dresser and examined the smiling young woman with the River Thames in the background. It had been almost a year since she'd seen Adrianna, and she wondered if her daughter would understand the change in her mother when she came home on holiday.

She set the frame down and picked up the one next to it. The face of a younger girl looked back from the photo, and Sophia was instantly racked with doubt about what she was about to do.

Rue was her baby, and the decision to take up her old life seemed like a betrayal to her dead child. Even as she endured years of her husband's drunken rage over Rue's death, she chose to weather the abuse without taking up the weapons that could have so easily obliterated her suffering.

In the end, it was Mr. Sinclair who saved her from having to make that choice. For that she owed an immense debt, and she was loyal. Mr. Sinclair needed her help, and he'd never once asked for anything in return for all the gifts he'd given her over the years.

Until now.

She put Rue's picture back down next to Adrianna's and reached for a green cameo vase, spilling its contents onto the white lace runner covering the top of the dresser: a matchbook with a phone number written across the cover, a business card for a tree removal service, a dead beetle that had crawled in and found it impossible to climb back out, and a key.

Sophia took the key and went back into the hall. The door was at the end, staring back at her as if it was taunting her—*We knew you couldn't stay away.* She marched toward it and placed the key in the lock. The door swung open as if an invisible hand had pulled it from the other side.

With a swift glide, she pulled back the thin woven rug and examined the pattern of the wooden planks underneath it. On the far left side was a section where the ends of the boards were too even, not staggered properly like the rest of the floor. She groaned as her aging knees pressed against the wood, and then she wedged the crowbar she'd carried from the pantry into a gap between two of the boards.

Sophia was a sturdy woman. With a grunt, she pushed down firmly and the old board popped up with a loud split. She did the same to the other two boards covering the hidden space between the floors of her house.

A strained breath expelled from her chest as she reached inside the floor. With both hands, she removed a wooden box, deeply patinated from significant age. She reached for the top but stopped as if it might burn her fingers if she touched it.

"Forgive me," she whispered with a slight glance toward the ceiling before removing the delicate chain holding the crucifix around her neck.

With a trembling hand, she removed the top of the box and stared at its contents. There would be no going back if she crossed the veil to her previous ways, laid hands on the old path, realigned her tenets and faith. She wondered if she was too cynical now, if it was possible to return to it with an open mind and a wide heart after all that had happened?

Her decision made, she opened the box and carefully lifted a metal bowl, charred on the inside rim from the many lifetimes of flames that had danced around its center. Four smaller bowls were removed next, followed by an elaborate silver chalice and a flat, polished stone with a star engraved across its top.

A smile rose on one side of her face when she extracted a large double-edged knife from its wooden scabbard. The blade had dulled, but the marks were still visible along each side. The knife had come from her mother, but the finely crafted scabbard had been carefully constructed from her own hands when she was sixteen. Feeling it again was like pulling a dark cloud from the sky, the one following her since the day she shoved her life into that dark hole.

Sealing the blade under the floor had been the only way to prevent Sophia from ripping it from the box, and to keep its alluring pull out of Adrianna's head. She would never allow her eldest daughter to be seduced by that world. Not after what happened to her Rue.

Sophia sat back on her aching knees and thighs and paused for a moment before completely unraveling the past nineteen years. She lifted the last item from the box—a small leather pouch. She opened it and let the silver charm slide into the palm of her hand—a sprig of rue adorned with a moon, a serpent, and a key.

As she placed the cimaruta around her neck where the crucifix had hung for so many years, she knew it had all been a lie to deceive her unbearable grief from knowing where it lived. But the grief had always been there, and she could feel it now without letting it destroy her.

The grand illusion had served its purpose. She was home

now. She was Strega, a fifth-generation hereditary witch from the old country, something that could never be put in a box and buried.

The bell on the door chimed as Sophia entered Shakespeare's Library, a tinge of anger spreading through her because it was a stark reminder that Alex was gone.

She fidgeted with the old charm tucked under her blue floral dress while she waited impatiently by the unmanned front counter. Her normal attire would have been much more conservative and age-appropriate than the bright spring dress she had on, but she wasn't feeling her age today. In fact, she felt like a new woman, like her clipped wings had suddenly grown back.

Apollo came out from the back room and looked around the deserted shop with annoyance. "I'm sorry. We're a little short-handed today. Can I help you find something?"

Sophia knew why they were short-handed. Alex had been a no-show and would probably be out of a job when Mr. Sinclair found her and brought her safely home—and he would.

He had asked Sophia for a favor, and that favor meant putting on her Strega hat to perform nothing short of a miracle. Never mind that he was asking her to swallow all that bitterness and reavow a life she no longer wanted any part of. He didn't know the extent of her deep-seated fear of what opening that box might bring, and had she refused, he would have accepted that refusal without reproach.

But here she was, standing tall and proud before her gods, not quite understanding how she could have been so quick to blame them for what happened to her Rue that spring day nineteen years earlier. She was back, and she would deal with all her baggage another time because there were more important things on her plate today.

"Are you the manager?" she asked.

"I am."

She prepared herself for the lie–something she didn't do well. "My name is Sophia. Alex Kelley is my niece."

Apollo made the connection with Alex's previous lie about a funeral for an uncle. "Oh, I'm so sorry for your loss. Alex told us about her uncle."

Sophia stared at him with a frozen expression, the rhythm of the lie interrupted and now slowed to a halt. "Her uncle?"

"Sophia. Nice to see you again." Katie came out from the romance section and interrupted the conversation that was about to get sticky.

"Yes, we were all very sad to hear about the funeral." Her eyes pinned Sophia's as she salvaged the lie. "Is everything okay? Alex hasn't shown up for work, and I can't seem to reach her on her cell."

Sophia took Katie's cue and pulled herself together. If this was to work, she needed complete focus. After all, she'd been alienated from her craft for nineteen years and was rather rusty on the fine points of illusion. A spell like the one she had planned required her undivided attention, which meant she needed Katie to distract Apollo while she worked her magic.

"Thank you," she said to both. "He was old." She looked at Katie and motioned toward the science fiction section with a slight flick of her head. "Can I speak to you in private?"

Apollo politely stepped back and allowed the bereaved widow her moment of privacy with Katie. Sophia wasted no time taking Katie by the arm and steering her down an aisle.

"*What* the hell was that?" Katie asked as she yanked her arm free. "Mind telling me why you're pretending to be Alex's aunt? And then you can tell me where she is."

Sophia wasn't happy about any of this. She'd spent the past two decades living by the dogma of the Catholic church in hopes of forgetting her past. And even though she knew it was all a convenient guise for denial, the part about not lying was a pretty universal tenet.

"She's in trouble," Sophia hissed. "Mr. Sinclair is taking care of things, but I need you to help me fix this job situation for her."

"It's too late. Apollo's already looking for a replacement."

"How many days has she missed?" Sophia didn't know Alex's schedule from one day to the next, usually finding out at the breakfast table each morning if she'd be home for dinner.

"Monday was her day off, but she hasn't shown up since then." An exaggerated shudder rippled through Katie's torso. "God, why is she doing this to me? I don't think Apollo is going to fall for another dead relative."

Sophia had no idea what Katie was talking about, and it showed through the blank stare she threw back at her.

"She missed a couple days last week when her *uncle* died. Hence the condolences to you—her *aunt*."

"Ah . . . I see." Sophia dismissively waved her hand. "I got a better plan."

Sophia had ears. She'd heard every detail when Alex told Greer about Katie's unique heritage. Having never worked with dragons, she had no idea if the spell would work on one, so she thought it best to bring Katie in on the plan.

"Do you like Mondays?" she asked Katie.

"Um . . . not my favorite day, but I have nothing against them."

"Good, because it's going to be Monday for a while."

Katie stood back and looked at the woman she knew as Greer's housekeeper and cook. "*That's* going to take a little explaining."

"Not everywhere. Just here. In the shop."

In general, time spells were tricky even for the most seasoned Strega. They could be just plain messy if you didn't get all the variables lined up just so. Even after reversal, Sophia had seen one or two overlap and linger between the physical and the astral planes. None of *her* spells, of course, but she still needed to be focused and very careful about what she was about to do.

"You walk in the shop, it's Monday," Sophia said with a *that's that* air of confidence. "As soon as you leave, no more Monday. Very simple plan."

Katie leaned back against the opposite shelf and grinned. "Well . . . What. Are. You?" she asked rhetorically, amused by the revelation that even the hired help wasn't immune to the weird and freakish bubble she was living in.

"Strega," Sophia announced proudly.

The word rolled off her tongue with a taste of pure truth, and in an odd sort of way, it released her from all the guilt she'd been storing up over the years.

Katie gasped and her grin spread wider. "Really? That's fucking awesome!"

Sophia's pride continued to swell as she lifted her arms toward the ceiling and began the incantation in Italian. She lowered her right arm back down and pulled something from her purse—a clear orb with a glowing green spot in the center. She hurled it at the north end of the shop. It stuck to the wall and spread like wildfire across the flat surface, consuming the posters and the hanging pictures as it made its way to each corner. She sent another orb toward the west wall, this one glowing blue in the center. The paintball working was completed with a red orb cast to the south and a yellow one to the east. The orbs met at the corners and spread across the ceiling and floor in unison, sealing off the room with an invisible shield.

Katie looked up, and the air in the center of the room was filled with letters and words that seemed to be floating from the pages of the thousands of books filling the shelves.

She shot a look across the room to where Apollo was sitting at the front counter, oblivious to it all. She took a few steps closer and realized he was frozen in place. Time had momentarily stopped.

"You are *bad*ass," Katie declared as she watched her boss hang in suspended animation.

When it was over and the walls and the air had cleared, Apollo looked up and noticed Katie staring at him. "What?" he asked.

She shook her head. "I was just trying to remember what day it was."

"It's the dreaded Monday," he grumbled as he buried his head back in his paperwork.

Sophia pursed her lips and walked toward the entrance. "I'll keep you posted," she threw over her shoulder as she walked out the door.

Except for the incredible smell of rising yeast and freshly baked bread, there was nothing remarkable about the place—until you pushed through the crowd and got a look at the amazing spread of pastries.

The floor was covered with worn linoleum marred by years of heavy traffic, and a vintage display case that came up to an average man's shoulders seemed to anchor the store to the corner lot on Mulberry Street. Adelina's had served New Yorkers for decades, and by the looks of the mob standing in line to order, it would continue to serve the city for many more.

Rhom surveyed the room with his trademark Rottweiler face. Satisfied by the innocuous nature of the crowd, he gave his approval with a firm nod.

The bakery had only been open for fifteen minutes, just in time for the brunch or early lunch rush. As you'd expect in a place where people waited at least a half hour just for the pleasure of serving themselves, there were no empty tables and plenty of standers waiting to pounce on the first vacancy.

"I don't like being an asshole," Rhom said, "but duty calls." He approached a table occupied by a man and two women. Not a word was said as he gave them a look that motivated them to leave.

One of the women slid out from the bench and Rhom slid in, drawing a few muttered comments from the lurkers who were there first but didn't dare broach the point. Thomas slid next to him while Greer and Loden took the other side.

"So, what do we do now?" asked Thomas.

Greer looked around the room, focusing on the guy with a flour-stained apron and greasy black hair hustling behind the huge counter. "I have no idea, but that cat didn't upchuck the name of this place for nothing."

Thomas bobbed his head and glanced around the table. "Yeah, there's something not right about that cat."

"You think?" Greer replied.

Thomas ignored the sarcasm. "Where'd she get that thing?"

"I have a feeling that cat found her," Loden speculated. "Seems to be on her side, though." He shrugged and slid back out into the aisle.

A woman with a high ponytail and running pants inched closer as he stood up. "Not leaving, love. But I'll make sure you get the table when we do."

"Where are you going?" Greer asked as Loden started walking toward the entrance.

"Well, I'm not going to jump the line." He nodded toward the back of the long mob of people.

"For what?"

"Cannoli. You don't come to Adelina's without getting cannoli."

"Bring me one," Thomas said. "And a double espresso."

"What the fuck do I look like? A waitress?" Loden smirked. "Don't worry. I'll buy a dozen."

He took his place at the back of the line, slogging along the front of the long display case, the slow progress making him want to buy one of everything. He wondered if that was the point. Clever marketing strategy; inflate the line with hooked regulars so those impulse purchases could fatten their asses and Adelina's profits.

Something dropped, and the sound of breaking china cut through the white noise of the voices and the ringing cash register and the crumpling bags being stuffed with pastries.

Loden glanced through the opened back panel of the display case, past the deeply scored Pane di Altamura loaves. He spotted a man with a tray in his hand bending down to pick up shards of broken china. He absently examined the contents of the tray: a glass of orange juice, a cup of coffee, a pastry stuffed inside one of Adelina's signature parchment bags. He couldn't see what was on the plate, but the small pitcher that had shattered on the floor left a pool of sticky amber liquid all over the linoleum and splattered across the lower edge of the man's white apron.

A woman was taking orders a few people deep from the register. Loden shuffled with the line past the tall display case and reached the counter. He gave the woman his order for eight cannoli, a dozen biscotti, and four espressos.

The man with the tray finished cleaning the mess on the floor and stood back up, revealing the contents of the plate.

Something triggered in Loden's head at the sight of a plate of French toast in an Italian bakery full of Italian breakfast delicacies.

Greer looked up from the table just as Loden turned to look at him. The two men held their stare for a moment, and then Loden nodded his head and turned his eyes back to the man walking past the counter with the tray of food.

THIRTY

Maelcolm pulled his phone from his pocket and placed the order. "Your food will be here shortly. I'll give you some time to eat and take a shower before we resume our conversation."

He placed the phone back in his pocket and headed for the door. As he reached for the knob, he looked back at me. "You will be a queen, Alex. The mother and the blood of a new race."

It took a moment for it to hit me, but the words settled in and I realized why I was here. Daemon had said something similar the night he grabbed me outside of Greer's house. *You, Alex, will make us kings.*

The prophecy was the prize, but I was the one who would create a race strong enough to keep it. It was in my blood. They needed my blood—a breeder.

The weight of the epiphany hung like a giant stone in my chest, dragging me toward the ground as my vision began to blur and I lost sense of my limbs.

As I began to slip toward the ground, Maelcolm's face appeared within a few inches of mine and then dissolved like particles of dust thrown into the wind.

*   *   *

My shins were cold. I looked down at the soft grass under my skin and followed the familiar shadow presiding over the altar, casting over the shiny black fabric partially concealing my legs. A breeze floated through the air, and the familiar smell of ancient rites anchored in my memory like roots of a tree. Then a ring of candles flared around the edge of the circle as the dark space lit up in a soft glow of blue light.

A hand rested on my shoulder, and my eyes closed as a euphoric smile spread across my face from the familiar feel of my mother's touch. But when I turned my head to look at the fingers resting against my robe, I saw the thin fragile hand of someone else. The veins of the hand telegraphed through translucent skin, and the joints of the fingers knotted and twisted from a lifetime of hard use.

I turned to see who was standing behind me. The old woman wore a robe like mine—silky and black, a long kimono held closed by a cord. Her snow-white hair reached down to her waist, and her eyes were the color of green quartz, nested in the center of folded skin as thin and fragile as tissue.

My robe hung open at the front. She glanced down at my exposed skin and walked past me to the altar. She reached for the same wooden box my mother had pulled the prism from, and removed something that bundled into a fat ball in her fist. Her arms circled me and cinched the braided cord of purple and silver around my waist.

"That's better," she declared with a light brogue, stepping back to examine me. "Now you look like a Kelley. A proper witch."

The voice was older and the eyes not as bright, but there was no mistaking the face that bore a remarkable resemblance to my mother's—and mine. I'd just been introduced to the grand matriarch of the Fitheach clan.

Isla Kelley stood before me in the flesh. But Isla Kelley was dead, so the woman standing in front of me was just as much of an impossibility as my mother showing up in a diner outside of Ithaca.

She came closer and finally let a smile peek through her smart and cautious façade. She pulled her white hair away from her face, revealing her left ear and the mark the gods had given her. "Let me see," she said.

I turned sideways and pulled my own hair into a lump of red waves on top of my head. "It's here." I pointed to the spot beneath my hair where the mark was.

She reached out to touch it.

"You can't feel it." My mark was different. My mother's was raised like a brand on top of her skin, and since Isla's was the result of a burn from lightning, I assumed hers was raised, too. "It's smooth and flat. It's part of me."

Isla ran her fingers over the spot. She didn't need to feel it. She could see it with her mind as clear as if it were painted in the air in front of her.

"The trinity is complete," she intoned.

Her face went solemn as she stepped back and looked over my shoulder. I looked in the direction of her stare as Maeve walked through the wall of candles illuminating the circle. She looked at Isla and then back at me, and then she fell to her knees and sank into the earth like a heap of black sails fluttering to the ground. Her fingers danced across the tips of the grass blades, combing each one as if she were flipping through a drawer of tiny index cards until she found the right one.

She plucked the blade and held it up to the moon. I focused on it and waited for some magical transformation to take place, but it was the ground beneath my bare feet that was the magic.

Isla's eyes lowered and her grin widened as she watched my reaction to the circle of grass rolling like a sea of turbulent waves. It seemed to reach upward around my mother's kneeling body, toward its missing part.

"Every blade is connected to a million others," Maeve said. "What happens to you, happens to all of us. You're being torn from your roots."

"I get it. It's a metaphor. But—"

Maeve stood up before I could finish the rest of my naive statement. She grabbed my hand and pulled me to the altar. She reached for a small knife lying on a wooden tray and held it over my hand, but as the blade came closer to my skin, she stopped and closed her eyes.

I made no attempt to pull my hand away, not quite believing my own mother would plunge a knife into my skin—or why.

Isla looked at Maeve with a pointed expression and then grabbed the knife from her hand. "Let's see what's inside." She brought the knife down firmly on the center of my palm, cutting swiftly through my flesh. It took a second for the pain to register and for the sharp gasp to leave my lungs. Isla's eyes went wide as the blood flowed from the wound and pooled into a thick black puddle in my upturned hand.

My mother dipped her finger into the blood and ran it across her lower lip, tasting it with the tip of her tongue as if it were a thin line of salt that required a mere granule to detect.

"I've feared this moment since the day you were born," she whispered as her eyes lifted to mine.

Ava poured herself a cup of steaming hot tea. A storm was coming and she could already feel the havoc of it in her bones. Not the kind of storm that brought lightning and torrential rain, but the kind that would wreck lives and leave a path of destruction that could upset the course of destiny.

She'd been getting messages from beyond the grave for days. They were ambiguous thoughts that weren't quite clear, but she knew they were coming from Maeve.

She took her cup and went back out to the front of the shop. It was Wednesday, which was book club day. For the past four years, the ladies of the Westside Book Collective had congregated at Den of Oddities and Antiquities for their weekly book review.

They were an interesting bunch, pulling their crucifixes out from under their blouses before entering the shop, liberally sprinkling reminders of God's grace between the appropriate passages of their book of the week. All the while perusing instruments of magic and books on the occult during their discussion breaks.

"Do you have any more copies of this?" Mrs. Cooper asked. She held up an old, weathered book simply titled *RUNES* in bold black letters. "I think both of my granddaughters might like a copy."

Mrs. Cooper was in her nineties but still managed to get around without the aid of a cane or a chaperone.

"I'm afraid not, Mrs. Cooper. All of our books are one of a kind."

"Really?" She examined the front and back of the book. "Isn't that interesting."

Ava had informed her elderly patron of this fact many times and suffered no annoyance in repeating herself. She liked Mrs. Cooper for her moxie and her determination not to crawl off somewhere and die like a ninety-something was expected to do.

Melanie came out from one of the aisles, carrying a box of antlers in the shape of corkscrews. "These are starting to grow roots on the shelf. We should probably run a special," she suggested before dropping the box on the counter.

"Hmm . . . probably a good idea," Ava agreed.

The ladies from the book club ended their weekly meeting

and began filtering out of the shop. When they were gone, Melanie leaned her back against the door and looked at Ava's cup of tea. "That's exactly what I need."

As she walked toward the cloth veil leading to the small kitchen in the back room, she heard the sound of breaking glass. She turned to see Ava stumbling out from behind the counter.

"Melanie!" Ava screamed.

The hot tea splattered across the glass case as the cup shattered against the floor. Ava's eyes squeezed shut as she grabbed for the edge of the counter to steady herself.

"Ava! What happened?"

"Our girl is in trouble, Melanie." The vision hit her hard, and for the first time since they began bombarding her days earlier, she knew what Maeve was trying to tell her. It was time to let go of old secrets, and it would take every ounce of magic that the two of them could muster to bring Alex home.

Melanie firmed up and stood tall. "What do we need to do?"

Ava looked at her with a bit of hesitation. "There's something you need to know."

Greer had worked and broken bread with Loden almost as long as he had with Thomas and Rhom. He was a pup in comparison, the youngest member of the crew with the charm and looks of a perpetual Lothario. For reasons Greer could only speculate on, he'd stopped aging at a time when most males were just beginning to grow into their oversized feet and inflated egos. Despite his premature elevation from son to warrior, Greer trusted every word that left his mouth and every instinct he followed. Today would be no different.

Loden pointed with his eyes. Greer followed his stare and spotted the man carrying the tray. Tall and thin with the wiry stature of a runner, he seemed innocuous enough. The man walked past the register and stopped at the order window. He set the tray of food on the ledge and spoke to someone in the kitchen. A minute later, he was handed a replacement for the tiny pitcher he'd dropped and broken on the floor.

Loden paid for his order and walked back to the table with the bag of pastries and a cardboard holder with the four espressos. His adrenaline hit Greer square in the nose as he approached.

"What is it?" Greer asked, a burst of his own adrenaline crawling up his throat.

"The guy with the tray." His head jerked in the direction of the counter. "Maybe I'm just looking for trouble where there isn't any."

"You? Nah." Thomas shook his head as he reached for the espresso and the bag of cannoli. He ate half his pastry in a single bite and closed his eyes. "Man, you weren't kidding about these things."

Loden slid into his seat, but the thought kept nagging at him like an abscessed tooth. "Greer, what's Alex's favorite food?" The strange question had everyone at the table looking at him.

Greer's brow furrowed. "You got something on your mind, just say it."

"What's Alex's favorite food?" he repeated.

"French toast," Rhom answered, eyeing Loden suspiciously.

Thomas nodded in agreement. Everyone at the table knew that. Alex spread the gospel about Sophia's French toast to the point of obsession. Not a dinner party went by that she didn't make reference to it as everyone cooed over Sophia's cooking.

"Well, I just think it's a little strange that the guy behind the counter is carrying a plate of French toast," Loden said as he focused on his cannoli, "in an Italian bakery. Who the hell is he taking a tray of French toast to?"

Greer's face hardened like a stone. He looked up as the guy with the tray walked past the cash register and headed toward the wall on the left side of the room.

"Get up," he ordered. Loden slid out of the booth so Greer could stand up for a better view.

Greer walked toward the counter, absently pushing past people as he followed the man with his eyes.

Thomas glanced at Loden and then Rhom. "Would someone tell me what the fuck is going on?" A lightbulb must have gone off in his head, because his expression suddenly changed.

The man kept walking toward the empty wall like he was going to run straight into it. He stopped within a foot of it and reached for the light switch. The wall opened, and he disappeared into the hidden doorway. Then it closed behind him, leaving no trace that it was ever there.

I looked at the blood that was now dripping from my fingers and waited for the show to begin. "Be careful," I warned my mother. "I'm dangerous when I bleed."

She laughed softly and then leaned in to kiss my forehead, the blood on her lower lip leaving a small smudge on my skin. "You won't hurt me. I'm your blood."

I thought about how I'd cut myself with the razor, hoping it would buy me a way out of Daemon's prison. But it didn't. Nothing happened because I couldn't take my own blood.

She cupped my arms and pulled me closer. "It's been a good fight, Alex. We've outrun this much longer than I ever imagined we could."

A heaviness filled my chest as an unexplainable feeling of loss began to throw a cloud over my head. "Outrun what?"

My mother ignored the question and continued with her declaration of defeat. "The game has changed. You'll be relying on your intelligence from now on, Alex. Do whatever you have to, and remember that no matter what happens I will always be with you."

I felt like I was being sent to the lions and my own mother

was opening the gate. Her mouth tensed as her hands dropped away. "Don't you dare lie down and die." Her face hardened with defiance.

"I'll find you and kill you myself before that happens," Isla hissed at me with a firm nod.

"Mother!" Maeve shot Isla a wicked glare. She motioned to a large black bowl on the altar. It was filled with water that looked like a liquid mirror. "Look," she said.

I bent over the bowl and gazed at my reflection. It took a moment to understand what she wanted me to see. It was such a subtle thing. But as I watched, I knew.

My head shook as I looked back at her. "I thought it was impossible."

An awkward smile softened her face, and then her lips began to tremble. "Close your eyes, my darling."

We'd learned to play this constant game of hide and seek, but I was afraid if I closed my eyes again, this time she'd be gone forever. Even though she said she would always be with me, I couldn't help but doubt her power to save me from what I was about to face.

Maelcolm was standing in front of me when I finally mustered the courage to open my eyes. His head cocked as he watched me return to the here and now.

"You saw her, didn't you?" His eyes darted discreetly around the room, looking for a ghost he couldn't see.

"My mother?" I knew whom he meant. "Yes. It's been quite a family reunion today."

A barely discernable tic appeared at the crease of his mouth, a telltale spike of discomfort or maybe even relief in his expression. "That is interesting," he said, turning to look me straight in the eye. "Why would you say that?"

I gazed back at the golden rings circling his blue eyes, identical to the ones that were now circling mine.

"You are my father, aren't you?"

The DESTINY
THIEF

THE CONCLUSION OF
THE FITHEACH TRILOGY

AVAILABLE NOW!

ABOUT THE AUTHOR

LUANNE BENNETT was born in Chicago and lived in New York City for several years. She makes her home in the South these days. When she's not at the keyboard, she's usually cooking or dreaming up new writing projects. If you'd like to know more, visit her at: luannebennett.com

I love to hear from readers. Email me at:
books@luannebennett.com

Made in the USA
Lexington, KY
18 May 2018